A. Hyatt Verrill's "The World of the Giant Ants" originally appeared in the fall 1928 issue of Amazing Stories Quarterly.

AUTHOR PORTRAIT

*A. Hyatt Verrill,
1871-1954*

THE WORLD OF THE GIANT ANTS

By
A. HYATT VERRILL

ARMCHAIR FICTION
PO Box 4369, Medford, Oregon 97504

*The original text of this edition was first
published by Experimenter Publishing Company*

Armchair Edition, Copyright 2018 by Gregory J. Luce
All Rights Reserved

Illustrations by Frank R. Paul

*For more information about Armchair Books and products, visit our
website at…*

www.armchairfiction.com

Or email us at…

armchairfiction@yahoo.com

INTRODUCTION

AFTER a great deal of deliberation, and with no little hesitation, I have finally decided to make public the contents of Dr. Henden's notebooks. Although I can in no way be held responsible for the incredible story they reveal, or be accused of attempting to perpetrate a hoax or a ridiculous example of imaginative fiction, still I have hitherto felt that I might be ridiculed for accepting the notes as genuine or believing they were written by a sane man. But the manner in which the stained and battered volumes reached my hand, and my knowledge of Doctor Henden and of the country and tribe in the territory near the locality where he met with the astounding adventures he recorded, convinced me that the notebooks, at least, were genuine. No one who knew Doctor Henden or who was familiar with his painstakingly accurate observations and his meticulous care to write of nothing which he had not personally seen and investigated, would dream of accusing him either of writing fiction or of recording hearsay evidence. Neither, I think, would anyone familiar with Doctor Henden's works, attainments and intellect, consider for a moment the possibility of his having lost his mind. Moreover, as will be seen by those who read the contents of his notebooks, the events he recorded, although seemingly impossible and preposterous, were viewed and studied, as well as described, by a man not only sane and free from hallucinations, but quite obviously far more observant and possessing a bigger mind and better powers of deduction and reasoning than most men. It is in view of these several arguments that I have at last decided to publish Doctor Henden's field notes, which record quite tersely and in abbreviated form, all of the events and occurrences of any importance during the two years intervened between the time when he vanished in the heart of South America and the time when I was in charge of an expedition searching for him and his notebooks almost miraculously came into my possession.

No doubt, the majority of those who read this will recall more or less of the details of Doctor Henden's quest, and disappearance, for when he set out from the United States, and when the world realized that he had vanished, the daily press carried full accounts of his undertaking, of his attainments and past life, and with more or less reasonable speculation regarding his fate. As a matter of fact, however, not one of these was within miles of the truth, and hitherto only I and the sponsors of the relief expedition have been aware of the actual facts, as far as they were revealed by his field notes.

But for the benefit of those few who may have but a dim remembrance, or no remembrance at all, of Doctor Henden's aims and disappearance, I will very briefly relate the facts as far as they were known to the world at large. Doctor Benjamin Henden was one of the best known scientists in the United States, or in the world for that matter. Although a comparatively young man at the time he departed—he was in his early fifties—yet he had won international fame in several branches of natural science. He was an excellent geologist, something of a botanist, and possessed a far greater knowledge of zoology than many professors of that science. In his early youth he had specialized in ornithology and later in entomology, and in the pursuit of these studies he had made a number of very successful expeditions to South and Central America, securing on these trips vast numbers of rare specimens and many new species. It is scarcely exaggerating to say that Doctor Henden had a more intimate first hand knowledge of tropical American bird and insect life than any man of his time. It was upon these expeditions to which I refer that Doctor Henden's interest was aroused by the aboriginal tribes of South and Central America and by the innumerable remains of past civilization in those countries. So absorbed did he become in these matters, that he completely forsook ornithology and entomology and became an ardent student of American ethnology and archeology. In a comparatively short space of time he had mastered all that could be learned from museums and books regarding these sciences, and again resumed his long abandoned fieldwork, this time, however, for the sole purpose of studying the living Indians and the remains of the prehistoric aborigines in South America. It is needless to even mention his numerous discoveries; the monographs and the volumes which he wrote, or the rather startling and wholly revolutionary theories he advanced as a result of his expeditions and studies. Suffice to say he brought many new races and cultures to light; founded an entirely new history of Central and South American civilizations, and solved many ethnological and archeological puzzles which for years had confronted all other researchers in his chosen fields. All this I have mentioned merely as a preface or explanation to show why Doctor Henden, who for twenty years had been known only as an ethnologist and archeologist, should have been so well able to record, observe and deduce matters which bore no relation whatever to either of those sciences.

In 1925 when he set out on his last ill-fated expedition, he stated publicly that he was in hopes of reaching a hitherto unknown district lying in western Brazil and eastern Peru, in which, it had been reported, there were mysterious unknown and unexplored ruins. In reality, as was revealed in his notes, he had a far more romantic and adventurous object in view. As all know, he reached Peru in safety, left Lima several days after his arrival, travelled by the Southern Railway to La Paz and thence into the Beni River district, and there dropped from sight in the impenetrable and almost limitless forests of the Bolivia-Peruvian-Brazilian hinterland. As was always the case, he went alone, accompanied only by a camp-boy and man-of-all-work—a West Indian negro who had been his companion on many expeditions, and he secured his porters, boatmen, guides, etc., as he went along. His knowledge of Spanish and Portuguese and of many Indian dialects made this comparatively simple, and he invariably argued—when the perils of thus penetrating dangerous territory were brought up, that he could accomplish more in a given time, could travel more swiftly and safely, and could be more certain of success when alone, than with a party. With every added white man the dangers and responsibilities were greatly increased, he affirmed and, as a clincher, he would always point out that no large expedition into the American tropics had ever been a success, whereas his own and many other "one-man" expeditions had invariably proved successful.

FROM the time he left Santa Cruz on the Beni, no definite word was received from Doctor Henden or his party. That he intended descending the Beni and exploring the Rio Grande had been well established, for he spent some time in La Paz and afterwards in Cochabamba, securing all information possible regarding the tribes on those rivers, and especially regarding the strange bearded Indians known as the Sirionos of the Rio Grande. Hence, when after two years nothing had been heard of Doctor Henden, and his friends organized a searching party to go after him and selected me as its leader, I followed the general route of these two rivers. Also, I followed Doctor Henden's example and went "light," being accompanied only by a camp boy—a half-breed Pano Indian—and secured my guides and boatmen at San Ramon, the last outpost of civilization in Bolivia. I regret that I am forced to occupy so much space with the wholly uninteresting details of Doctor Henden's last trip and with a brief account of my own in search of him or traces of him, but I fear it is essential if my readers are to understand the more important matter to follow and are to accept it as fact rather than fiction.

I found no trace of the missing men until I reached the country of the Sirionos. These Indians were in themselves enough to cause anyone to wonder if he were dreaming or in his right mind. Entirely nude and wearing immense bushy beards and heavy mustaches, they resembled Australian Bushmen more than any Indians, while the bows and arrows they used seemed fashioned for a race of giants rather than for use by rather undersized humans. The bows were often ten feet in length and five inches across, while the arrows were an inch or two in diameter, eight to twelve feet long and with feathers projecting six inches or more from the shafts and from two to three feet in length. To an ethnologist of Doctor Henden's type they would have afforded months of study, and very obviously he had visited and studied them, for, once amicable relations were established, the Indians told of the visit of a white man many months previously. That they referred to the missing scientist I felt sure, for they had been vastly impressed by his black companion. Moreover, they described the doctor very well and imitated some of his mannerisms—they are wonderful mimics— so accurately that anyone would have recognized to whom they referred. According to the Sirionos, Doctor Henden had remained in the vicinity for several weeks, during which time he had made enquiries regarding the tribes and the fabled ruins, which were his objectives. None of the Sirionos knew anything definite regarding either, but while Doctor Henden was there a party of Indians arrived from the Zanteca River and claimed to have accurate knowledge. They conversed with the scientist for a long time. As a result, two of these strangers left with the Doctor when he departed the following day and from one of these the Sirionos understood that the route would be largely through the jungle. But just where the river was to be left or in what direction they were headed, not one of the tribe knew. Hence my only course was to make my way to the Zanteca River natives in the hopes of there finding some Indian who knew what route those who accompanied Doctor Henden had followed, for to go blindly into that vast wilderness would have been worse than hopeless.

Fortune favored me. At the village on the Zanteca I found one of the two who had started out with the scientist. He had not, however, accompanied the Doctor to the end of his journey, and he knew nothing of his whereabouts or fate. He and his fellow tribesman had merely guided the Doctor to the first of the ruins and had refused to go farther, because, he said, the country beyond was inhabited by wild hostile tribes and by beings which no man could resist. In fact, his tales were so bizarre and so utterly preposterous that I put them down as mere figments of the savage's imagination and superstitious dread of any unknown place or people. He consented, however, to guide me to the ruins where he had last seen Doctor Henden alive. Of that journey it is not necessary to speak. It was filled with all the usual hardships of travel through the jungle, but eventually we arrived safely at the ruined city. I should like to describe the wonders of this lost and forgotten centre of some marvelous prehistoric civilization, but this has its place elsewhere. Moreover, Doctor Henden describes it fully and far more lucidly and accurately in his diary than I could do.

It was after I had reached these ruins, that the great earthquake occurred. Although it was only slightly felt in the United States, it was exceedingly severe throughout South America and particularly in the district within several hundred miles of the Andean chain. It was coincident with the violent eruption of Mount Misti in Peru, which annihilated Arequipa with immense loss of life, as all are aware, and utterly destroyed many towns and villages in Peru, Bolivia, Ecuador, Chile, and elsewhere. In the jungle, there would have been little or no danger to us, but in that ancient ruined city amid the immense buildings and monuments, we were in as imminent danger as if we had been in one of the Andean towns. Moreover, it occurred in the night and we were awakened by the crash and thunder of falling walls and monoliths. The Indians were panic-stricken, and dashed shrieking from the courtyard in which we had camped. It was a fatal mistake on their part, for while the patio was fairly safe from falling debris, being roofless and large enough to leave plenty of clear space in the centre, even if its walls did fall in. Outside of the court yard stones were being tossed about and walls were falling on every side. Pedro, my half-breed Pano, remained with me, and throughout that terrible night we cowered in the centre of the court, quite powerless to aid the Indians, and sick and nauseated with the heaving, undulating motions of the solid earth beneath us. When at last the tremors ceased, dawn was breaking and, convinced that there was no more danger—for even if the quakes recurred, there was no remaining masonry to fall—we ventured from our refuge. Outside, the ruins were devastated. Nothing remained standing. Debris was piled high everywhere, and with the faint hopes of finding some of the Indians still alive—perhaps safe in hiding or only wounded—we moved about shouting and hallooing. For a time only the echoes of our voices broke the silence. Then, I from a spot where the great central temple had stood majestically and impressively before the earthquake, we heard a faint sound as of some one striving to reply to our calls. Climbing with great difficulty over the heaped-up masses of broken stone and fractured idols, and guided by the human sounds, which, now that we were nearer, were evidently uttered by someone in agony, we came at last to the remains of the temple court. I had expected to find an injured Indian. Instead, imagine my utter amazement at finding the body of a negro wedged fast beneath an immense fallen column. He was clad in a single garment of some coarse silk-like cloth, his body was covered with scars, some recently healed and some showing merely as bluish-white welts against his black skin, and he was obviously on the point of death. But he was conscious and still able to speak. And the first words he uttered—speaking between agonized gasps, for his chest was crushed and his back broken—caused me greater amazement than finding him there, for he spoke in English. But even more astounding was what he said. He was, in fact. Doctor Henden's servant—the Jamaican, Tom—and I bent low and hung on his words, elated, despite my sorrow at Tom's plight, to think I was near the scientist or at least was about to learn of his fate. But I was doomed to disappointment. The wounded man's life was ebbing fast, and the little information he was able to communicate was given in disconnected sentences or rather words, interrupted by heart-rending groans and gasps for breath.

As nearly as I can repeat them they were as follows: "I Tom—Doctor Henden boy—getting away—killed—come through tunnel—dead city—earthquake—tunnel fall in—I die—better die than slave ant men—maybe all killed—black fellows fight—Doctor Henden teach them—all in book—in pouch."

With the last words he choked, a spasm shook him, and death came to relieve his awful sufferings. Much of what he had said was utterly incomprehensible to me at the time—though later, when I had read Doctor Henden's diary, it all became quite clear. But that the scientist was dead; that Tom had escaped from some tribe whom he called the "ant-people;" that he had reached the ruined city by way of a tunnel which had been destroyed by the earthquake and in doing so had lost his life; those things were quite plain. But I was at a loss to understand what he meant by the book and pouch. However, with the utmost difficulty, Pedro and I pried the stone from Tom's body and dragged him out to give him decent burial, I discovered that he wore a leather pouch or wallet strapped to his waist. Opening this, I found a few bits of dried fruit, a few grains of some cornlike cereal and a rather bulky package wrapped in a transparent parchment-like material. Unwrapping this, I disclosed two small books and hastily opening the stained, worn and rubbed covers, I hastily read in one, "Field Notes, 1925-26, B. Henden," and in the other "1926-7 Notes, B. Henden."

Very probably there are many who will censure me for not putting aside the two little volumes and giving my attention to the dead negro. But I felt, and I still feel, that at that time the scientist's whereabouts or fate was of far greater importance than the corpse of any man, and that it was my first and most pressing duty to examine the books which so miraculously and providentially had come to my hands. My first glance, however, convinced me that it would take hours—even days—to read the thousands of closely written and almost microscopic words, covering the hundred and more pages of the books, and which I noticed were written for Doctor Henden's personal use, being abbreviated, lacking in punctuation, disjointed and often forming almost a sort of shorthand. In fact, they were written precisely as Doctor Henden, myself and innumerable other scientific men jot down notes when in the field or when making some experiment; notes intended to refresh the writer's memory in writing about it later, or merely to be used as references, generally almost incomprehensible to anyone else.

On one point, however, I was satisfied. On the last space, the final portion of the inner side of the back cover of the second volume, was an almost illegible entry as follows: "Decided T. attempt reach Tupec, going through tunnel. Believe he can make it. Giving him my notes. Only proof. T. can bring party through from Tupec. Has full instructions; forces, arms, etc. Chelomeans attack today.—Chelomeans victorious. Reds annihilated. Am mortally wounded. T. Leaving at once. No use rescue party now. My last words—" Sorrowfully I closed the book. What tragedy, what sufferings, what heroism must be concealed behind those few terse words written by a dying man as impersonally, as succinctly as though he were recording the habits of some insect. And what startling story, what amazing discoveries might still be hidden within those closely written pages! But my wildest conjectures fell far short of the reality, as will be seen by those who read Doctor Henden's notes as I have transcribed them.

Reading through his records, I found that Dr. Henden had not—after the first few entries—either dated his notes or kept them regularly. Sometimes he noted that a week, a month or some other period had elapsed since he had last written of his experiences. But more often there would be no reference to time, although it was apparent that considerable time intervened between the records. Hence, in compiling the notes for publication, I have omitted all dates and references to time (except when noted by the Doctor) and have set down the story as though it were a continuous and uninterrupted record of events. Also, I have somewhat elaborated the notes and have filled in words and sentences to make them more readable, and I have omitted strictly scientific observations and data which add nothing to the interest of the account and would be incomprehensible to the average person. Aside from such changes and additions, I have written nothing more than the amazing story recorded by Dr. Henden in that remote corner of the continent whence there was but one avenue of escape, which now is sealed forever. To Doctor Henden, any avenue of escape would be useless now anyway.

The Story of the Notebooks Revealed

CHAPTER ONE

THE Indian guides that I secured on the Zanteca tell me the first ruins are only two days farther ahead. I am looking forward to reaching these ruins with a feeling of greater excitement and thrill than I have ever experienced on any of my many expeditions. And yet it seems such a wholly preposterous wild goose chase that I have undertaken. At times I feel that I must have absorbed some of the superstition and credulity of the aborigines, among whom I have spent so much time. Certainly, that for which I am searching seems beyond the bounds of all probability and scientific reasoning, I have no doubt there are unknown ruins ahead, for there are countless undiscovered ruins in the country, but that there could be any such creatures, such monstrosities, in existence seems incredible, and were it generally known that I had the faintest belief in the Indians' tales of such things, my fellow scientists would laugh me to scorn. Hence I have let it be thought that my present expedition is solely for the purpose of discovering and studying the ruined city of Tupec which, for more than two hundred years has been thought to exist somewhere within the vast unexplored region I am now entering. But I am truly convinced that there must be some basis of fact in the innumerable tales I have so often heard from so many and widely separated tribes who could not, under any circumstances, have heard the story from one another. The aborigines, from my observations and experience, do not fabricate tales from whole cloth, as we say. They must have a basis or fact of some sort to build upon, and while no doubt many of their stories are fantastic and highly exaggerated, somewhere there is some portion of truth in them. This I have repeatedly proved and my most noteworthy discoveries hitherto have been made by following up the Indians' myths or legends and tracing them to their foundation. Hence this tale of the bizarre, terrible beings who dwell beyond the ruined city, and the nightmarish details of the story, must, I feel, have some basis, and I am determined to find out what that basis may be. If I succeed and there is even one thousandth part of truth in the stories, then I will have made an epochal discovery and will have entirely upset all preconceived ideas of archeology, ethnology and several other ologies, not only as relating to South America but to the world in general. But if I find nothing more than the semi-mythical city of Tupec, I will have accomplished a great deal.

* * *

I HAVE been sounding the Zantecas regarding the tales of weird beings dwelling in the interior beyond Tupec. They were loth to speak of it but know the tale. There is one curious fact in regard to it, however. If no human being can enter the territory and if no one has ever been there and returned, how can anyone know anything regarding it? If there is any truth in it the story must have been handed down from remote times, perhaps from the days when Tupec was inhabited and a civilized race dwelt in this district. Strange that such a race ever should have disappeared. What could have destroyed them? The Europeans never entered here and there are no records to show that the early conquerors had any knowledge of the existence of ruins even. If accounts of Tupec are within a mile of the truth the inhabitants must have been a very highly advanced race and very numerous. One of my greatest efforts will be to try to ascertain why or how the city was abandoned and why the civilized race vanished. I wonder if it had any connection with the stories of those weird beings beyond; if the Tupecans as I might call them, started that tale. It's all idle speculation and by tomorrow night I should know whether such a place as Tupec really exists, or whether it is merely some insignificant ruin or even remains of some forgotten Spanish fort or outpost.

* * *

TUPEC exists. I feel as if I had been dreaming as I write this. We reached the ruins day before yesterday. All I had heard had not prepared me for anything so marvelous or of such incalculable archeological value. Nothing in Mayan-Toltec, Aztec, Chibcha, Incan or pre-Incan remains even approaches these. There is not the remotest similarity between the Tupecan architecture, carvings, monoliths and culture and any of those that I have mentioned, with two exceptions. In some respects they are striking features that are common to these ruins and the ruins of Tiahuanaco in Bolivia and the Cocle ruins of Panama discovered last year by my friend andconfrère, Verrill. I am beginning to think that all three civilizations were merely different stages of the same race's advancement, Tupec being the last and ultimate stage. Also I am already convinced that the people who built and lived in Tupec were a white race and not indigenous to South America. Perhaps—but no, that is too wild a theory—I was about to say that perhaps the tales so common in tropical America and relating the existence of a white race, may have had their foundation in the existence of some remnants of this Tupecan people, who still dwell somewhere in the fastnesses of the unexplored districts. I shall spend many days, perhaps months, here. Years would be required to make an exhaustive study of the place.

YESTERDAY my Zantecas cleared out. They left suddenly and without notice. Something frightened them; perhaps they were nervous when I began excavating in a spot I deemed to be a cemetery. Only my two Panos and Tom are now with me. Even if the Panos desert I shall remain here, for Tom and I can take care of ourselves and can find our way out, but in that case I fear I shall be forced to abandon my intention of penetrating farther into the district in search of the gigantic terrible beings of the Indians' yarns.

* * *

I WAS right. The inhabitants of Tupec were white. I have found two well preserved mummies. Even a superficial examination proves they were not of the Amerind, Mongol or any other known race. They are nearer the Caucasian, but not the same. I have also discovered that they had a written language. Tom stumbled on a cache of beautiful ceramic tiles decorated with symbolic figures and glyphs. Their arrangement at once caused me to suspect they were some sort of record, and I am now certain of it. The same figures appear in many places and always in orderly arrangement exactly as we would use letters in inscriptions. Moreover the discovery of these tablets proves the truth of the theory advanced by Dr. Tello of Lima in which he claimed that the decorative pottery vessels with human, vegetable and other figures in innumerable slightly varied positions or forms were symbols employed in recording events and various matters by the pre-Incan races of Peru.

I have been puzzled by the numerous sculptures and paintings of strange creatures which are everywhere. Some are quite easily recognizable as representing birds, mammals and insects with which I am familiar, but many, although obviously as well and carefully drawn and as accurate reproductions of their subjects as the others, are not like anything known to science today. There are strange creatures that resemble dragons, or I might rather say pterodactyls; there are elephant-like creatures with claws and canine teeth; human beings or monkey-like creatures with tails and shaggy hair, and, very commonly, the figures of some insect-like thing with enormous jaws, six legs and no eyes. These are usually shown in connection with figures of semi-human beings with triangular heads, exaggerated bowed legs, immense outstanding ears, attenuated bodies and bald heads, or with monstrosities resembling overfed hippopotami with innumerable legs and antennae. In several places I have found sculptures of these creatures side by side with those of men, and of equal size, and on some ceramics, and also in carvings, these men, attired in truly remarkable costumes and armed with strange weapons, are shown battling with the beasts. Probably these are allegorical or symbolic records, possibly showing man's constant struggle with the lower animals and with insect pests, the latter being exaggerated to indicate their numbers or dangerous characters. Or again, they may be indicative of human enemies, the beast forms being given as symbolic of contempt or derision. If I could only decipher the inscriptions I might discover the key to these matters.

* * *

I HAVE made a most astounding discovery, a discovery which has completely upset all my former ideas and conjectures.

The weird figures I mentioned are representations of those beings so vividly described in the Indians' stories. Strange I did not think of it at once. Do or did these things exist, or did the Tupecans know the same tales and did they merely depict the creatures of their stories? I am inclined to think that at the time Tupec was inhabited, many creatures known to us only as fossils, still inhabited this land, and that these were the beings that gave rise to all these weird tales. Perhaps they were rare and were regarded as sacred or looked upon with awe. But unquestionably the Tupecans battled with, them, as recorded by the carvings and ceramics. Is it not possible that some of these prehistoric creatures still exist in the fastnesses of the unexplored areas into which I hope to penetrate?

THE WORLD OF THE GIANT ANTS

* * *

ANOTHER discovery. While exploring the inner portions of the central temple—a magnificent structure—I came upon the cleverly concealed and evidently secret entrance to a subterranean passage. Tomorrow I intend to explore this. It may lead to another portion of the city or to some monument or statue whence the Tupec priests uttered words or oracles to impress the people, or it may lead to some point outside the ruins. But wherever it leads it is highly probable that it may contain objects of inestimable archeological value.

* * *

I AM writing these words by torchlight within the underground tunnel. This is our second day within it and we have not yet reached the end. It must be fully twenty miles in length and appears to have been cut by hand. Yet in some ways it has the appearance of a natural formation, perhaps the channel of some subterranean stream, long dry and improved by man. Moreover, it contains innumerable galleries and side passages—a perfect labyrinth; almost, I might say, like a gigantic ant's nest. But I have found nothing of any ethnological or archeological interest except some skeletal fragments of human beings and parts of some unknown prehistoric creatures. The former show signs of having been intentionally broken or crushed. The latter, as nearly as I can determine from a superficial examination by torchlight, are horny or chitinous plates or scales from some huge reptile. Among them is one great, curved, serrated-edged horn which reminds me of a gigantic shark tooth. I regret I am no paleontologist and possess but a very superficial knowledge of fossil creatures. I plan to continue to the end of the tunnel if our torches and supplies permit. Otherwise I shall be forced to retrace our way to Tupec. This would be extremely difficult had I not taken the precaution to mark the way by means of smudges of smoke upon the walls wherever there was a turn or a branch opening. Much to my surprise, my Panos are still with us. They appeared more terrified at remaining in Tupec, than in accompanying me through this tunnel. The two fellows are fairly chattering with insane and unwarranted terror, however. Even Tom is nervous, but I have always observed that nearly every man is afraid of underground unknown passages. I wonder what purpose this tunnel served. Was it a secret exit to be used in case of necessity—if the city were attacked and conquered for instance? Does it connect Tupec with some other ancient ruins? Anything of this size and character must have possessed some immensely valuable or important feature. However, I shall know very soon.

* * *

A MONTH has passed since I last penned words in my diary. A month of such nightmarish, impossible events, such amazing experiences, such horrible incredible happenings, that I would be laughed to scorn were I to relate them to my fellow men. But I doubt if I will ever see a fellow man, other than Tom, again. I am writing more from force of habit than with any hope that my notes will ever be read, for I can see no chance of escape from this fearsome, awful place. All the tales I had heard were nothing compared to the reality. I am in the land of the Indians' tales and am among the monstrous, hideous beings they described; creatures more awful, more savage, more incredible than the wildest imagination could invent, and yet possessing an intelligence, an organization and a devilish ingenuity and purpose, that make them the equals of most human beings.

I can scarcely force myself to believe that I am not dreaming or am not in the delirium of fever; that I will not awaken to find it all the fabric of a sleep-befuddled brain. And that Tom and I still live, is perhaps the most amazing thing of all.

We traversed the tunnel to find it closed by a massive stone door which could be readily opened from within, by means of cleverly designed levers and a simple mechanism, but which—too late—we discovered could not be opened from without.

If we had only known! If we had only guessed what lay beyond; if I had only stopped to investigate before rushing blindly on, how different would have been our fate. I could then have wedged the door so it could not close behind us. I could have made a closer study of the mechanism. I could have somehow arranged it so that we could retreat within the passage and close the portal in our rear. But I did none of these things. When the door at last swung open and revealed a vast strange country beyond, we—or rather I, for I assume all responsibility as leader of the party—carelessly allowed the door to swing to, and we found it irrevocably locked when, terrified beyond our senses, we again attempted to reenter the tunnel.

THE WORLD OF THE GIANT ANTS

Before us, as we emerged from the passageway, stretched a strange country, as I have said. On every side it was surrounded by immense, snow-capped ridges. As nearly as I can judge from my knowledge of geology, the entire place is the stupendous crater of an extinct volcano. In fact, the land appears to be the very bottom of a long-dead crater, for the surrounding mountains must be fully twenty-five thousand feet in height. And as there are no such mountains rising above the country of the outer world, I feel sure that the immense territory here must be at least ten thousand feet below the level of the rest of the surface of the continent. It is like the bottom of a huge well or giant mine-shaft. Everything points to this. It is hot, damp, humid. The sky is overcast and the mountains veiled in vapor. The vegetation is that of prehistoric days and is rank, primitive and viscous. Fungi are everywhere and of preposterous proportions. There are mushrooms higher than my head, russolas, towerlike trees among clusters of agaricus that would serve as shelters for a mounted horseman. Lichens and liverworts form deep carpets; club-mosses and hepaticae here reach the dimensions of cedar trees and cabbages; parasitic vines and plants are of gigantic size and incredibly rapid growth; the trees are fleshy-leaved and pithy, and the air is so heavy, so laden with moisture and so reeking with the odors of decaying vegetation and the overpowering scent of the inhabitants, that it is oppressive and difficult to breathe. No doubt these conditions have brought about the unique, the terrifying and incredible conditions of animal life which exist here, just as the environment of the giant dinosaurs resulted in the development of reptilian life to the nthdegree. But I am wandering, theorizing, and cannot waste my all too little space by recording such thoughts. I must set down the facts; my observations. Just why I should do this is rather a puzzle. I feel sure we shall never escape from this place. It is equally certain that my notes will never reach the outside world. And yet, such is man's psychology, that even when all hops is abandoned, he still goes on, following his accustomed habits, planning his future; and I am writing this exactly as if I expected to return to civilization at any time and planned to elaborate my notes to form a report on this impossible place.

At first, when we emerged from the passage and gazed upon the bizarre country, we saw no signs of inhabitants. There was no town, no village in sight. But presently one of the Indians—whose eyes are always keener than those of civilized man—saw some creature moving about in the dense jungle upon the plain below us. We were woefully in need of food, and as there appeared to be no danger from hostile savages, we descended the hillside—which I noticed even then appeared to be an artificial mound rather than a natural formation, in the hopes of securing game. It was when we reached the first vegetation that I became aware of its remarkable character. Very warily we approached the spot where the Pano had seen the creature, for we did not know what sort of beast it might be—whether carnivorous or a ruminant, whether it might prove ferocious or timid—and we had no mind to be either unexpectedly attacked or to lose our dinner. Presently we heard the sounds of some creature ahead, the rustling of foliage, and a strange crunching, creaking noise which I may best compare to the sound of a heavy cart passing over corn stalks. With my revolver drawn and with the Indians holding their bows in readiness for instant use, we pressed forward. The next second I staggered back, unable to believe my eyes, while the Panos screamed with terror, and turning, dashed madly from the spot. Stretched along the limb of a low tree was what at first sight appeared to be a gigantic serpent, its huge body of mottled green and brown undulating slightly and moving slowly forward. But the next instant I realized it was no snake, for through an opening among the leaves I caught sight of legs; stout fleshy legs, covered with coarse hair and terminating in disk-like horny feet that clasped the bark of the limb. Then, as I gazed, fascinated and incredulous, the thing reared its head, a huge, rough, dull-red head with immense expressionless staring eyes and vicious saw-toothed horny jaws. Seizing a thick fleshy leaf between these, the mandibles ripped through the leaf with the crunching noise I have mentioned. It was absolutely unbelievable, positively impossible, but true. The thing was a caterpillar, a monstrous gigantic larva fully ten feet in length! A scream from the Panos broke the spell in which I stood transfixed, gazing at the thing. With Tom at my side, shaking and actually pale, we turned and hurried towards the cries. What we saw seemed to freeze the blood in my veins and caused Tom to drop to his knees, chattering and mouthing in abject terror.

Side by side, the two Indians were battling furiously with a most terrifying, fearsome creature. That he was human or semi-human no one could doubt. But he was a monster, a being fit only for a nightmare, and with a shock I recognized him as the original of some of the weird figures I had found at Tupec. His head was hairless, misshapen and almost triangular in form, with immense outstanding ears. His body, thin almost to emaciation, was black as night and covered with close-growing wooly hair, and his short legs were enormously bowed. His back was towards me, and he was leaping about, with his immensely long arms aiming sharp, terrific blows at the Indians, who were already torn, and bleeding from dozens of deep wounds. Broken arrow shafts protruded from one shoulder and a thigh, of the creature. Evidently the Panos had used their weapons effectively, yet the missiles imbedded in his body did not appear to affect the creature's vitality in the least. And he was at too close quarters for the Panos to use their bows.

His ferocity was terrible, and the worst of it was he fought silently, not uttering a sound, although at every blow of his hands—and with horror I noticed that these were armed with sharp, long claws—the Indians screamed and groaned in agony and deadly fear. All this I took in at a first glance. Without hesitation I raised my pistol and fired point-blank at the thing's back. I knew I had not missed, but instead of falling dead or wounded as I had expected, the creature wheeled, and at sight of its face, a cry of horror escaped me and I fell back, trembling, shaking. Never has living man seen such a face. The great, staring, expressionless, lustreless, lidless eyes in the black triangular-shaped head; the huge, drooling mouth with flappy lips revealing toothless gums, and the utter absence of a nose, but with two yawning black holes for nostrils, were those of a fiend of the eternal pit, rather than of anything of flesh and blood. For the space of a second the thing stared at me. Then, without a sound, it turned and recommenced its attack upon the Panos. As rapidly as I could pull trigger I emptied my revolver into the bestial monster until, fairly riddled with bullets, it slumped to earth. But it was too late. The Panos had been fairly ripped to pieces. One was already dead and the other was breathing his last. And I had no time to aid him even had his condition warranted it. From the dense growth of vegetation sounds were issuing, sounds of approaching things, being attracted perhaps by the shouts of the Panos, perhaps by the sounds of my revolver shots. Who or what they might prove I did not know and I had no wish to remain to see. Already, within the space of a few short minutes, I had seen more than enough. The place was too terrible, too monstrous. Thinking only of escape, only of putting as much distance as possible between us and more of those fearful black things

Without hesitation, I raised my pistol and fired point-blank at the thing's back

in human form, I shook and cursed Tom into action and raced madly towards the mound-like hill whence we had issued from the tunnel.

Once I glanced back and the blood seemed to freeze in my veins as I saw a crowd, a horde, of the terrible beings in pursuit. But they were not fleet of foot, we were gaining on them, and felt that if we could reach the hill and the tunnel, we might yet escape. Imagine my horror, my frenzy, as we gained the hill and found the gate to the passage irretrievably closed against us.

Madly we tore and beat at the massive stone portal, hurled ourselves against it, wasted our puny strength in vain efforts to swing that ton or more of rock. And each moment, as we struggled, and as sweat poured from our skins and cold dread chilled our hearts, those fearsome beings were approaching us. Presently they were close at hand, silent, ominous, and so sure was I that we were about to die an awful death, that I placed my pistol to my temple and pulled the trigger before I remembered that in my blind terror I had forgotten to reload the weapon. Before I could slip a cartridge into the cylinder, the things were upon us. I drew back, cowering, trembling, while Tom, paralyzed with fear, was a pitiable sight. I expected the creatures—I cannot even now call them men—to fall upon is and rend us as they had the Panos. But for some inexplicable reason, they did not. Though they made no sounds, yet they seemed to be conversing, carrying on some sort of argument among themselves, debating perhaps what end to make of us. Realizing we were not to be summarily destroyed, I regained some measure of courage and hope. I peered intently at them, trying to fathom their thoughts, their intentions, by watching their gestures and expressions. But their flat, noseless, triangular faces were expressionless, and their huge, dull eyes gave no hint of the reactions of the minds behind them. But from their actions and attitudes I judged that we were as strange to them as they were to us. And being rather familiar with the psychology of savages, I took heart, knowing that the savage in his calmer moments seldom destroys that which excites his wonder or curiosity. Nevertheless, one of the things had killed the Indians, and the Indians must have been as strange to the thing's eyes as were ourselves. But very possibly, I thought, the Panos had been the aggressors. Seeing the black being, they had very probably taken no chances, but had shot at it, and the pain of the arrow wounds had enraged it and it had flown at them in a frenzy. All the time that these thoughts were racing through my brain the black beings were standing around us, gazing unwinkingly at us, staring fixedly; their loose lips slobbering over their toothless gums in a most horrible manner. Then two stepped forward and stretched out claw-fingered hands towards Tom. He shrieked in terror and drew back, but the beings did not even indicate that his agonized screams had been heard. As easily as though he had been a mere child, they lifted him, stood him on his feet, and with their faces close to him, sniffed at him, passed their hands over his skin and his garments, and having apparently satisfied themselves on some score, they passed him to their fellows and turned to me.

It was a terrifying, an indescribably awful ordeal I underwent. The reek of the things was nauseating, a strange pungent odor that reminded me of something I had smelled before but overpowering in its acrid strength, while the hideous faces of the brutes as they sniffed at me and the feel of the rough hairy skin and animal-like claws as they touched me, caused me to shiver and shrink from them. But they showed no desire to injure us, although I well knew that a single stroke of those talon-like fingers could rend me to the bone.

Presently the terrible examination was at an end. Again the things seemed earnestly though inaudibly discussing us, and once more I felt sick with fear at what fate they might decide should be ours. Then, seizing poor Tom roughly by the scruff of the neck, and urging me more gently but no less insistently, the things turned from the hillside, and with us, captives in their midst, hurried towards the jungle whence they had appeared.

Turning to one side before we reached the spot where the Panos had met their end, the beings conducted us along a sort of roughly worn trail. Even in my extremity and my fear I could not avoid noticing the weird character of our surroundings; the giant fungi, and the preponderance of parasitic plants. And what animal life I saw amazed me even more. Once a dark shadow fell across our path, and there was the rustle as of huge wings.

Startled, I glanced up. My eyes stared incredulously, for above us a butterfly flew slowly. But such a butterfly no other mortal had ever gazed upon; a scarlet and orange thing of indescribable beauty fully a yard in length and six feet across the velvety wings. Like a flash my mind reverted to that first astounding discovery we had made, to that huge larva browsing on the leaves and in my suddenly awakened interest in entomology and my speculations as to whether this glorious insect were the image of that larva, all my worries and fears were momentarily forgotten. The next second our captors appeared to be seized with sudden panic. They released their grasps on us, darted in to the shelter of nearby plants and giant toadstools, and crouched, trembling, in the shadows. Wondering what had frightened them, but realizing that some dread danger must threaten, I followed their example and dragged Tom, dazed and incapable of thought or action, into the shelter of a broad-leaved vine. Then to my wondering, incredulous ears came a strange sound, the vibrant humming of a distant airplane.

Human beings, civilized men must be near. Forgetting all else, I sprang into the open, gazing expectantly at the vapor shrouded sky, ready to shout, to wave my hands, to use every effort to attract the attention of the airship's occupant the instant it appeared.

With astonishing rapidity the humming increased. It became a roar. At any instant I expected to see the machine flash into sight above the tree tops. Suddenly it burst into view, and as my straining eyes rested upon it my face blanched, and with a cry of terror I flung myself headlong into the undergrowth.

CHAPTER TWO

I HAD expected to see an airplane, a fabric of metal and machinery made by the hand of man, and with a fellow being, a civilized man or men, within it. Instead, the apparition that roared into the range of my astounded vision was a living thing, a huge, winged creature flying low above the trees; a thing to fill the stoutest heart with mad terror; a creature of fearful, menacing aspect. Brief as had been my glimpse of the thing before I sought safety in hiding, I had recognized it as the original of those figures in Tupec, which I had mistaken forpterodactyls. And instantly, too, I had recognized it for what it was. Its great, staring, many-faceted eyes, its immense multiple jaws, with the outer serrated mandibles, the short vibrating antennae, the gleaming black and golden thorax and stream-line abdomen terminating in a needle-like point, were unmistakable. It was a hornet! a gigantic, predatory insect belonging to the group of solitary hymenoptera. No doubt it was searching for some victim which, having been stung into a state of helpless paralysis, would be buried alive, inert but conscious, until the hornet's grubs emerged from their eggs and devoured the living flesh, so thoughtfully provided by their savage parent. Scores, hundreds, thousands of times I had watched solitary wasps and hornets as they seized spiders, larvae and even locusts, and after paralyzing them carried them to their nests to be stored away as a live food supply for their young. And now, now I was shaking, shivering with abject terror, as overhead circled a hornet as large as an eagle, a rapacious terrible insect large and powerful enough to swoop upon me and plunge its numbing, paralyzing sting into my own body. Cold sweat broke out upon my temples at thought of such a fate, at thought of being buried alive but incapable of movement in some underground chamber, until hungry, loathsome, wriggling maggots threw themselves blindly upon me and gnawed at my palpitating living flesh. From the actions of the savages near me, I knew my fears were well justified. They were even more terrified than I, if such a thing were possible, for no doubt they knew from dire experience the extent of the danger that hovered over them. Only Tom appeared oblivious to this newest peril. But he had no knowledge of the habits of hornets, and, moreover, his brain had been so surcharged with fright that it held no space for further fears.

How long that fearsome giant insect hung on humming wings in the air above us I shall never know. It seemed like hours, and each moment I expected it to descend and seize a victim from among us. Again and again I felt that its great eyes or its delicate waving antennae had located us as it swooped downward, its great, horny, clawed legs outstretched, its ravening jaws open, its abdomen thrust forward with shining, dagger-like sting unsheathed. But either it was not certain of our character or our location or else it hesitated to risk its membranous wings among the foliage and branches, for each time, with an angry buzz, it drew off, until at last it dashed with terrific speed from the spot and the humming of its vibrating wings grew faint in the distance.

Not until then did our captors rise, and again, seizing us, proceed on their interrupted journey. By now, too, much of my first terrible fears of the beings had worn off. Possibly familiarity was beginning to breed contempt or again it may have been a subconscious feeling that as we had not hitherto been harmed we would remain alive and whole. But largely I think it was due to the tremendous scientific interest my strange surroundings had aroused and to my realization that we faced far greater dangers from the other denizens of this world than from our captors. Two distinct emotions cannot exist coincidently in the human brain, and my interest in the overdeveloped insects, the strange vegetal growths and the innumerable abnormalities on every side overrode my fears and drove terror from my mind. Moreover, I had made an astonishing discovery, or rather, I might say, realization had come to me once fear had fled and my brain had cleared sufficiently to co-ordinate and function in more or less normal fashion. I was in an insect world, in a land where, for some inexplicable reason, evolution had proceeded along insect lines; where vertebrates had taken second place, and where the conditions of the rest of the world had been reversed and super-insects dwarfed and dominated man. Thinking thus, I studied the savages more closely. And as I did so, my senses fairly reeled as I made a second and even more astounding discovery. The creatures were almost as much insects as men! To be sure they walked upright and possessed but four limbs and they had more or less human-like forms, but their heads and faces were totally unlike those of men; their eyes were distinctly insect-like; their digits were more claws than fingers; their immense ears savored of short, heavy antennae, and the manner in which the first one I had seen had continued fighting while apparently oblivious of his wounds, was astonishingly like the actions of a wounded insect. It was unthinkable, preposterous to even dream that they were insects; that any insect could have evolved or developed such human-like characteristics. But was it not possible that in this land, where I had abundant proof of conditions which favored the dominance of insects, such vertebrates as there were might have assumed insect-like characters?

Scientifically I could see no reason for assuming that this were not only possible but highly probable. Environment has an even greater influence upon the development of living organism than heredity. In a land where all the environment was adapted to the survival and the development of insects there would most assuredly be a tendency for vertebrates—even man—to evolve certain characteristics which would enable him to exist, and which, therefore, would inevitably be insect-like. It was an amazing idea with astounding possibilities and, incredible as it may seem, I was actually beginning to rejoice that fate had decreed that it was to be my privilege to study such abnormal and undreamed of conditions of life. As yet I had seen only the fringe of the land, had observed but a few, an infinitesimal portion of its marvels. What wonders might yet remain, what incredibly astonishing objects and events might be in store, what astounding discoveries might be made—provided I lived to make them—were impossible even to guess. In such a land, amid such surroundings, almost anything might be possible, but my wildest dreams, my most fantastic conjectures, were far short of the truth.

WITH my mind busy with such thoughts, with my fears of our captors dissipated, I gave even more careful attention to our surroundings. Repeatedly enormously overgrown insects were seen. Mostly they were inoffensive, harmless things even in their enormous size. Somehow, too, a remarkable sensation of disproportion possessed me. Instead of the insects and plants appearing of gigantic size I had the feeling of being dwarfed, of being a Lilliputian accompanied by equally Lilliputian beings moving through a normal land among normal creatures. In fact, the exact sensation one might have were one suddenly reduced to the size of a midget, perhaps six inches in height, and found oneself in a brushy, weed-filled pasture. Once this sensation of inverted proportions had entered my brain I could not rid myself of it, try as I might. It was exactly the same as the effect of an optical delusion, like looking at the well known representation of shaded cubes which, when gazed at fixedly for a space, suddenly turn upside down, after which it is next to impossible to force one's optic nerves to see them in their original position. And, up to the present moment, I still feel as though it were Tom and myself who were abnormal—insignificant beings the size of cucumbers amid ordinary sized surroundings. Thus the immense bamboo-like growths assumed the character of ordinary grasses as they would appear to a toad or to the white-footed little deer-mouse; to a sparrow's eyes the sluggish caterpillars for which he sought would appear no larger than the giant, bristle-clad larvae, I saw; the mole, or meadow mouse, following his well-worn pathways across a meadow, might well have gazed upon much the same surroundings as those through which we passed as our captors led us along their trail. So possessed with this strange hallucination did I become that I began to wonder whether the insect life and vegetable growths about me were actually of gigantic size or whether in some inexplicable manner my brain had been affected in such a way that I was seeing things with distorted vision. So insufferable did this doubt in my mind become that, in order to test my senses, I grasped the edge of a russet-hued toadstool that reached to my shoulder and wrenched off a handful of the fungi. As the thing broke, a nauseating, overpowering odor almost choked me, and from the sickly-gray decomposing mass three horrible, corpse-white, wriggling maggots dropped. One struck my shoulder with a thud, and a feeling of sickening repulsion ran through me at its touch. Another fell to the earth in front of me, and before I could avoid it, I stepped squarely upon the thing and my foot was buried to my ankle in the horrid pulpy body. If my eyes and brain were deceiving me, so were my hands, my nerves, my feet, and I was convinced that whatever my sensations of proportion might be, I was in a land where normal men were puny as compared with the insect and plant life. Also, I found myself wondering what the beings who had captured us ate; where and how they lived; how they communicated with one another, and whether they were the only vertebrate denizens of the country. So far we had seen no other vertebrates; no birds, mammals or even reptiles or batrachians, but that, of course, did not prove their non-existence. And if such higher forms of animal life existed what, I wondered, would they be like?

Would they, too, be gigantic? Would they also have acquired more or less of the insect characters? Or would they have remained normal in size and character? It was fascinating to speculate on such matters, and I longed to be able to communicate with the black beings in order to learn something of themselves and their country. But every effort to do this failed. They were apparently dumb, my words meant nothing to them, and signs were obviously incomprehensible.

By now, Tom also had recovered from his first overwhelming terror, and although still shaking with fear, his brain was beginning to function and he was taking note of his bizarre surroundings. Once or twice he uttered exclamations of surprise, and once, when a giant cricket nearly two feet in length leaped unexpectedly across the pathway, he gave vent to a startled cry and sprang back. And gradually, as I managed to get him to converse, I found that he had none of my sensations of being dwarfed, which was a vast relief to me, for it was convincing proof that everything was of gigantic size except the savages who had come with us.

We had now passed through the densest part of the jungle and had entered an area of immense grasses or bamboos. Suddenly these ended, and before us was a cleared open stretch, in the centre of which was a circular ring or mound of stones. As we came within sight of this, scores of the black creatures swarmed over the edge and came hurrying towards us. As they came forward in a close-packed mass, their triangular faces and great staring eyes were so strikingly insect like that they appeared more like a swarm of ants than like a crowd of human beings. In a moment more we were surrounded. The creatures were evidently tremendously excited. Their heads swung from side to side on their long, thin necks; they moved about with nervous quick motions; their antennae-like ears seemed actually to vibrate, and their saliva-dribbling lips twisted and grimaced, while from them there issued an almost inaudible indescribable droning, as though their vocal cords were vibrating without producing articulate sounds.

In the midst of the horde as we were, the odor of their bodies was almost more than I could bear, and my eyes smarted and ran and I coughed and sneezed as though afflicted with hay fever. All the time we were being urged onward towards the stone mound where, between stumbling, walking and clambering, and being pushed and shoved, we at last found ourselves on the summit. It was a broad wall or barrier of stone surrounding a circular sandy area or hollow in the centre of which was a roughly built stone pile—I can scarcely dignify it with the name of building—perforated by innumerable apertures or openings. Straight towards this we were hurried, and still surrounded by a crowd of the creatures although the great majority remained outside, we were led through one of the openings and along a downward-sloping, winding and inky-black passage.

THROUGH endless tunnels and galleries we were led, and gradually our eyes became somewhat accustomed to the darkness and I could distinguish the shadowy walls and at times more or less of the interiors of the chambers we passed or entered. Everywhere the walls of the tunnels were plastered with dried mud or were built up with stones, and everywhere the place reeked with the smell of the beings and with a different, sickishly-sweet odor that issued from certain galleries or rooms. In some places I caught glimpses of figures moving about, but whether they were males or females was impossible to say. At last we were conducted into a fairly large chamber where a very dim light entered through a crack or crevice in the ceiling. And as I glanced about, expecting to find some sort of ruler or chief presiding over the place, I rubbed my eyes and could scarcely credit my senses. Instead of a king or ruler or even a council of the beings who had captured us, I saw the most astonishing sight I had yet beheld. Here and there about the chamber were insects of huge size. Partly reared on his stout legs was a long-bodied, rudimentary-winged rover-beetle nearly a yard in length, with his big eyes staring at us with an oddly vapid, peaceful expression that was almost ludicrous. Then, having apparently lost interest in the newcomers, he settled back lazily upon the floor. Near him was an immense, hairy-bodied, bee-like fly with a fat overfed body as large as a pumpkin, and preening its antennae with one foot, so strikingly like a paunchy man stroking his mustache after a full meal, that even Tom chuckled at the sight. In another spot a drowsy-looking, wingless nymph reposed upon its belly; a soft-bodied, immature thing with glassy, sightless eyes and undeveloped pulpy legs; the yard-long young of some species of hymenopterous insect, helpless as a human baby.

Beyond this were several smaller insects I could not identify, while curled up like a sleeping puppy, and so obviously slumbering that I could almost fancy it snored, was a great, wooly-coated caterpillar. What did this mean? Were these things prisoners like ourselves? Were they destined to be killed and eaten by the savages, and were we destined for the same fate? There seemed no other explanation of this aggregation of strange creatures to which we had been added, unless the savages were acquiring a menagerie and regarded Tom and myself as exhibits. Then, for the first time, I noticed that the creatures I have mentioned were being tended by members of the tribe who had captured us. Several of the beings were offering the insects food, waiting upon them, caring for them. Even as I watched in surprise, two of the things approached Tom and myself, bearing bunches of tender leaves. They offered them to us as if expecting us to devour them as eagerly as the caterpillar, which had uncoiled itself and was crunching avidly at the leaves given to it. They seemed greatly disturbed when we refused to dine on the leaves, and scurried about excitedly. Presently one returned with a fragment of a mushroom—evidently they had misinterpreted my act in breaking the fungus as I had walked along—while a second brought a piece of stinking meat. The meat almost turned my stomach, although the giant fly had ceased stroking its antennae to dine on the same flesh. I was ravenously hungry and, having tasted the fungus, I managed to swallow some of it. Tom, however, could not stomach it, and again the beings, who seemed so solicitous of our welfare, scurried off to return with some sweet, sugary, pasty material which Tom found palatable, declaring that it tasted like condensed milk. This I noticed was also eaten by the mild-eyed rover beetle, as well as by the nymph. With something of dread that we would be forced to subsist upon the same fare as that provided for the insect occupants of the chamber, I squatted down, leaned against the wall and wondered what would be the ultimate end of it all. Our captors apparently paid little heed to us, leaving us unwatched and unguarded when they frequently left the room to return with more food. And, strangely enough, now that they had us here and had fed us, they appeared to take little interest in us. It was inexplicable behavior, and I could only surmise that eventually we would be taken before the ruler of the beings and that our fate would then be decided. Still, there was something in the attitude of our captors which puzzled me greatly. They somehow acted as though we were guests rather than prisoners, and finally, in order to test the matter, I rose to my feet and walked boldly towards the entrance to the chamber. Tom, worn out with his fear and the strain he had been under, was fast asleep, and I did not disturb him. The two beings still in the room glanced up as I turned towards the doorway, but they showed no signs of interfering with my actions. Stooping low to pass through the portal, I stepped into the passage and sauntered onward. Several of the beings met me, several overtook me, but not one showed the least interest in my movements or offered to molest me in any way. I was fairly astounded. For all I could see, I was at liberty to go anywhere I pleased, and I wondered if I would be permitted to reach the open air and even to leave the home of the beings. I was strongly tempted to test it, but I feared I would lose my way in the multiplicity of galleries and passages and would be unable to return to Tom.

There would be plenty of time to discover how free we were later, and turning, I walked back and re-entered the chamber where the strange insects and Tom appeared to be all wrapped in sleep. Feeling tired and drowsy myself, I decided there was nothing better than to follow their example, and stretching myself beside Tom, I closed my eyes. Then, as I dozed off and my half-conscious brain reverted dreamily to the events of the day, I suddenly burst out laughing as a fantastical idea entered my mind. Why hadn't I thought of it before? Why hadn't this solution of the case occurred to me? Now I understood why Tom and myself were there, why those giant insects were in the chamber, why they and ourselves were being fed and tended by the strange beings. Yes, my knowledge of entomology, of the life histories and habits of insects should have made it all clear to me at first sight of that great rover-beetle, the paunchy fly, the helpless nymph, the drowsy caterpillar. Like their prototypes of the outside world, that dwell within the nests of ants and bees and are not only suffered to remain but are actually fed and tended by their hosts, these insects about me were inquilines.

They were lazy, improvident guests of these beings who despite their human forms, were themselves so ant-like. Inquilines that perhaps had come uninvited, or that, perhaps, had been brought here as Tom and myself had been. And it was this thought that had brought a chuckle of laughter to my lips. The thought, the conviction, that we two were nothing more than inquilines; creatures to be regarded with the same tolerance and as on the same plane as the insects that shared the underground chamber with us.

CHAPTER THREE

I AWOKE greatly refreshed and much easier in my mind. Tom was already awake, but our insect companions appeared to be still slumbering. I had no idea how long I had slept, and the chamber was too dark to permit me to see my watch. I was on the point of striking a match in order to learn the hour, but realizing how scanty was my supply of matches, I thought better of thus wasting one of the precious things. But I was longing to smoke, and at last, unable to resist longer—for I had not had a whiff of tobacco since entering the country—I decided that I could afford one match for lighting my pipe and could determine the time with the same light. The effect of the lighting of the match was astounding. As the flame flared up, momentarily lighting the room, every occupant came to life instantly. There was a rustling of wings, the scratching of chitinous feet, the sound of scurrying bodies, and strange clicking noises. Instantly everything was in confusion. The rover-beetle rushed scurrying into a dark passage; the aldermanic fly spread its wings and flew blindly about, bumping into walls and against the ceiling; the wooly caterpillar uncoiled and hurried out of sight as if it had a pressing engagement elsewhere, and the savages who were within the chamber threw themselves on the floor in a paroxysm of terror. Only the pulpy, helpless nymph remained placid, utterly unmoved, utterly oblivious to everything, just as any normal, nymph should be. I was so surprised at the effect of the sudden light upon the creatures, that I held the match until it scorched my fingers.

But after all, I thought, it was not really surprising in the least. Insects invariably react to a light in darkness. They may be attracted by it and blunder into it—the proverbial moths and the flame—or, in the case of many beetles and other insects, they exhibit fear and seek safety by hiding themselves in the darkest crevices they can find. And the insect denizens of the chamber were all inquilines, creatures whose lives are spent in darkness. Merely because they were of gigantic proportions was no reason why they should be any more intelligent than ordinary insects or should not possess precisely the same habits, characteristics and reactions as the normal sized insects of the same genera. Somehow, quite unconsciously, probably because Tom and I had been treated like the other inquilines, and perhaps partly on account of their size I had begun to regard the huge insect inhabitants of the land as sentient, intelligent beings, more or less like higher forms of life or even like primitive humans. In fact, the effect of my match upon the creatures brought me suddenly to the realization that, without knowing it, I had been brought into a curious psychological state, wherein I had been regarding the overgrown insects like fellow men or, to put it another way, I had unwittingly placed myself, mentally, on a plane with the insects. And this knowledge explained in a measure the ant-like characteristics of the black savages. Through countless generations they had lived among insects, had inhabited a land where insects dominated. If I, a civilized, and I flatter myself an unusually intelligent man, so quickly and unconsciously acquired this amazing psychological state, the wonder was that the poor, ignorant, semi-human savages had not ages ago lost what little intelligence and human characteristics they had possessed. And it was not surprising that they, too, had been terror-stricken at the flare of a match. When I came to think of it, I had seen no signs of fires anywhere, and the chances were that they did not even know how to make a fire. But my discovery of their fear of flame was most opportune and did much to encourage me. Fire would be a weapon with which I could rule the beings, and I doubted if even the most courageous of them would attempt to interfere with us, once they had seen me produce the phenomenon. But I soon found that I possessed an even more potent and terrible power than fire. Telling Tom of my plans and explaining as well as I might what I believed our position to be, we rose, and leading the way, I started down the passage. As on the previous day, no one attempted to interfere with us. And presently I noticed that, as we approached them, all the savages within sight raced off as though the devil were at their heels. Moreover, they came pouring from chambers and galleries and filled the passage to overflowing as they crowded and struggled to get out of our way, until the tunnel before us was packed with a milling, excited throng. At first I thought that word of my match had been spread and that the savages were terrified for fear I would again strike a light. Then, suddenly, the truth burst upon me; it was the smoke from my pipe. Perhaps the sight of the smoke was enough to strike terror to their hearts or, more probably, the odor of the tobacco was the cause of their fright. But whatever the basic cause, the result was in our favor, for not only was it obvious that we had nothing to fear from that time on, but in addition, we had merely to follow the retreating mob in order to reach the open air. The instant they reached the exits to the tunnels, the creatures scattered and ran, and we found ourselves quite alone, with the faint light of dawn just breaking through the heavy veil of mists that shrouded the land.

THE smell of the fresh air and of vegetation was most welcome after the musty, malodorous atmosphere of the subterranean chambers, and we sat there taking deep breaths and waiting for the sun to rise. I had determined that as soon as it was light enough to see, I would go in search of food. The bit of musty fungus I had eaten had merely taken the edge off my ravenous hunger, and Tom confessed that he felt famished. Somewhere in the land there must be edible fruit, vegetables or game, and I was determined to find out what alimentary resources the country possessed. I still had my revolver and a belt full of cartridges, and though I am no expert marksman, I felt confident that I could manage to bring down any ordinary sized animal or bird we might find. Also, there was a chance that there might be fish in the streams or pools I had seen, and, all else failing, we might be able to fall back upon some form of insect. More than once, when among Indians, I had eaten dried grasshopper meal, fried caterpillars and roasted palm grubs, and from personal experience I knew that, when one's natural repugnance to such things was overcome, that food was nutritious and palatable. And I could see no reason why a grub, larva or grasshopper should not be equally edible, if it happened to be several feet long, instead of an inch or two. In fact, at that moment, I could picture dining off a grasshopper's drumstick or a beetle-grub steak with intense satisfaction.

Meanwhile I loaded my pistol and chatted with Tom, while in the distance, the shadowy forms of the savages lurked about, watching us fearfully and ready to take flight at the first movement on our part. They were, after all, a most timid and harmless lot, and I wondered that I had been so terrified by them in the first place. But then again, I had seen a demonstration of their fighting ability and I thoroughly appreciated the fact that, should they screw up their courage to the proper pitch, they could make short work of us without much danger to themselves. But it requires the highest degree of both mental and physical courage to attack an unknown being, and more especially a being who is regarded with superstition or, who is regarded as a superior being. And I could not imagine those triangular headed degenerate savages possessing any mental courage no matter how much physical valor they might have. Now I felt perfectly secure as far as any danger from our recent hosts was concerned.

Presently, too, the light had increased sufficiently for us to start on our hunt. Leaving the savages to their own devices and to their underground retreats, we clambered over the stone wall, walked across the open space and found ourselves in the jungle. On every hand strange noises and rather terrifying sounds issued from the shadows and thickets. Some of these I recognized. The siren-like, deafening screech from a clump of bamboos was unquestionably that of a giant cricket. The piercing, ear-splitting note was probably from some awakening grasshopper. The crunching rending noises were caused by hungry larvae devouring the moisture-laden leaves, and the loud, clicking noises, like a hammer striking metal, were, I decided, produced by beetles. The whole place appeared to teem with life, and at every turn we caught glimpses of the busy insects. Probably the number of insects in this place is not any greater in proportion to the area and the vegetation than elsewhere, but owing to the fact that they are all, or nearly all, of exaggerated size, they appeared far more numerous. Also, as we were relatively small, we were better able to discover the insects. Had we, too, been built on the same proportionate scale as human beings in an ordinary land, I doubt if we would have noticed any greater abundance of insect life than in an ordinary meadow or forest. But as it was, we were not only enabled to see practically every insect within reach of our vision, but I was afforded a most marvelous opportunity of studying their lives and habits. It was, in fact, like looking at everything through a powerful microscope, and my hunger was forgotten in my interest in watching the strange life about me. Even Tom, who was not in the least given to an interest in natural history, and always considered all forms of insect life as "bugs" to be destroyed, became quite excited and fascinated as I pointed out the habits of the creatures about us. From the limb of a spreading tree a fat-bodied spider the size of a tea-tray, and with hairy legs as thick as a rolling-pin, was industriously spinning a web of gleaming silken strands, each strand the size of stout cord. And when a blundering gnat as large as a sparrow flew blindly into the half-completed web, and the ferocious owner dashed at it, enveloped it in coils of silk and gloatingly proceeded to devour the captive, we watched the tragedy with almost hypnotic fascination.

Tom glanced nervously about. "Wa-lla," he ejaculated, "Ah don't wantin' for to meet sco'pions an' tarant'las here 'bout, Chief. Nor cent'pedes neither. A cent'pede mos' surely be as big as dem bo'on'strictors, an' a sco'pion de bigness of a cow. No, Chief, Ah don't longin' fo' meet none of dem folk."

But fortunately we met neither centipedes, scorpions nor predatory arachnids, though I could fully appreciate Tom's fears of such an encounter, and fully realized the dangerous character of such creatures, if of the same proportions as the other insects. A scorpion six feet in length, a mygale or tarantula weighing a score of pounds or a centipede twice as long as a man would indeed be a formidable enemy.

BUT even without these to reckon with, there was, I felt, no little peril in wandering through this jungle of strange forms of plant life. Many of our commonest insects are predatory, still more are carnivorous, and, for their size, insects are the most savage, ferocious and utterly fearless of all creatures. To be sure, as a rule insects are very particular as to their food, and a species which devours caterpillars, for example, will attack and eat nothing else. Hence, I reasoned, that if human beings were not included in the menu of any of the insects in this land, we had comparatively little to fear, for it is rarely that any insect attacks another creature except for the purpose of eating it. But, on the other hand, I had witnessed the terror of the black savages when the solitary hornet had approached, and, for all I knew, the giant insects of this country might have acquired a liking for human flesh and blood. A tiger-beetle a yard in length would be a bad customer and would be far more dangerous than a tiger. An aphislion with its enormous scissors-like jaws a foot in length would be able to shear a man's head from his shoulders. And if there were ants, as I felt there must be, they might and probably would prove the most dangerous of all the preposterously overdeveloped fauna of this strange land. In addition to all these unknown dangers which might confront us at any moment, there was the danger that the vertebrate beasts inhabited the jungles. Although I had so far discovered no sign of the presence of mammals, lizards or even birds, yet it seemed highly improbable that such did not exist. And if they did, how could I be sure that they, too, were not relatively as large as the insects?

I trembled at the thought of meeting a carnivorous beast or bird under such conditions. Even a shrew—the tiniest of mammals—would be large and powerful enough to destroy us, as readily as our ordinary shrews destroy a husky stag-beetle. But a little later, when we met our first mammal, all my conjectures had not prepared me for what I saw. The creature was some sort of gopher or ground-squirrel, and quite unexpectedly it darted from the jungle across our pathway. And, so strangely had my surroundings affected me mentally, and so accustomed had I become to seeing familiar things enlarged to incredible size, that I was speechless with amazement, for the creature was no larger than an ordinary woodchuck. Recovering my self-possession in time, I brought the marmot down with a lucky shot from my pistol, and we were assured of at least one meal. I felt immensely relieved, also, to find the marmot of normal size. If the form of mammalian life was normal in this land of abnormalities, there was no reason to think that others were not normal as well. But as I speculated upon this, and again resumed our way, I wondered how ordinary sized vertebrates ever managed to survive in a land of giant insects. But I believe now, from what I have observed, that the only vertebrates which havemanaged to exist, are those that dwell in subterranean holes or burrows and are nocturnal in their habits. Whether all other species have been completely exterminated, or whether they were never indigenous to the land, I cannot say; but my opinion is that the latter is the case and that the absence of large carnivorous birds and mammals is one of the chief causes of the ultra-development of insect life here.

So engrossed had I become in my thoughts, and so closely was Tom scrutinizing the thickets fearing a surprise by some dangerous creature, that I failed to watch my step. Suddenly and without warning, my feet flew from under me and with a terrified yell I found myself sliding, rolling down the steep side of a pit-like depression. To be sure it was not more than five feet in depth, but to me it held all the terrors of an inferno. At the very instant I had lost my footing I realized what it was. And as I struggled to regain my feet, and to scramble up the sandy slope, my hair seemed literally to stand on end and I fairly screamed with terror, for I had fallen into the trap of a monstrous ant-lion. A few feet from me, and clearly visible, as with fear-dilated eyes I glanced backward, two enormous scimitar shaped jaws were protruding from the loose sand at the bottom of the pit. Once within reach of those horny, dagger-sharp, living blades and I would be seized, sliced as with gigantic scissors, and the blood slowly sucked from my palpitating body. Many a time had I watched helpless struggling ants and other insects as they slid to the bottom of an ant-lion's trap and were seized and sucked dry by the flat-bodied, powerfully-built, ravenous creature concealed under the sand. Now, as I fought madly to escape from the shallow pit, I realized how those unfortunate insects must have felt.

Meantime Tom stood paralyzed above me, his mouth gaping, his eyes rolling, and utterly bereft of enough of his senses to aid me. But the worst was yet to come. As I slowly, as if in a nightmare, clawed my way upward, slipping back an inch for every two I gained, the lurking terrible creature at the bottom began throwing showers of sand and dust at me, exactly as I had seen countless ordinary ant-lions throw dust at escaping ants. With quick upward jerks of his flat spatulate head and broad pincer-like jaws, he would toss a few handfuls of sand over me with devilish accuracy. Half blinded by the dust, frightened out of my wits, expecting each moment to reel back into those waiting jaws, I might as well have been trying to find hand- and foot-holds in water as in the sliding loose sand. Then, when I was becoming exhausted and felt convinced that I was doomed, Tom recovered his wits, and bracing himself firmly, extended a tough branch within my reach. The next instant I was panting, spent, breathless and shaking, but safe on firm ground.

It had been a close shave. Maddened, and in a paroxysm of hate and resentment, I whipped out my pistol and was about to blaze away at the now quiescent ant-lion when Tom reminded me that my ammunition would be more valuable for getting food and that a few good sized rocks would serve equally as well as far as the ant-lion was concerned. Suiting his actions to his words, he picked up a convenient stone and hurled it at the beast. But the creature was protected by a layer of sand, and the only result was to cause it to hastily bury itself deeper.

WE proceeded with far greater caution after that experience. It was fortunate that we did so, for not only were the ant-lion traps fairly numerous, but in addition, we soon discovered that the earth, in spots, was riddled with holes and burrows in any one of which we might wrench an ankle or break a leg.

To recall all the forms of insect life we saw would be impossible, and to fill my notes with descriptions would be a waste of paper of which I have none too much. Ground-beetles seemed to be the most abundant things, and though they rushed madly about in a strangely excited and yet purposeless manner, and several times almost knocked our legs from under us, they appeared to be quite terrified whenever they came near us. Perhaps it was the strange scent of human beings, though they smelled so abominably themselves, that I cannot understand how they could detect any outside odor. Dipterous insects were also very common, and these appeared quite familiar and of ordinary size until I realized that their iridescent, jewel-like, gauzy-winged insects, the size of our common bluebottle flies, belonged to genera, members of which, ordinarily, are so small, that they are scarcely visible to the untrained eye. Once, too, a great dragon-fly dashed into sight, alighted with stiff outspread wings and keen eyes upon a dead tree top, and then darted after a passing fly and snapped it up at a single gulp. He was a truly magnificent creature, although a bit terrifying at first; a gleaming thing spreading fully ten feet. From his round head, with its terrible jaws, to the tip of his tapering plated body, he was a mass of dazzling blue, scarlet and silver. Tom remarked that if he could only be caught and tamed, he might serve as a living airplane to carry us back to civilization.

Butterflies were numerous, and while I recognized some genera, others were quite strange to me. Thehelioconidae appeared the most common, as they usually are in the tropics. One species—a gray and white mottled chap spreading about three feet—had a most interesting habit of settling upon the earth, waving its wings slowly, and emitting a remarkable clicking or ticking sound like snapping clam shells together. Several very large species were observed, the largest being a shining green beauty spreading at least eight feet across the wings and evidently one of the morphos. But the most beautiful and interesting butterflies were tiny fellows the size of our ordinary danais or medium sized papilios. They flitted nervously and jerkily from one resting place to another as we approached them, invariably alighting with their heads towards us and with their feathery antennae and ruby-like eyes watching our every movement in a most intelligent and fascinating manner.

They were most delicately fashioned and beautifully colored things, too. Their legs and bodies appeared to be dressed in garments of thick soft fur of almost metallic lustre, their wings were in some cases edged with delicate feathers; in other cases they were entirely of the most intricate lacework, and their colors were indescribably lovely. For the most part they were pastel shades of lavender, buff, red and green, often set off by shining flecks of gold or silver. I longed for a net in which to capture and examine some of these, and it was not until I had watched them for a long time that it dawned upon me that they were in reality prototypes of our own microlepidoptera, things so minute that they can only be examined through a powerful lens and so delicate that it is practically impossible to capture or preserve them without ruining their beauty and their details. But here were microlepidoptera large enough to study at a considerable distance and with the naked eye, and I wondered if somewhere in this land there were any minute forms of insect life, creatures as small in proportion to the lacy, feather-winged beauties as are our minute moths in proportion to the big shingidae. Strangely enough, too, a great many genera and families of insects appeared to be entirely wanting. I saw norepiptera, none of the carnivorous predatory beetles, no termites, no arachnids other than a few spiders, no millipedes or centipedes and no mosquitos. For this I was duly thankful, for the thought of mosquitos the size of dragon flies or larger was disconcerting, to say the least. Aside from the gopher I had killed, one or two field-mice which darted out of sight instantly, and a fleeting glimpse of some creature I thought to be a hare or rabbit, we saw no mammals. We did, however, find several snails, one or two of large size, but no larger than many marine molluscs. And we had a hearty laugh over our terror—after it had passed—when an enormous overgrown toad leaped from the shadows and descended like a falling elephant to the trail ahead of us. To our affrighted and startled eyes, he appeared a most gigantic and terrifying beast, although in reality he was no larger than a good-sized dog, and quite harmless. As he squatted there, eyeing us speculatively, winking first one eye and then the other as if doubting his own vision, the while his yellowish-white throat palpitated to his breathing, he seemed most astonishingly and ludicrously human. Finally, having apparently satisfied himself that we really existed, he opened his wide toothless mouth, yawned prodigiously and, as if deciding we were most uninteresting and ridiculous beings, he leaped back to his damp retreat.

So far, our search for food had not been very successful and it began to look as if we would fare badly unless we resorted to insect flesh for sustenance. We had not gone entirely hungry, however. From time to time we had found nuts and seeds; once or twice we had found berries, which, from a botanical viewpoint, I knew must be edible, and Tom had discovered—with the born instinct of the West Indian negro—a species of cane with a sweet sap, which he munched avidly, declaring it was as good as inferior sugar cane.

But by far the greater portion of edible fruits, berries and even tubers that we found had been completely ruined or partly devoured by the innumerable insects. In fact, the only real edibles of any account which we found were located by means of the insects. If we noticed flies, beetles and other creatures hurrying in any one direction, we soon learned that by following them we were usually led to an accumulation of ripe fruits or to a bush laden with berries. Of course the greater portion of the fruit was far beyond our reach, and often we gazed longingly at the luscious-looking fruits surrounded by butterflies, hymenoptera, diptera, etc., in the lofty tree tops.

WE had been wandering thus for several hours when I at last suggested that we should light a fire and roast our game. No dry fuel was near, and noticing a fairly open forest a short distance ahead, we turned towards it. We had proceeded but a short distance, when, to my surprise, I came upon a well-marked, carefully smoothed pathway, a road of bare earth, perhaps two feet in width and leading almost in a straight line in either direction as far as we could see. Evidently, I thought, there were human beings in the country, men who were far above the black savages, and, whether hostile or friendly, far preferable as hosts. Mentally deciding that as soon as we had eaten we would investigate the pathway and find where and to what it led, we set about gathering dry sticks in readiness for the fire. Busy with this, while Tom was engaged in skinning and cleaning the marmot, I failed to maintain as careful a watch as I should, until, instinctively warned by the sixth sense that one develops in the bush, I straightened up and turned my eyes towards the pathway. My amazement at what I beheld forced an exclamation from my lips, and at this Tom also glanced up. One glimpse, and dropping the carcass, he leaped to his feet, and with rolling eyes and terrified features, he sprang behind a sheltering tree. Hurrying towards us down the pathway came a huge reddish-brown creature; a creature fully five feet in length with enormous head, great rounded fixed eyes, short club-shaped antennae, rough, powerful legs, attenuated waist and turnip-shaped abdomen. From head to tail he was sheathed in shining horny armor like a coat of mail. Clamped fast in his enormous, triangular jaws he held a huge section of green leaf that waved like a banner above his head. Behind him came another and another, an endless procession, each carrying its green burden until the moving stream of leaves appeared like a strip of jungle marching through the forest.

Instantly I recognized them for what they were. They were leaf-cutting ants, the bane of all tropical agriculturalists, but hundreds of times larger than any leaf-cutting ant ever before seen by mortal eyes. Like their prototypes so abundant throughout tropical America, the gigantic terrifying creatures before us were bent only on their own affairs. They turned neither to right nor left, as they rushed past us, intent only on reaching their underground nest and placing their bits of leaf within the chambers where the decaying vegetation, carefully watched and tended, would develop the edible fungi on which the ants subsisted. I have said they were hurrying, but the term conveys no idea of the terrific speed at which they traveled.

They moved with the rapidity of racing motor cars, at a speed of fully fifty miles an hour I should say, and this added to the illusion of a moving, steadily flowing stream of leaves. For a moment I was astounded at the speed of these huge ants, but an instant's reflection convinced me that it was quite to be expected, that it was really no faster in proportion to their size than the movements of ordinary ants. I had repeatedly timed the progress of various insects, and I knew that the larger ants easily traversed forty to fifty feet or approximately one thousand times their own length in one minute. Hence, at the same proportionate rate, there was no reason why the giant insects I was watching should not move one thousand times their length or fully a mile in a minute. Tom was absolutely helpless with terror and was gazing with horror-filled eyes at the ever-flowing, endless procession of rushing, ferocious looking giant ants. For a space, I confess, I partly shared his fears, but unless these overdeveloped ants possessed intellects and habits wholly unlike those of their normal relatives, we had nothing to fear, if we were not so foolish as to step into their pathway or interrupt their business-like progress. But I could not convince Tom that the creatures would not tear us limb from limb if they caught sight of us or suspected our presence. In fact, he shook and quaked with new terror when I spoke, filled with dread that the onrushing ants might hear me. I laughed gaily and assured him that the ants were stone deaf as far as our voices were concerned. And gradually, as he noticed that the passing creatures gave no heed to my voice, he began to believe me. But it was not until I had thrown the entrails of the gopher into the ants pathway, and he had watched them halt and remove the obstruction and again resume their interminable march without offering to devour the offal, that he could realize that we were in no danger. So, feeling quite safe as far as the ants were concerned, we lit our fire and prepared to cook our meat and eat our long delayed breakfast within a stone's throw of the ant column. But if the ants had paid no attention to our proximity before, and had given no sign that our voices were audible to them, they showed immediate and unmistakable evidences of knowing something was wrong the moment the fire was lighted.

At the first whiff of smoke blown across their roadway, they came to an abrupt halt, milled about, stroked one another with their feet, touched antennae, and seemed tremendously excited. Some dropped their burdens and started off in various directions through the forest, and two of these scouts headed directly towards us. Tom sprang to his feet screaming, but I seized him by the coat and forced him to remain beside me, although I admit it required no little courage and self-possession to stand there in the face of the ferocious-looking, expressionless beasts who rushed down upon us. But I trusted to the intelligence of the ants and to our fire and I was not disappointed. As the two came within range of the thickest smoke, they halted, reared themselves on their hind legs—reminding me of great tawny bears as they did so—pawed the air, rubbed their antennae, and wheeling, scurried around to the other side of the fire. Once more they dashed up until they felt the heat of the flame, whereupon they again retreated. Over and over again they repeated these tactics, often passing within a foot of us, and each time they came near, Tom trembled and shook until his teeth chattered. But as far as the ants were concerned we might have been forest trees or bits of stone. All their attentions and senses were centered upon the fire and smoke, totally new things to them. At last, having satisfied themselves that it was some phenomenon that was to remain fixed, and that it was not likely to attack them, they hurried back to the waiting column. Then, having apparently conveyed the information they had gathered to their fellows, they picked up their discarded bits of leaves, fell into line, and once again the procession was in full motion. Convinced that he had nothing to fear, Tom sank back to the earth, while I chaffed him and poked fun at him for being afraid of leaf-carrying ants with whose habits he should have been so thoroughly familiar. Somewhat shamefacedly he admitted that he was quite aware that the "drougher ant" of Jamaica and other tropic lands was a strict vegetarian and confined itself to certain definite vegetable growths at that, but, he added, as he ravenously attacked a gopher leg; "Dis Gent'man, he don't been tha same, Chief. He don't been right an' proper ant all. Chief. He been distinc' specie of bug an' too monstrous for truf. No, Chief, Ah knows a cat eats mice an' Ah can shoo her off. But b'lieve me, Chief, Ah aint desi'ous of strivin' to shoo off no lion. No, sir."

CHAPTER FOUR

OUR hunger satisfied, the question arose as to our next move. We were homeless, friendless waifs, in a strange, bizarre and dangerous land. To return to the hospitality of the black savages was not to be considered. And we well knew that it would be a waste of energy to attempt to regain the outer world by way of the tunnel from Tupec. There was a chance, however, that there might be other means of leaving the place, and our only feasible plan appeared to be to thoroughly explore the country in the hope of discovering some trail or passage by which we might escape. I have already said that at our first view of the place it had appeared to be surrounded by lofty mountains. But I knew from experience that mountain ranges might seem continuous and unbroken from a distance and yet might be cut by numerous passes, ravines and canyons, and it is rarely indeed that a long mountain range cannot be surmounted in some spot. To be sure, it seemed an almost hopeless task to think of tramping around that vast territory searching for an exit, maintaining a precarious existence meanwhile, and constantly facing unknown perils. I knew only too well how slow one's progress is in a tropical untamed land, and I knew that months, years in fact, might be required to really explore the place. But in a way, time meant nothing to us. Aside from the fact that my supply of ammunition was limited and that our garments and shoes would not last forever, there was no valid reason why we should not devote the rest of our lives to our search. For that matter, if we did not attempt it, the rest of outlives would be passed here anyway. At any rate, we would be doing something to occupy our minds and bodies, and anything was better than to remain inactive and hopelessly awaiting whatever might befall. As I thought on such matters and discussed them with Tom, it occurred to me that my position was highly amusing. I had set out on this trip, lured on by the wild tales of weird people and strange beings in the unknown interior of the country: I had determined to penetrate the district beyond Tupec, and I had looked forward with enthusiastic interest to making epochal discoveries. And now that I had penetrated to the locality, had actually reached the fabulous land and had met the beings—as well as even more amazing things—all my interests and efforts were bent on getting away from the very spot I had so long desired to enter.

There was no doubt that I had made epochal discoveries, but of what use to discover things unless such discoveries could be made known to the world? Also it struck me forcibly, for the first time in my life, that man's desire to explore, to see strange sights, to discover amazing facts, was not a question of personal gratification or a thirst for individual knowledge, but was really due to an inherent, egotistical vanity; a love of publicity and a longing to be applauded, praised and regarded as famous by his fellow men. Throughout my own career I had rather prided myself on fighting shy of publicity, and had flattered myself that all my studies and investigations had been carried on solely for the benefit of science and adding to my own store of knowledge. Yet here was I, amid the most amazing things that any scientist ever dreamed of, and thinking only of getting away from them, of returning to humdrum lands and uninteresting civilized human beings. Still, I did feel an intense interest in the place and its strange denizens, and I knew that, had I been free to leave whenever I desired, I should have elected to remain for a long time and should have found the greatest delight in studying the animal and plant life of the land. Thus musing on the complex psychology of mankind and the reaction of the human brain to conditions and environment, I lit my pipe, and, as one place seemed as good as another for a beginning, led the way through the forest towards the nearest mountains. I should have liked to have crossed the pathway of the leaf-carrying ants, for beyond that line of march, the forest was more open, the land sloped upward, and I surmised that from the higher land I might secure a widespread view of the place and could thus be enabled to pick some promising objective point. But despite my knowledge of the ants' habits and herbivorous characters, I had no desire to attempt a passage of their highway. To try to dash across amid that throng of hurrying insects would be far more perilous than to undertake to dodge among countless racing automobiles on a congested avenue. Ants at best are short-tempered things, and while they might not go out of their way or neglect their own affairs to attack us—as long as we minded our own business and did not interfere with them—yet I felt quite confident that they would resent any trespassing on their right of way and would show their resentment in a most unpleasant and terrible manner. Even if they did not fall upon us and tear us limb from limb, but merely regarded us as temporary obstructions—much as they had treated the gopher's entrails—I had no desire to be picked up by those great terrifying jaws and tossed to one side. So, abandoning all thoughts of crossing the stream of ants, we turned our backs upon them, and keeping to the open forest, tramped onward. Here in the forest, life was comparatively scarce. Far above our heads we could hear the sounds of insect life, the crunching of leaves by giant larvae, the droning of buzzing flies and bees, the high-pitched screech of tree-crickets, and innumerable noises I could not identify.

Once, too, a terrific roaring bellow struck terror to our hearts and we halted, cowering behind a tree, for such a sound I felt could only issue from the throat of some huge carnivorous mammal. But presently, as the roar was repeated and I gazed fixedly in the direction whence it came, expecting to see a crouching tiger or other feline, I burst into a peal of laughter. Clinging to the rough bark of an outjutting limb, his great golden eyes blinking, squatted a huge tree-frog; a gigantic hyla with moist skin so perfectly matching the color of the lichen-covered bark that had it not been for his eyes and the movements of his throat, as he again gave vent to his bellow, he would have been invisible.

On another occasion we were startled by what might well have been the screech of a steamship's siren, a terrifying sound that rose and fell and quavered and drowned all other noises. For a moment I was perplexed, but as I caught sight of an object clinging to a tree trunk I knew instantly what creature had produced the ear-splitting cry. As Tom also saw the thing on the tree he gave a howl of terror and clung to me shaking with fear. I really could not blame him, for nothing we had yet seen, was more horrifying in aspect or more monstrous in form. Its fat abdomen was perhaps three feet in length; its heavy spike-covered legs ended in great anchor-shaped claws, that were buried deep in the bark; its goggle eyes wore a fishy, ghastly expression—reminding me of a long-dead human—and between short, murderous-looking palpi or fore-legs we could see a long, needle-pointed tusk or beak. But despite its fearsome aspect I knew the thing was harmless, devoid of life, and picking up a stick, I stepped forward and with a laugh aimed a blow at the thing. As the stick struck the monster it crackled, collapsed and dropped in a dozen pieces to the ground. It was merely the cast-off skin of a cicada larva, or so-called "locust," and the siren-like screech from the tree top was the triumphant love call of the mature insect which had recently emerged from the discarded pupa-case.

ANOTHER time Tom had a surprise, which amazed him so that for several moments he was quite incapable of speech, and sat gazing, unable to believe his eyes, until my peals of laughter brought him to his senses. In order to remove a twig from one shoe he had reached out one hand to rest it against a tree to steady himself. The next instant a two-foot section of the rough, gray bark had detached itself from the tree trunk, had sprung suddenly into life, and on broad rustling wings had flitted off, showing a flash of flame color as it did so. Fifty feet away it had vanished as suddenly and as completely as though it had dissolved in air, and Tom, as I said, sat gazing incredulously at the spot where it had disappeared. I had recognized it as a catocola moth, a giant specimen to be sure, but possessing the same habits and practically the same colors as our familiar catocalas of the northern forests. Like them its upper wings were colored and patterned to precisely match the bark of the tree on which it rested, like them its under wings—visible only in flight—were gaudily colored in orange and black, and like them it flitted but a short distance, before again alighting on a tree trunk, where it became instantly so camouflaged as to become invisible. Tom was loth to believe this possible, and in order to prove the facts, and to accustom him to unexpected experiences, I approached the tree where the moth had vanished until within a few feet of it. Then, while Tom stared at the bark incredulously, I tossed a pebble, and once more the apparent piece of bark took flight Tom shook his woolly head and gazed after the flitting insect reflectively. "Pears to me, Chief," he observed, "we folks don't been design' for to abide here no ways so conven'ent like tha bugs. Could Ah absolve mahself into a tree bark like dat gent'man do, Ah wouldn't be afraid of nothin'. Ah'd jes' transfo'm mahself into the bark an' laff at whatsoever was a—s'archin' fo' me. Yes, Chief Ah mos' surely would."

THE WORLD OF THE GIANT ANTS

To me, the most astonishing thing about all the life we had seen was the fact that in their habits, characters and even appearance, the insects, mammals and batrachians were so very similar to those I was familiar with elsewhere.

About the only difference was the discrepancy in size, and, in the case of mammals at least, even that distinction was wanting. Only the human denizens of the land appeared to have developed unusual physical characters and habits—characters and habits strikingly insect-like as I have already said. If, as I assumed, this was due to the predominance of insects and the environment, why then had not the insects developed higher forms, greater intelligence and at least some of the characters that we associate with human beings? As I speculated on this, my memory went back to my college days and I recollected the words of my professor of zoology. In the course of a lecture he had stated that one of the peculiarities of man's mind was that it could not conceive of anything totally unlike anything ever before seen, smelt, heard, tasted or felt. In other words, man's imagination was completely restricted to the experiences of his five senses. No man, he had declared, could describe a color, a sound, an odor, a texture or a form entirely new or unknown. Even the writers of the most imaginative fiction were at a loss to do this. If they attempted to describe the denizens of another planet they invariably compared them to something familiar: they were like this that or the other with slightly altered details; a color was invariably described as resembling one or more of the visible rays of the spectrum. "And yet," he continued, "we have no reason to assume that the inhabitants of another world—or even of some unknown part of this world—have the slightest resemblance to anything we have ever seen. There is no valid scientific reason why any of the lower forms of life—even the insects—should not, somewhere in the universe, have evolved and developed to the same or even greater heights than the primates in our circumscribed world."

The truth of this statement, coming from a scientist of world-wide reputation, could not be denied or even doubted. And yet, here, in a land where most obviously every condition was most admirably adapted to the ultra-development of insect and batrachian life, the insects were still insects in character, in intellect, in habits; the batrachians were still batrachians, and while man had degenerated, the other forms of life had not progressed beyond acquiring greater size. There were the ants for example; the most intelligent, the best organized, the most human-like, if I may use the term, of the insect-world. Theoretically ants, in a land like this, and where they reached undreamed of proportions, might be expected to exhibit marvelous intellect, amazing progress, and might even be more advanced than human beings. Yet the leaf-carrying ants, which were the only species I had observed, were still ants, gigantic in size to be sure, but still behaving exactly like any ordinary leaf-carrying ants.

NO, there was not a thing I had met so far which I could not have described fully and intelligently from my former experiences and observations; not a thing which was absolutely new to my eyes, nose, ears, tongue or touch.

After all, I thought, there is much truth in the old saying that there is nothing new under the sun. But there is equal truth in the equally trite proverbs regarding pride going before a fall and a modicum of knowledge being a dangerous thing, as I was to discover very soon. Absorbed in my reflections and cogitations, I had failed to note our surroundings until I was aroused by a surprised ejaculation from Tom. I glanced up to find that we had reached the end of the forest and that before us was a grove, or I might say orchard, of large shrubs or small trees with thick, fleshy stalks and soft green foliage. That they had been planted purposely and were cultivated growths was evident, for they were arranged in orderly rows and the earth beneath them was bare of grass or weeds. For a brief instant new hope sprang to my breast, for here, I thought, was proof that intelligent civilized or semi-civilized men dwelt in the land. But the nest second my heart sank and I involuntarily slipped back of a tree. From between the rows of plants one of the hideous black savages appeared.

But it was not the semi-human being that riveted my attention and caused me to gasp with incredulous amazement, but the creatures that accompanied him. For the fraction of a second I mistook them for some species of pachyderm, some creature related to the hippopotami, and in a flash I remembered the carvings at Tupec showing the same beasts. But that they were not pachyderms of any sort was instantly apparent. In fact they were not mammals, for the dozen or more ungainly creatures forming the herd which the black savage was driving and urging onward all possessed six legs!

Incredible as it seemed they were insects—great round-bodied, short-legged beasts the size of heifers; soft and flabby-skinned, with drooping dewlaps, small elongated heads, goggle-eyes staring upward from the occiput and with short rudimentary antennae and elephant-like trunks which were folded up between the front legs. Some possessed rudimentary wings in the form of fleshy pads above the abdomen, some were brown, some pale green, some mottled, and several were a livid, sickly whitish. But all were alike in one respect, for near the rear end of the abdomen of each was a swollen protuberance with teat-like appendages. It was in fact this peculiarity more than anything else which enabled me to identify the things. Despite their enormous size, despite their striking resemblance to lumbering pachyderms, I knew they must be aphids, plant-lice, as they are more commonly known. It was equally apparent that they were domesticated, for they behaved precisely like our own domestic cattle. Every moment or two one or more of the beasts would stray aside and, extending its proboscis, would feel about on the stem of a bush as if searching for food.

And each time, as the black herder started in the direction of the beast, it would fold up its proboscis, and kicking up its heels in a most ludicrous and ungainly manner, would hurry after its companions, who, taking advantage of the herder's diverted attention, would invariably stop to graze, as I might express it, by climbing up the nearest bushes and inserting their noses in the soft, fleshy stems. The poor black was having his hands full, but between tossing pebbles at his charges, whacking them with a light switch which he carried, and constantly darting first to one side and then the other, he managed to keep them going in the direction he desired. Scarcely had the first herd and its driver passed when another came into view followed by a third and fourth. So astonished had I become at discovering that the semi-human blacks had actually domesticated the giant aphids and were apparently using them as milch cows, exactly as do many species of our common ants, that I completely forgot myself and my surroundings and hurried from the shelter of the forest in order to secure a closer view of the remarkable beasts. Instantly, all was confusion. The blacks, the moment they caught sight of me, deserted their charges and scurried off with every indication of terror, and the aphids, as startled by the apparition of a strange being as ordinary cattle are at the approach of a stranger, stampeded, thundering off in every direction at a speed of which I should never have thought them capable. But they did not go far. Instead of rushing off among the rows of small trees, they commenced clambering up the stems. So indescribably ridiculous and so absolutely astounding was the sight of these great lumbering beasts climbing up the straight smooth stalks, that I fairly roared with laughter. A few of the beasts continued upward for a dozen feet or more until they gained the lowest branches, but the majority instantly forgot their fear as soon as they found themselves on the stalks, and with bovine complacency, at once fell to work sucking the sap, oblivious to all else.

For a moment or two I watched them, and then, feeling rather sorry for the terrified herders and the commotion I had caused, and being anxious to study their actions further, I withdrew and rejoined Tom where he was hiding, still terrified, in the forest. No doubt the concealed blacks had been watching my every movement, for a few moments after I had again entered the forest, they crept timorously forth, and after a deal of difficulty again rounded up their charges. Of course I knew that the aphids were perfectly harmless and incapable of either offensive or defensive actions—unless by chance they should step on one—but nevertheless I was rather amazed at the manner in which the triangular-headed blacks manhandled the big beasts, pushing and shoving them about and dragging them down from their perches by tugging at legs or snouts. I was still more astonished at the almost monkey-like agility of the blacks as they ran up the stems of the trees, and herding the escaped aphids from the limbs, forced them to descend to the ground. Presently the herds were again moving steadily onward and anxious to discover where they were going, and with what purpose the savages were driving them, I waited until they were barely visible in the distance and followed after.

CHAPTER FIVE

BY now, as will have been surmised, I had completely lost any lingering fears of the savages. And even Tom, seeing my example, did not dread them greatly. This was due partly to our experience when we had left the subterranean chamber and had realized that the blacks were far more afraid of us than we of them; still more it was due to the evident fear of us exhibited by the aphids' herders. But I think that the last sensations of dread I had felt had vanished mainly because of the innumerable and far more dangerous things I had met.

Compared to a five-foot, leaf-carrying ant, the blacks seemed comparatively harmless. A roving wasp or hornet was a far more dangerous foe than a dozen of the savages, and I would rather have faced a score of the beings single-handed than to have repeated my experience with the ant-lion. To be sure, they were the largest living things we had encountered, fairly good-sized for men and almost equal to my own stature. But almost any insect is fully one hundred times as strong for its size as a human being, and I was well aware that any predatory beetle or hemiptera of the size to be expected would be a match for a small army of the savages or for several well-armed beings like myself.

Hence, quite unconsciously, I had been mentally comparing the savages with the giant insects of the place, and without realizing it, I had come to think of them with something of contempt. Perhaps I can best explain my feeling by comparing myself with a man who, surrounded by hyenas and seeing the beasts tearing some creature limb from limb, becomes terrified at their ferociousness and brute strength until he comes face to face with a lion or a tiger.

Added to all this, was the fact that my scientific interest had been aroused and that—even had I still feared the blacks—I doubtless should have forgotten my own peril in my anxiety to study them and their habits. At any rate, the fact remains that I had no fear whatsoever of the beings who were urging on their aphid cattle far ahead of us. Rather, my mind was bent on not frightening them, and it struck me as rather amusing to think how quickly our positions had been reversed and that, within twenty-four hours of my first sight of the savages, I was the hunter rather than the hunted and was taking every care not to terrify them into flight. Then, for the first time, I realized how rapidly the hours had passed. It was already late in the afternoon; my appetite warned me that I should be searching for food rather than following the creatures ahead. And it behooved us to find some place in which to pass the approaching night. Regretfully I decided that it would not do to continue farther. I was about to turn aside and hunt for provender and a spot in which to camp, when the herds and their drivers suddenly vanished as if the earth had swallowed them.

As a matter of fact that was precisely what had happened, as I discovered a few moments later when we reached the spot where they had disappeared. Here were several yawning openings in the side of a hill or mound, and from the sounds issuing hollowly from within, I knew that the savages and their charges had entered the subterranean passages. It was useless to follow them without a light, for it would, I knew, be inky black within the passages. Deciding to remain in the vicinity until morning and then investigate, I abandoned all entomological researches for the time, and with Tom, vastly relieved by my decision, set out in search of dinner. We were rather fortunate. As in other lands, with the approach of sundown the majority of the insects went to rest, while nocturnal mammals—and apparently most, if not all of the vertebrates of the place, were nocturnal—came forth from their hiding places. Scarcely two hundred yards from the edge of the forest we came upon several largo hare-like creatures browsing in an open space. As they were not at all shy and we approached within a short distance of them, I easily shot one while Tom knocked over a second with a well-thrown club of wood. At the thunderous echoes of my pistol-shot, pandemonium broke loose in the forest, and on every side were the sounds of beating wings, sharp cries, strange clickings and the rustle of unseen creatures aroused and frightened by the unwonted sound. Seeing how easily Tom had killed game with mankind's first and most primitive weapons, I was sorry that I had wasted my ammunition. Hence, as I gathered fuel and Tom prepared the hare I had shot, my mind turned to the matter of equipping ourselves with bows and arrows which would enable us to secure game, protect ourselves quite effectively, and hoard the cartridges, which might be far more valuable later on.

Very soon the fire was blazing, and as the flames lit up the shadowy forest and the pungent smoke drifted upward through the trees we soon discovered that we had created a most unpleasant situation for ourselves. From every side insects came winging towards us, attracted by the light. Myriads of gnats and midges the size of bumble-bees swarmed about, tumbling into the flames blundering with seared wings over the ground and upon ourselves, crawling over us and making life miserable. Great crane-flies with yard long attenuated legs and flimsy wings flitted through the smoke and dropped, crippled and injured, about us. Moths of every imaginable size and color, from tiny things no larger than our own "millers," to great eagle-like sphingidae andbombycids as big as albatrosses, dashed back and forth on whirring pinions that blew the fire about and drove the smoke in our faces, while humming, clumsy, armor-clad cockchafers, longicorns and other beetles dove blindly at the light. Dodging the larger things, brushing the smaller from our persons, and kicking aside the cripples that seemed bent on wandering over us, we managed to stick it out until the hare was broiled. Then we retreated to the shadows, and with our backs against a tree, proceeded to dine

We soon discovered that we had created a most unpleasant situation for ourselves

off the half-burned, half-cooked meat. But even then we were not to be left in peace.

NO sooner did we commence to eat than scores of insects swarmed about us, attracted by the odor of the meat. Mainly, they were coleoptera and neuroptera. Hard-shelled beetles representing several families and genera, were numerous and among them I recognized some familiar forms. There were many of the tumble-dung groups; a number very similar to our lady birds or lady-bugs, as they are popularly called; some shimmering, iridescent chaps gleaming like burnished metal, and a few magnificent purple and gold buprestids.

All of course were far larger than anything in other lands, and the same was the case with the disgusting looking cockroaches, the big brown crickets and one or two stupendous green katydids. But none of these were as troublesome as the caddis-flies which swarmed about; frail phantom-like things that were constantly completing their brief lives and were dropping dead upon us and our food. They were even more of a nuisance than the buzzing gnats and flies which seemed determined to share our meal. Many of these were no larger than normal insects, and, glancing towards the dying fire, I was surprised to see myriads of tiny, minute forms of insect life attracted by the light of the smouldering coals. How far, I wondered, did this diminution in size extend?

Were there actually microscopic insects in this land? I remembered the old jingle about fleas having little fleas to bite them, and a somewhat surprising idea occurred to me. Did the same conditions exist in other lands? Were there actually forms of insect life as much smaller than the common sphinx moths as these minute things I was watching were smaller than the six-foot moths darting through the air about me? So small were many of the midges and flies, that they appeared like motes of dust in the firelight, and if species existed in other lands as small in proportion, they would be wholly invisible to the unaided eye—perhaps invisible—even through a powerful lens of a microscope. It was a fascinating thought and I wondered it had never occurred to me before. By now it was black dark in the forest, and among the trees, fireflies made their appearance. But such fire-flies! In the tropics the big fire-flies, or rather fire-beetles belonging to the elater or snapping-beetle group, are famous for the brilliance of the steady luminosity of their thoracic spots and the abdominal segments. Often, in the past, I had kept a phial containing one or two of these fellows to enable me to discern the hands of my watch by their light during the night, and here were light-giving elaters hundreds of times the size of any known tropical species. Their twin thoracic spots gleamed like the headlights of a motor car and fairly dazzled our eyes when they came winging towards us. The greenish luminescence of their abdomens illuminated the earth beneath them, as they crawled along or winged among the trees, as though they carried concealed arc-lights. As hundreds of the creatures appeared and flew aimlessly about, trees, earth, branches and every object in the forest, became outlined in a soft radiance as bright as moonlight. Very fortunately for us, there appeared to be no biting insects, and the absence of these I attributed to the scarcity of vertebrates. But whatever the reason, we neither saw nor heard mosquitoes; the gnats and midges, though insistent and a nuisance, did not offer to test the quality of our blood, and as there seemed to be no other solution of the problem, we decided to sleep where we were. To be sure, there was no little danger in doing so. A wandering hungry ant might find us and make short work of us, and I shivered as I thought of the possibility of their being army-ants in the country. I had witnessed many demonstrations of the voracity and destructiveness of these insects, of the ordinary army-ants which march through the tropical forests in countless millions, their armies often hundreds of yards in width and extending in dense formation for miles, and which march on irresistibly killing and devouring every living thing in their pathway. I had seen houses invaded by these ferocious, highly organized, perfectly trained insect soldiers, who had passed on, leaving nothing behind them but the bones of dogs and cats and not a living insect or existing vermin. And I had known of more than one instance of human beings having been surrounded, overcome and devoured by the army-ants. In this land of giant insect forms, if army-ants existed, what monsters they must be! In my mind's eye I could picture them— six, perhaps even ten feet in length—judging from the size of the leaf-carrying ants we had seen—sweeping across the land in a vast, all-devastating army and coming upon us as we slumbered. And the thought was far from reassuring or pleasant. There was also the danger of some prowling beast, of whose existence we were ignorant, falling upon us.

But there was nothing else to be done, and we had beheld so many amazing things during the day and the previous night, and had become so accustomed to being terrified by real dangers, that the idea of passing a night in the forest did not greatly frighten us. I deemed it wise, however, to have one of us remain awake while the other slept, and although I doubted his ability to keep his eyes open for long, Tom offered to take the first watch. Handing him my revolver, and cautioning him not to use it except as an ultimate resort, and telling him to arouse me at the first sign or sound of danger or if anything unusual occurred, I curled myself up in a moss-covered space between two tree-roots and fell instantly asleep. Several times I woke with a start, thinking some huge beast had stepped upon me, only to find it was some wandering beetle clambering over my recumbent body. At last I came to my senses with a start, with the feeling that I had overslept, and wondering why Tom had not called me. But as I rubbed my eyes, and gazed about, I broke into laughter. It was broad daylight and Tom was snoring lustily, doubled up where he sat. He had been utterly oblivious of his surroundings throughout the night, and yet nothing had happened. We were still safe and sound, and I felt quite confident that we had little to fear in case we were forced to spend another night under the open sky. But I had no intention of doing this. Before the sun set on us again we would have some provision made for sleeping safely and securely as well as comfortably.

If we ran no danger of being attacked by the living denizens of the land, there were other very grave risks from the dampness, miasma and chilly air. Even now, in the forest, it was cold, and my hands felt numb and my teeth chattered as I hastily gathered firewood and started a cheery blaze. This brought to my mind another matter of importance to be attended to. I possessed but one box of matches and Tom, who was not a smoker, had none. I must discover some other means of kindling fire without delay. There might be flint or stone of some sort which would serve with the aid of my hunting-knife and proper tinder, or again I might be able to rig up a bow-drill with which to ignite punk. The thought of a bow-drill brought back my decision of the previous afternoon to fashion bows and arrows. This I knew would be a rather difficult problem, and I mentioned it to Tom, as I thought he might know more of the properties of tropical woods than I. It was fortunate that I did so, for he solved the problem instanter by suggesting that we return to the spot where the two Panos had been killed and secure their bows and arrows.

OUR breakfast was very meagre and consisted of a few fruits we were lucky enough to find. But soon after we started off in the direction, which I assumed would carry us to the scene of the Indians' deaths, we surprised a huge land-frog dozing in a clump of palmettos. Tom gazed at him quizzically a few moments and then, picking up a hefty club, grinned as he cautiously approached the fifty-pound batrachian. "Seem to me. Chief," he observed, "he mighty like a crapaud in he aspec's. Yes, Chief, he cert'y possess tha same look an Ah been goin' to as'tain' is he as fit fo' to eat as they."

Reaching the side of the still unconscious frog, he dealt the creature a terrific blow on the head and the batrachian collapsed without a sound. As Tom had said, there was no reason why the huge frog should not be edible, in fact, most palatable, for the big West Indian land frog or "crapaud" is a highly prized delicacy and is most delicious. I judged that this immense fellow belonged to the same genus—even unobservant Tom had noticed the resemblance—but I was also aware that two species of the same genera may vary greatly in their edible qualities. However, Tom had not been mistaken. One of the frog's legs was soon broiling over a fire, and the flesh proved as white, as tender and as savory as the most fastidious could wish. One hind leg was ample for our meal, for it was twice the size of a turkey's leg, and having cooked the other leg and the thick white loins, Tom wrapped these in fresh green leaves, tied them with flexible vines, and slung them over his shoulders. We had enough food on hand for the rest of the day, and more, and feeling fresh and strong after our feast, we proceeded on our way towards the scene of the recent tragedy. Fortunately I possess a very highly developed sense of direction, and within an hour or two we began to recognize familiar landmarks. But to travel in the general direction of some spot and to locate a certain small point in that direction are two very different matters. Moreover, in our flight from the savages, we had raced blindly towards the tunnel entrance and had taken no heed of surroundings; also, we had been led as captives along a trail that passed far from the scene of the Pano's end. Hence it was a long and apparently hopeless task searching for the bodies of the Indians. When, after weary hours of retracing our way—as nearly as was possible—from the tunnel entrance to the jungle and back again, we at last found the spot which I felt certain was where the black savage had fought with the Panos, we could find no trace of either dead bodies or skeletons. That we were not mistaken in the locality was certain. The earth showed the imprints of our shoes and of bare feet. The plants were wilted and drooping where they had been crushed and broken by the struggling men, and if any doubt had remained in our minds they would have been dissipated when Tom picked up an empty pistol cartridge, and a short search revealed others. One thing puzzled me. Quite an extensive area was bare of living plants and appeared to have been recently dug. Was it possible, I wondered, that the black savages had buried the bodies of their fellow and of the Indians? I could scarcely believe that such primitive, degenerate beings would bother to do this, but there seemed no other explanation of the recently turned earth and the absence of corpses. If they had done so, no doubt they had also taken possession of the Indians weapons. I was about to give up in despair and was roundly berating our ill-luck, when Tom uttered an exclamation, and pushing his way into a clump of wilted vegetation, drew out a bow. A moment later we had secured the other bow and five of the eight arrows. Then, as we were diligently searching for the balance of the weapons, I noticed a bit of smooth, straight cane protruding from the freshly turned earth.

Recognizing it as the end of an arrow-shaft, I seized it and tugged at it. It seemed rather firmly embedded, and as with a final pull it moved, I staggered back, momentarily horrified. About it the loose earth had come away and had exposed the partly decomposed shoulder of the black savage I had killed three days previously. And as I dropped the broken arrow, and drew hastily back, the earth about the swollen black flesh began to move and heave as if the body were coming to life. It was a horrifying, ghastly sight, and, hardly knowing what to expect, I gazed fascinated at the spot. The next instant a clod of earth fell away and a huge black and red beetle emerged. Instantly, I recognized the creature and knew why and by whom the bodies had been interred. It was a carrion or burying-beetle, a vastly enlarged edition of the common burying-beetles with which I was familiar. Like those, it, and probably a number of its fellows working in unison, had dug away the earth under the bodies until they had dropped into the excavations, and had then covered them with soil to provide a food supply for their larvae when they emerged from the eggs deposited beside the decomposing flesh. It was all so ghastly, so ghoulish and so repulsive that I shuddered, and abandoning all thoughts of searching for the other arrows, I called to Tom and we beat a hasty retreat from the vicinity.

BUT we had accomplished our purpose. We each possessed a powerful bow and most efficient and deadly arrows, for I was well aware that the tips were poisoned and that even a slight wound caused by the weapons would produce death in a few moments. Tom was quite as well aware of the deadly character of the things as I was, and he handled them most gingerly. But even so I felt that we ran a grave risk, in case we should stumble or by chance scratch ourselves, and I at once took steps to safeguard ourselves by cutting some sections of hollow reeds and slipping these as sheaths over the arrow-points.

Neither of us had ever used bows and arrows, and if we were to secure game with them or intended to use them to protect ourselves, it was highly important that we should test our skill or lack of skill and should practice until we were proficient archers. So, setting up a target of reeds tied together in a bundle as large as a fair sized animal, we spent the next few hours shooting the arrows we made for practice, or rather at it. Knowing that any game we might meet, or even enemies, would be at short range, we confined our efforts to a distance of thirty yards, and much to my surprise I found that we rapidly acquired proficiency and were presently making hits at every shot.

Quite satisfied with our progress, and well tired and hungry, we dined off cold frog's leg. The next step was to endeavor to discover some sort of fire-making apparatus. In this I was successful, and with Tom's aid and suggestions, for he had the primitive man's knack of such matters, I at last had the satisfaction of creating a smouldering heap of dust by means of a bow-drill and spindle. In fact it took us longer to find some highly inflammable tinder which would spring into a blaze from contact with the spark than it had required to ignite the material in the first place. At last, satisfied that we could kindle fire whenever we wished without sacrificing matches, we again set out, this time heading towards the locality where we had seen the aphids driven into the underground passages. I was still anxious to investigate this matter farther, but as we strolled along we did not forget to keep our eyes and senses alert for some camping place for the approaching night.

It would have been a fairly simple matter to have erected a shed or lean-to—a benab as the Indians call such temporary structures—but the main question was to provide beds or substitutes, for I had no wish to spend another night reposing on the damp earth. Tom suggested hammocks, and when I asked if he knew how to weave a hammock, and if he realized the length of time necessary to do so, he replied that he had often used a sheet of flexible inner bark for the purpose. But our most diligent search failed to reveal a single tree with bark adapted to hammock making. In fact, it was late in the afternoon before a solution of the problem occurred to us, and then, as is so often the case, the solution was thrust upon us and was in no manner due to our own intelligence or inventive abilities. We had seen several huge spiders' webs, and I had half facetiously remarked that we might make hammocks of spider silk, when upon glancing at a nearby sapling, I noticed several oblong, grayish objects hanging from the branches. For a moment I rather vaguely wondered what they were, and with the investigative tendency which has led me into innumerable successes and misfortunes—including my present predicament—I stepped closer to examine them, As I had half-expected, I discovered they were the cocoons of some bombycid moths, or as they are more commonly known, moths of the silk-worm group. In nearly all countries the moths of this family are among the largest of insects. In the United States, for example, the Cecropia is our largest lepidoptera, spreading over six inches. In the East Indies the Atlas moth attains the largest dimensions of all living lepidoptera—aside from the moths in this strange land of course—with a wing spread of a foot or more. And here I had already observed giant bombycids with a wing expanse of over ten feet, which in proportion to the other huge insects of the place was rather small, if anything. The cocoons much resembled those of the Atlas moth, or rather more, those of the Ailanthus silk worm of the Orient, which has been introduced into the United States. Like these they were pendant, being attached to the branch from which they hung, by stout silken strands, and like them they were gracefully tapered from the thick central portion to the two extremities. The cocoon of the Atlas moth is about five to six inches in length by over one inch in diameter, and hence the size of the cocoons before me was not greatly surprising. They were, in fact, about nine feet in length by two feet in diameter, or approximately twenty times the size of the average Atlas cocoons.

For a moment I stood admiring the beautiful texture of the silk of which they were composed, and the intricate manner in which it was woven. Then I uttered a triumphant shout that brought Tom to my side on the run. Here, ready made for us, were ideal hammocks; silken couches such as no other human beings had ever possessed.

Tom grinned from ear to ear as I explained matters and, armed with my hunting-knife, he climbed up the smooth stem as he had many a time climbed coconut palms. But it was a far more difficult matter to cut down the big cocoons than to dislodge a bunch of coconuts. The silk was tough and elastic, and the hunting-knife was not the best of tools for cutting through it. But Tom was strong and persevering, and presently the first cocoon came tumbling down. The next soon followed, and tired and exhausted, Tom descended.

From the resounding thuds with which the things had struck the earth I knew that they contained living pupae or chrysalids. But as it would be necessary to cut the cocoons open in order to use them, the presence of the pupae did not trouble me. Tom having done his share, I straddled a cocoon. Being rather more familiar with their construction than Tom, I readily found the loosely-woven aperture at one end, inserted my knife-blade, and ripped the thing from end to end. Then, calling Tom to help me, we stripped off the thick, tough outer envelope and revealed the thin, papery structure containing the dormant chrysalis within. Rolling the latter to one side, we trimmed away the edges of the cocoon and presently were in possession of a strong, light and most perfect hammock of spun silk. Slung by its own silken strands between two trees, it proved most comfortable and luxurious. Before sundown the second hammock was ready. Well satisfied, but tired with our unwonted labors, we dined on cold frog, slaked our thirst at a nearby brook, and flung our weary bodies into the hammocks so providentially supplied by nature.

CHAPTER SIX

WE were not disturbed during the night, and as we had no fire, the insects did not bother us much. Having breakfasted, we folded up our hammocks, slung them like packs on our backs, and went on our way. Peering into the thickets in search of game as we proceeded, we followed along near the edge of the forest with the dense jungle on our right. There was a fair-sized brook here, and anxious to learn if it contained fish, we crept to an overhanging spot on the bank and gazed down at a clear, calm pool below. Presently, from the dark shadows, a large fish moved slowly into sight. But we had no fishing tackle and I was about to withdraw regretfully when I remembered how the Indians secure fish by shooting them with arrows. Although I was only a beginner with these primitive weapons, I decided to try my hand at the game.

Unsheathing an arrow, I fitted it to my bow and rose as slowly and quietly as possible. At my first movement the fish darted out of sight but he was either bold or hungry and soon reappeared. He remained far below the surface, however, and I knew that to attempt to get him at that depth would be futile. Tom, however, was resourceful, and unwrapping the last remnants of our food, he cut off a few tiny shreds of meat and tossed them onto the water. Instantly the fish rose to the bait and as he did so, I discharged my missile. I could scarcely have missed. The fish was within five feet of my poised arrow and I distinctly saw it strike him just back of the gills. But to my amazement, the point failed to penetrate his body, and as the fish darted off, the arrow floated harmlessly upon the surface of the pool.

Tom was as puzzled as I was and insisted the fish must be "Obeab" or a "Jumbie" to have resisted the arrow. But I knew there must be some good reason for the seeming miracle, and I became more than ever anxious to secure the denizen of the pool and to learn the explanation. Without fish hooks, without a net, this seemed a hopeless desire, however, until Tom again proved his resourcefulness.

Searching through his pockets, which invariably contained as miscellaneous an assortment of odds and ends as the pockets of the proverbial small boy, he produced a large wire nail. By means of stones and my hunting-knife, and at the expense of bruised fingers, he at last succeeded in bending this into hook-like form. Unstringing his bow, he attached the crude hook to the string, and having baited it with a bit of frog's meat, he stretched himself full length on the bank and dangled his improvised fishing-tackle in the pool. The fish, which had never before seen a hook or a line and was therefore wholly unsuspicious, lost no time. With a rush he seized the baited hook, and the next instant was flapping upon the grass at my feet. Instantly I knew why my arrow had failed to injure him. He was a ganoid fish, one of those strange hold-overs from prehistoric days, which, like the sturgeons and a few other species, wear a coat of bony armor on the skin in place of scales. I had seen similar species in the rivers of Guiana, and as I examined his gleaming coat of mail, his exterior skeleton in fact, I no longer wondered that my arrow had been turned aside. But despite his peculiarities, he proved excellent eating, and we lunched sumptuously that day. Having thus provided for our midday meal, we again resumed our tramp. We had by this time become so accustomed to the magnified forms of insect life, that we gave little attention to them, except now and then, when some new or most unusual creature attracted us. And, having so far been unmolested, and having encountered nothing dangerous—with the exception of the hornet on the first day—we became rather careless and thereby came very near meeting a most horrible end. We were crossing a small open space in the forest when a dark shadow fell across our path.

Glancing quickly up, I was terrified to see a huge, fearsome-looking creature swooping like a hawk upon us. At my first glimpse I had mistaken it for another giant hornet. Its huge eyes had the same ferocious expression; it possessed the same broad, transparent, powerful wings; its extended clawed feet were similar, and its deep-orange and blue thorax, slender waist and tapering abdomen were hornet-like. But the powerful, sharp-edged biting jaws of the hornet were missing, and in place of the dagger-like sting of the hornet, there was a long, horny appendage. As with a sharp startled yell I leaped to one side, Tom following, I realized the nature of the malignant thing. It was a gigantic ichneumon-fly, an insect even more terrible and repulsive in its habits than the predatory hornet.

The hornet may sting its victims into a coma and place them within its nest to be devoured alive by its young. But the Ichneumon reverses the process. Swooping upon some caterpillar or other insect, it clings fast to the struggling creature and deliberately deposits its eggs under the unfortunate victim's skin. In due time the eggs hatch, the young ichneumons devour the tissues of the living body within which they find themselves, and the doomed creature, with the hungry maggots within him, continues to live, to eat and to suffer untold agonies as the parasites gnaw at his vitals until they have attained their full growth. Then, transforming to chrysalids, they leave the shrunken almost devoured creature to die a lingering death, and eventually emerge from his carcass as full grown ichneumons. All this flashed through my mind as I dodged the swooping creature and escaped it by a hair's breadth. For a brief instant I had thought that perhaps the ichneumon was attacking us in error; that it had mistaken us for larvae or some other natural prey and that, finding itself mistaken, it would draw off and continue on its way.

But hope died in my heart as, baffled, the ichneumon checked its swift descent and with amazing speed turned and dashed at me. I felt sick with fear as visions of becoming the victim of the loathsome awful thing swept through my mind, and frantically I leaped aside, screaming as I did so. Visions of becoming the victim of the loathsome awful thing swept through my mind. But for a man to dodge a winged insect is a difficult and hopeless undertaking as anyone who has ever disturbed a hornet's nest or a bee-hive is aware. And to seek safety in flight was, I knew, suicidal. The ichneumon could move ten feet to my one, and the instant I took to my heels it would soon be upon my unprotected back. I shuddered at thought of

THE WORLD OF THE GIANT ANTS

Visions of becoming the victim of the loathsomething swept through my mind...

feeling those grasping claws upon my body, of feeling the sharp stabbing pain as the creature's ovipositor penetrated my flesh and deposited an egg in my quivering tissues. All this, of course, occurred in an instant. The enraged insect was swooping at me again, and in a few moments more would have fastened its claws upon me, had it not been for Tom. He, poor fellow, was as terrified as myself, although he had no knowledge of the creature's habits and the awful fate in store for him if the ichneumon accomplished its purpose. As I dashed and dodged about and Tom came within the insect's range of vision, the creature became confused and, suddenly abandoning its attack on me, it hurled itself at Tom. Luckily for him, he reached the shelter of a tree in the nick of time, and the insect, unable to check its rush or to turn in time, bumped against the opposite side of the tree trunk. For the fraction of a second it clung there, apparently a bit dazed and stunned. But that fraction of a second was enough. With a rush, my presence of mind returned to me. Whipping out my pistol, I sprang close to the momentarily quiescent insect and fired two shots in rapid succession into its thorax. Acrid, ill-smelling juice oozed from the bullet holes, the great wings quivered, the hooked claws slowly relaxed and, still alive but incapable of flight or action, the terrible thing dropped to the earth. And as with fiendish hate we beat it to a pulp with sticks and stones, I thanked Heaven that I had retained my pistol and my ammunition.

SO shaken and unnerved were we from this awful experience, that we were quite unable to walk or even stand, and for an hour or more we sat there, pale, nervous and trembling. But the attack of the ichneumon had taught us a lesson. It had proved that we were surrounded by dangers at every step, that at any instant we were liable to be attacked from some unexpected quarter and by some unsuspected creature and that if we were to survive for long, we must be constantly on the alert; the least carelessness might result in our deaths, or worse.

Hence, when we started forward once more, we proceeded with the utmost caution and it was well that we did. Suddenly, from the dense growth of canes at the edge of the jungle, came the sounds of some immense creature rushing towards us. The canes swayed, crashed, snapped and were crunched underfoot, as though a herd of elephants were approaching at breakneck speed. Not knowing what terrible thing might appear, what gigantic creature might be about to attack us, we rushed for shelter and cowered, trembling, behind a huge tree. The next instant the canes parted. Nothing had prepared us for the thing that burst upon our astounded eyes. It was a monster, a veritable dragon, fully fifty feet in length, and the exact counterpart of the carvings I had seen at Tupec. With incredible speed, it rushed from the canebrake, leaped across an immense fallen tree, raced through the forest and vanished in the distance. Never have I seen any living creature move with such agility and rapidity on four feet. It appeared, sped past us and vanished, all in one flashing movement. But brief as had been its appearance, I had obtained a fairly good view of the creature. Its scaly body that gleamed like metal was vivid green from the tip of its big blunt snout to the end of its immensely long tail. Its stout, powerful legs ended in long-toed feet, armed with great recurved claws, a foot in length. Beneath its throat hung a great fold of loose skin or a dewlap. From the back of its broad, scaly head rose a crown or crest of serrated, upright plates of blue, and along the entire length of its back and tail extended a row of upstanding thin scales two feet or more in height. Despite its gigantic proportions and its dragon-like appearance, I knew that it was merely a super-lizard of the iguana group, and, unless varying vastly in habits from all its fellow species, a most omnivorous beast, ready to devour anything of vegetable or animal nature that came its way, although it was by preference a vegetarian. Obviously, it had not been after us and had probably not seen us, but I trembled to think of what would have happened had we been in its way and had been trampled under the feet of the hurrying monster. I realized, also, how powerless we would be to protect ourselves from such a beast, for my pistol and our arrows would prove as ineffective against his scale protected hide as against an elephant. Tom of course was once more quaking with terror and clung close to my side as we hurriedly left the spot and moved directly away from the area wherein the huge lizard had vanished. It was evident that giant insects were by no means the only denizens of the place which we had to fear and guard against. If iguanas reached such giant proportions, there was no reason to believe that other reptiles would not attain an equally great size. What, I wondered, would a snake be like? What if we stumbled upon some deadly serpent—upon a bush-master or even a rattlesnake equally overgrown? Bush-masters in the tropics attain a length of eight or nine feet—larger by far than any ordinary iguana—and hence these most deadly of snakes might be expected to be fully one hundred feet in length if they existed here. And a boa or anaconda! Eighteen to twenty-five feet in length is not unusual for these under normal conditions, and here they might easily grow to a length of two hundred feet if developed in equal ratio to the iguana and the batrachians. These were disconcerting thoughts, and the only comfort was that such things might not exist and that, judging from our experiences so far, they must be scarce if they did exist. And, after all, I thought, a boa or anaconda one hundred feet long or more would probably take no more notice of a puny man six feet in height than an ordinary boa of twenty feet would give to a humming bird or a squirrel. Moreover, all the big snakes are very sluggish and such gigantic serpents as I was imagining would not, in all probability, be capable of rapid movement and could readily be avoided. No, snakes, if they existed and were of immense proportions, would not be nearly as dangerous as the livelier, more active and voracious creatures, such as lizards, and especially the carnivorous Solopendras. Then I chuckled. I had been disturbing myself, working myself into a nervous state, by imagining utterly impossible perils. How could there be huge snakes when there was nothing for them to eat? All the mammals we had seen were tiny things, not enough to supply a meal for even an insignificant snake, and I could not imagine a boa depending upon insects for its sustenance. So, dismissing all further thoughts of giant serpents, I passed the time, as we tramped along, mentally reviewing more reasonable possibilities and now and again stopping to examine some particularly interesting form of insect life. One thing struck me forcibly, though it had not before attracted my attention. There were no birds. Not a chirp, trill, nor song of a bird had I heard since I had entered the place. To be sure, amid such a chorus of insect noises as came incessantly from tree-tops and underbrush, it would be difficult to distinguish a bird's note. But in all our wanderings, we had not caught a glimpse of a feathered creature. If birds were non-existent, it was small wonder that insects teemed, and I reasoned that in all probability the absence of birds was one of the principal reasons why the insects had developed to such proportions. From an ornithological viewpoint, I rather regretted the lack of bird life. What astonishing things they would be if they occurred here. I let my imagination run wild and tried to visualize brilliantly-hued warblers and tanagers as large as eagles; partridges as big as ostriches; hawks the equals of Sinbad's Rok, and humming-birds the size of pheasants. But on the other hand, our own dangers would have been enormously increased. A hawk, an eagle, even a crow or a crane would have been an ugly customer, if built on the same proportionate scale as the insects and reptiles, and I thanked our lucky stars that birds of prey did not occur here. Meanwhile, we had left the denser parts of the forest behind, and presently emerged at the edge of an open space which, to my surprise, I recognized as the spot whereon was the home of the black savages. To be sure, we had reached it by a different route from the one we had followed the first day. But it was unmistakable, for in the distance was the mound with its wall of stones, and even from where we stood, I could distinguish the moving figures of the beings. Nearer at hand was a smaller hill, and beyond this and perhaps a quarter of a mile from it, was a broad expanse of green which I recognized as the orchard or grove wherein I had first seen the aphid-cattle. A few moments study enabled me to locate the spot where I had seen the aphids driven into the underground passages, and still anxious to learn more of this interesting incident, I hurried across the plain with Tom at my heels.

WE were just in time. As we neared the place, several aphids came lumbering forth from the entrances in the mound and, knowing our appearance would alarm them, I dropped behind a boulder with Tom beside me. One after another the grotesque, overgrown insects emerged, to be followed at last by a black herder who, rounding up his charges, commenced driving them in the direction of the grove. Determined to reach the subterranean chambers before the rest of the aphids came forth, I sprang up and hurried forward. Sounds from within assured me the occupants were still there and, quite forgetting our danger, I entered the nearest aperture. The place smelt abominably. It was worse than any cow-shed or stable, for mingled with the stench of dung and the sharp pungent odor of the blacks, was that sickly sweet smell I have mentioned as being so nauseating in the burrows of the savages. Tom coughed and choked, and I felt suffocated, but my scientific ardor was aroused and I hurried on. As I had conjectured, the place was dark as pitch, but presently I saw a glimmer of light ahead, and turned into a side passage. From the direction of the light came the sounds I had heard; low grumbling noises, the soft squashy sounds of moving heavy feet, and a strange swishing noise. The next moment we came to the entrance of a large chamber faintly illuminated by a shaft from above, and I halted dumbfounded. The place was divided into two or three sections by mud walls and was crowded with the aphids. And, moving about among them, were a dozen or more of the black savages actually engaged in milking their insect-cows! It is a well known fact that many species of our common ants not only make use of aphids as we use cows, and even watch over and tend their plant-lice herds, but in addition build underground stables or shelters in which they keep the aphids during cold or inclement weather. But to come suddenly upon such things, to unexpectedly find aphid-cattle in their subterranean shelters, to actually enter these and see aphids as large as real cows, and to watch these being milked by human beings instead of by ants, was astonishing. And the manner in which the blacks obtained the milk—if milk it can be called—was most interesting. Ants, I knew, stroke the aphids with their feet in order to induce them to exude the desired "honey-dew" as it is called, and it has always been assumed— and accepted as fact—by scientists, that the stroking produces a pleasurable sensation upon the nerves of the aphids and that this causes them to produce their sweet excretion. But the savages before me were beating and lashing their charges with switches and sticks in anything but a gentle or pleasurable manner, and at each stroke, the aphids, grunting and protesting, but unable to move because they were securely tethered fore and aft, were exuding the thick, greenish-yellow fluid.

Obviously it was pain rather than pleasure which caused the aphids to give up their secretion, and I was instantly convinced that it was the irritation of the ants' claws and no pleasurable stroking that caused our ordinary aphids to produce honey-dew for the ants' delectation. Surprising and interesting as was this discovery, even more amazing was the manner in which the blacks were gathering the "honey-dew." Beside each aphid under treatment, there squatted a hideous black, and as the viscid material dripped from the appendages of the aphid above him he would catch the fluid in his great toothless mouth. When at last his mouth could hold no more he would close his lips, scurry to a large trough-like affair of clay and empty the contents of his mouth into it. Each black was, in fact, a living milk-pail, and as Tom watched the process and it dawned upon him that it was this substance which he had swallowed on the first night among the savages,—and that it had unquestionably been prepared in the same manner, he uttered a disgusted and far from elegant exclamation. At the sound of his voice, the occupants of the cow-pen became panic-stricken. Catching sight of us, they dropped their sticks and switches and huddled among the cattle, while those who had been catching the milk hurriedly emptied their mouths by the simple expedient of swallowing the contents, and scurried like rats between the legs of their aphids, who, also alarmed, milled and struggled and snorted, crushing their masters and trampling upon them. Whether the unfortunate savages were badly injured or killed or not, or how the disturbance was finally quelled and affairs straightened out, I cannot say. Regretting that we had been the cause of all the trouble, and having seen enough, I hurried from the place. How or where we lost our way I cannot say. But it was soon evident to both Tom and me that we were not moving towards the opening whence we had entered.

In vain we attempted to retrace our steps. Over and over again we stopped and listened, hoping to hear the sounds that would lead us back to the scene we had just left. And over and over again, when we heard the sounds and at last reached the spot whence they emanated, we discovered it was a different chamber. Presently, in the dim light ahead, we saw the form of a scurrying savage, and feeling sure that eventually he would enter some passage whence we could reach the outer air, we dashed after him. The next moment he vanished, and coming to an abrupt halt, we found ourselves at the entrance of a large room, the contents of which caused me to rub my eyes and stare incredulously. Everywhere over the floor swarmed immature savages. I cannot call them babies or infants, for they were such unspeakably horribly repulsive and hideous things that they deserve only to be called larvae. They were a sickly livid-gray in color, almost shapeless, with stubby pulpy limbs and faces which seemed all mouth and eyes. Apparently, too, they were all of approximately the same age, and when we first saw them they were in charge of several undersized blacks, who I surmised, were females, but who seemed to scent our presence and almost instantly vanished. I had no mind to enter the stinking place nor to make a closer inspection of the infantile stages of the beings. But the next chamber we saw was, if anything, worse. Here again were countless of the young, but these were much larger, they were more active, and the manner in which the horrid things crawled, squirmed and wallowed in their own filth and over one another was disgustingly like a mass of maggots. Another and another chamber was passed, each containing its quota of young, and each lot being apparently older and more advanced than the preceding. Everywhere, too, the sweetish, fetid odor of the aphids' milk was overpowering, and I noticed in my hurried glances into the nurseries, that the young savages were being fed on this substance.

Even in my disgust and hurry to get away from the place I could not help wondering what became of such an innumerable supply of young savages. No doubt the percentage of infantile fatalities was very high, but even if a tenth of the young reached adult size the whole country would, I thought, be overrun with the savages in a few years. And yet there did not appear to be a great number of the blacks, and they were restricted to the vicinity of their homes.

Evidently, all young were reared in unison and all identity to parentage was lost. Indeed, it was probable, I thought, that even the mothers were ignorant of the parentage of their offspring, for I could not imagine such degenerate creatures having either morals or marriages of any sort. They were, in fact, scarcely a step above the brutes, scarcely above the insects; and once more their amazingly antlike characters and habits struck me forcibly. The way they herded the aphids, the extensive use of the honey-dew, the manner in which the young were cared for; even the appearance of the grub-like young, were all more ant-like than human. Was it possible, I wondered, that they had -developed such habits and characters through watching ants? But all conjectures and speculations were forgotten, when, a moment later, we saw bright light ahead and emerged from the passage into the open air.

CHAPTER SEVEN

FROM the summit of the mound which marked the entrance to the savages' homes, we had a very good view of the surrounding country. I had not, of course, noticed this before, for we had left the spot before it was fairly daylight, and the mountains and forests had been shrouded in mist. But now we could see across the wide areas of jungle and forest, across plains, valleys and hills, and had an unobstructed view of a large portion of the surrounding mountains. Now I understood a matter which had puzzled me. I had often wondered how the savages had first happened to see us. Not since that first day had I seen any of the blacks in the jungle or forest, and yet the Indians had been attacked and we had been captured several miles from the area to which the savages appeared to confine their activities. But I could readily see that from their mound they had spied us as we entered the place and had deliberately gone after us. To me, however, the terrain of the ranges was of far greater interest and importance than anything else, and I studied them carefully, searching for a spot which might offer a pass or opening. They were mostly rugged, sheer cliffs, unquestionably of volcanic structure, and hence, I knew, liable to be much broken and cut with fissures, canyons and ravines. Moreover, they did not appear to be as high as I had first estimated them. Assuming that the lowest limit of perpetual snow was approximately eighteen thousand feet above the sea, I judged from the extent of gleaming ice that crowned the summits, that the highest peaks were not over twenty or twenty-one thousand feet above the surface of this place. But as no such lofty mountains had ever been reported from the surrounding country—the highest known being the Pakina range, not exceeding fourteen thousand feet above the continental surface, as any such peaks would be visible for hundreds of miles, I felt sure that the surface of the land in this strange territory must be about six thousand feet below the surface of the country beyond the mountains. But unless I could discover a pass, it mattered little to us whether the mountains were twenty or fifty thousand feet in height. To scale a range twenty thousand feet high, and with several thousand feet of their summits entirely covered with glaciers and frozen snow, and with a temperature below zero, was I knew, an impossible feat. But some ten or twelve miles beyond where we stood, almost in a direct line with a distinctive three-peaked mountain, I could distinguish a deep purple shadow which might indicate a canon. It seemed the most promising spot to explore, and so, leaving the savages' mound, we turned our steps towards the mountains. Fortunately, as it seemed at the time, our route led along the edge of the cleared land where it bordered on the forest. Here it was far easier walking than in the forest or jungle; there was less danger of being surprised by dangerous creatures, and it was less damp and oppressive for the sun had dissipated the miasmic mists and vapors here in the open.

SOON, too, we reached the aphid orchard and found it delightfully cool in the shade of the orderly arranged, broad-topped bushes. From twelve to sixteen feet or more above our heads the branches were interlaced to form an almost continuous roof of vegetation, while underfoot the earth had been packed down until firm and smooth by countless herds of aphids passing over it. Several times we saw black herders dozing in the shade while their cattle grazed contentedly in the branches above them. Some were sound asleep and were quite unaware of our proximity, while others, who were awake, hurriedly sought refuge in the bush-tops as soon as they saw us approaching. Glancing up at these, I noticed in several places that rude structures of interlaced twigs and leaves had been constructed where large limbs forked from the main stems. At first I thought them arboreal homes of the savages, but presently I realized that their true purpose was to serve as shelters for the aphids in case of sudden showers. Here again the savages exhibited most amazingly ant-like habits, for I was quite familiar with the aphid-sheds or shelters erected by many of our commonest ants and in which their tiny plant-lice cattle are protected from the weather. One discovery often leads to another, and as I moved about, the better to observe the sheds, I noticed several odd creatures among the aphids. They were most grotesque and weird-looking things. They were slightly larger than the aphids but were far less clumsy and bulky, with slenderer bodies, longer, thinner legs and brighter, more intelligent eyes. In fact, as they peered down at us, their expression was so droll and quizzical, that both Tom and myself laughed gaily at them. Their forms and colors were, however, their most astonishing features. All appeared monstrosities. Some were humpbacked, others were broad and flattened, some had projecting rhinoceros-like horns on their heads, and several were armed with wide-spreading horns that would have been a credit to a Texas steer. Some were brown, some green, some mottled with yellow and black, and a number were most gaily marked with diagonal stripes of intense rose and vivid green. Although I should have recognized them at a glance, yet they were so huge, so exaggerated in all their details, that it was not until one of them leaped abruptly from its perch, and sailed through the air for fully fifty feet before it alighted on another limb, that it dawned upon me that they were leaf-hoppers, hemiptera closely related to the aphids. But in their appearance, their actions and their agility, they no more resembled the heavy, slow-moving, bovine aphids, than a deer resembles a cow. Even as I watched them, interesting events were transpiring over my head. Scarcely had the giant leaf-hopper made his astonishing jump through space when a black savage materialized from somewhere among the leaves, and grimacing down at us, as though thoroughly out of patience at our presence, he ran scrambling and swinging from branch to branch in the direction of the grotesque creature. Every moment I expected to see the leaf-hopper leap again as the black approached him, for I well knew how wary these insects are and how exasperating it is to attempt to capture one of our ordinary species.

I was therefore greatly surprised to see the black follow and reach the side of the creature, straddle its hard back, and deliver resounding blows with a short club upon its savage-looking horns. For a moment the leaf-hopper shook its head menacingly, backed around the stem to which it clung and squatted down as if determined to remain there indefinitely. But as the blows still continued to fall it thought better of the matter, gathered itself together, and before our astounded eyes it leaped back towards the bush whence it had come. Thereupon the savage dismounted, retired to the shelter of his leafy retreat, and the leaf-hopper, burying its proboscis in the soft bark, resumed its interrupted feeding. Here, then, was still another ant trick. The blacks had domesticated the leaf-hoppers as well as the aphids for the sake of their "honey-dew." Truly indeed they must literally have followed the time-honored advice of "Go to the ant thou sluggard."

To me, accustomed as I was to the marvelous habits of insects and the wonders of their every-day lives, the insects of this place had been a revelation, and I was being continually amazed at observations and discoveries I made. But to Tom, who never before had dreamed that such things existed, the most ordinary habits of the insects, thus revealed by their immense size, appeared to savor of the miraculous or supernatural. But even I could appreciate his feelings when, having watched the leaf-hopper's amazing jump with its savage black rider, he stood gazing, open-eyed and with sagging jaw. And I thoroughly agreed with him when, as we resumed our way, he shook his head dubiously and remarked: "Ah ain' never seed nawthin' in no circus tha' equal, Chief. Lordy, but that mos' surely was travelin'!"

Then as a sudden idea came to his somewhat childish mind, he halted in his tracks, and exclaimed, "Fo' tha' Lo'd, Chief, Don't it been possible we kin cotch some o' them beas's an' ride 'em our own sel's? Yes, sir. Chief, they'd mos' cert'nly move we over this place mos' exped'ently. An' can they keep on a-leapin' like that fo' long they'd ca'y us clean 'crost that mountings in scarce no time 'tall."

"Hmm," I muttered, wondering if, after all, there might be anything in Tom's wild idea. "I don't believe we could catch them in the first place, Tom. We might steal one or two from those black rascals, but I very much doubt if we could control them, guide them or manage to do anything with them. They're accustomed to their black savage owners and would be frightened and wild if we went near them. And I don't know as I am very anxious to attempt to ride one on such a jump. It would be worse than riding a bucking bronco."

Tom sighed a bit regretfully. "Yaas, Chief," he admitted, as he moved on again. "Ah, 'spec' you' right. Ah calc'late as how they's like the Coolie buff'loes we has in Jamaica. They mos' humbuggin' ugly beas's an' don't stan' no foolishness from white men or negroes, but they gentle like kitten wif tha Coolies an' any little Coolies boy or girl can ride he an' driv he about any place. Yaas, Chief, an' Ah took notice some o' them beas's been mos' surely like them Buffloes in aspec's. They got tha same ho'ns an' tha same hump on he back. But Wa-laa! T'ank de good Lord the buff'loes caint go a-leapin' 'bout like dem folks."

WE reached our objective point without further adventure and without encountering anything of particular note. I was elated to find that as I had suspected, there was a deep ravine or canyon cutting into the mountain at this point and promising a pass. But we were doomed to disappointment. After long hours of laboriously climbing over loose rocks, toiling up the cliffs and always ascending, we came to the end of the canon, a cul-de-sac with precipitous walls impossible to scale. Our efforts, however, had not been without some results. In one spot, a few hundred feet above the valley and just beyond the limits of the vegetation, we had found a deep fissure or cave near the base of a cliff. This I had at once realized would provide an ideal dwelling and, finding we would be forced to remain in the country for a time at least, we decided to take possession of the cave. It was large and dry, and a chimney or volcanic blow-hole extended from the roof of the cave to the open air far above, thus providing ventilation and sufficient light.

Nearby a brook trickled down the mountain side, fed by the melting snows far above, and within easy distance was the jungle. The question of food did not worry us, for since we had discovered that the big land-frogs were palatable we could always be sure of a meal by hunting up one of the creatures, and a short search would always result in the discovery of the hare-like animals which were easily killed by arrows or even stones. A little later, too, Tom rigged up a coop-trap in which he captured many of these creatures alive.

As there were practically no insects on the bare mountain side, the only species we had seen being a few butterflies and some harmless beetles, we felt we would rest undisturbed in our cave during the night. But there was always the danger of being attacked by some roving lizard or other beast, or by some predatory hornet or ichneumon, and our first step was to protect our new home from invasion. This we accomplished by constructing a door of light poles bound together to form a grid-like affair. It was not a difficult job, for the entrance to the cavern was not over six feet in width by eight feet in height. To be sure, any fairly large beast could have torn the frail screen to bits or could have pushed it aside, but I trusted to the instinctive fear of traps which seems to be common to all wild animals, and I had little dread of anything attempting to reach us past the screen. There was no place in which to sling our hammocks, but as we felt sure we would be free from insect invaders, and as the floor of the cave was dry, we gathered dead leaves and dry moss and soon had comfortable beds prepared. Partly for the sake of warmth, for the air was chilly and cold at night, and partly to prevent being overwhelmed by insects attracted by the light, we built our fire within the cave. It was well that we did so, for no sooner had darkness fallen than hundreds of insects came buzzing, whirring about. But very few were small enough to find entrance through the openings in our door, and they bumped and banged themselves aimlessly against the screen while we remained cozy and comfortable within. And as we at last threw ourselves upon our couches and I smoked an after-dinner pipe, I felt more at ease and far safer than at any time since we had reached the strange country.

From the cave's altitude we were able to look down upon a vast area of the land, which lay spread like a map below us. Without difficulty, we located the mound whence we had emerged from the tunnel from Tupec. We could see the open area with the semicircular wall of the black savages home in its centre. The orderly rows of bushes where the aphids pastured appeared like a neatly laid out garden; and we could even identify the area that we had covered on our wanderings. And a very small, an almost negligible portion of the whole place this was. In fact, as I compared the limited district we knew with the whole vast expanse of plains, forests, jungles, hills, valleys and marshes, it seemed a hopeless, endless task to explore the whole or even a small part of it. This, however, did not trouble me, for I had no interest in the place aside from a possible way of escape, and I had no intention of exploring the land, more than was necessary, as we would move from one spot to another in our search for an exit. But as I studied the topography, and as the light increased and the drifting vapors and fogs were dissipated, I began to notice many features of the land which interested me.

Not far from the base of our mountain, and a little to the east, was a broad expanse of green which had a rather unnatural appearance. In fact, the edges were so straight and even and the low vegetation appeared to grow in such oddly rectangular areas, that I felt convinced that they were cultivated fields. Very possibly, I thought, they were fields of the blacks, perhaps additional pastures for the aphids herds. Farther off, and covering an area of several hundred acres as I judged, was an almost bare spot dotted with a few large trees and, as I gazed at this, I started and uttered an ejaculation of surprise, for unless my eyes woefully deceived me, I could distinguish a number of buildings clustered there. And when Tom also saw the structures, I knew that there was no fault with my vision and that human beings, perhaps semi-civilized men must dwell there.

But the next instant my hopes fell, for close nearby I noted a second orchard of the aphids' shrubs. No doubt it was merely a larger settlement of the black savages, and I sighed regretfully as I turned my eyes towards another quarter. But Tom, whose eyes were far sharper than mine, was making discoveries on his own account. Urging me to look in the direction he indicated, he pointed towards the cultivated fields and insisted that he could see men moving about and working. For a long time I stared, longing for a field-glass to aid my vision, until at last I, too, caught the movement of tiny figures. But so distant were they, so foreshortened as we gazed down from our height, and so concealed among the vegetation, that I could not distinguish any details. Tom insisted, however, that they were not blacks, such as we had met; that they were brown or reddish, like Indians, and that they were cultivating the fields. Presently, too, he made out a road or pathway leading from the fields, and wildly excited, he cried out that he could see a village at the end of the roadway. Once he had pointed it out I, also, could see it, and this time, I felt convinced that the little settlement was not the home of the blacks. Instead of the circular wall of stones and the minute black dots marking the openings to underground burrows, I could see fences or walls built in straight lines and forming a large irregular square enclosing a number of buildings apparently of thatch and surrounded by plots of green, like small gardens. Here and there a spreading tree or a palm rose above the edifices and, in every respect, the place had the appearance of an Indian village. Instantly I determined to investigate. If there were Indians, the chances were they would be peaceful. On all my expeditions I had never yet met a hostile Indian, except where they had suffered at the hands of whites or blacks, and here, where I well knew no other civilized man had penetrated, I felt confident the Indians would prove friendly. Still there was a chance that, never having seen a white man before, they might become terror-stricken and attack me before waiting for explanations.

This, however, was a rather remote chance; moreover it was a chance that must be taken. Not that I was so overwhelmingly anxious to partake of the aborigines' hospitality; nor was I obsessed with ethnological ardor.

Tom and myself were living quite comfortably and we did not particularly feel the need of the companionship of other men. But the Indians—or whoever they might prove to be—would know the country and, even if they could not lead us to some exit from the place, they would prove of the utmost value as guides and in aiding us in innumerable ways during such time as we were searching for a means of escape. Moreover, they possessed cultivated land and, doubtless, vegetables, fruits and grain, and we would I knew, soon be sorely in need of a change of diet if we were to preserve our strength and health. Though I gave little thought to it at that time, I remember now that I wondered how on earth the Indians could cultivate the land and raise crops where insects were so numerous and of such size.

Somewhat to my surprise, Tom appeared as ready and willing to make our way to the distant village as I was. I had expected him to be nervous and frightened but he had become so accustomed to visiting wild and savage tribes with me in the past, and had faced so many far more terrifying things here in this land, that the idea of visiting human beings—no matter who or what they might be—appealed to him as about the only normal thing we could do.

HAVING breakfasted well, and having prepared an ample supply of food—for we had, I knew, a long and weary tramp ahead of us, we rather regretfully left our snug cave and, after fixing the location of the village in my mind and noting landmarks, we started on our way.

The first few miles was down hill and easy going, and from our point of vantage on the mountain side I had picked out a route which appeared to be less difficult than striking blindly through the forest and jungles. In a general way it followed the courses of the streams and, as I had foreseen, we were enabled to proceed far more rapidly than on our former tramps.

Very soon, too, the country took on quite a new and different character. The jungle became more open with fewer of the giant fungi and with more of the palms and tree-ferns. The flat land gave way to rolling hills, and presently, although I had not been aware of it when looking down from above, I realized that we were steadily ascending. From our cave, the cultivated lands had appeared only a few miles distant—certainly not over ten miles. But as we tramped on and on, toiling up the hills and maintaining our course by occasional glimpses of the mountains, I began to realize how deceptive distances might be, when viewed from a considerable altitude. By mid-day we had reached the end of the elevation and found ourselves on a broad, fairly level plateau, rising well above the surrounding forests and jungles, and covered with brushy areas and open park-like groves of big trees. Even a cursory examination convinced me that the place had, at some time, been under cultivation.

The decayed remains of trees and bushes that had been cut down were still visible. There were large piles of stones which had obviously been picked out of the earth as it was ploughed or turned over. Here and there were fragments of low mud walls, and in several places, among the weeds and brush, were stray stalks of a corn-like plant quite new to me, as well as a large grass bearing heads of grains, somewhat like wheat. That any Indians should have cultivated such an extensive territory and should have done so in such an apparently thorough manner, was astonishing. The ordinary jungle Indian usually cultivates very small fields in the forests and, as soon as the soil loses its fertility, he moves his gardens to a new spot at a considerable distance. But I was aware that the Quichuas, Aimarás and other Andean tribes were excellent agriculturalists. Moreover, in this land, where mammalian and bird life was almost lacking, man would of necessity fall back on agriculture unless, like the blacks, he copied the habits of the ants and domesticated giant insects. There was another peculiarity of the place which caused me considerable surprise and which I could not understand. Insects were scarce and, come to think of it, I could not recollect having seen any huge forms of insect life—with the exception of several flashing dragon-flies, one or two beetles, whose stench identified them as carybidae, whose prey was caterpillars, and sailing high in air some insects, which I took to be flies or bees. I had not seen a butterfly, a moth, a larvae, or even a ground-beetle. But I had little time to puzzle over these matters. We had reached the edge of the deserted, brush-grown fields and before us saw a low mud wall and beyond it fields of waving grain. Not desirous of taking any chances, we crouched back of the wall, peered into the grainfields searching for Indians, and endeavored to orient ourselves and recall where the village was situated. This was not difficult. From our hiding place, I could look back and see the big scarf in the mountain side which I had hoped was a pass and, in the opposite direction, I could pick out a peculiarly formed peak which I had noted as a bearing. According to my calculations, the village lay a few hundred yards beyond us and to the left. But I could hear no sounds of life, no barking of dogs, no human voices, such as usually emanate from an Indian village. But it was mid-day and the chances were that the inhabitants were lazing away the hottest portion of the day and taking their siestas.

It was a good time to visit them, and I was about to rise and proceed in the direction of the village, when my attention was attracted to the luscious looking ears of corn so near us. The sight of this reminded me that I was hungry and, anxious to test the edible qualities of the new cereal, I leaped the wall and started towards the nearest stalks. The next instant there was a loud humming from overhead, a sharp cry of warning from Tom, and I glanced upward to see a huge winged creature dropping like a falling meteor towards me. Without stopping to question what manner of enemy it was, but almost subconsciously supposing it a bird of prey, I dodged into the shelter of the corn stalks. I was not an instant too soon. As I crashed into the thick growth of ten foot stalks, the creature struck the spot where I had stood an instant before.

And as, momentarily, it alighted upon the earth, and I had a good view of it, I was utterly dumbfounded. It was no rapacious bird, but a gigantic bee, a great fuzzy black and buff insect with a body the size of a beer keg and with dusky semi-transparent wings fully five feet across. There was no question that it was angry and that it had deliberately attempted to attack me. Its eyes gleamed savagely, its strong mandibles clashed together like the action of some carnivorous beast gnashing its teeth; its antennae were laid back like the ears of a fractious mule, and its big abdomen rose and fell, constantly unsheathing and withdrawing a terrifying stiletto-like sting. And it was buzzing with the roar of a steam saw-mill as it peered in my direction, as if considering whether or not to attempt to resume its attack. There was no doubt that it was one of the solitary bees related to our common bumblebees and, I reasoned, in all probability its nest was close at hand and its fiery temper had been aroused when it had spied me so close to its home.

ANYONE at all familiar with bumble-bees, or anyone who has ever purposely or inadvertently disturbed the nest of one of these insects, knows from dire experience what short and ugly tempers the owners possess, and how unpleasant they can make it for the trespasser. And here was a thoroughly aroused and irate bumble-bee, several hundred times the size of our common garden variety, ready and waiting to inflict dire retribution on the being who had unwittingly approached too closely to its home. I was in a pretty fix. I could not rise and seek safety in flight and I was not at all sure that the giant bee would not advance upon me at any moment. Bees are most intelligent creatures, and if this big fellow's brains were developed in proportion to the rest of his body, he must possess true reasoning powers. In that case he would realize that all he had to do was to crawl over the canes beneath which I cowered, thrust his eighteen-inch sting between the stalks and kill me as readily as a man spears an eel. All this, of course, passed through my mind in a fraction of a second. Then, before the bee could make up its mind as to its next move, before I could even wriggle deeper into the corn, there was a sharp twang from the direction of the wall and a five-foot arrow sang through the air and buried itself in the bee's body. Tom had come to my rescue. With, rare presence of mind he had used his weapons to good effect and, too late, I bethought myself of my revolver. The arrow had struck the bee just back of the thorax, and with, an angry buzz that was more like a roar, it swung itself about, twisted into a half-circle and with a single bite of its powerful jaws, snapped the arrow-shaft in twain. Furiously it beat its wings, striving to rise, but the muscle or some nerve was severed and the poor creature rolled over and over. Its struggles became weaker and weaker as the poison on the arrow did its work, until at last it lay dead and harmless before me. Not until then did I rise, and hurrying to Tom, grasped his hand and thanked him fervently for his timely action and complimented him on his marksmanship.

My words were cut short by a distant roar from the sky. The next instant we were racing as fast as our legs could carry us in the direction of the village. One brief glance had been enough. Fully a dozen of the giant bees were speeding towards their stricken fellow, and we had no desire to be in the vicinity when they arrived. Onward we dashed, keeping to the scant cover and dodging among the scattered trees, while behind us the roar of buzzing wings grew louder. Indians, no matter how savage and how wild, would be preferable to the angry insects, and intent only on reaching the village, we sped on. Suddenly, ahead of us, loomed a wall; beyond it were the roofs of buildings. To scale the barricade in our spent and breathless state was impossible and, even in my terror of the bees, I realized that should we appear suddenly over the wall we would probably be shot down instantly. Somewhere there must be a gate or an opening, and panting, stumbling, we dashed along the mud wall. It seemed endless; my legs felt as if they would collapse beneath me, but the increasing buzz of the bees spurred me on.

The next instant we turned an angle in the wall. Before us was a low arched opening, and with a final spurt we bent our heads, and dashed through it.

CHAPTER EIGHT

AS I stumbled through the gateway, amazement and terror drove all fears of the pursuing bees from my mind. Enclosed by the wall was a large courtyard or plaza of bare, clean-swept earth, broken here and there by small beds of plants. Grouped near the centre were a number of mud-walled buildings with roofs of straw. But at the time I saw nothing of this. My gaze, my entire consciousness, was riveted upon a large circular area of hard-packed earth within a dozen yards of where I stood. Covering it were piles of freshly-cut grain, and staring at us, where they had been interrupted in their work of threshing by our precipitate arrival, were the inhabitants of the place. I had expected to see Indians. Naked primitive savages perhaps, but still men and women. Instead, the beings I saw were monsters. So astounded, so terrified was I, that, for the moment, I was not sure whether or not they were human. Their color was a coppery-red; their great round heads were supported on necks so slender that it seemed impossible that they could support them. They had enormous chests, attenuated waists and short paunchy abdomens, and each had six, strong, powerful limbs. They were insects! Seven foot giants, thoroughly human in their attitudes, their occupation and in their surroundings, but unquestionably insects nevertheless.

As my stunned senses realized this, and, shuddering, I recoiled, I recognized them as monstrous ants. Any one of the creatures could have torn us to pieces with ease; but despite their awesome aspect, their powerful fearful jaws, their unwinking staring eyes, there was something reassuring about their appearance, an intangible, indescribable expression of intelligence and peacefulness on their faces. In fact they appeared to be as astounded at our wholly unexpected advent as I was about to dash pell mell into their midst. Neither did they appear alarmed nor angry, and they made no hostile move.

All this I noted almost instantaneously. The next instant the roar of the buzzing bees galvanized us into life and action and with yells of terror, we dove for the shelter of an open shed. Glancing over my shoulder, and drawing my pistol as I ran, I witnessed a most incredible and amazing thing—a sight that caused me to halt in my tracks and to forget fear, giant ants, everything. As the first of the maddened bees swooped down with extended sting ready to deal me a death blow, one of the red creatures on the threshing floor darted forward and threw itself directly in the bee's path. I expected to see the creatures instantly attacked and destroyed. Instead, the bee checked itself in mid-flight, swerved sharply to one side, and circling, came to rest at the creature's feet. One after another the other bees did the same until a swarm of the huge insects surrounded the man-like ant, humming in subdued tones, fawning upon him. Stepping among them, he stroked their heads and backs, uttered strange scarcely audible whistling sounds and appeared to be conversing with them. The next moment one bee after another spread its wings and took flight, until presently all were again sailing, like tiny black specks, high in the sky. Nothing I had hitherto witnessed in this marvelous land approached this for sheer incomprehensible wonder. Dazed as I was by my fright, my surprise and my topsy-turvey brain, yet I reasoned that the bees were domestic creatures, the property of the beings before me, and that the red giant had called off the chase and had saved my life. And with this knowledge, like a flash of light came an even more astounding thought. The bees were actually engaged in watching the ants' property, in guarding the grain fields, and had attacked us, not because we were near their nests, but because we had trespassed on their domains. But wonders had only just begun. The huge red ant was approaching Tom and me. He came slowly, cautiously, as if striving not to alarm us. Every few moments he would halt, rise on his hind legs and wave his fore feet and antennae in a strange manner, and would utter the same whistling or hissing sounds he had employed with the bees.

Tom, of course, was nearly insane with terror and I felt shaky and far from easy myself. But the fellow had shown friendliness rather than hostility by calling off the bees, and I reasoned that, if he or his companions desired to attack or seize us, they could have done so readily, either singly or en-masse. In many ways, his actions were strikingly similar to those of strange Indians when meeting a civilized man for the first time; the actions of a man trying to make friends but still a bit suspicious. And why should I assume that these giant ants must be hostile or dangerous? Why should I fear them any more than I would have feared the unknown savages I had expected to meet? So, summoning all the nerve I possessed, and comforting myself with the thought that I was at the ants' mercy anyway, I stepped forward, moving my own arms in much the same manner as the ant. For an instant it hesitated, as if rather doubtful of my peaceful intentions. Then, evidently reassured, he stepped close to me, extended his antennae and with his great, horny, hook-clawed feet resting lightly against me, he examined me thoroughly.

I confess I trembled, felt chill and in deadly fear as his immense round head moved close to my own and I had a close-up view of the terrible mandibles that could have severed my neck as completely as a

The next moment one bee after another spread its wings and took flight.

guillotine. But his gentleness and the purring sounds he uttered gave me courage, and I managed to stand the ordeal. Bad as it was, it was not as terrible as the examination I had undergone at the hands of the black savages. At last, apparently satisfied, he stroked me with his antennae and turned towards Tom.

A SHRIEK that would have roused the dead, had there been any near, rose from Tom's lips, and cowering and shaking, he clung to my coat. For a space, the ant regarded him critically standing on his four rear legs, his body raised and his head turned first to one side and then the other, as he actually "sniffed" with his antennae. Then, perhaps deciding Tom was of the same species as myself, or perhaps recognizing him as my servant, he turned to me and half-led, half-urged me towards the watching throng on the threshing floor. For a moment I feared that I was to be forced to pass an examination by each ant in turn. But luckily I was spared this, and while the individual who had made the first advances explained matters to his fellows, the others kept turning curious glances at us. But as I stood there, the centre of interest, I could not help thinking how puny I seemed by comparison with the ants and how superior they were to man in many ways. I am speaking only of physical superiority, but since then I have become convinced that these ant-men, as I must call them, as well as others, are man's superiors in mentality also. Our advent might have been expected to completely disorganize the ants for the time being. The arrival of an inhabitant of Mars or Venus on earth would most assuredly disorganize human occupations, and we were unquestionably as strange and remarkable to the ant-men as a Martian would be to ordinary humans. But nothing of the sort occurred. No sooner had the fellow explained matters—and I would give a lot to know what his explanation was—than they again resumed their work of threshing the wheat and gave no further heed to us. Whether or not the one who had checked the bees' attack and had introduced us, so to say, was a leader, an officer or an official, I cannot say. But he seemed to take charge of us by common consent, and with gestures which were unmistakable in their meaning, indicated that we were to follow him. For a moment I thought we were to be conducted to underground chambers and that possibly we would once more find ourselves inquilines. But instead, our guide led the way to one of the buildings. I noticed, now that I had recovered my self possession, that these were built of pellets of mud neatly piled and cemented together and that the straw roofs were not true thatch but were in reality roofs of clay supported and held together by straws. In form they varied greatly. Some were roughly rectangular, others circular, others oval; but all were alike in having dome-shaped roofs. Near them, as I have mentioned, were plots of vegetation, and as we passed some of these, I saw that they were seed-beds or nurseries and were filled with young plants.

With this discovery came a rather dim recollection of having somewhere or at sometime seen similar beds. Then suddenly, it dawned upon me. Why had I not thought of it before? It had been in southern Texas, where I had been on an entomological trip, and I had spent hours watching the marvelous habits of the famed Agricultural Ants. I had watched them busily clearing their tiny fields, pulling up the weeds, cutting down small sprouts. I had seen them garnering their crops of grass seeds. I had seen the minute grains threshed out by the insects, and had—quite ruthlessly but in the name of science—dug up one of their underground storehouses or granaries. There could be no doubt about it. The ant-men among whom I found myself were agricultural ants, very similar in habits to their little Texas cousins, but far more advanced, far more intelligent, and—as might be expected in a different environment—possessing certain distinct habits and characters. Evidently, too, they were, like most agricultural creatures, including human beings, peace-loving and friendly, and I felt sure that neither Tom nor myself had anything to fear.

By now we had reached the first building and, glancing within as we passed it, I saw that it was more than half filled with ears of the corn-like cereal. The next was partly filled with the wheat-like grains the ants were threshing out, and as we passed the door, two of the fellows arrived carrying receptacles full of wheat, and entering the building, dumped the contents into a huge bin.

Here was proof that the agricultural ant-men were far ahead of their Texan prototypes in intelligence. They had erected out-of-door storerooms; they had learned to build roofs; they had constructed bins of mud walls; they had discovered how to form basketlike receptacles. With my interest and my scientific thirst for knowledge thoroughly aroused, and anxious to study these most remarkable creatures, I felt actually grateful for quite by accident finding myself among them.

We had now come to a smaller, round building and this our guide entered. Then, having hissed or whistled again, and having rubbed me with his antennae, he left us and hurried off.

THE WORLD OF THE GIANT ANTS

The room was bare of any furnishings of course, and it contained no food; in fact nothing except a number of the basket-like utensils I had seen in use. Rather curious to discover what type of weave the ants had employed, I stepped forward and examined these. To my surprise I found them formed of strong broad leaves firmly glued or cemented into shape. I was puzzled to know how this was accomplished or what the creatures used for their glue, but I was soon to have this puzzle solved. I also noticed that one wall of the building was provided with numbers of arched openings or holes reminding me of a country post-office with gigantic mail-boxes. Wondering what purpose these served, I stepped close to them and peered within the ones at the height of my eyes above the floor. Some were empty, except for soft shredded straw scattered over the lower portion or floor, but to my amazement, several were occupied by ants apparently sleeping. Could it be, I wondered, that this was actually a dormitory or barracks. It certainly looked that way, and perhaps we, too, were supposed to make ourselves as comfortable as possible in the niches. They were certainly large enough to accommodate us, being about three feet in width and height and fully nine feet in depth. But they were stuffy, dismal places and were far too much like the tombs in a Latin American cemetery to appeal to me as sleeping quarters.

But I soon made another discovery. Noticing what appeared to be a rear door to the building I passed through it and found myself in a long, gently-sloping corridor leading into a hill or mound, and with its walls, as far as I could see, riddled with the same oven-shaped apertures. Unquestionably these were the living quarters of the ants. From the main corridor, too, side galleries led to right and left and these also contained hundreds of the niches. Examining some of these, I found those of one corridor completely filled with the dormant pupae of the ants. Another was devoted to the larvae, and later, I found that the eggs were also stored in these pigeon-holes. I noticed, too, that the air in the corridors devoted to pupae, larvae and eggs seemed much warmer than elsewhere and presently I found that the passages actually were warmed by artificial means. In mud-walled receptacles designed for the purpose, were piles of some material which gave off considerable heat and a rather fragrant vapor or steam. It appeared to be decaying vegetable matter, although there was none of the unpleasant odor of rotting material, and ultimately I found the stuff was a form of fungus, or rather I think, a plant closely allied to the yeast-mold, which threw off heat as it developed. Moreover, it was not a natural growth but was a culture obtained from the masticated grains of certain grasses which were then fermented until the spores developed.*

I LONGED for a thermometer to enable me to test the amount of heat thus produced, but I judged it to be about 120 deg. F. Here was a solution to the heating problem which would have been a wonderful boon to civilized man. At no expense whatsoever, and with practically no care, a house or other building could be perfectly heated. And, when once started, the plants increased. There was practically no limit to the extent of heating that could be produced from the first culture. Moreover, the vapor thrown off by the growing plants contained a large amount of free oxygen so that the air was kept constantly fresh and invigorating. In this ultra-tropical land, human beings had no need of artificial heat, however, and perspiring freely and feeling as if I had been in a Turkish bath, I hurriedly returned to the outer room. As there appeared to be no restraint upon us and no reason why we should not go wherever we wished, I urged Tom into activity and some semblance of common sense and stepped from the building. Several ants hurried towards us, and for an instant I thought we were to be forced back to the hut. But after waving their antennae and feet, and, as nearly as I could judge, interrogating us on some matter, they scurried off and left us to our own devices. Threshing was still in progress, and as I passed close to the threshing-floor I noticed for the first time that the ants were actually -using mechanical means to separate the grain from the chaff. I had been too nervous and disturbed to notice this before, but now, with the utmost interest and amazement, I watched them.**

EACH great ant was provided with a short section of a log of wood. Moving on the hind-feet and guiding the roller with the front feet the creatures pushed the sections of logs with the middle pair of legs, presenting as they did so, the appearance of men pushing wheel-

[* Scientific observers have reported that the agricultural ants actually use small pebbles for threshing the seeds of grasses which they cultivate.]

[** The fermenting leaves in which the leaf-carrying ants of the tropics propagate their edible fungi, develop considerable heat. Many authorities are of the opinion that these ants thus produce artificial heat purposely.]

barrows. While some thus trundled their wooden rollers around and around the area, others scattered the heads of grain before them; others followed after, gathering up the waste straw and tossing it to one side; others deftly swept the grains of wheat, as I must call it, into their leaf baskets, while still others were constantly engaged in tossing fresh sheaves of the grain into the arena.

Every individual worked with machine-like efficiency and clock-like precision. Never did one get in another's way; never did they stop their work to rest or converse; and yet, as far as I could see, no one was in charge. In fact, the impression conveyed was that of a machine with each cog of its mechanism performing its allotted task and functioning without jar or apparent effort and with mathematical precision. Everywhere, where the ants were working, it was the same. A short distance from the threshing-floor another group was busily winnowing the grain. Here, too, the advantage of six legs was very obvious. Standing on their hind legs and grasping a leaf-basket with the front feet, the ants would scoop this full of the threshed grain, raise it high and pour the contents in a steady stream to a basket on the ground before them. And as it descended, they would vigorously wave a stiff fan-like leaf with the middle pair of feet, thus blowing the light chaff aside. The creatures were all so human, so evidently actuated by intelligence and reasoning powers, that I momentarily expected to hear them speak. But aside from the low hissing or whistling sounds they emitted, they were inarticulate. All communication appeared to be carried on by means of antennae and feet. And while at times their gestures were so expressive and obvious that even I could guess their meanings, yet I felt convinced that it was not merely by signs that they conversed but by means of some vibratory or other waves emanating from their antennae. In fact, once or twice, I was astounded to discover that I grasped their meaning even when they did not gesticulate. It was a most remarkable sensation; something like the sensation one has, when, listening to a conversation in some utterly unknown and incomprehensible foreign tongue, a word is suddenly caught which is intelligible. I do not mean to convey the idea that the ants' antennae, wireless, as I might call them, was intelligible to me. But as I watched them at that time, and later, I would now and then receive flashes of detached fragmentary communications. Not words or phrases by any means, but simply meanings or thoughts, so to say. I would have given a great deal—provided I had had it to give—to have been able to communicate with the ants, for there were a thousand and one things I should have liked to have asked them. But as it was, and still is, I can only observe and form my own conclusions; can only guess at many things, and can only solve puzzles by theories or conjectures deduced from my knowledge of the habits and characters of related insects in other lands.

Wandering from the busy threshers and winnowers, who by the way scarcely glanced at us, although they must have been consumed by curiosity, we approached one of the seed-beds where several ants were carefully transplanting the tender seedlings. It was while watching them that I again, marvelled that these creatures could carry on their agricultural pursuits successfully in a land so teeming with destructive insects. And once more, I became suddenly cognizant of the scarcity of insects here. It dawned upon me that with the exception of the bee watch-dogs—still sailing like buzzards far above us—and a number of immense dragon-flies that were constantly flashing to and fro, I had not seen an insect of any kind since we had entered the ants' domains. But the next moment the riddle was solved and another astounding discovery and amazing proof of the ants' super-intelligence was made.

In removing some of the young plants, two wriggling grubs or naked caterpillars were exposed. Tossing these to one side, the ant uttered a low hiss and, instantly, from some hiding place among the adjacent buildings, a gigantic green and purple beetle rushed forth and pounced upon the larvae. Reaching out a foot, the ant patted the magnificent beetle and stroked him exactly as a human being would stroke a faithful dog, whereupon the beetle squatted down with his bright, fierce eyes fixed on the earth ready to pounce upon any stray larvae that might appear. There was no doubt about it; the beetle, like the bees, was domesticated, was kept by the ants to destroy insect larvae.

WITH a sudden flash of comprehension, I realized that the dragon-flies were also allies of the ants. No wonder there were so few injurious insects here. The ever-hungry beetles would devour every grub and larvae they could find; the alert, keen eyed, swift winged dragon-flies patrolled the air and destroyed all flies, moths and other winged pests, while overhead the droning bees kept constant guard and were ready to swoop upon any trespasser they saw, as we knew from dire experience. Perchance, for all I knew, other domesticated carnivorous insects might guard the fields and storerooms by night; but with the corps of daylight patrols I doubted if such were required.

No doubt, also, the ants themselves destroyed countless larvae and eggs, as well as insects incapable of flight, as they tilled the fields. Here again the ants exhibited intelligence and common sense in advance of our human farmers. Despite every effort of scientists and the government, our farmers still persist in destroying birds, mammals, reptiles and carnivorous insects, and as a result, are constantly fighting a losing battle with insect pests. Despite numberless pamphlets and monographs and widespread propaganda and lectures proving beyond question that birds of prey, crows, snakes and countless other forms of wild life—as well as innumerable insects—are the farmers' best friends, the human agriculturalist will still adhere to his hide-bound superstitions, ideas and beliefs and will ruthlessly destroy the very creatures that, if protected and encouraged, would save him countless thousands of dollars annually. Yet here were ants, giants to be sure, super-ants it is true, but nevertheless ants, who protected themselves and their crops by encouraging those insects, which naturally preyed upon their enemies. And in a land where insects were a thousand times as large and as numerous as in the north, they had, by so doing, practically exterminated insect pests throughout their domains. With my mind filled with such thoughts, and deeply regretting that I could not demonstrate the matter to a committee of grangers, I left the ants busy with their seedlings and walked towards the rear of the buildings. Here were several large trees, and as I neared one of these, I noticed a group of ants busily engaged upon some work which rather puzzled me. And when I approached closely enough to witness their operations, I found I had stumbled upon the most interesting and surprising thing of all. In the shade of the wide-spreading branches was a great pile of freshly cut leaves trimmed into regular forms. Close to these were several ants, as I have said. As I reached them, one of the creatures selected a piece of leaf, spread it with his fore feet, and grasping a second piece of leaf with his middle feet, he extended the two leaves towards one of his fellows.

Reaching down, this second ant picked up a curious elliptical object from among a pile of straw beside him. Holding this in his front feet, he pressed one end of it against the edge of the leaf held by his comrade. Instantly, from an orifice at the extremity of the object, a thick viscid fluid emerged and left a mucilaginous trail along the leaf-edge as the ant moved the thing slowly back and forth. As I gazed fascinated at this sight, the first ant passed the leaves he held to a third who quickly pressed the edges of the two pieces together and handed them to a fourth. He in turn picked up another leaf, held it for a fifth ant to smear with the gum-like material, and then passed all to the sixth ant, who dexterously pasted the last bit to the others and formed a basket-like receptacle such as I had already seen. Here, indeed, was ample proof of intelligence equal to many human beings.

Anxious to learn what sort of glue they were using, and what the paste containers were composed of, I edged around until I stood beside the first ant who was using the glue. Imagine my surprise when I saw that the yellowish, spindle-shaped objects were the living larvae of some insect! Larvae which, like many other larvae, possess a sticky liquid silk with which they spin their cocoons and which, when irritated or disturbed, they excrete from their heads. And these great ants were availing themselves of this habit and were using the larvae's store of cocoon material to cement leaves together to form baskets! I was aware that certain ants are known to use their own larvae in a somewhat similar manner, gumming the edges of leaves together to form their own nests. To be sure, I had never personally witnessed this, but I had read numerous descriptions of the remarkable habit, and I knew that it had been observed and studied by such eminent scientists as Bruce, Agassiz, Wood, LeConte, Bates, Putnam and others. But here beside me were ants using larvae as living mucilage bottles to form utilitarian articles, and if I were not greatly mistaken they were using the larvae of some other insect and not their own. Of this I soon convinced myself. Without interference on the part of the ants, I examined the larvae and found they were the young of a lepidopterous borer. While doing this, an ant arrived, carrying a couple of large baskets filled with straw and sawdust and containing a number of fresh larvae. Setting this down, he picked up the ones that had been used and hurried off. Anxious to see what he did with those whose supply of gummy silk had been exhausted, and thinking perhaps I would thus learn more of their origin, I scurried after him. He moved much more leisurely than had the racing leaf-carrying ants we had seen, but I had hard work to keep pace with him, while Tom, fearing to be left alone, panted after me. My expectations were soon fulfilled. The ant headed for a number of small trees near the further side of the plaza. Reaching these, he busied himself placing the sluggish larvae in neat round holes in the tree trunks. Then, while I watched, he ripped off a section of bark from another tree, exposing the sappy, hole-riddled wood, and began extracting the larvae concealed in their burrows. Among them were several brown pupae and these he carefully placed to one side. Also I noticed several images which, as I had already assumed, were rather handsome steel-blue feather-winged moths very similar to our peach-tree borers, although of course far larger, being over a foot in expanse. The trees, I saw, were conifers, and as I could find no others in the vicinity, I was forced to the conclusion that they were raised and maintained for the sole purpose of providing a food supply for the borer larvae which were of such economic importance to the ants. Just how the larvae and their adults were protected from the carnivorous insect attendants of the ants was something of a mystery. Possibly the beetles, bees and dragon flies had been taught not to molest them, just as our farmers' dogs and cats are trained not to attack chickens or other live stock, or possibly the borers' habits were sufficient protection.

But the thing which puzzled me far more than this question was, how and where the giant agricultural-ants had learned the trick of using borer larvae for cementing leaves together to form baskets. Their own larvae, as I soon determined, could never have been used for such a purpose, for they possessed no sticky secretion. Had the ants seen some other species using their young, and had they learned to imitate the process, substituting the borer larvae for their gumless young? Had they accidentally discovered the borer larvae exuded a sticky material, which had by chance fallen on leaves and had fastened them together? Or had they actually invented the process by using their brains and their reasoning powers? I could not say, and I do not know. It was one of the questions I should have liked to ask them had I been able to converse with them.

And now I had begun to realize that I was hungry. So interested had I been, so astonished at every turn, that I had quite forgotten that I had not eaten since early morning. However, Tom still carried our food supply, and seating ourselves in the shade of a large tree, we proceeded to eat our meal. Oddly enough, this simple matter excited the ants tremendously and caused more interest and curiosity than they had hitherto shown.

Evidently their sense of smell was marvelously keen, for though no ant was in our vicinity when we started to eat, they came scurrying from every direction the moment we began munching our cold meat. For a moment I feared they were angry or that the smell of meat had aroused their savage instincts, for there was something about their expressions and the businesslike manner of their approach that was not reassuring. But it was soon evident that they had no intention of molesting us. As they came close they rose on their hind legs, "sniffed"—I can only describe their actions by this word—with their antennae, hurried about and watched us intently. Then, as if utterly unable to understand the matter, they formed a circle about us and remained, with antennae pricked forward and eyes staring, exactly like a crowd of human beings, watching animals fed in a menagerie. Suddenly I laughed as the explanation of their behavior dawned upon me. Being strictly vegetarians themselves they could not understand us devouring flesh. To be sure, their domesticated allies were some of them carnivorous. But to see a dragon-fly or beetle devour a larvae or a moth was one matter and to see us strange beings eating what must have appeared like carrion to them, was quite another. We humans think it nothing strange or unusual to see a cat eating a rat or a chicken eating worms, but we would be filled with amazement and disgust were we to see an apparently intelligent human being dine on a mouse or a snake or witness a ruminant devouring a haunch of mutton. That my surmises were correct was soon proved. One of the ants scurried off and presently returned carrying a leaf basket, which he rather hurriedly and timidly placed by my side.

It was filled with ears of the corn-like cereal and with the wheat-like grain. Perhaps the kindly fellow thought we were forced to eat the meat through want of anything else and was offering us what he considered proper fare. At any rate his hospitable intentions could not be mistaken, and being thoroughly tired of a meat diet anyway, I helped myself to the contents and passed it to Tom. The corn, though hard, was edible, but the uncooked grain was beyond us. Tom declared, however, that it could be cooked And that if he could crush it, he could make some substitute bread, and I knew that the corn, if picked green, would be delicious. No doubt the ants were disappointed and puzzled more than ever when they found we preferred the meat to their fare, but despite our wishes to please our hosts, we could not manage to satisfy our hunger on the flinty grains. Not until we had finished our meal did the crowd of ants leave us. Evidently, too, their day's allotted work was over, for instead of returning to their former occupations, they betook themselves to the storerooms, whence they emerged, each carrying corn or grain, and proceeded to dine in the open air. I could not but envy the way in which their great horny mandibles crushed the hard-shelled cereals, and I was thankful indeed that they were friendly and not hostile and preferred the products of their fields to our flesh and bones.

Having dined, they filed into the building with the niches and quickly took possession of the openings. Apparently each had its own pigeon-hole, and while the majority vanished down the passages, others stowed themselves away in the niches in the wall of the first room. By the time all had retired, every cavity was occupied, and it was evident that Tom and I must shift for ourselves.

Although these ants had none of the rank fetid odor of the black savages, still they smelled unmistakably of ant, and the outer air was preferable to that within. Moreover, there were no insects to trouble us, except for the domestic beetles which appeared to confine themselves to larvae, and so we slung our hammocks between two of the trees and were soon sleeping soundly.

CHAPTER NINE

THE ants were early risers. They were up before dawn, and like workmen streaming towards factories, were hurrying to their tasks before the sun rose. Seeing that the majority were headed for the grain fields, we joined the throng, for I was anxious to study their agricultural methods, and I dared not visit the fields unaccompanied, while the bee-guards were on duty.

Without stopping to think, I lit my pipe, and instantly the entire orderly system of the ants was disorganized. Still, they appeared far less afraid of the flare of the match and the sight and smell of smoke than had the leaf-carrying ants or even the black humans. Their actions in fact savored far more of curiosity than of fear, although the tobacco smoke evidently irritated and troubled them. Every time a whiff of smoke reached an ant, the creature would shake its head, sneeze—if I can use that term to express the action—rub its face with its fore-legs, twitch its antennae, and act temporarily confused and almost intoxicated. Realizing that if I were to accomplish anything, and fearing that the ants might think better of their hospitality, if I persisted in troubling them, I put out my pipe and forbore smoking for the time being. For that matter I had not intended to take more than a few puffs, for my tobacco supply was woefully small and I doubted if I could secure any substitute in the country.

Apparently puzzled at the sudden cessation of the incomprehensible smoke, the ants again fell into line and proceeded on their interrupted way. Again I noticed that there appeared to be no leader, no chief or officer, and that no orders or directions were given. Yet the ants seemed to work in unison, to know just what to do, where to go, how many were required at each spot, exactly as though all were controlled by a single mind. Indeed, the more I watched and studied the ants, the more I became convinced that this was in a way the case. So intensely communistic and socialistic had they become, that a sort of mental telepathy or similar unconscious means of communication existed among them, and the thoughts or ideas of one were common to all. In other words, the mental reactions or stimulations of the ants were identical in every individual, and were, in effect, a single unit, just as their physical actions were so well coordinated that in effect the labor of a number was the labor of a unit.

To be sure, when we first arrived, a single ant had taken charge, and as I have said, he apparently had to explain what he had learned of us to his comrades. But in that case he was dealing with a matter totally strange and foreign to all their lives, experiences and mental processes. I had no doubt that, in the case of any unusual or wholly new event or experience, the ants would be confused, disorganized and at a loss, for their synchronized minds would not function in unison, except when dealing with matters with which all were perfectly familiar.

I noticed, too, that all the ants I had so far seen were apparently of one class. All appeared to be sexless workers. There were no warriors, such as are common to most ant communities, fellows with overdeveloped jaws and physical characters adapted for defensive and offensive duties. All I had seen were exactly alike in every detail, and I wondered if, through countless generations and with the domesticated insect allies to protect them, the warrior class had gradually been eliminated through evolution or if, being no longer needful and merely a burden on the community, they had been destroyed as they developed. Of course, somewhere, there would be a queen or queens, and there must be consorts or drones. Possibly, I thought, the ants I had found sleeping in their cells on the day previous had been males who performed no manual labor, and I determined to investigate later and satisfy myself regarding the breeding habits and social system of the ants.

We had now reached the grain-fields, and with perfect system and as if by mutual consent and understanding, the ants began their task of weeding, cultivating and reaping. They worked with marvelous rapidity and precision, and their six legs and powerful mandibles enabled any one of them to perform the work of several men. Neither did they require tools of any sort. A nip of the chitinous jaws was sufficient to cut down a stout stalk; their powerful, hard, hooked claws hoed and raked the earth as well as any steel implement, and weeds were uprooted and tossed aside by their powerful jaws.

VERY few injurious insects were found, and these were instantly pounced upon and destroyed by the big Carib-beetles who roamed about among the toiling ants. I wondered how, with insects so ruthlessly and completely eliminated, the corn and grain could be pollinated. But of course there were the bees, and, presently I discovered that there were innumerable lady-beetles, as they are called. These, I noticed, were unmolested, the ants evidently being aware of their usefulness, and I hunted about, until I found the beetles' larvae—ferocious-looking, flat-bodied creatures with short, stout legs, rough, hairy bodies and stupendous, serrated sickle-shaped jaws. At sight of me they backed away, snapping their great jaws, shaking their ugly heads and lashing their stubby tails in a most menacing manner. Although comparatively small in relation to the ants and other insects, yet they were far too large and powerful to be treated with impunity. They were in fact, about the size of large tom-cats, with jaws twice the length of their bodies, and I knew that a single bite would sever a man's wrist or arm.

They were, however, most interesting creatures, and apparently represented several species. Some were almost naked, being sparsely clothed with stiff bristles, while others were covered with warty protuberances, thickly set with short, barbed hairs to which the owners had attached bits of leaves and empty skins of small insects.

Thus camouflaged, they were wonderfully protected and concealed. Indeed, as I watched one of them resting motionless and completely hidden under his cloak of empty skins of former victims, a small thrip came flitting by. Seeing the skins of his fellows clustered together on the leaf, and mistaking them for a little colony of his species, he dropped unsuspectingly to the spot. Scarcely had he alighted when the crouching larva sprang forward with surprising agility and seized the unfortunate thrip in its hungry jaws. Very quickly the juices were sucked from its still palpitating body, and, a moment later, its empty skin was added to the collection of trophies on the larva's back. In a way, it was an old story to me. Countless times I had watched our own insignificant aphis-lions capturing and devouring their tiny prey in the same way, and following almost identical habits. But despite this it seemed like a new discovery and a most astonishingly interesting one to see these twenty-pound aphis-lions doing the same thing. Often, in my entomological days, I had marveled at the lack of interest in insects' habits and lives exhibited by the average man. Over and over again I had tried to arouse an interest in such matters among my layman friends, but without success. But now I realized why men and women give no heed to the most remarkable habits of insects about them, and yet become intensely interested and engrossed in the far less remarkable habits of birds and mammals. It was merely a matter of size. Were our insects the size of our mammalia and birds, the public would find as much or more interest in them. Even I, who had made a deep study of entomology and was thoroughly alive to the fascination of insect life, was being thrilled, excited and engrossed by the revelations of the giant insects about me, in a way I had never experienced when observing insects of normal size.

Presently, I noticed a new arrival. At first I mistook him for an undersized bumble-bee, for his colors were much like those of the big fellows who had attacked us. But as he blundered about among the corn-tassels and I had a closer view, I discovered that he was a honey-bee. Also, as he was busily engaged in loading his pollen-baskets with the yellow dust of the corn flowers, I discovered that he was one of the sting-less bees so abundant in tropical America. Thinking to have a little fun at Tom's expense, I called him to me, showed him the big bee, and quite casually extended my hand and poked the insect with a finger. Tom yelled and grasped my arm, but too late. The bee, angry at being so rudely interfered with, uttered an ominous buzz, swung about and struck viciously at me with its abdomen. But it was all bluff. He possessed no sting, and I laughed heartily at Tom's expression of combined terror and amazement.

Somewhere, not far distant, I knew the bee must have a nest and a store of honey. Honey would, I thought, be most desirable, and I watched the departing bee as, laden with pollen, it spread its wings and flew off. It headed directly towards the ant village, and I mentally decided to have a thorough search for its hidden sweets when I returned to the buildings. But I would no more have dared to leave the vicinity of the toiling ants and approach the village alone with Tom, than I would have dared to enter a den of hungry tigers. Ever in the air above, the great bees wheeled about, looking like the tireless-winged vultures of the tropics, and faintly to our ears came the droning of their pinions like the distant exhaust of airplanes. As long as I was with the ants I felt safe from the giant bees, but I felt sure that the moment their eyes detected Tom and myself alone they would swoop upon us and wreak vengeance for the death of their companion. I need not have worried, however. The bees, like ferocious watchdogs, once they had learned that we were to be treated as friends of their masters, would not have molested us. But at the time I was not aware of this, and whiled away my time as best I might, watching the ants, studying the habits of the few useful insects that I saw, making friends with the ferocious Carib-beetles. Something about these big coleoptera appealed to me. Despite their almost overwhelming pungent odor, which is a characteristic of their family, they were very dog-like in their behavior, and they were gloriously magnificent in their colors of metallic red, green and blue ornamented with sparkling dots of gold and silver. Lying on the ground in some shady spot, their bright roving eyes watching every move of the ants, they would wait patiently until their keen vision or the signal from an ant apprized them of the presence of a larva. Then, with a bound and a rush, they would be upon it, exactly as a terrier springs at a rat. Despite their fierce aspect and their somewhat nervous dispositions, they were quite docile, and although at first they showed distrust and fear of Tom and myself, and edged away whenever we approached them closely, I very soon managed to win the confidence of one or two. Digging about with my hunting-knife in spots which, to my entomologically-trained eyes, promised the presence of hidden larvae, I unearthed several and kicked them within view of the beetles. Thereafter, two of the creatures followed me about constantly and watched my every movement. Tom, however, fought shy of them. The negro, I have always noticed, is very timorous when near strange dogs, and Tom could not overcome his fear that one of the beetles might snap at him at any moment.

As mid-day approached and our appetites warned us that it was time to lunch, the question of our food arose. There were apparently no mammals in the vicinity for us to shoot, and the only edible substances seemed to be the corn and grain. Many of the ears of corn—it was not true maize but so very similar, I always think of it as corn—were in the green milky stage and, somewhat hesitatingly, as I was not sure how the ants would take it, I pulled off several of these.

The ants, however, gave no heed to my actions and, gathering a number of the ears, we prepared to lunch on green corn. But while the cereal was edible in a raw state, it was not particularly tempting and I decided to try roasting it. I realized that to build a fire might cause a panic among the ants, and I was somewhat torn between my desire to dine on roasted ears and my dislike of exciting or frightening the creatures, who had so far shown nothing but friendly and kindly feelings towards us. But my curiosity to witness their reactions, my appetite, and my insatiably experimental mind decided me. Gathering some dry corn stalks, for there was no better fuel near, and moving a few yards from the ants to a spot where the grain had been harvested and the earth was bare, I kindled the fire. The reactions of the ants were as remarkable as they were unexpected. At the first whiff of smoke they had swung about, their eyes staring and their antennae pointing in our direction. Then, as they saw the flames and sparks, with one accord they dropped their work and came hurrying towards us. For an instant I felt sure we were in for it, and bitterly I regretted my actions. But instead of attacking us as I had feared, the ants dashed directly for the blaze. Almost too late I realized that they were actually about to throw themselves into the flames. Without stopping to think of consequences, I seized the foremost ant, shouting to Tom to follow my example, and with all my puny strength, shoved him roughly back. For the fraction of a second he resisted, struggling and snapping his jaws. Then, apparently realizing that there must be some reason for my actions, he fell back and gazed, fascinated, towards the fire.

TOM, meanwhile, terrified at the ants as he was, had nevertheless obeyed me and had succeeded in driving back two ants. He had been less fortunate than I, however. One of the creatures had snapped at him and had torn one sleeve of his coat completely off and had left an ugly cut on his arm. But our interference, brief as it was, had checked the impetuous rush of the creatures. It was hopeless for us to think of holding back the whole mob, but the first three were now more cautious and, as they drew closer and felt the heat of the blazing cornstalks, the others leaped hastily away.

One individual had approached too closely and had badly singed one of his feet, and limped off to some distance. The others, perhaps through co-ordination of mentality or perhaps through reasoning, now realized that the fire was dangerous and stood quietly regarding it, antennae and postures expressive of the utmost wonder. I was amazed. Every intelligent wild creature I had ever known had invariably exhibited instinctive dread of fire. Even the leaf-carrying ants had been wary of it; yet these ants were attracted by it and would have blindly thrown themselves to destruction like stupid moths and gnats had we not forcibly prevented them. But after all, why should they be afraid of fire? They had never seen it, and no doubt their first impulse at sight or smell of anything new was to rush upon it. In fact, now I came to think of the matter, I had often observed that this was a common trait of ants and that their brains appeared to be incapable of either fear or caution. But it argued well for these ants' intelligence that they should have understood our actions and should have resisted their natural impulses. However, I was convinced that it would not be wise to kindle fires within the ants' reach, and I foresaw a rather dismal prospect of subsisting upon raw food while we were with them. But as we had this fire—or rather the coals, for the stalks had quickly been consumed—I decided we might as well follow out our original intention and roast the corn. The ants looked on with intense curiosity as we did this. When at last I raked the ash-covered, somewhat blackened ears from the smouldering coals, I handed one to the nearest ant. As he sensed its heat, he hurriedly drew back and stood regarding it suspiciously. His attitude, his muscles tensed ready to leap away, his forward-turned antennae and his every expression were exactly like those of a skittish horse regarding the approaches of a stranger. But as Tom and I sank our teeth into the truly luscious corn, the ant gingerly touched the ear, became more confident and at last bit off a piece and tasted it.

Instantly he became excited and, apparently summoned by him, his comrades crowded about, smelling and tasting the roasted corn. Very evidently it did not appeal to them, for each in turn ejected the masticated kernels from his mouth. But it was equally certain that they were vastly astonished at discovering that such a great change could be wrought in their cereal by placing it in the fire. Finally one of them picked up the ear and hurried with it in the direction of the village. What he did with it I cannot say. Perhaps he desired to test it on the young ants; possibly it was to be presented to the queen, or for all I know it was to be preserved as a precious relic and a great rarity for future generations to marvel at. I am not sure whether it was the effect of my fire or the time that caused the ants to cease their labors in the fields and turn towards their homes. Naturally, Tom and I joined the crowd, and as we passed along, I tried to count the ants in sight.

Much to my surprise I discovered that there were not over two hundred and, as far as I could judge, practically the entire population was present.

Of course there might be many in the buildings and underground chambers. Many more might be in distant parts of the fields or gardens; and there might be others engaged in other pursuits. But when we had started out, no others were in sight, none were threshing, winnowing or making baskets, and I felt convinced that the entire colony did not number over three hundred individuals.

But when we reached the village, I was astonished to find at least another hundred busily threshing and winnowing. Presently I noticed that these appeared to be somewhat smaller, lighter in color and softer-boiled than the others. Then I caught sight of several ants carrying off broken fragments of papery, parchmentlike material, and the solution dawned upon me. The threshers and their companions were newly-emerged ants which had hatched from their pupae during our absence, and the objects being disposed off were the remains of their pupae skins. A new wonder filled my mind. A wonder at a fact which had never before impressed me during my long study of insects. Here were creatures, who until a few hours previously had been inert, helpless things incapable of voluntary movement or thought, and yet, no sooner had they cast off their pupal coverings and emerged as ants, than they fell to work upon the tasks of the old experienced adults and apparently as expert, as skillful and as accustomed to the by no means simple processes, as though they had been doing the same things for years and perhaps after vigorous training.

It was far more wonderful than the newly-hatched chicken scratching for its food; it was as remarkable as it would be for a newly-born infant to step into a motor car and drive it through traffic or to solve a problem in trigonometry. Unquestionably it was inherited instinct, and I wondered if, in future generations, the human race will have developed to a similar extent and if, some tens of thousands of years hence, the new-born members of our race would be able to take the places and the duties of the aged without undergoing the long and, in a way, wasted years of training and instruction.

But even more remarkable than their aptitude at age-old tasks of their ancestors, was the fact that they showed no curiosity or interest in us. Certainly that could not be inherited instinct. I felt positive that no member of the tribe had ever seen human beings. Moreover, when we had arrived the new generation must have been in an advanced pupal stage and almost ready to emerge. Hence they could not by any possibility have inherited a knowledge of us from their parents. Why then, I wondered, did these newly-hatched ants appear to regard us with the same indifference as they regarded their fellows? The only way I could account for it was to assume that the ants from the very beginning, regarded everything they saw, smelt, heard or experienced, as matters of course. In that case, I decided, they would fall easy victims to enemies or to any untoward or unusual event. If they emerged to find themselves surrounded by deadly enemies, they would assume instinctively that all was well. If they emerged to find the crops being devastated by insect-pests, they would think it nothing unusual. And yet, in that case, their inherited instincts would force them to undertake work, to do things that would be impossible of accomplishment.

And it must have required generations to have domesticated and trained the insect-allies. No, whichever way I tried to solve the mysteries of the ants' lives, instincts and intelligences, I ran, figuratively speaking, against a stone wall of evidence in rebuttal, and at last I gave it up in despair.

This time, still desiring to learn where the queen or queens were secluded and to discover more about their home life, I followed the ants into the passages leading from the exterior buildings.

There was little difficulty in locating the Royal Chamber. As I entered, my attention was centred on the other occupants of the place, rather than upon the queen herself. A dozen or more ants were working busily, and my first hasty glance showed me they were actually making bread. By this I do not mean that they were kneading dough and baking it in ovens.

But they were cracking and masticating the grain with their jaws, mixing it into a pasty dough with some sticky substance and patting it into loaves or pellets with their feet. Curious to know what they were using, I went closer and discovered that it was honey, as I had already half-suspected. As fast as the little loaves of sweetened flour were formed, other ants would pick them up and carry them to the queen, who was so enormously fat and lazy that she was actually unable to feed herself. The bored expression in her eyes, the blasé, indifferent manner in which she opened her mouth to receive the pellets of food from the jaws of her servants, was indescribably ludicrous, and was amazingly like many old dowagers I had seen. In fact, the whole scene was far more like a dream than a reality. I thought of the old nursery rhyme, for here, literally, "The Queen was in her parlor, eating bread and honey."

CHAPTER TEN

THAT night we dined in royal style. It was a comparatively simple matter to locate the bees' store of honey in a hollow tree, and as the owners were stingless and powerless to harm us, we helped ourselves. Tom rigged up a crude sort of mill consisting of a flat stone and a rounded cobble and, after the manner of Spanish-American women and Indians, he ground a quantity of corn and grain on this rough, and ready metate. Mixed to a paste with water and wrapped in corn husks, these were baked in hot ashes, and when dipped in our honey, proved most delicious after days on a meat diet. In order not to attract the ants and endanger their lives and limbs, we built our fire at some distance from the buildings and waited until all the ants had retired, before lighting it. Evidently the ants, once they had ended their days' work, were not easily disturbed, for despite the fact that they must have scented the smoke, which blew across the buildings, no ant put in an appearance.

Despite my interest in the ants and the friendly manner in which they had received and treated us, I was still as anxious and impatient to escape from the country as I had been before. No civilized man would have been content to remain indefinitely in such a place, even though we wanted for nothing in the way of creature comforts and were literally monarchs of all we surveyed, in a truly magnificent and interesting land. In fact, when I tried to analyze my own feelings and discover why I should be so intent on leaving the place, I was rather at a loss. I had neither kith nor kin in the outside world and I was surrounded by the very things in which I was and always had been most interested, and I had enough material for study to last me the rest of my life. I finally came to the conclusion that I was actuated by a combination of causes. The desire to make my discoveries known; the gregarious instinct of the human race; the inborn restlessness of the explorer, and most important of all, that peculiar and inexplicable kink in the brain of man which never permits him to be content or satisfied but is forever urging him on, forcing him constantly to seek something better or something beyond his reach. It might be called ambition, desire, purpose or any one of a thousand different names, but that did not explain it.

It was this urge, this insatiable longing for something he has not got, that has led man to all human progress, civilization and attainments. And while possessed by all men, no matter how primitive and savage, yet Nature has so ordered things that the more advanced, the more cultured man becomes, the more he develops this desire. Thinking upon this matter as I lay in my hammock, I concluded that in this lay the real, the greatest distinction between man and the lower animals. Not a single creature I could bring to mind possessed this mental state. Here, for example, were these ants. In their actions, their habits, their intellect, they were fully the equals of many races, they had learned to till the soil, to raise crops, to domesticate and train other creatures. They had made at least two quite notable discoveries or inventions, and in unity of effort, in social life and organization and in successful communism, they were far ahead of average human beings.

They had completely done away with leaders and the necessity of rulers and consequently they had eliminated oppression and caste. There was no poverty, no riches among them. They had attained, to a measure, the state which many of my fellow men prate of as Utopia. But to what purpose? Boiled down to actualities, all they did was to eat, toil, sleep and propagate their species. They possessed no arts, no sentiment, no culture, no romance, no literature, no history, and while they were no doubt perfectly happy and contented, I felt that almost any fate would be preferable to leading such an existence. Their very unity of purpose and their co-ordination of brains and effort had utterly destroyed all individuality, all personal rights and considerations. No member of the community could possess anything more or less than his fellows; there could be no striving for something better, no incentive for progress. And yet, how could this be when I had proof that there must have been progress, must have been individuality, must have been an inherent desire to better themselves in the past? Surely some one ant must have thought of training the other insects to destroy the insect-pests that beset them. Some individual must have invented the use of a roller for threshing grain, even if he only discovered it by accident. Some one ant must have visualized utensils for carrying the grain and must have found the way to make baskets. Some ant must have constructed the first building.

Such ideas, such conceptions could not have come suddenly to all at once. Such things could not be the result of inherited instinct. Even in the cultivation of their lands, the garnering of their crops, the use of the grains, they showed the result of invention, of progress. And if their lives from time immemorial had been purposeless, as I had assumed; if they had been satisfied with things as they were; if they had not possessed some sort of urge or ambition, why should they have accomplished all these things? The more I thought of it the more confused and puzzled I became. Did all living things possess to greater or less degree that never-ending desire for improvement? And, come to simmer it down, so to speak, did the human race with all its super-intelligence, its boasted progress and enlightenment, really accomplish anything more than did these ants? When all was said and done, were not all our lives, all our efforts, all our civilization, our wars, everything devoted to enabling us to eat, sleep, toil and propagate our species? And to what end? Men toiled that they might eat and sleep.

They ate and slept that they might toil, and eat and sleep again. They propagated, their species and reared their offspring, in order that their offspring might live to toil and toil to live, and they themselves toiled and lived with the sole aim of enabling the younger generation to take their places and toil and live in an endless circle. What did it all mean; what did it all lead to? Why was man—for that matter, and the lower animals also—created to go on forever in this way and get nowhere? And why was I who, by a mischance, found myself so situated that I need not toil to live nor live to toil, so anxious to return to a land where I would be, to all intents and purposes, of no more importance and where I would possess no more true freedom or individuality, than belonged to one of the ants sleeping in their underground cells? Like so many other problems and puzzles that I had faced since entering this land, it was insoluble as far as I was concerned and, I therefore gave it up and lost myself in sleep.

I had determined to set out on a further search for an exit from the country without more delay, and the following morning we started on our way. I had rather wondered how the ants would take our departure. I did not think they would hinder us, but I did assume that our leave-taking would arouse some curiosity. But I was disappointed. Not an ant paid the least heed to us, and that was not surprising, for I noticed that a second crop of the creatures had hatched out during the night and that all the ants in sight were newly-emerged individuals who had never seen- us before. What, I wondered, became of the older ants? At this rate the colony would soon increase until the food supply could not support them and the village would be overcrowded. Of course they must swarm; new queens must leave the place and establish new colonies, but as yet we had seen no swarming, no signs of young queens and still there had been two broods of new ants since we had arrived. In some ways obviously, their habits were quite different from any ordinary ants, and I rather regretted leaving them until I had thoroughly studied their lives and habits.

LEADING from the gate in the wall was a well-marked pathway which we followed, partly because it afforded easier walking and partly because I was rather curious to know whither it led. Perhaps half a mile from the village we had left, we were greatly surprised to come upon another wall exactly like the first, though evidently much newer, as in places the mud plastering was still damp. Within it we could see the roofs of houses, and beyond, tilled fields wherein ants were laboring.

Like the wall, the buildings were of recent construction, and in fact were not entirely completed, for a number of ants were working upon them. The fields too, were freshly tilled. Piles of weeds and pebbles culled from the soil were scattered about, and ants were still weeding and preparing the fields for planting. Here then was a newly established colony of the agricultural ants, and I at once jumped to the conclusion that it was a community started by young ants with a new queen from the parent colony. But if is a rash matter to jump at conclusions in this land where everything is strange and new. As I approached the nearest ants I saw that they were not young but old individuals, and, among them, I recognized the fellow whose foot had been burned in our fire. For a space I was puzzled, but presently the solution came to me. Among these ants it was not the young but the old who went forth and established new colonies.

As fast as enough young had emerged to manage the fields and carry on the studies of an established community, the older ants left and started a new village and fields. Being experienced and, in the social organization of the ants, of less value when aged, they were better fitted for this pioneer work. Also, it occurred to me, that it was quite possible that although the newly emerged young instinctively carried on the work to which they had been born, they might not inherit the knowledge of starting new communities. At any rate it was a far more human habit than most ants possessed when establishing new colonies. The young were brought up in a new environment and became thoroughly able to take care of themselves and their own progeny, before being forced to go forth and face the world and its dangers.

Each generation in turn would establish new colonies, leaving the younger ants to continue with the old communities, and thus the larger and more important colonies were always maintained by young, virile, active and more numerous ants. What, I wondered, became of the old ants eventually? How long did they live under normal conditions? Did they continue to move on indefinitely until they died of old age or did they at last find a quiet and toilless old age in some colony? Or again, were they put out of the way, killed off as so much deadwood, when they became too old and stiff in their joints or too feeble in intellect to be of further economic value? In all probability, I decided, they gradually decreased in numbers, either through natural deaths, through accident or other causes so that, after having started a certain number of colonies, their places were taken by the succeeding generation. I wondered also, how they managed to subsist until their fields were producing grain, and also whether they brought their own queen with them, or carried off a new one each time they moved on. Even whilst I was pondering on these matters, the first question was solved.

A number of ants arrived, each carrying its burden of grain or corn, and hurrying to the storerooms, deposited the load and hurried off. All were young ants, unquestionably from the colony we had just left, and supplying the immediate needs of their elders from their own stores. It was a striking proof of the splendid cooperation of these creatures, and a good demonstration of filial duty. They might permit the old ants to leave home— might even drive them forcibly away— but they had no intention of permitting them to starve to death before the new colony was on its feet. By the very order of things, and as a result of their habits and customs, this was most essential, for the entire existence of the race and the successful spreading of communities depended upon the older ants being supported and maintained in health and strength until a colony was productive and a new generation or two had appeared. It was not so easy for me to settle the question regarding the queens. The ants made no move to interfere with us—perhaps they assumed that we were moving to the new colony along with them—and I wandered into the passage which I assumed would lead to the Royal chamber. I was not mistaken.

There was the obese, complacent, blasé female and her court. But whether she was the aged mother of countless offspring or a youthful flapper I could not determine. To my eyes all queens looked alike, although to the ants they were doubtless as distinct in forms and features as are women to the eyes of men.

For several hours thereafter, we came upon colonies of the agricultural ants in various stages of development. Some were well advanced and the crops were bearing or were even being harvested, and in one or two we saw numbers of newly-emerged ants. Here was a wonderful field for study with an opportunity to make most interesting discoveries and to observe and to record all the similarities and differences existing between these ants and our own, and to make comparisons and reach conclusions as to the effects of heredity and environment. At any other time and under other conditions, I should have welcomed the opportunity, but as it was, I made only the most cursory inspection of the various colonies and kept to my main purpose of searching for an outlet from the place. Passing the last of the ants' farms, we swung into the woodland once more and headed towards a spot on the mountain ridge which I had previously selected as our first goal. We had traveled perhaps ten miles, and had just killed a fine fat hare for our mid-day meal, when, glancing through the trees, I noticed a moving object which rather puzzled me. At first sight I took it for one of the black men, bending over as if searching for something. Then I saw that it moved on all fours.. It did not, however, resemble any other creature I had met, and as well as I could judge, on account of the distance and the shadows of the trees, it appeared to be jet black in color. It was, I judged, about ten feet in length, and it moved about with a peculiar, indescribable manner of most efficiently searching every nook and corner in its vicinity. Had I been in any other land, 1 should have thought it a giant black bear, for its movements were far more ursine than feline. Even here, where I had almost convinced myself that there were no large mammals, I felt fairly certain that the strange creature must be mammalian. And that it might be and in all probability was a powerful and dangerous beast, I did not question. But no matter how dangerous it might be, there was nothing we could do save remain silent and motionless where we were, in the hopes that the thing would move on without seeing or scenting us. For a time I thought this would be the case, for the creature came no nearer and in fact at times actually moved away from us. Then, as if finally locating that for which it was searching, and with a confident manner it had not hitherto shown, it turned and came hurrying directly towards us.

"Wa-laa!" muttered Tom between chattering teeth. "He been smell tha blood what drap from the rabbit. He been a-trailin' we 'long o' tha blood, Chief." There was no doubt about it. He had crossed our trail, had smelt the hare's blood—and perhaps our own scent as well—and was after us. I had already drawn and cocked my revolver, and Tom had unsheathed his arrows in readiness to defend ourselves to the best of our ability. But I well knew that a pistol bullet was of little avail against such a huge, powerful beast and I doubted if the arrows had power enough to penetrate its thick hide. If need be, we would fight for our lives, but as long as there was a chance of escaping without facing the beast, I intended to avoid battle. If the creature had smelt the hare's blood, there was a possibility that it would be satisfied with the hare and would not attempt to attack us. To be sure, the hare would be scarcely more than a mouthful for it; but it probably had never before smelled a human being; nearly all wild creatures have an instinctive fear of man, and while it was devouring the hare, we might be able to get far enough away to be beyond its reach. So, dropping the hare, and in terse words explaining my ideas to Tom, we hurried as fast as our legs could take us in the opposite direction. Once I looked back, and through the intervening foliage I saw the dark bulk of the monster -where it was busy with the hare. A moment later, Tom yelled and spurted by me like a deer, and behind me I could hear the crackling of branches and the running footsteps of our savage pursuer. It was hopeless to think of outrunning the thing in the forest, and, shouting to Tom, we raced for a large tree, whose outjutting slablike hips extended several feet from the trunk and formed a small niche or open space with a narrow opening. Here we could be attacked only from the front, and exhausted and spent, we reached our hastily selected refuge not a moment too soon. As we dodged between the big bark-covered walls and swung about, the ferocious creature was less than twenty yards behind us. And as, for the first time I had a clear view of the beast, I saw to my absolute and complete amazement, that it was an ant. He was so monstrous, so gigantic that it did not seem possible even in this land of impossibilities. But there could be no doubt about it. He was far larger than the agricultural ants, nearly twice the size of the leaf-carrying ants, and far more formidable than either. From head to tail he was shiny, jet black, reflecting the light like burnished steel. His head seemed all eyes and terrific jaws. In fact the jaws were far larger than the head and were as keen-edged, as heavy and as deadly as battle axes. His great eyes wore a terrifying, savage glare; his antennae were drawn back, his jaws opened and extended and his great clawed front feet were raised ready for action as he rushed upon us. Never have I seen a more inexpressibly ferocious beast, and, had we been in the open, he would have made short work of us, for despite his size he was as quick and agile as a panther.

Raising my revolver, I blazed away. My first shot went wild, but my second tore a gaping hole in one eye. Partly blinded, no doubt, he swung slightly to one side and banged into one of the outspreading hips of the tree. This was our salvation. Before he could recover himself, I fired the other bullets into him at short range while Tom drove three arrows at the great beast now within a dozen feet of us. The arrows might as well have been straws. His thick polished coat of chitinous mail turned them aside as readily as would steel armor. It even proved efficacious against some of the pistol bullets when they struck a glancing blow, but the others crashed through his shell. From the gaping wounds, thick, yellowish juice oozed, emitting a sickening, acrid stifling odor. But despite the damages done by my bullets, the creature was far from dead or even mortally wounded. Half-blinded as he was, riddled with holes, he staggered off a few yards, and shaking his head and clashing his jaws, gathered himself for a second charge. As he stood there for a moment, I reloaded my weapon with trembling fingers, and I noticed for the first time that his abdomen ended in a sharp point and that from this protruded an immense barbed sting. Instantly I placed him. He was one of those strange solitary ants of the tropics; those giants of their family who possess both stings and powerful fighting mandibles, and who roam the jungles alone, blindly attacking every living thing they find, devouring any creature they can conquer, and are so savage, so poisonous that even those of normal size are regarded with terror by the Indians. And this one, gathering strength for another attack upon us, was a monster of monsters, hundreds of times the size of the largest known to science. All this flashed through my brain during the few short seconds it required to reload my pistol. The next instant I was feverishly kicking, scraping, pawing dead leaves, twigs and bits of bark into a pile at the entrance of the tiny refuge where we stood. As the giant ant's muscles tensed and his great jaws opened, I scratched a match and touched the flame to the little pile.

As the match flickered and went out and a tiny flame ran through the dead leaves, the ant charged. Though his rush lacked the speed and strength of the first, for he was evidently weakened by his wounds, still it was terrifying enough, and with cocked revolver I awaited him, determined to withhold my precious ammunition to the last, and hoping against hope that he would be checked by the rapidly-spreading fire. As he felt the heat and smelled the smoke, he hesitated. Then a pile of leaves flared up, the flames scorched his feet and head, and hastily he drew back. For a moment he stood there, shaking hid head, rubbing his burned legs and peering at the flames. Then, as if deciding the fire was a new enemy to be summarily dealt with, he leaped forward and regardless of the smoke and flames, savagely attacked the blaze with jaws, sting and feet; throwing the firebrands aside, biting at the flames with such ferocity as I have never witnessed in any beast.

Again and again I fired at him. Tom, his fear giving way to primitive savage frenzy, was belaboring the creature with his bow, pelting him with clods of earth and yelling like a fiend. But our case seemed hopeless. The giant ant was rapidly destroying the fire; he was within six feet of us, and my bullets apparently had no effect. Then, suddenly, help arrived from a most unexpected quarter. There was a rustle of leaves, the swift patter of hurrying feet from behind the tree, and the next instant a huge beetle rushed upon the scene. I say huge, but in comparison to the maddened ant he appeared puny. In his large, soft abdomen, his embryonic wings, his steel blue color, he closely resembled one of the blister-beetles, or as they are more commonly termed, Spanish-flies; but that he was a distinct species and a new genus to me I knew at a glance.

As he caught sight of the fiendish ant he halted, his protruding glistening eyes fixed on the scene. Then with his short club-shaped antennae sheathed in their recesses out of harm's way; with his useless wings half raised; with his abdomen curled sharply upward, he raced for the ant. It seemed the height of folly, a suicidal act for this soft-bodied, harmless-looking creature to attack the giant ant. I expected to see the latter turn, snap the beetle into bits and resume his attack upon us. But nothing of the sort happened. Busy with the fire, the ant failed to see the beetle until it was upon him. With a leap so swift the eye could scarcely follow it, the beetle sprang at the ant, alighting upon its back. Instantly there was a sharp report like a miniature explosion, a misty cloud enveloped the two insects, and Tom and I staggered back almost overcome by a smarting, burning, choking terrible sensation, as if we had been exposed to mustard-gas. Scarcely able to see through the tears that filled my burning eyes, I saw the great ant stagger back and the beetle spring lightly from its perch. The next moment the ant was writhing and twisting, while the beetle, always maintaining a safe distance from the terrible sting, the clashing jaws and the thrashing feet, darted back and forth, like a dog worrying a wounded bear. But each time, instead of nipping at his struggling foe, he would swing quickly about, raise his abdomen and would discharge a cloud of vapor with a loud report. I was scarcely as much amazed by his temerity in attacking the ant as by his methods. I was, of course, familiar with the habits of the common Bombardier-beetles, those little ground-beetles who, when angered or frightened, discharge an infinitesimal quantity of ill-smelling gas from their abdomens to the accompaniment of an almost inaudible pop.

But the beetle before me was of a totally different genus, one of the blister-beetle family I felt sure, and the vapor he was discharging at his fallen foe, was obviously having a deadly effect. In fact, the huge ant was even now helpless, barely able to move, and after one or two more of the beetle's gas attacks he remained quiescent and evidently quite dead. Here was a most marvelous exposition of the triumph of science over brute force. The soft-bodied, short-jawed, inoffensive beetle had easily defeated and destroyed the gigantic armed and ferocious ant without even exposing itself to serious danger. But what if he turned his attention to ourselves? What if he should discharge his deadly gas at us? Grateful as I felt for his timely intervention, I was half minded to shoot the beetle at once, for my eyes still smarted from the effects of the slight amount of gas we had been exposed to and I knew that a full charge would render us helpless, if it did not destroy us at once. I also realized that the odor and the intense burning properties of the vapor were precisely like the smell and effect of the oily secretions exuding from the blister-beetles. In fact, it was this strongly irritant material, which has given them their popular names and has caused them to be used in medicine in the form of plasters and counter-irritants in many lands. If then this huge beetle was, as I felt sure, a member of this family, it was no wonder that his secretions were sufficient to destroy the ant, especially when concentrated and discharged in large volume directly upon him.

As all these thoughts rushed through my mind, I watched the triumphant beetle closely, expecting at any moment to see him turn towards Tom and myself. But I need not have worried. He was examining the dead ant, feeling him with his antennae, smelling of the carcass and, as nearly as I could judge, he was greatly puzzled to account for the wounds caused by my pistol balls. No doubt it was the first time he had ever destroyed an enemy by his gas attacks and then had found the defeated insect's life-juice exuding from a dozen or more gaping holes. Puzzling as it must have been, it apparently made little difference to him. With his stout short jaws, he quickly tore a large opening in the ant's abdomen, and began devouring the creature. He ate ravenously, and at last, gorged to repletion, he balanced himself on his hind legs, meticulously cleansed his head, antennae and jaws, brushed the crumbs from his waistcoat—if I may use the metaphor—and with a regretful glance at the store of food still unconsumed, he trotted off and disappeared in the forest.

With deep sighs of relief Tom and I stepped from our shelter. For a moment we stood gazing at the remains of the giant ant. Tom stooped, picked up one of the huge disarticulated jaws and grinned. "Seem like to me," he chuckled. "This been a mighty fine sort of cutlash, Chief. Ah been goin' to ca'y it along, an' if Ah comes to fightin' another of dis gent'man Ah boun' for to use it far bash in he haid."

Tom's idea was excellent. The jaws were as large and as strong as butchers' cleavers, with edges almost as keen, and the rounded knob-ended joints with which they had been connected with the muscles before the beetle had devoured the tissues, made excellent handles. They would, as Tom had said, serve as most vicious and deadly weapons at close quarters and, moreover, they would prove useful as tools or implements and would save much wear and tear on my hunting-knife. But the almost skeletonised ant was to provide us with still another addition to our armament. Protruding from his half-devoured abdomen was his immense sting, a needle-pointed rapier of chitin over eighteen inches in length, as flexible as tempered steel and almost as light as wood. With some difficulty, I cut it free from its tissues and muscles, and cautiously examined its shining black length with its sharp recurved barbs near the tip. A tiny scratch from that poison-soaked weapon would mean death and, mounted on a stout shaft, it would be a most formidable spear. To find and cut such a staff was easy, and having bound the sting to its four-foot shaft, and having protected its point by a bamboo sheath, we left the scene of the recent drama and resumed our interrupted journey.

CHAPTER ELEVEN

HAVING sacrificed our prospective meal, we searched about for possible game and were at last forced to fall back upon frog. Tom killed the big batrachian with a blow of his ant-jaw axe and thus proved the efficiency of his new weapon to the entire satisfaction of us both. We lunched beside a fair-sized stream, and the cool limpid water appeared so attractive that we decided to have a swim before resuming our journey. Stripping off his scanty garments, Tom dove from the bank, and through the clear water I could see his brown body swimming, like a giant frog, far below the surface. Like all of his race, he was almost amphibious, and I watched him, as he moved slowly along, close to the overhanging bank near to the bottom of the stream. Then, just as I was on the point of plunging in to join him, I saw him veer aside, strike out furiously and shoot to the surface. Wild terror filled his eyes, his face was distorted with fear, as he swam madly for shore. He had seen something to terrify him I knew, and I peered towards the bottom of the stream, in an effort to discover what it might be. But the commotion caused by his frantic movements obliterated everything, and while I thought for an instant that I caught a glimpse of some huge dark creature, scarcely more than a shadow, I could not be sure it was not merely the effect of the disturbed water. The next instant Tom was on dry land stammering and quaking, and it was several minutes before he could speak coherently or I could make head or tail of his gibberish.

"Lordy!" he managed to exclaim at last. "Wa-lla, Chief; Ah been see the mos' frightsome al'gator Ah ever see. Yes, indeed, Chief. An' fo' tha Lard yo' come nigh to losin' yo' negro Tom, Chief. He been miss grabbin' me by no more'n a inch, Chief."

"Alligator!" I ejaculated. "Are you sure, Tom?"

As I spoke, I crouched on the bank and again peered into the depths but could see nothing. Still Tom insisted that a monstrous saurian had attacked him and that he had barely escaped with his life. Unquestionably he had seen something, but I could not believe it an alligator or crocodile. The clear water, the smooth pebbly bottom were not such as the saurians prefer. And in all my experience I had never before known one of the reptiles to lie in wait and snap at passing objects far below the surface. Always, they rise and seize their prey at or near the surface, or when below, rush at it.

Also, knowing Tom's character and how easily he became terror-stricken at any unusual sight, and how objects under water are distorted and magnified, I felt that it was far more probable that he had seen an overgrown and harmless salamander or even a tadpole. So sure was I that no alligator was lurking below that I rose, prepared to dive down myself and investigate. But Tom begged me not to attempt it, and, remembering how many unexpected perils had been met, I thought better of my impulse and decided on a wiser plan.

The discarded portions of the frog, on which we had lunched, were near at hand, and dragging these to the bank, we attached them to the end of a tough vine, weighted them with stones so they would sink, and lowered them into the stream at the spot where Tom insisted he had seen the reptile. For a moment nothing happened and then, from among the stones under the bank, a huge horrible head darted out, seized the bait, and with a jerk that tore the vine from our hands, dragged it back among the stones. I was amazed. Even in the brief glimpse I had had, I knew it was no alligator, no crocodile. The immense curved jaws armed with huge spike-like teeth were not those of a saurian or of any reptile with which I was familiar. And yet what else could the monster be?

All my curiosity was aroused and I determined to discover what manner of rapacious beast lay in wait there. Gathering the remaining portions of the frog, we bound them and a number of stones together with vines, attached them to a stout vine and fastened this to the tip of a long, strong pole. This we fastened securely so that it extended several feet from the bank. Stretching myself at full length, and with my ant-sting-tipped spear poised, I told Tom to drop the bait into the stream. As the ripples caused by its fall smoothed out and the frog-meat slowly sank, I lowered my spear until its point was but a foot above the spot whence the creature had appeared. With both hands gripping the shaft, I waited ready to plunge it into the monster the moment he emerged from his lair. For a space I feared he would not expose himself, that his hunger had been appeased and that our bait would not again tempt him. But I had not counted on the thing's insatiable appetite. Once more that fearsome head lurched forward with wide-spread, ravenous jaws. But this time the bait was further away, and following the monstrous ferocious head, came a foot or two of pale, livid, fleshy body. With all my force I drove the spear downward, aiming for the point where the head and body joined. I felt the spear bury itself in yielding flesh, the shaft was wrenched from my grasp, and as I sprang back, the stream frothed and churned and was transformed to a miniature maelstrom by the wounded maddened monster. Keeping well back from the shore, Tom and I watched with fascinated eyes, expecting each moment to see the terrible thing rise from the waves and dash at us.

Gradually the commotion subsided, the water cleared, and cautiously we approached the bank. With a yell, Tom leaped back, pointing excitedly. Then I, too, saw. Close to the bank, half- floating, belly up, and still wriggling and twitching spasmodically, was the body of the thing. I shuddered as I looked at it. Never had I seen a more diabolical looking beast. Its flattened segmented ten-foot body with its rows of short, clawed, stout legs resembled that of a giant centipede. Along the sides were rows of great warty protuberances bearing short, stiff bristles. Its immense flat head was covered with broad plates of chitin, and its enormous terrible jaws were still opening and closing viciously. As it moved feebly in its death throes, it turned partly over and its big cruel eyes glared at us balefully.

No wonder poor Tom had been terrified. To meet such a monster under water would have been enough to drive the bravest man half mad with fear. But the monster's days were over; my spear had proved its worth and the ant poison had done its work thoroughly. But as I had felt sure, the beast was no reptile. He was an insect; the larva of some gigantic species of Corydalis, a monstrous hellgromite or dobson; a stupendous prototype of the ugly, savage, aquatic larvae of the neuropter, common in our own brooks and so much in demand by anglers as bait for black bass.

Fortunately Tom had discovered the beast in time. Still more fortunately, his discovery had probably saved us both from horrible deaths, for I had no doubt that scores, hundreds of the creatures lurked in the stream and in other streams, and bathing, with such monsters about, would be far more perilous than diving into a nest of man-eating crocodiles. At last the huge creature ceased to move, and approaching it cautiously, we threw rocks and sticks at it. Our attack brought no response, not even a tremor. Feeling convinced it was quite dead, we managed to throw a loop of vine over one of its jaws and dragged its head within reach, so that I might retrieve my spear. The struggles of the monster had snapped the staff of the weapon, but the sting itself was uninjured, and with considerable difficulty, I wrenched it free from the dead hellgromite's flesh. Then, having again bound it to a new shaft, and feeling quite elated at our destruction of the monstrous larva, we resumed our way.

We had been delayed and interrupted so frequently that we had made but little real progress. It was mid-afternoon; we were miles from our cave, too far from the ants' villages to return to them, and with the mountains still in the distance. It was evident that we would, be forced to pass another night in the open, but this did not greatly trouble us. We had our hammocks, we felt quite well equipped with weapons, and while we had learned that we were surrounded by many known and still more unknown enemies and dangers, we had grown so accustomed to facing such perils that night held little terror for us.

I preferred not to sleep in the forest, however, and as we proceeded, we searched the country for some open spot wherein to camp. An hour or two after our destruction of the hellgromite we reached the edge of the forest and came to the verge of a broad, rather sandy plain or prairie bare of vegetation with the exception of bunches of coarse grass and clumps of cactus and agaves. Some of the cacti were of the giant candelabra variety and were even larger than the largest of those on the deserts of our Southwestern States. They were in fact, real trees and amply strong enough to sustain our hammocks. Here was an excellent camp-site. We would be in the open, away from the myriad of gnats, moths and beetles; we could not be attacked without warning except from the air—and it was dry and free from the miasmic mists of the forest. Selecting a clump of several large cacti at a short distance from the forest edge as a likely spot for our camp, I directed Tom to gather some dry firewood from under the trees, and sauntered on in advance towards the group of cacti. Never dreaming that any danger could be near in this open country, I gave little attention to my immediate surroundings.

Suddenly, and without the least warning, a two-foot circular section of the earth sprang up within a few yards of my feet. To my startled eyes it had precisely the appearance of a man-hole cover thrown open. Then, as the lid dropped back, exposing a round hole, a chill ran down my spine. From the aperture two great, hairy, brown arms appeared, each tipped with immense black talons. Before I could regain my wits, before I could move, a horrible head followed. A rough, hairy, brown head with immense down-curving, tusk, like black fangs, and with a group of small, flaming-red, piercing eyes. I needed no second glance. The thing was a giant tarantula—one of the trap-door spiders—a deadly, terrible creature. Confused, unable to decide on what to do, I stood there, inert and helpless, as the fearful creature climbed swiftly and silently from its silk-lined burrow. A moment and he would pounce upon me. I could almost feel the agony of his gripping claws, could almost sense these awful fangs burying themselves in my neck. Then life, action, sense came back to me. With a wild cry, I whipped out my pistol and fired. But my hand shook, the bullet went wild, and striking the sand a few inches in front of the crouching tarantula, it flipped a shower of dust and pebbles into the thing's eyes. Surprised, dazed, partly blinded, confused, the giant spider sprang quickly back, bit viciously at the offending sand and momentarily forgot his human prey. Taking careful aim, I pulled the trigger, and from the great hairy thorax I saw a puff of dust and fur fly as the missile struck.

But it served only to infuriate the beast, to remind him of my presence.

Again I levelled my weapon and pulled the trigger, but only a click followed.

The revolver was useless. I had forgotten to reload after my battle with the ant. To turn and run would be worse than hopeless. In less than a dozen steps the monstrous spider would be upon my defenceless back. And I had no time even to turn. I saw the great tarantula gather his feet together for a spring. I saw him hurl himself forward. Unconsciously, instinctively, I thrust out my hands to ward him off. Like a ten-inch shell, he came hurtling upon me, his terrible talons outspread, his awful fangs ready to bury themselves in my body, his dozen red eyes gleaming like coals of fire. In my mad terror of the deadly creature, I had forgotten that I still grasped my spear. Not until my staring, dilated eyes saw the tarantula upon me, not until I felt the impact of his body against the weapon, did I remember it. Then, with a rush, recollection and swift action returned to me. Grasping the shaft with, both hands, taking a backward step, I lunged forward and upward with all my strength.

I felt the weapon go home; I dropped the shaft and plunged headlong to one side. One great claw snatched at my coat and ripped the sleeve from shoulder to wrist; vile-smelling, horrible liquid spattered me. Stumbling to my feet, not daring to look back, I rushed blindly away, until tripping over a stone, I sprawled at full length on the sand. Dazed, shaken, trembling and utterly spent, I stared back, expecting to see the monster about to finish me.

But he had other matters to occupy his mind, if he possessed any. In a perfect paroxysm of rage he was writhing, twisting, rolling about; biting with indescribable ferocity at his own body, his own legs and at my spear which had transfixed him. It was a horrible, a terrible sight, and Tom, who had witnessed the entire affair, had dropped senseless from sheer terror; had actually fainted, for the first time in his life. What my bullets had failed to do, my spear had accomplished. The tarantula's minutes were numbered. Already his struggles were becoming weaker, and by the time I had reached Tom's side and he had recovered consciousness, the gruesome, horrible beast was still in death. My spear, however, was ruined. The dying spider, in his convulsive rage, had bent and broken the tough chitinous blade beyond all hope of repair. I was maddened at my loss, for twice the weapon had served me well and I owed my life to it. But if the gigantic spider had robbed me of my trusty javelin, he was to supply me with a substitute. His great, curved, pointed fangs were larger and heavier than the ant's sting, and while they bore no poison, as I knew, they were not to be despised as weapons. With difficulty overcoming my repugnance at the task—and utterly unable to coax or threaten Tom into approaching the dead creature—I hacked and cut its fangs free. Unlike the ant's sting, which was beautifully tapered, perfectly cylindrical and straight as an arrow, the spider's fangs were curved, thickened on the convex edge and possessed deep longitudinal grooves. As spears they were useless, but their similarity to the ancient English bill-hooks was striking, and I knew they would prove most effective weapons. Passing one to Tom and keeping the other myself, we carefully retraced our way to the forest, keenly searching each square foot of the desert as we advanced.

After my experience, we had no desire to sleep on that open plain. The horde of night insects in the forest was far preferable to prowling tarantulas.

Only stopping long enough to cut and fit handles to our new weapons, we hurried into the forest until we were beyond sight of the plain, before preparing to make camp. It was already very late; we had no time to lose, and quickly we lit a fire, cooked our meal, and slung our hammocks by the light of the flames. But we slept little that night. As before, myriads of insects attracted by the fire, buzzed, blundered, crawled and flew about us, and I was far too nervous and upset by the afternoon's adventure with the tarantula to sleep well.

Altogether it was a nightmarish time. But dawn came at last, and with the new day and the welcome, light, our spirits rose. Very soon Tom secured game—a hare and a strange creature quite new to me, and which resembled a porcupine without spines. We breakfasted well. By the light of morning, the experiences of the preceding day seemed dream-like and unreal; but there were our tarantula-fang bill-hooks to prove their reality, not to mention the ripped sleeve of my coat. We had no mind to attempt to cross that stretch of sandy plain, however. Where one giant trap-door spider dwelt, others probably dwelt also, and I knew the ferocious character of the creatures far too well to take any chances with them.

So, although the route was far longer, we decided to follow the forest edge to our objective point. Hitherto, all the spiders we had seen were rather small and were of the geometrical orb-weaver group, quite harmless as far as we were concerned, although ugly and terrible in appearance.

This had already caused me a great deal of surprise and no little wonder, for in a country where other insects were so abundant and of such huge proportions, it might be assumed that the spiders or arachnids would be proportionately abundant and of proportionate size. Yet, until I had met the tarantula, we had seen no spider of any sort more than three feet in length. We had met none of the predatory jumping-spiders so abundant in other lands, none of the wolf-spiders, the funnel-makers or the long-legged web-makers. Nor had we seen any of the arboreal mygale group which are usually so abundant in the tropics. Why, I wondered, were spiders relatively so scarce? I could not explain it, could find no hypothesis to account for it, but I was duly thankful that they were rare. Before the day was done, however, I was to discover the answer to the question. We had passed well beyond the scene of our adventure with the tarantula, and were in a district where the country was broken and outcrops of rock projected above the earth. Several times I had noticed large, dark-colored insects winging back and forth above the plain, but had given them little attention, knowing they were neither solitary hornets, ichneumon-flies nor giant bees. But as we stopped to rest for a time, my eyes idly followed the creatures. Presently one of them swooped quickly towards the surface of the plain, vanished for a few moments, and reappeared, carrying some object in its jaws and forefeet. Somewhat curious as to the prey it had secured, I watched it as, turning, it came flying heavily in our direction. As it drew near, I saw that it was a wasp, a big dark-blue, dusky-winged, slender-bodied fellow perhaps three feet in length and that its burden was a big fat-bellied spider. Its similarity to our own familiar mud-wasps was striking, and like them, it evidently had the habit of preying upon spiders. Knowing the manner in which our own mud-wasps sting their victims into a comatose state, and then wall them up in their mud nests to provide food for the young wasps when the latter hatch out, I had no doubt that the big wasp humming past us was bound for its nest on a similar mission. A few rods beyond where we sat, it volplaned down to a rocky ledge and vanished.

Anxious to learn more of its habits, I rose and cautiously approached the spot. Clambering over the rocks I soon detected the wasp. It was clinging to its nest and was so busily engaged in forcing the stupefied spider within it, that it paid no attention to my presence. The nest was a beautiful structure, a perfectly symmetrical urn-shaped affair of smoothly-moulded clay with its base attached to the rock; a perfect example of the workmanship of the potter-wasp group, and as true in form and as gracefully designed as though modelled by an expert human potter on a potter's wheel.*

But unlike the potter-wasps with which I was familiar, this species was evidently gregarious, for clustered on the rocks near the first nest, were a dozen others. Some had the orifices tightly sealed, indicating that their owners had stored their supply of living provender within and had completed their maternal duties. Others were partially completed; others were ready for occupancy but were still empty; while on several the big wasps were resting, as though they were tired out with their labors.

While I watched, two more wasps arrived with their spiders, and I realized that here was one reason for the comparative scarcity of the arachnids. No doubt, I thought, there would be numerous colonies of these wasps scattered throughout the country and the aggregate might be sufficient to keep down the spider population. Still, I had noticed that all the spiders captured by these wasps appeared to belong to the wolf-spider group, and I could not see how or why the decimation of their numbers should have any effect upon the spiders of other species

[* Many of our solitary wasps construct clay nests of beautiful vase or pot like form. For this reason they are popularly known as "Potter wasps."]

dwelling in remote spots, in the jungles and forests. As a matter of fact, however, I was really more interested in the wasps' nests than in the spider problem. Seeing the graceful, vessel-like nests had put an idea in my head. If wasps could mould pottery, why should not Tom and myself do the same? Hitherto we had been forced to roast or broil all our food and we had sorely felt the want of utensils for holding water on several occasions. Calabashes, gourds, large nuts or similar objects appeared wanting in this place, and we had fallen back upon sections of bamboo. Somewhere near there must be a clay bed, and mentally deciding to hunt this up and try my hand at the ceramic art, if we failed to find an exit through the mountains, upon my return, I rose, and calling to Tom, we again trudged on. But our way was beset by difficulties we had not foreseen. Everywhere among the rocks were wasps' nests. Whichever way we turned, we came upon them. Many were like those I had seen, but others were immense, rough, irregular affairs containing many cells. We had literally stumbled into a hornets' nest, but fortunately for us the mud-wasps, like their ordinary prototypes, were docile, peaceful insects and did not offer to attack us. Still, I did not care to tempt them too far, and finding we could not continue on our route without passing through the wasp colonies, we swung far to one side and headed for a defile or valley which was sparsely wooded. But here we were no better off. Although the mud-wasps were left behind with the bare rocks, the valley fairly swarmed with black and yellow wasps. And these, too, were spider-catchers. The air fairly vibrated with them and I knew perfectly well that they were quick-tempered fellows, very different from the good-natured mud-wasps. Everywhere, too, the trees were festooned with their gigantic top-shaped nests of gray paper, and as we watched them from a safe distance, scores, hundreds of the big yellow-jackets were constantly arriving, each carrying a stupefied spider.

No wonder the spider-world had not multiplied or grown to gigantic proportions. Betwixt the mud-wasps with their penchant for prowling wolf-spiders of the open, and these paper-makers, who apparently captured woodland spiders only, there was little chance for the arachnids to increase in numbers or in size. No doubt, too, there were many other colonies of wasps and hornets who depended upon spiders and which I had not chanced to find, for it would be most unusual and quite contrary to all known habits of insects, to have the entire spider-eating wasp population of the vast territory confined to one small area. Why the mud-wasps should be here I could well understand, for their habits required the presence of the rock ledges near the edge of the open plain; but wherever there were such conditions, there would no doubt be mud-wasps. While I could not see that the haunt of these black and yellow fellows was in any respect different from countless other wooded valleys, still there might be certain details—as the presence of trees suitable for paper making—which would appeal to the hornets. At any rate, it was obvious that they had taken complete possession of the place, and I for one had no longing to dispute their rights.

CHAPTER TWELVE

MAKING a wide detour, we passed through a stretch of jungle and came out upon a grass-covered area ascending at an easy angle to the first slopes of the mountains. Scattered about, and half-hidden in the grass, were scores of what I at first took to be great rounded boulders. Suddenly I halted, staring, for one of the rocks had seemed to move. Squinting in the brilliant light, shading my eyes with my hand, I gazed, wondering if it was an effect of the shimmering heated air rising from the plain; if it was an hallucination of my brain due to a coming attack of fever, or if I had merely imagined it. Then once again the massive boulder heaved itself upward, moved slowly forward for a few yards and again remained motionless. I hurried forward filled with amazement and curiosity at this seeming miracle. Then abruptly I roared with laughter at my own stupidity. The thing was no rock but a gigantic turtle, a stupendous land-tortoise. The dome-shaped carapace was strikingly similar to those of the giant tortoises of the Galapagos Islands but immeasurably larger, being fully ten feet in length and rising for several feet above the waist-high grass. I stood awed and impressed at thought of the countless centuries which must have passed since this huge creature first emerged from its egg. The Galapagos tortoises are estimated to be from two to five hundred years old, and if these fellows in the grass about me grew at a proportionate rate, then their ages must be measured by thousands of years. And as we came near and the mammoth tortoise raised his great head and looked at us curiously, his bleary eyes seemed to gaze upon us puny beings with all the wisdom of the ages.

Immense age, too, was indicated by the countless deep wrinkles on his skinny neck, the worn and battered scales upon his enormous feet, his scarred and battered shell, and the blunted worn-down edges of his jaws. What marvelous stories these multi-centenarians could tell could they but speak! What amazing events they must have witnessed in the transformation of the world about them! But the hoary old patriarch within a few yards of us was not interested in anything aside from the grass within his reach, and, after assuring himself that we were not to be feared and that he need not withdraw his wrinkled neck and elephantine feet within his shell on our account, he worried a bunch of grass from the earth and munched it slowly, deliberately, like a toothless old man. Having devoured all the herbage within reach, he reared himself ponderously, lurched forward a few yards and again sank down.

Something in his movements reminded me most forcibly of an Army Tank, and seized with a sudden boyish impulse, I handed my weapons to Tom. With some difficulty, I scrambled onto the giant turtle's back. Of course he paid no attention to my presence, for through his immensely thick carapace, he could not have felt my movements, and my weight was no more to him than that of a grasshopper upon the back of an ordinary tortoise, and he continued to graze as calmly as ever. As far as I was concerned, I might as well have been standing upon an upjutting rock. Grinning from ear to ear, Tom stepped towards the beast's rear and dealt a resounding blow upon its stout scale-covered tail. Instantly I felt as though I were experiencing a terrific earthquake. The great carapace rose upward, it shook, swayed, rocked, and sprawling flat on my stomach, I clung desperately to the rough surface with hands and feet. Like a dismasted ship in a hurricane-lashed sea, the tortoise lurched forward, thoroughly startled at the treatment he had received, and at each forward heave of his ponderous legs progressed a dozen feet or more.

Tom, elated at his success, and bellowing with laughter, followed after, belaboring the turtle's tail and paying no heed to my frantic shouts to cease. The beast's pace was by no means slow and Tom was forced to run to keep up with us. But the rolling, rocking motion was more disturbing than that of any laboring ship, and at last, unable to stick it out longer, I allowed myself to slip earthward and landed safely on all fours in the grass.

Instantly, as Tom ceased his efforts, the turtle came to a halt and resumed his interrupted breakfast as if nothing unusual had occurred. It had been a most unique and remarkable experience for me, and I assured Tom that as a means of transportation, the turtle was even more tank-like than in his appearance.

Passing through the herd of the giant tortoises, I remarked that here were creatures who had nothing to fear from any enemies. No living beast, not even a dinosaur, if such had existed, could have made any impression on those mighty shells. The fiercest, most savage insects, would have found the thick scale-protected skin of neck and legs impervious to mandibles and stings. Even man, unless equipped with a powerful rifle, would find it difficult indeed to harm the beasts, and, once they withdrew within the shelter of their shells, they would be as secure and safe as though barricaded in a battleship's turret. They were harmless, useless creatures provided by Nature with ample means of protection in lieu of means of defense, and yet I knew that, should civilized men ever invade this country, they would want only destroy these monstrous tortoises as ruthlessly as they had exterminated the giant turtles of the Galapagos.*

FOR the first time since entering the place, I felt thankful that it was not inhabited by my fellow men.

Beyond the turtle plain we came to broken country, and throughout the day we climbed, toiled, tramped and searched the mountain side; but all in vain.

Every ravine and canon we explored proved a blind lead, and when night fell we camped where darkness found us among the rocks, too tired and spent to retrace our way to a better spot or to worry over discomforts. Nothing disturbed us, there was no reason for any living creature dwelling in such a desolate spot. Even the customary ground-beetles were lacking. With daylight we had a magnificent view of the country, for we were at a higher altitude than we had previously attained in our explorations. Far below us stretched the green, sloping plain dotted with the brown, rounded backs of the giant turtles. In far distance we could distinguish the farms and villages of the agricultural ants. Barely visible on the opposite side of the valley was the low, swampy, jungle-covered area with the aphis groves beyond. Like a vast brown patch the desert plain of the tarantulas broke through the greenery, and we could make out the rocky ridge where the spider-eating mud-wasps had their nests. So far, we had covered a large part

[*These tortoises often reach large size. Specimens have been known large enough easily to carry two or three men upon their backs.]

of this familiar area, but there was an immense amount of territory still unknown to us and this I studied carefully. Here, once more, I saw the expanse of orderly arranged trees, which we had seen from our cave on the other side of the valley, and which I had assumed was a second settlement of the black humans with their aphis orchards.

But I was now much closer to it and the more I studied it the less it looked like the settlement and orchards of the blacks we knew. I could not exactly describe or analyze why or how it appeared different and, at the time, I did not give very great attention to it, for I thought it in no way strange that two settlements of the race should vary considerably. In another spot, and much nearer to us, was a group of half a dozen or more low, rounded, dome-like objects, standing prominently among the vegetation. They were quite different from anything I had hitherto seen, and in general appearance were more like huge beehives or Kaffir kraals than anything else. I longed for glasses with which to examine them and, as I had done scores of times before, I blamed myself and figuratively kicked myself for an unmitigated ass for having left my equipment, including my field-glasses, at Tupec when I first started to explore the tunnel. But to regret my lack of foresight was futile, and I strained my eyes, and Tom did the same, trying to puzzle out what the structures were, whether in fact they were structures or natural formation, and trying to pick out a route that would lead us to them. If they were indeed artificial things, buildings of any sort, then in all probability they might be the homes of human beings. A short time previously I should have said certainty rather than probability, but experience had taught me not to jump at conclusions, and after the agricultural ants, I realized that, even if artificial, these beehive-like affairs might be the homes of some form of insect life. But whatever they might prove to be, I had made up my mind to have a look at them at close range.

From former experience I knew that the puzzling affairs would prove far more distant when we began to tramp towards them than they appeared to be when viewed from the heights. But I planned to cross the valley and thoroughly explore that side, retaining our cave as a headquarters, before continuing on the side where we now were, and it would be only a few miles out of our way to visit the dome-shaped things. Descending the rocky slope was far easier than ascending it, and very soon we were again in the turtle pasture. Crossing this, and searching for game, for we were very hungry, we swung to the north and entered an expanse of thorny jungle where we secured two of the odd mammals which I have likened to porcupines minus spines. Like all other mammals we had seen they were rodents, but I noted, as I cleaned and skinned them, while Tom prepared his fire, that they were of a very primitive type and undoubtedly new to science. In many ways they were more closely related to the capybaras and guinea pigs than to the porcupines, and to my surprise, I discovered that they were marsupials, pouched mammals. Here, indeed, was a great discovery. The only American marsupials hitherto known were the opossums, which are carnivorous. And here was a marsupial rodent.

This set me to thinking, and I wondered if it were possible that the hares and marmots of the place were also marsupials. In fact for the time being my discovery of a new order of marsupial mammals on the South American continent quite obsessed me, until I recollected that, unless I escaped from the place, this discovery along with all my others, would die with me and might remain unknown to the world for centuries or perhaps forever.

Regardless of their peculiarities and their interest from a zoological viewpoint, the creatures proved excellent eating, and when we at last resumed our tramp, only the clean-picked bones of the beasts were left. However, I had no fears about future meals, and within the hour Tom knocked over one of the little marmots. As I had rather expected and had hoped, he, too, proved to be a marsupial, and later I discovered that the same was the case with the hare-like creatures. Yet, despite the fact that I was daily, hourly in fact, making astounding scientific discoveries and finding all previously conceived ideas completely upset, it came as something of a shock when Tom stumbled upon the nest and eggs of one of these animals. We were walking through a patch of forest, carpeted with dense ferns, when Tom exclaimed that he had found a bird's nest. I hurried to him, for we had neither seen nor heard birds, and I had instantly assumed that he had found the eggs of some reptile or possibly of some huge insect. But my first glance assured me that I was wrong and Tom was right. At the base of a cluster of ferns, and filling a slight depression in the earth, was a bulky nest of dead leaves and down, containing five elliptical pale-buff eggs slightly speckled with bluish-green. They were about the size of hens' eggs and, so I at once assumed, were eggs of some gallinaceous bird, perhaps incapable of flight. Tom, however, was far more interested in their edible properties than in the identity of the owner, and picking up one of the eggs, he deftly sliced off one end. With a startled surprised cry he dropped it as if it were red hot.

THE WORLD OF THE GIANT ANTS

"Lord A'mighty!" he exclaimed. "He been got a rat inside he."

I STARED incredulously at the contents of the egg revealed by the smashed shell. Squirming feebly in the mess upon the earth was the embryo of a four-footed creature! For a brief instant I thought it a reptile, but the bedraggled scant hair, the ears, the whole appearance of the embryo precluded that and proved it to be the inmate of the egg of a mammal. It was astounding. And yet I knew that the Platypus or Duck-bill of Australia lays eggs, as does the echidna or spiny ant-eater. Excited at this fresh discovery I examined the now defunct embryo and readily identified it as the young of the hare-like creature we knew so well. The long ears, the rudimentary tail and the greatly developed hind legs were unmistakable. Moreover, in its embryonic state, the creature appeared far more like a kangaroo than a hare and a new idea flashed to my mind.

Was it not possible that the kangaroos had evolved from rabbits or vice-versa? Here were creatures, evidently very low in the scale of mammalian evolution, who resembled hares as much as kangaroos, who were marsupials, who laid eggs. They were true missing-links, and more than ever before I regretted my inability to make my discovery known to my fellow men and to add to the world's knowledge of life and evolution. No scientist was ever in a more exasperating and unenviable situation. I was making epochal and revolutionary discoveries that could be of no benefit either to myself or to the world. Even my discovery of the hare's eggs (for I must thus refer to the creatures) was of no real benefit, for they were unfit for food, and food to Tom and myself was of far more importance than scientific facts.

So, leaving the nest and its contents undisturbed, we proceeded on our way.

I gave little attention to our surroundings. My mind was far too busily occupied with theories and speculations. I wondered if all the marsupial mammals of the place laid eggs. I wondered if the young emerged from the eggs, blind and helpless, or if they hatched out quite as able to care for themselves as newly-hatched chickens. And I wondered whether the females incubated the eggs or left that duty to the air and sun. In fact my mind harked further back, and I began to wonder if the black savages we had met might not also deposit eggs. Had I not personally viewed their young being cared for in their subterranean chambers, I might even have speculated on the possibility of these being marsupial humans, for nothing seemed too wildly unreasonable or bizarre in this weird land.

Filled with such thoughts, I failed to note that we had left the wooded area behind and were now in a brush-covered country. Presently, however, I was aware that the sunlight had disappeared and, thinking it must be clouding over, I glanced up. Above the trees to our right hung a dark cloud blotting out the sun, a funnel-shaped lowering cloud with its whirling, twisting stem descending earthward; an ominous-looking cloud presaging a tornado.

And it was coming directly towards us. We were in its path and death was imminent, for a brief instant I hesitated, confused, searching about for the safest direction in which to flee. Ahead the way seemed more open. There was less brush, and even if we failed to out-race the coming, twister, we would be free from the danger wind-hurled trees and branches. The next instant we were running at our utmost speed while behind us we could hear the roaring of the oncoming cloud and the day became as dim as twilight. Panting, exerting every effort, straining every muscle, we dashed through the shrubs and bushes that tore at us and held us back like clutching fingers. At any moment I expected to feel the first blast of the tornado, to see the brush torn up by the irresistible force of the revolving gale, to be hurled aside bruised, helpless, perhaps broken and mortally injured. Then, above the roar of the cloud, came a staccato patter like rain or hail upon the vegetation close to us. Heavy falling objects fell upon the leaves and earth about me and pelted my back. As I caught sight of them I screamed like a maniac, and halting in my mad race, stared with bulging eyes at the black menace in our rear. It was incredible, impossible, too fearful to be real. But it was, there was no doubt of it. All about us great winged insects were dropping to earth, insects a foot or more in length, insects dropping like falling leaves from the vast army, the countless millions of their fellows who formed the roaring black cloud now passing directly above our heads. Thousands were falling about us, striking us with the force of descending wild-ducks killed in mid-flight. Thousands covered the earth, the bushes. As rapidly as they fell, their flimsy dark wings dropped from their bodies, and aimlessly, excitedly, they rushed hither and thither, climbing over us, scratching our exposed flesh with their horny claws, causing us to shake, shiver and tremble with terror and loathing.

At my first sight of them I had realized that they were ants, swarming ants equipped with temporary wings; ravenous, creatures able to overwhelm us, to tear us to bits, to devour us alive. It was horrible beyond words, enough to drive anyone mad, and screaming, fighting, beside ourselves, we staggered backward inch by inch, away from the main cloud of the ants. Still we remained unharmed, untouched, unbitten. Not one of the myriads of hurrying creatures had offered to molest us, and gradually our first mad terror decreased, and a measure of confidence returned to us. We might yet live to escape. The main body of ants had passed on, the thousands that had fallen had scattered and were intent on hurrying away, and now only a few were dropping down from above. But we were almost smothered in their cast-off wings. Wings lay six inches deep over the ground and covered the brush-like icy snow.

Then common sense returned to me and I remembered that swarming ants are almost as harmless as swarming bees; that they are far too much occupied with their own affairs and their new queens to bother with anything else, and that our danger—if ever there had been any—was over.

The swarm had passed on. Only a slender line of laggards streamed across the sky above us, and glancing back, I saw, for the first time, that they rose from the locality of the dome-shaped structures I had seen.

Was it possible these were giant ant-nests; that the swarming insects had issued from them? Avoiding the few hurrying ants that remained under foot, swinging to one side out of the reach of chance stragglers from above, I hurried towards the spot I had seen. Presently we left the brush behind and before us saw the group of bee-hive-like objects. There was no doubt of it. They were ants' nests. Ants were scurrying about them, winged ants were still issuing from the apertures and were taking flight. But they were ants quite distinct from any we had hitherto seen. They were far smaller; they were frailer, weaker things, and their undersized blunt mandibles convinced me that they were no fighters and that we were not in any great danger from them. At our approach, a few turned from their duties and rushed towards us, but the instant they came within scent of our persons, they turned tail and scurried off, evidently as much afraid of us as we had been of their swarming fellows. In color they were a peculiar greenish-gray, a most unusual shade for ants, and I wondered how, with such small dull jaws, they could hold their own, how they erected such huge structures, and what they depended upon for food. By now the last of the winged ants had vanished and the others had retreated to their homes, evidently having been warned of the presence of unknown beings by the ants who had first inspected us. Stepping closer to better examine the great, rough-surfaced mounds, I discovered that instead of being constructed of mud or earth, they appeared to be formed of some woody substance. Possibly, I thought, it was a material akin to paper, such as the paper made by hornets; and taking out my hunting-knife, I chipped off a bit of the surface. I gave vent to an ejaculation of surprise. Under the dull-gray outer surface, my knife had exposed a green sappy interior.

It was exactly as if I had cut away a bit of the outer bark of a living tree.

A MOMENT later I knew that this was the case. Here and there upon the surface of the structures small shoots were sprouting out. About the bases of the nests I found slender roots, and on one were a number of good-sized, fleshy leaves. The things were not artificial; they were living, natural vegetable growths. Like the famous ant-tree of Java, they were distorted, bulbous, pithy roots of some tree or plant within which the ants dwelt.*

GREATLY I longed to examine the interiors, to determine whether they were filled with natural chambers and galleries like the Javanese ant-tree, or whether the ants had tunneled their own passages and rooms. But the apertures were far too small to admit my body— even had I wanted to enter—and I knew it would be a hopeless task to attempt to dissect one of the tough gnarled roots with my knife. As I stood there, examining the huge warty root and trying to place its family botanically, I decided that it was not a root at all, but the short, stocky trunk of some unknown genius, in some ways very much like the yaretta plant of the high Andean deserts, and which is used extensively as fuel. Like the yaretta, it grew in dome-shaped masses; like the yaretta, the leaves and flowers were insignificant and sprouted directly from the bark; and for all I knew or could determine it might, like the yaretta, belong to the celery family. Presently, too, I realized

[* The remarkable ant-plant of Java and the East Indies appears to be designed by nature as a home for ants. The large tuber-like root is filled with natural passages and chambers very similar to those of an ant's nest. Within these, certain species of ants always dwell and probably are beneficial to the plant.]

my right hand felt numb and swollen, as if it had been stung or bitten by some poisonous insect. Glancing at it, I was surprised to see that it was red, inflamed and puffed up. Yet I was certain I had not been bitten by an ant and I was equally certain I had not been stung. Then the truth dawned upon me. It was the juice of the plant.

No wonder the ants were free from molestation. Dwelling within this plant, whose juices were so irritatingly poisonous, they were perfectly safe. No enemy would venture within, and Nature had made them immune to the poison, just as it provided them with natural poison-filled nests wherein to dwell.

It was indeed fortunate for me that I had not attempted to investigate the interior of the ants' natural dwelling place. The minute quantity of sap, juice or oil which had exuded from the tiny incision I had made, had played havoc with my hand already. It was swelling rapidly; pains were shooting up my arm; I felt feverish and ill. I was ignorant of the nature of the poison. I did not know whether it was an alkaloid, an oil or an acid, and even had I known, I possessed no antidotes, no medicines of any sort.

To continue on our way was impossible. To remain here would be worse. I realized I was in for a period of severe illness and helplessness, if not death, and we must reach some shelter, some spot where we would be safe and where food could be obtained. I thought of the cave, but that was far distant; it could only be reached by a stiff climb, which I knew I could not accomplish, and time was pressing. Then I thought of the agricultural ants. Their colonies were near, they were safe, there was food in abundance, and I felt sure we would be permitted to return and remain there. Telling Tom of my plan, we hurriedly left and headed for the nearest ant-farm. Until I started to walk I did not realize how badly off I was, how weak or how feverish. It was only by using my utmost will power, by forcing my muscles to act, that I could set one foot before another. Tom was all anxiety, solicitous of my welfare, and did everything possible to aid me. He almost carried me, and he constantly spoke cheering words, vowing that, once he got me to the ants' village, he would find "bush" with which to cure me. Had it not been for him, I would never have reached our goal; I would have dropped in my tracks, to die miserably and be devoured by the loathsome carrion-beetles. By the time we saw the walls of the agricultural-ants ahead of us, the whole right side of my body was paralyzed; I could scarcely see or hear, and I was hardly more than a moving corpse. With amazing speed, Tom stretched my hammock in the shade just within the wall, and dropping into it, I lost consciousness.

How long I remained utterly dead to my surroundings I shall never know. Tom was far too busily occupied trying to save my life to keep count of days or weeks. But he won. His intimate, almost uncanny, knowledge of tropical medicinal herbs was my salvation. When I opened my eyes and regained my senses, the fever had left me, the swelling of hand and arm had gone down, and Tom assured me that all I needed was rest and good food. Poor, faithful black Tom! How he must have worked, worried and suffered! Knowing his terror of his surroundings, his fright at every unusual thing, his fear even of the friendly agricultural-ants and his worry over me, I could partly appreciate the agonies of mind he must have undergone while alone during my illness. And in all those endless days, I doubt if he ate one square meal or slept; two hours at a stretch. He did not dare to leave me to hunt and secure game. He subsisted on raw wheat and corn, for he was fearful of lighting a fire so near the ants. Only for the purpose of gathering his "bush" did he leave my side for a moment. He did not even possess a utensil in which to brew the herbs and roots, but was forced to pound and bruise them and macerate them in cold water. The poor fellow was thin, drawn, haggard. He was so emaciated, he was like a living skeleton, but he was as cheerful as ever and grinned delightedly from ear to ear, as he saw me open my eyes and knew that he had won the battle for my life.

The first thing I did was to send him on a hunt, declaring I was perfectly safe and that meat was needed as much for his benefit as for mine. He demurred at first but finally went off, to return very soon with two of the hares.

Regardless of the ants, we kindled a fire and soon Tom was gnawing ravenously at the broiled meat and I felt new strength coursing through my veins as I partook of the tenderer tidbits—the livers and hearts of the creatures.

The ants, Tom informed me, when he had at last satisfied his hunger and could talk, had been most friendly. Seeing Tom helping himself to their stores, which he did with trembling limbs and terror-filled mind, for fear they would resent his act, they had regularly brought corn and grain to the spot where we were camped. Evidently to them we were a new kind of inquilines dependent upon their bounty. But they had not brought honey as Tom had hoped they might, and despite my demonstration of the bees' harmlessness, he could not summon enough courage to attempt to rob their hive. His greatest fear had been of the giant bumble-bees and the savage carib-beetles, and he still quakes with unreasoning terror whenever one of these savage-looking but docile creatures comes near.

My convalescence has been rapid, but I have not yet regained sufficient strength to walk about or to sit up for long. But time has not hung heavily on my hands, for I have busied myself writing these notes of our experiences so far, although I do not expect any living man ever to read them.

I have practically abandoned all hopes of escaping from this place, and I am resigned to whatever Fate may have in store for me here. I might be far worse off; and with faithful Tom for company, I feel sure I could endure life and even find a measure of contentment here for years.

I have said that a month had elapsed since last I recorded anything in my note book, but that is merely guess work. It may have been three weeks or six since we entered the valley. It seems years ago to me. I wonder what our next experiences will be, what new and amazing discoveries I shall make, what adventures we will have. There is no more to record at present. Tomorrow I shall make an effort to walk a short distance. I think we will make our home here among the friendly ants.

CHAPTER THIRTEEN

MUCH has happened since last I wrote in my note book. There have been many remarkable occurrences. I have made many marvelous discoveries, and we have had innumerable strange adventures. In fact, nothing that the most fertile imagination could invent, nothing the wildest fiction could relate, would begin to equal the reality.

When last I wrote, I was recovering from the illness brought upon me by the poison of the strange ant-tree. During my convalescence I had thought much upon our situation and our future, and I had decided that it was almost hopeless to expect to leave the place. I determined to make the best of things and yet, not to give up calmly. But I realized that it would undoubtedly be many months— perhaps years—before we could find a means to escape, if ever we did, and that if we were to live in anything approximating comfort and security, we must have a permanent home or a headquarters. The cave I have

THE WORLD OF THE GIANT ANTS

rise my astonishment when, a short time later, they came trudging back, each ant carrying a load of sticky mud with which they immediately began plastering the shack.

mentioned was excellent, in its way, but it had many disadvantages, and having considered various locations, I decided that we could do no better than to remain where we were with the friendly agricultural-ants. Here we were in the centre of things, so to speak. We were safe from enemies, for none dared trespass where the giant bumble-bees were ever on guard. There was abundant game within reach, and the ants' grain, corn and honey were also available. Moreover, I had become rather attached to the good-natured, hardworking, peaceful ants, whose hospitality had stood us in such good stead. Thus have I decided, and Tom agreed with me, for he, too, liked the ants and no longer feared them. We started work on erecting a hut to shelter us, for I felt sure that before long we would have rainy weather with torrential downpours. To erect a fairly comfortable shack is an easy matter in the tropics, and, although my strength had not fully returned, I was quite able to perform much of the lighter work, while Tom could gather the material and do the heavier work. The hut, as we planned it, was to be of the Indian type, an affair of bamboo, canes and small posts with the framework fastened together with bush rope of lianas (vines), and with a "shingled" roof of palm leaves. I had helped to construct scores of such shelters, and Tom was perfectly familiar with their erection, for they are widely used by the West Indians. Very soon he had collected the material required and with my help, the corner-posts and framework were set up without any difficulty.

As we worked, the ants seemed greatly interested, but whether they were merely curious or whether they mildly resented our taking possession of their land and placing a house thereon, I could not feel sure. But on the third day, when the shelter had begun to assume the form of a building, they became quite excited. They examined the hut from every side, climbed over it, and presently hurried off. Imagine my astonishment when, a short time later, they came trudging back, each ant carrying a load of sticky mud with which they immediately began plastering the shack. Nothing I had seen had surprised me so greatly. Not only had they recognized the structure as a house, but they had decided to aid us and to complete our shack in the manner which they considered proper. Of course it may have been nothing more than their instinct, their natural tendencies to construct mud buildings excited by seeing a framework suggestive of such a building. But I prefer to think that it was their almost human intelligence and their kindly, hospitable desire to aid us. At any rate, the work went on apace, and in an incredibly short time we found ourselves in possession of a mud-walled, snug home, far more elaborate and solid than we had planned. At first I feared that our ant neighbors might carry matters still farther and turn their attentions to the interior of the edifice. But either they thought that that was a matter for ourselves or else they reasoned that as we had not elected to use their cell-lined buildings, such things were not adapted to us. But if they very wisely refrained from furnishing our home with tiers of pigeon-hole-like cells, they were not yet through with us. No sooner had they completed plastering the hut to their satisfaction than they began bringing corn and grain and storing it within the shack. In fact, I began to fear that they had mistaken our purpose and had assumed that we were building a storehouse, and that they would fill it to overflowing and force us either to sleep in the open or to erect a second dwelling. Enough was as good as a feast, and not knowing how to induce them to cease provisioning our new home, I decided to try a gentle hint and slung our hammocks within the dwelling. This had the desired effect, and at last the helpful ants withdrew and left us in sole and undisputed possession of our own home and supplies. It was very evident, however, that to their minds we were helpless creatures, true inquilines, who must be humored and cared for. Daily they brought us food, and I was highly amused when one of the creatures appeared lugging in a huge squirming larva and deposited it beside Tom, evidently thinking that all meat was alike to us. Indeed, it was a constant puzzle to the ants as to why we should devour some forms of animal life and not others, and, almost daily, they brought offerings of dead or living insects. One of the big Carib-beetles had taken up his abode with us, and although his overpowering odor was most unpleasant and he was far from welcome on that account, we permitted him to remain. Needless to say, we found a ready means of disposing of the well meant but superfluous offerings, by feeding them to the ever-hungry beetle.

By the time I had fully recovered my strength and felt able to go about and take long walks, we had become thoroughly accustomed to dwelling among these ants. We had even grown to distinguish individuals. At first they all looked precisely alike. Now, however, we realized that there were slight differences. One would have a slightly malformed antenna or foot; another would be a shade lighter or darker on abdomen than thorax or vice-versa; another would possess tiny warts or pimples, and so on indefinitely. To amuse ourselves, we had given many of them nicknames. We had a Tom, a Bill, a Jerry, a Pat, a Daddy Long-Legs, a Fatty, a Skinny and many others, while one unusually dark colored individual, who was particularly assiduous in its attentions, had been dubbed "Black Baby" by Tom. Moreover, the swarming or emergence season was over for the year, and there was no change in the personnel of the colony.

I HAD also learned much about the family and social life of these strange ants. Among other things I had discovered that we were not the only inquilines by any means. Within their multitudinous chambers I had come upon a regular entomological collection of these easy-going, lazy, self-appointed guests. There were moths, caterpillars, beetles, flies, hemiptera, neuroptera, hymenoptera and even snails. I learned that the larvae of the Carib-beetles were inquilines, and that the big bumble-bees had their -homes in the ants' burrows, reminding me of the burrowing owls who dwell with the prairie-dogs, and I came to the conclusion that it was this close association, rather than true domestication, which had led to the savage beetles' and ferocious bees' positions among the ants. But by far the most surprising and interesting of the inquiline were other ants. I had never heard or known of ants maintaining other ants as inquilines, and I considered I had made a truly remarkable entomological discovery. These ant-inquilines were a very distinct species and genus, and in many ways more closely resembled termites than true ants.*

THEY were soft-bodied, colorless creatures, owing no doubt to the fact that they never emerged from the underground chambers, and, as might be expected in the case of such creatures, they were perfectly blind. In size they were slightly larger than the ants whose swarming had so nearly overwhelmed us, being about two feet in length, and they were exceedingly sluggish in their motions. But they possessed a most remarkable habit of burrowing or digging. They were literally born miners, and whenever one of the creatures was placed on soft earth or found itself in a strange spot, it would instantly commence digging like mad until it had completely vanished within its new burrow. At first I was puzzled as to the food eaten by these ghost-like inquilines, for I saw no stores of grain or other food near them. But soon I solved this riddle, and in so doing was more than ever impressed and amazed at the unfathomable ways of Nature. In several of the chambers I had noticed great globular objects hanging from the roofs. At first I took them for the nests of some inquiline, some wasp, or hornet, and I rather avoided going too near them. Then, quite by accident, I bumped my head against one of the objects, and as I drew hastily back, expecting an angry hornet to emerge and resent my actions, I was astonished to see the thing move slowly along the ceiling. In the dim light it had a most remarkable effect, and approaching closely, I discovered that the thing was alive. The globular mass was the enormously distended and swollen abdomen of an ant. So large was the abdomen in proportion to the rest of the

[* These white ants or termites (they are not true ants) are among the most destructive of creatures in the tropics. Unseen and unsuspected they will completely devour the interior of a board, timber or piece of furniture, and the first warning of its condition will be when it collapses in a shower of dust. In a remarkably short time they will riddle a good-sized plank or timber and completely ruin it. Voluntarily they never expose themselves to light but remain in the darkness of their chambers and passages gnawed in wood.]

insect that its head, thorax and feet were almost invisible, and the three-foot body appeared suspended by a stem, like a gigantic apple, rather than supported by legs and feet. The contact with my head had disturbed the weird creature, and from tiny orifices between the widely separated and stretched segments of the abdomen, a thick fluid with a sickly-sweetish odor was exuding.

There was no question as to its identity. It was one of those strange honey-ants; those remarkable insects who, fed and waited upon by its fellows, becomes filled with a peculiar matter resembling honey, until, so distended that it is practically helpless, it becomes a living honey-pot and provides a source of food for its more active companions.*

TO have found a colony of honey-ants, even of such immense size, would not have surprised me greatly. But to find such honey-ants in the home of the agricultural-ants, was most remarkable. That it was not a member of these I felt positive, and I came to the conclusion that it, too, was an inquiline and that in return for its bed and board, it provided the agricultural ants with its syrupy secretion. But I was destined to make an even more surprising discovery. As I was examining the creature and its fellows, several of the blind, white digger-ants came into the chamber, and climbing up the walls, made their way unerringly to the honey-ants and proceeded to help themselves to the contents of the latters' abdomens.

This then was the food of these pale-bodied, sightless creatures. Inquilines themselves, they were provided with food by other inquilines, who in turn were maintained by the rightful denizens of the place. Here, indeed, was a matter for entomologists to puzzle over, for evolutionists to explain. Had the honey-ants been the first inquilines and had the blind diggers taken advantage of their presence?

[* Many species of ants are prized by the natives as delicacies. The queens of the big drougher (leaf-carrying) ants of tropical America are eagerly hunted and eaten by the Indians. The queens' bodies are enormously distended with eggs and have a sweet, rich flavor, much like condensed milk. The true honey-ants are very different. Certain members of the colonies of these ants remain quiescent and are fed and gorged by their fellows. Their abdomens swell to huge size and become filled with a peculiar honey-like material which provides food for the ether members of the colonies. They are, in effect, living honey-pots.]

Had the reverse been the case, and had the agricultural-ants introduced the honey-containers to feed their other inquilines? Or was it all a matter of evolution, of Nature creating or developing one insect to support another? And what did it all mean? Of what benefit were the pale, sickly looking burrowing ants to the agricultural-ants; what purpose did the honey-ants serve as far as the agricultural-ants were concerned? And why should the industrious, busy, intelligent agriculturalists support these lazy, apparently useless inquilines within their homes? Personally I could find no answer, but I felt that somewhere, in some manner, the owners of the burrows must benefit by the presence of these and other inquilines, and that the whole involved affair must be the result of a purposeful scheme of an all-wise Creator.

I have hitherto spoken of the agricultural ants as friendly, peaceful creatures, but by this I do not mean they were inoffensive or cowardly.

On the contrary, I found them most valiant and courageous when necessity arose and, once their temper and fighting spirit were aroused, they became possessed with an almost insane fury. The first occasion on which I discovered this trait was a few days after I was able to be about. I had taken a short walk along the roadway leading from one colony to another, and was perhaps a mile from our shack, when my attention was attracted by thrashing, crackling sounds issuing from a thicket near the path. Cautiously, for I had no desire to walk blindly into danger, I approached the spot. Beyond the thicket was a small open space and within this two creatures were engaged in a terrific duel to the death. So rapid were their movements, that for a moment I could not be sure of their identities, except that they were ants. But as for an instant they drew apart and awaited another opportunity to rush at each other, I saw that one was a member of the agricultural-ants' community, while the other was an enormous red warrior with huge, terrible jaws, overgrown head and powerful legs. He was of a species I had not before seen, but that he was one of the fighting or soldier caste and no ordinary worker was obvious. As he stood there, reared on his hind legs, his big head thrust forward and his terrible jaws opened threateningly, he reminded me of the pictures of old Roman gladiators. And if he represented the helmeted, sword-armed gladiator then, I might say, the other represented the "fisherman" gladiator with net and trident. That the latter stood any sort of a chance against his powerful fighting-machine foe seemed unworthy of consideration, and for a moment I was tempted to come to our friend's aid by firing a pistol bullet into the warrior facing him. But I was rather anxious to witness the outcome of the fray and decided to

THE WORLD OF THE GIANT ANTS

He reminded me of the old Roman gladiators.

withhold my interference until I saw that the agricultural-ant was getting the worst of it. The next second they rushed. The big warrior fairly hurled himself forward, and I held my breath, my nerves atingle with excitement, expecting to see our champion thrown, mortally wounded, to the earth.

But what the farmer lacked in brute strength and power was made up for by his superior intelligence and agility. Lowering his head, he dashed in like a flash, and, like a football player, tackled his enemy low. The very impetuosity of the other's rush was against him. He stumbled over his adversary, his great jaws clashed murderously but harmlessly, and as he sprawled headlong on the earth, I saw that our friend had severed one of the soldier's legs as he had rushed beneath him. But the warrior was not crippled or out of the fight by any means. Before the agricultural-ant could turn, he was on his feet, and mad with rage, was rushing at the other. One nip with those giant jaws and all would be over. But with a quick side leap, our friend escaped the other's vicious side-swiping mandibles and, wheeling like a flash, he flew at his enemy's rear, and snapping right and left, tore great pieces from his foe's abdomen before the latter could turn. However, things were not going entirely in his favor. The other swung about, caught the agricultural-ant before he could escape or dodge, and for a moment the two were a whirling, writhing, confused mass of swinging legs, snapping jaws and armored bodies. The next instant they had broken from the clinch and I saw that our neighbor had lost two legs and an antennae, and had several ugly gashes as a result of the mix-up. But his injuries seemed only to increase his anger and his ferocity. He fairly danced with rage, his body quivered, his eyes glared and his jaws worked convulsively. Never had I seen a creature more completely the embodiment of fury. With a rush, he went at his enemy. Regardless of the other's strength and size, he flung himself at him. Dodging beneath the other's head and jaws, and locking his legs about the soldier-ant's body, his own head and thorax too close to permit the other to use his deadly jaws, the agricultural-ant severed his enemy's neck with a single bite. Even when the immense head of his foe rolled on the earth, its jaws opening and closing spasmodically, the victor still clung to the lifeless body, tearing at it in a paroxysm of rage, and not content until the body was literally torn to bits. Then, his mad fury satiated, he stepped back and calmly and systematically cleansed his body, examined his wounds, nipped off a broken dangling leg, and quite unaware of the presence of spectators, went limping triumphantly on his way.

I WAS very curious to know what had brought on the battle, why the victor had been so far from his fields or paths, why there should be such enmity between the two species and what sort of an ant the beheaded fellow was. More than ever I regretted my inability to communicate intelligibly with the friendly agricultural-ants, for I not only had my natural curiosity to appease but somehow, by some intuition or perhaps merely because of the stranger's appearance, I felt that in him and his kind, lay a most deadly and ever present danger. And had I known but half the truth at the time I would have been far less easy in my mind; and I could have taken steps which might have prevented the terrible catastrophe and the awful experiences that were to follow.

As I have learned by bitter experience, the worst failing of these otherwise admirable ants, and for that matter of all the ants I know, is their entire lack of forethought in some directions; their failure to be in a constant state of preparedness for events which they should know by experience are certain to occur. They prepare for the future as far as storing food is concerned; they provide walls to keep out unwelcome visitors and trespassers, but they seem utterly oblivious of danger and make no attempts to forestall calamities or to protect themselves or their communities. To be sure, they have the bees and beetles, but the former are too few in number and their resources for offense and defense are too limited; and the beetles are scarcely more than scavengers. Yet the agricultural- ants are surrounded by enemies. Countless times in the past they must have suffered grievously from their natural foes. Still they continue to live on with a care-free, false sense of security. If ever there was a living proof of the fallacy of universal peace and international disarmament, it is these ants. But I am getting too far ahead, and must try to set down my records and my experiences in the order of their occurrence, as far as I can co-ordinate them in my memory.

It was a few days after the ant duel that I took my first long tramp with Tom, our object being to explore a spot on the mountain where Tom had discovered a small waterfall or series of waterfalls descending through a narrow gorge or cleft. In such a spot there might be a chance of climbing out as soon as the next dry season came on, and the water vanished. By now, I had forgotten to note, the wet season was evidently near at hand, as I had suspected it would be. Although no heavy rains had fallen, we had had a few showers; the summits of the mountains half way to their bases were hidden in clouds, and from the increased flow of the streams and the innumerable trickling rills on the mountain sides, I knew that heavy rains must be falling on the mountain tops, and probably on the country beyond the ridges.

The ants, too, were preparing for the rainy season. They had harvested all their crops, had worked over the soil and had planted their seeds and young plants. Constantly, too, they were adding to the plastering of walls and buildings, and a small army of the creatures was busily engaged in digging trenches about their fields, evidently designed to carry off the surplus water when the torrential rains arrived.

Our route that day was new, and as we walked along, traversing a pleasant rolling district covered with dense forest and cut by many streams, I noticed that the insect life had altered greatly with the advance of the seasons. Butterflies and moths were very scarce; there were no caterpillars seen, but we noticed innumerable cocoons and chrysalids attached to trees, limbs and bushes. Some of the former were composed of such delicate, thin, tough silk that we determined to secure them on our return, for they would serve excellently for blankets and for garments. We would very soon be in dire need of clothing, and I had already given considerable thought to the problem of making new wearing apparel to replace our worn and tattered rags. I had thought of many things, but here, ready-made for us, was tough, strong cloth which only needed to be cut and sewed into form to provide excellent clothing.

Bees and hornets were also scarce; the few beetles we saw were arboreal species; but flies, gnats and neuroptera swarmed, while by far the most abundant insects belonged to the orthoptera, a family which on our previous trips had not appeared numerous. Crickets and grasshoppers were everywhere. Katydid-like insects filled the forest with their strident notes from the tree-tops, and woodland cockroaches scuttled over the earth and dodged into hiding places on the bark of the trees. In one spot Tom came to a sudden halt and his eyes grew wide with wonder. I could scarcely blame him. In a small opening ahead of us a shaft of sunlight cast a subdued golden-green light, and dancing about in this were a number of beings, who might well have been fairies. So fairylike were their pale, semi-transparent, graceful bodies, their gauzy iridescent wings and their flowing draperies, that even the most prosaic and non-imaginative person might have been converted to a firm belief in the existence of woodland sprites. Silently as wraiths, they circled and floated in the golden haze, their movements orderly and rhythmic, their motions graceful and following a well defined system, and as ephemeral and unreal as a fragment of gossamer rainbow. For a long time we watched them, fascinated and charmed by their supernatural beauty and phantasmal dance, and Tom found it difficult to believe me when I assured him they were no fairies, but merely a species of May-fly enjoying their nuptial festivities during the few short hours, which nature had allotted them as their span of life. Poor, happy, care-free, beautiful things! An hour before they had been ugly, crawling aquatic larvae. Before the day was done they would be lying lifeless and forgotten upon the forest floor. And yet, to them, their lives probably seemed as long and as filled with adventure, love, sorrow, joy and experiences as our lives seem to us.

It was after we had left the dancing fairy-like creatures, and my mind was occupied with thoughts on the mysteries of life and nature, that in approaching a partly fallen tree trunk an apparent mass of dead and dried leaves suddenly sprang into life and fluttered off on dull-orange and purple wings. Tom promptly collapsed and sat staring incredulously. "Lordy!" he ejaculated. "Ah boun' say, Chief, there been plenty obeah roun' 'bout here. The fairies a—dancin' back there; they been dead leafs a— turnin' to but'flies, an' Ah aint goin' be surprise' no more if one o' tha trees turns into a el'phant or a man. No, sir, Ah—"

AS if to test his statement and to bear out his expectations, a limb of the tree suddenly came to life, and raising itself on legs, and rearing up a long-neck topped with goggle eyes, it peered searchingly into Tom's face. The sudden transformation of apparent dead leaves into butterflies had been surprising enough to Tom, although I had recognized them as a species closely related to the tropical Kalimas, those most remarkably camouflaged of all protectively-colored butterflies or lepidoptera.*

BUT to be taken at his word and to see a rough, bark-covered limb of the tree come to life before his eyes, was too much for Tom. He was too astonished to move, too amazed even to be frightened. He sat there, eyes staring and rolling, wide lips parted, jaw sagging. And, had such a thing been possible, I verily believe his kinky wool would have stood on end. It was an astounding thing to see leaves become butterflies, but once they had become animated, they were obviously and unmistakably butterflies. But the limb, although indisputably alive, was still, to all intents and appearances, a tree branch.

It was the same color, it was covered with the same mottled, lichen-dotted bark, slender twigs took the place of legs, a small warty knob formed the head, and the grave serious-looking eyes seemed nothing more than imperfections on the end of a twig. Having apparently satisfied itself that Tom was harmless, or perhaps assured that the negro's boast was not to be taken seriously, the animated limb

[* Many common butterflies simulate leaves when at rest. The most remarkable case of protective coloration, as it is called, among butterflies is the Kalima. The under surfaces of the wings ate colored and veined like a dead leaf and are of the same shape when folded. When at rest the Kalima assumes the exact position and location of a leaf upon a twig and is almost indistinguishable from the true leaves about it.]

moved slowly, deliberately along the trunk for a few yards, halted, raised itself at an angle, and instantly became transformed into a limb indistinguishable from those about it. I was convulsed with laughter at Tom's expression. It seemed an incredible, an impossible thing to him; something supernatural and savoring of witchcraft was taking place. But after my first momentary surprise at the great size of the apparition, it seemed perfectly natural to my eyes. It was, as I knew, merely one of those strange, almost weird orthoptera, commonly known as "walking-sticks" or "stick-insects," which have been formed and fashioned by nature to exactly imitate a twig or branch for their self-protection. They are among our commonest woodland insects in the north, especially in late summer and autumn, and they are fairly abundant in the tropics. Our own species reach a length of six inches or more; I had seen and collected specimens over a foot in length in the tropics, but here was a giant at least twelve feet long. I tried to explain the matter to Tom, but until I approached the harmless creature and prodded it with a stick, forcing it to come to life again, he refused to believe it was merely a curiosity of the insect-world. I wondered, as at last we left the giant walking-stick to itself, if these big fellows went through the same seasonal transitions as their small northern cousins. I wondered if they were green and soft in the spring; if they simulated the luxuriantly growing and budding branches during the summer, and if they turned russet and yellow and ended their lives by dropping earthward with the falling leaves in the autumn, as the northern species do.

Also, I was somewhat surprised that we had not come upon any representatives of those even more remarkable and astonishingly-protected creatures, the "walking-leaves" or "leaf-insects." They are mainly tropical and are noted for the exactitude with which the veins of their wings, the foliate legs, and the markings upon them, match the leaves among which they rest. No doubt, we had passed near many of them without discovering their presence; but thought of them did not make me any easier in my mind. They are carnivorous creatures, very savage and bloodthirsty, and if they grew to the gigantic proportions one might reasonably expect in this place, they might prove far from harmless.*

[* In Borneo a species of Mantis is colored and formed to exactly imitate the flower of a handsome orchid. Lying motionless among the leaves, the creature pounces upon butterflies and other insects which mistake him for an orchid flower.]

I DID not at all relish the idea of being suddenly pounced upon by a hungry leaf-insect or mantis several yards in length, and I kept a sharp watch for suspicious-looking clusters of leaves as we proceeded on our way.

So intent was I on avoiding possible attacks from such sources that we very nearly came to grief. We were passing under some unusually large trees draped with tangled lianas and gigantic air-plants, when Tom sniffed audibly. "Mus' be a mighty sweet flower 'roun' 'bout," he remarked.

I also noticed the almost sickish sweetness in the air now that he mentioned it. But overpoweringly sweet odors from blossoms are so common in the tropical forests that I gave little heed to it. The next moment Tom gave a yell like a Comanche and almost bowled me over as he dashed from behind the tree.

"Wa la!" he exclaimed, "Tha' mos' surely been obeah 'bout here. Ah been went for pick tha' flower an' he turn to snake an' try for nip me."

Laughing at Tom's fears, and supposing that he had come upon some other protectively-colored insect, I stepped around the tree. Covering a fleshy-leaved vine depending from the tree-top, were clusters of strange blossoms.

In color they were dull purple and russet with golden-yellow striping, and the sweet odor emanating from them was cloying in its heavy, sickish perfume. In form the flowers suggested orchids; and the stems and leaves of the vine were very similar to those of a gigantic vanilla vine. Tom, maintaining a safe distance in my rear and ready to turn and run at an instant's notice, repeated his assertion, that, when he had attempted to secure one of the flowers, it had turned into a serpent and had struck viciously at him. Such a thing I knew was impossible, even in this land of many surprises, but I felt that there must be some basis for his terror and that, in all probability, some insect was concealed among the blossoms or foliage.

Possibly, I thought, there might be a real snake there, and I had no intention of taking any chances of being bitten. But despite my most painstaking scrutiny of the vine and its odorous flowers, I could detect no signs of animal life. Telling Tom to indicate which flower he had approached, I extended my bill-hook spear until the point touched the blossom. Instantly, from behind the petals, five long, green tentacles shot out and entwined themselves about the spear. Thunderstruck at this phenomenon, I attempted to withdraw my weapon only to find it

Instantly, from behind the petals, five long green tentacles shot out and entwined themselves about the spear.

held irresistibly by those clinging tentacles. With all my strength I tugged and wrenched, but my efforts were futile. Slowly the tentacles contracted and the spear was drawn towards the centre of the flower, while the petals folded inwards, closing like the segments of an orange-peel dredge-bucket. Then, as the tip of the weapon touched the surface of the blossom, the petals flew back, the green tentacles released their grasp, and I sprawled backward, overbalanced by the sudden freeing of the spear.

IT was Tom's turn to laugh, and he took full advantage of the opportunity. I certainly could not blame him for having been frightened and for having mistaken the tentacles for snakes. And while I knew that the tentacles were vegetable and not animal, I was fully aware of the narrow escape Tom had had. If those powerful tendrils had seized him, there would have been no escape, for there was no doubt that the plant was carnivorous, that it was as relentlessly bloodthirsty and savage as any wild beast, and that the sweet, beautiful blooms were designed to lead unsuspecting creatures to their destruction.*

THE whole thing was a marvelously designed and perfected trap. Any object touching or approaching the flowers was instantly seized by the concealed tendrils coiled behind the handsome petals, and was drawn to the flower's centre and enfolded by the petals, where, if the capture was a living creature, it was digested and devoured by the plant, or if inedible, as in the case of my spear, it was cast aside. Even as we watched, a huge green-bodied fly flew towards the clustering flowers and alighted on the velvety-looking petals. The next instant he was buzzing and struggling helplessly in the grasp of the tendrils and was being drawn towards the centre of the blossom that had attracted him. A moment more and the flower had closed and the unfortunate

[* Many plants are carnivorous. Our common northern Pitcher-Plant has leaves which contain water and which are lined with hairs so arranged that insects may crawl in but cannot emerge. Attracted by a sweetish secretion of the leaves, flies and other insects enter to find themselves prisoners and eventually die and drop into the water where they decay and are absorbed by the plant. The Venus Fry Trap plant also devours insects, closing its trap- like leaves upon them. In the; tropics carnivorous plants and flowers are even more common and many carnivorous orchids are known.]

insect had been added to the list of the plant's victims.

But a fly, even a giant two feet in length, was scarcely more than a morsel for the plant, although as greedily seized and eaten as a peanut by an elephant.

Unquestionably the normal food of the strange vine was insects, for there were no other forms of animal life, except the gigantic lizards and an occasional tree-frog, which could fall into its trap. But its tendrils were strong and powerful enough to capture and hold a man, and as I looked more closely at the flowers, I saw that the inner surfaces of the petals were covered with sharp, barbed thorns which would anchor a body immovably, once the petals had closed over it. I had, during my travels, seen many strange carnivorous plants but, even aside from its enormous size, I saw nothing to compare with this flower for devilish deception and deadliness.

Very fortunately for us, the thing's activities were confined to its immediate vicinity. Beyond reach of its tentacles there was no danger; however, I had a peculiar horror of the plant and an irresistible feeling that it might dash at us as we passed, and we gave it a wide berth as we at last continued on our way.

Very little transpired during the balance of that day. We met nothing more that was especially noteworthy or remarkable, and we had no further adventures. Once, to be sure, we had a distant glimpse of one of the giant iguanas, but he was too intent on chasing a hare to see or scent us and vanished from sight in the jungle. Evidently these creatures were far from abundant, for which I was duly thankful, for we had seen only two—or perhaps we saw the same individual twice.

When, soon after mid-day, we reached the cataract, we found far too much water flowing down the gorge to make a thorough examination of its possibilities as a means of egress from the valley. From a distance it had appeared a mere cascade, but when we got close, we found it a truly impressive waterfall thundering down for hundreds of feet. But from the formation of the rock and what I could judge by a careful scrutiny of the gorge, it held a promise, once the dry season returned. It was certainly the best and most encouraging prospect we had yet found.

Our return to the ant colony was also without incident, except for one discovery which at the time seemed of little importance. In one spot we came upon a great pile of rotting leaves and vegetation, evidently of artificial construction. Upon investigation, this proved to be a nest or breeding place of those strange bombardier-beetles, one of which we had seen destroy the giant solitary-ant which had attacked us. No adults were present, for which I was grateful, but the compost pile was alive with the immature larvae.

One other discovery I made, which was most important to me but has little if any scientific interest. My tobacco had been exhausted for some time and on this trip I found an excellent substitute. This was the inner bark of a tree, which I take to be closely related to or identical with the Kipa tree, whose bark is so widely used in place of tobacco by many tribes of South American Indians. It was the similarity of the tree to the Kipa that first attracted my attention, and a trial pipe-full of the shredded, papery bark proved that it was fully the equal of the Kipa.

Hence, although our journey was without definite result, from the point of view of escaping, still it was not fruitless, and I felt well repaid for the day's work.

CHAPTER FOURTEEN

IT was several days after our expedition to the cataract that we had a most terrifying adventure and a most narrow escape from an awful fate. We had turned southward and were following the course of a good-sized stream, when, stopping to rest for a few moments in a rather dense patch of forest, I noticed an unusual number of insects. Even during the height of the dry season I never saw so many insects at one time during the day. But now myriads of flying, crawling, hopping, running and creeping things were all about us. A few late butterflies flitted erratically past on frayed wings. Great green tree-crickets whirred through the air, alighting momentarily to again spread their stiff wings and continue on.

Huge brown cockroaches blundered about. Bees and flies buzzed and hummed. Beetles scurried over the ground. Crickets and grasshoppers traveled by huge leaps. An ugly looking praying-mantis, with his lobsterlike claws raised and clasped as if in supplication, scurried by and paid no heed to the abundant insects about him. And, as if in chase of the myriad insects, and yet paying no attention to their proximity, several big warty toads and a couple of tree-frogs hopped ponderously past us. Once or twice, also, we caught glimpses of fleeing hares and marmots, and then, with the rush and roar of a charging rhinoceros, a gigantic dinosaur-like iguana tore through the forest.

THE WORLD OF THE GIANT ANTS

It was as if the entire population of the place was on the move; as if every form of life was migrating in unison; and, unable to account for the exodus, I noticed that all were headed in the same direction. Somehow it reminded me of a picture in the geography of my schooldays, a picture supposed to represent a prairie fire with the herds of wild horses, antelopes and other creatures fleeing from the onrushing flames. But there was no fire in the forest near us, no conflagration of any sort to drive the denizens of the forest en masse before it. Fire, I felt sure, had never existed until our arrival, and even had it been possible that by accident we had set fire to the forest, there was no smell of smoke, nothing to indicate a conflagration.

Yet here were countless creatures all hurrying from something and obviously terrified and seeking only their own safety, for the most ferociously carnivorous and predatory species moved side by side with their natural prey, and made no effort to molest them. Even ants were numbered in the throng, and to my amazement I saw one of the giant solitary fellows hurrying past, all his savagery gone in his fear of some unknown danger! So numerous were the creatures, that to attempt to move on our way was impossible, and only by flattening ourselves against a tree-trunk could we escape being overrun by the onrushing hordes. For perhaps ten minutes this continued. Then the numbers of the creatures sensibly diminished; only the slower moving species continued to pass us, and as the last stragglers and cripples struggled along, I was conscious of a strange, rapidly increasing sound from the direction whence the hordes of creatures had come. It was a roaring, swishing noise, more like the sound of descending rain upon a roof than anything else, and for a moment I thought it was caused by a torrential downpour upon the forest and that the deluge was the cause of the creatures' flight. But the sky was still bright; there was no feel of rain in the air. For perhaps ten seconds I stood irresolute, undecided whether to advance or to follow the example of the affrighted creatures and retreat. Then suddenly a terrible premonition, an awful fear swept over me. Shouting to Tom to follow, I sprang forward and rushed headlong after the fleeing insects. But too late, hardly had we covered fifty yards when I leaped back with a warning yell. Before me, like a flowing, living stream, was a vast column of gigantic ants. My worst fears were realized. Army-ants were on the march. No wonder the wild denizens of the forest had fled in mad terror. Too late I had realized what that roaring sound presaged. Thousands, millions of the voracious ants were marching through the forest, devouring every living thing in their way, leaving the country over which they had passed absolutely devoid of life. If ever we were caught by them, we would be beyond all hope and only our clean-picked bones would remain when the army had passed on. Turning, hoping yet to outdistance the advancing hordes of terrible creatures, I turned and raced in the opposite direction, with Tom at my side. Ten, twenty, fifty yards we covered and then, converging upon us, came the other far-flung wing of the ant army. We were surrounded, hemmed in. To try to break through that cordon of five-foot creatures, creatures as large as wolves, a hundred times more ravenous, a thousand times more fearless, more powerful and more immune to injuries or attack, was suicidal. And now, appallingly close at hand, we could hear the sounds of countless millions of advancing bodies, the ceaseless clashing of countless millions of terrible jaws blending into a uniform swishing roar. Yelling orders at the top of my lungs, resorting to our last hope, I frantically gathered leaves and twigs, while Tom, terrified beyond speech, but mechanically obeying, did the same. Piling them in a heap, I touched match to them with shaking hand, and praying as I had never before prayed that the leaves might ignite, that fire and smoke might yet save our lives. Never had leaves seemed so loth to take fire. Shaking until my teeth chattered, I held the flickering match, while close upon me I heard the first of the advancing ants. By the time the leaves ignited and the flames darted up, the foremost ants were within a dozen paces. Blind as they were, depending wholly upon the senses of smell and hearing, the fearful creatures turned towards us unerringly. But as the pungent, reeking smoke reached them, they halted. And as though at a spoken word of command, the whole vast army in their rear came instantly to rest. It was a brief respite, and madly we availed ourselves of the few short seconds. Regardless of burns, scarcely sensible of the heat and pain, we grasped handfuls of the blazing leaves and twigs and hurled them towards the ants. Some of the creatures, scorched and half-suffocated, squirmed and twisted in agony; others hurried in a frenzy to one side, while the bulk moved deliberately, as with one accord, a few paces backward. By now the fire had spread, and all about us the forest floor was smouldering, burning, sending up a dense choking smoke and breaking into little spurts of flame where the leaves were thicker or drier than elsewhere.

THE WORLD OF THE GIANT ANTS

THE army was checked; even the fearless, irresistible ants dared not cross that hot smoking area. But we had no time to lose. In a few moments the thin layer of leaves, the few dry twigs would be consumed, and once again the ants would be upon us. Turning, we dashed forward. If we had delayed five seconds we would have been irretrievably lost. Though the main army had been checked, though our fire had thrown back the curving, crescent-like vanguard or skirmishers, the leaders of that marvelously organized army had not been out-generaled by our defense. From either side of the main body flanking parties had rapidly advanced, and now, as we rushed onward, they were hurrying at incredible speed to cut off our retreat. Less than twenty feet separated the two converging columns, and as we dashed for this narrow opening, panting, almost insane with terror, three of the great warriors scurried forward to intercept us. At point-blank range I fired two bullets through the head of one. With all my strength, I swung my tarantula jaw bill-hook at the second, and I saw Tom lop the head from the third with his weapon. Before us the way was clear. Behind us came the ants in full cry. Though far slower in movement than the other ants we had met, yet they were steadily gaining on us. Our mad pace could not last for long. We seemed doomed to destruction when, ahead, we saw the gleam of water. Without hesitation, forgetting the perils of possible aquatic beasts as dangerous as the ants, we plunged into the stream and with our last remaining strength, struck out for the further shore. Drawing ourselves upon the bank, we lay helpless, gasping for breath, while the baffled ants, reaching the brink of the stream, moved rapidly up and down, searching vainly for a spot to cross. I felt certain we were safe, at least for a time. The river was far too wide for even the army ants to bridge. But for all I knew, there might be a narrow or a shallow spot further up or down the stream, or a fallen tree might partially bridge it. It would be more than reckless to remain long where we were. But we could not proceed until we had recovered somewhat from our strenuous exertions, and as we strove to calm our palpitating hearts and to regain control of our lungs, we watched, fascinated, our enemy ants, separated by a scant one hundred feet from where we sat. Their perseverance, their organization, their ingenuity were almost uncanny.*

AGAIN and again they attempted to cross the stream by means of living bridges. Several of the ants would select a firm spot on the bank, and holding to roots and bushes with their tremendous jaws, would allow their bodies to swing suspended in the air. Others would rapidly clamber down these, and grasping their fellows by their jaws, would extend the living chain by their own length. Over these would hurry others, until link by link, the bodies of the ants extended the chain sufficiently to reach from shore to shore.

Then, the last ants releasing their hold of the bank, the living bridge would swing free and would be swung outward and towards our side by the current.

Several times we fairly trembled and were ready to rise and dash off as the ultimate links of the ant-chain seemed about to lodge against the bank where we sat. But each time the current proved too swift, the living bridge failed to make connections, and the ingenious ants were carried past us and were forced to scramble back to safety on their own side of the river. But I felt that ultimately they would succeed, and that sooner or later a bridge would be formed, and that over the suspended bodies of their fellows the whole vast army would come swarming to our side. I had exhausted my final cartridge; both Tom and myself lost our priceless weapons when we threw them aside to swim the stream. But even unarmed and defenceless, it was better to face the dangers of the forests and jungles than to remain so dangerously close to the ant army. At last, our breaths and strength partly restored, we rose and hurried with all possible speed upstream and towards a distant spot where we could cross the river just above a branch which would effectively prevent the army ants from reaching us. Fortunately for us, we met no dangerous creatures on our way. The entire district appeared to be devoid of life and I decided that every living creature had sensed the oncoming army and had hurried away for safety.

[* The organization and discipline of the common army ants, such as we encountered, are almost incredible. Although blind, these ants move in regular columns, send out scouts, maintain a commissary and hospital corps, build bridges and manoeuver with military precision and order. Members of the army that are injured are placed at one side and are examined by the ants detailed for the purpose. If too badly injured to recover, they are destroyed whereas, if only slightly wounded, they are carried to the rear and cared for until able to resume their places. Broken or injured legs are often amputated. When reaching streams or fissures, the engineering corps hurry forward and form living bridges over which the army passes.]

THE WORLD OF THE GIANT ANTS

Spent and weary, we reached the walled-in lands of the agricultural-ants at last, and never have I seen a more welcome sight than the little group of mud buildings, our humble shack, and the good-natured, peaceful ants among whom we had found refuge.

IT rained quite heavily a day or two later, and each day the rains became heavier and of longer duration, but at no time during the wet season was there so much precipitation or such prolonged rains as in other portions of the tropics with which I was familiar. Nevertheless, time hung rather heavily on our hands, for we were more or less confined to our shack and it was hopeless to try to do any serious exploration work in search of an exit through the mountains.

To while away our time, we busied ourselves with many matters. We made a number of new and better arrows than those we possessed, and we made several spears. We also gathered a quantity of the silkiest, toughest cocoons and managed to make ourselves some fairly serviceable garments. They were, of course, most ludicrous and crude, for our only cutting instrument was my knife, and we had neither thread nor needles. But by means of bone awls and the fibres of the cocoons, ravelled out and twisted together for thread, we succeeded fairly well. The clothing consisted of baggy gaucho-like trousers which were little more than bifurcated bags, and short ponchos in place of shirts. Ponchos, of course, were the simplest things to make, for they were nothing more than squares of material with a slit in the centre. They were very serviceable, however, and as we discovered that the outer covering of the cocoons was impervious to water, they served us excellently as raincoats too. We had become so friendly with the ants and so accustomed to them, that I jokingly slipped a poncho over one of the creatures. It was a most amusing sight to see the big ant wearing this typically Indian garment, and for a few moments he seemed rather proud of it. But it evidently was more of an impediment than an advantage, and he soon stripped it off. The ants were, however, vastly interested in everything we did, and we constantly had an attentive audience watching our operation and task. Personally, I devoted an immense amount of time trying to establish some means of communication with our hosts. But I am convinced that they either communicate among themselves by means of vibratory waves emanating from and received by their antennae, or else by a means akin to mental telepathy. I did, however, make some progress. By repeatedly making use of precisely the same gestures or signs when I did anything, required anything or wished to communicate any thought, I established a sort of sign language. It was truly remarkable to find how quickly the ants grasped the idea. In a very short time they had learned to recognize my sign for food, and as soon as I made it, they would rush off and return with corn or grain. From this it was but a step to teach them one sign for corn and the other for the threshed grain, and in a month I had accomplished wonders in the way of this primitive means of communication.

It is during this time, also, that Tom first started keeping pets. He has captured a young specimen of the hare-like marsupial and it soon became very tame and amused us both with its antics and its frolicksome ways. One of the porcupine-like creatures followed. Soon afterwards two marmots were added to the collection, and one day Tom returned from his traps with a moat remarkable creature, which, as nearly as I could identify it, was closely related to the Solendons.*

HAVING exhausted the mammalian inhabitants of the region I suggested to Tom that we try our hands at domesticating insects. At first Tom could not see anything at all attractive or interesting in the idea of making pets of the giant "bugs," as he still called them. But I pointed out the success of the ants in domesticating beetles and bees, and, half humorously, suggested that with a body-guard of tame hornets or other dangerous insects, we would have no fear of enemies. Tom took this quite seriously and he spent a long time considering whether he would start with a young hornet or an immature solitary ant. He plied me with innumerable questions regarding their habits, their food and where he would be likely to find a nest which he could

[* The Solendon is a most interesting and remarkable mammal, which combines characteristics of the rodents and the insectivorae. As far as known, they are represented by only two species, one inhabiting Cuba, the other Santo Domingo. In many ways they more closely resemble certain fossil creatures of the Pleistocene period than any living creatures. It is about fifteen inches in length with short neck, long trunk-like nose, rat-like tail, front feet like a mole, extremely weak eyes and keen ears, and covered with a combination of hair, wool and scales showing the complete evolution from skin to true hair.]

safely rob of the young. In fact, he appeared quite disappointed when I told him that it would be a rather dangerous matter to attempt to raid a solitary ant's nest, and that a young hornet was a most uninteresting and helpless grub. But the discussion had given me an idea, and I recalled the Bombardier-beetles' nest we had found and suggested that we visit it, and, if it contained young, secure some of them and try to domesticate them.

NOT only was I curious to learn more of the creatures, but, if it were possible to domesticate them, they would prove far better guardians than the most ferocious of dogs. By good fortune, we found the heap of fermenting material contained a number of the beetles in the pupal stage; quite capable of movement and feeding, and yet soft-bodied, harmless things and with their gas-glands and explosive apparatus still undeveloped. Four of these we carried back to our home and installed in a compartment by themselves. They grew very rapidly, and, to my surprise, I discovered that they were vegetable eaters in their immature stage, although carnivorous when fully grown. They also appeared amenable to domestication, and I began to have high hopes that we would find them very similar in their characters to our common skunks in the States. These odorous beasts are easily tamed and never make use of their natural means of defense when with their masters or friends, but are quick to recognize enemies or strangers and to make themselves both felt and smelt. Needless to say our miniature menagerie was a vast source of curiosity and interest to the ants. Undoubtedly, they regarded our pets as our natural inquilines, and I was greatly amused when one of them brought us several specimens of the honey-ants with one of the big-bellied females, evidently thinking they were an essential portion of any real inquiline colony. But when we established our nursery of bombardier-beetles, the ants grew wildly excited. In them, of course, they recognized traditional enemies, and I could well imagine their feelings in the matter.

To them it must have been much the same as it would be for a guest in a hotel to start rearing rattlesnakes or cobras in his suite. No doubt, had they been able to communicate with us, they would have ordered us either to rid ourselves of these newest pets or else betake ourselves elsewhere. But as it was, they merely showed their displeasure by giving us the cold shoulder for several weeks. Gradually, however, their curiosity overcame their fears or their dislike and, finding that the creatures appeared to be harmless, they soon became as friendly as ever, perhaps reasoning that bombardier-beetles in captivity were no more like their natural wild fellows than were the Carib-beetles or giant bees. At first, also, we had been much afraid that these guardians of the colony, and especially the Carib-beetles, would fall upon our pets and destroy and devour them. But we soon found we had nothing to fear on that score. The big ferocious beetles were as well trained to differentiate between friend and foe as any watchdog at home. And like our dogs, they appeared to distinguish instinctively between living creatures to be attacked and those to be left unmolested. Many a dog will live in perfect amity with cats belonging to his master or mistress, and yet will fly at any strange feline, and our friendly Carib-beetle, and the others, made no attempt to molest any of our live stock, although they would instantly attack others of the same species in their natural state.

They appeared to take naturally to the rapidly-growing bombardiers, and would frolic and play with them exactly as an overgrown mastiff will frolic with a playful puppy. And never did the young bombardiers show any tendency to use their deadly gas. Brought up with us and with the ants, they had no hatred or fear, and though they would rear and raise their tails in a most threatening manner when teased or irritated, they always bluffed. In fact, they were so good-tempered and apparently so thoroughly weaned from their natural habits, that I very much doubted if they would prove of any value as guardians in case of an attack, and I was rather anxious to test them.

By the time they were fully grown, the rains were over and we were again able to make extensive trips through the land. Several times one or more of our pets accompanied us, and as we walked along and the bombardiers scurried about, examining every nook and cranny, now and then locating and devouring some grub or larva, I rather wished that we might run across a solitary ant, just to see what our companions would do. But I had no need to come upon one of these terrible creatures to satisfy myself. As we were passing through a patch of jungle, three huge red ants suddenly rushed at us. Instantly I recognized them as of the same species I had seen duelling with the agricultural ant. Remembering the savagery and ferocity shown by the red ant on that occasion, I realized we were in the most imminent peril.

Quickly fitting an arrow to my bow, I discharged the missile at short range and saw it strike fairly between the thoracic segments of the leader of the trio. Tom also transfixed one of the creatures; but the arrows seemed to have little effect other than to halt the creatures temporarily until they could bite off the arrow shafts. The next second there was a rush and our attendant bombardiers hurled themselves at the enemy. As instinctively, as intelligently and as efficiently as though they had never known confinement, the four beetles followed their natural and instinctive tactics and the episode of the solitary ant was reenacted before us. I verily believe that a single bombardier could have worsted the three red giants. But with the four of them, the battle was so short, sharp and decisive that it was literally a massacre. Within ten or fifteen seconds, the three red ants were stupefied, dying from the bombardiers' gas, and the triumphant four were gorging themselves on the flesh of their victims. I was more than satisfied. With our bombardiers accompanying us, we need have no fear of savage ants, and I was also pleased to discover that the beetles did not draw the line at any one species of ant, but attacked the red fellows as quickly as the black solitary ants. Tom was tremendously elated and enthusiastic, and he declared emphatically that he believed our pets could vanquish an entire army of the army-ants. But when it came to setting the bombardiers in hand once more, we had no little trouble. Indeed, for a time, it looked as if we might have to leave them to revert to their natural lives. Their savage fighting instincts had been aroused; temporarily they had forgotten they were supposedly domestic animals, and they turned on us savagely, rearing up, opening their jaws and lifting their tails as if about to attack us with a discharge of their deadly gas. But Tom, oddly enough, considering his fear of wild animals, appeared to be absolutely unconscious of danger in the case of his pets. Talking to them as he might to a rebellious dog or a fractious horse, he advanced boldly, slapped the creatures with his big black paws, grabbed them by the necks and half-urged, half-dragged them away from their unfinished feast. I fairly gasped, expecting the beetles to turn on him; but evidently they recognized their master and, finding they could not frighten him, they submitted and trotted along beside us as docile as ever.

IT was upon the return from this trip that we met with the most exciting event that had as yet transpired. On our way back towards the ant colony, we came upon a column of the leaf- carrying or drougher-ants. They made no effort or attempt to attack us, but our bombardier-beetle companions went at the moving column with a concerted rush. I had expected to see them overwhelmed or destroyed, for hundreds of the droughers were hurrying along their pathway. Unquestionably, I thought, they would destroy a few of the ants; but even their agility, their ferocity and their deadly gas could not combat hundreds of the ants. But I had yet to know the fear the bombardiers inspired in the minds of their natural prey. No sooner had our pets leaped to the attack, than the hurrying ants abandoned their burdens, and scattering in every direction, made good their escape, leaving their fellows to their fates.

In one respect, however, the leaf-carriers had an advantage over the bombardiers. They were far more agile and quicker in their motions than the solitary ants or the big red fellows, and they were of a race that deemed discretion the better part of valor. Instead of stopping to give battle, they turned and ran, and only one unfortunate, overpowered by the bombardiers' gas, fell a victim to the beetles' ferocity. As we waited for our allies to satisfy their insatiable appetites for ant flesh, my attention was attracted to the objects the fleeing ants had dropped. To my amazement, I discovered they were ears of corn. Where had the ants secured these, what were they doing with them? The answer to my mental query flashed across my brain instantly. The droughers were inveterate thieves in other countries, as I knew. In a single night they will carry off a bag of rice or a sack of corn, kernel by kernel. There was no wild corn here. There could be but one explanation. They had been robbing our friends, the agricultural-ants. There had been a raid and probably a battle. Had our friends been defeated? Had they been destroyed? I feared the worst, and calling to Tom, and, regardless of their resentment, beating and luring our bombardiers into obedience, I hurried in the direction of our hut.

CHAPTER FIFTEEN

IT was even worse than I thought. During our absence the droughers had swept down upon the peaceful agriculturalists and had left death and destruction in their wake. That the owners of the property had put up a stiff fight was evident. Everywhere dead and dying ants were lying about, and there were far more bodies of the raiders than of the agriculturalists.

No doubt their insect allies had aided them in their defense, but against the hordes of leaf-carriers, resistance had been futile. As I glanced about at the victims of the battle, I noticed several of the big red warriors I have mentioned. For a moment I was puzzled as to their presence among the raiders. Then, as I examined them more carefully and discovered that they were of the same species as the droughers, I realized the truth. They were the soldier-caste of the robbers, professional fighters. No wonder the agriculturalist had flown at the red warrior he had met in the forest. He had recognized him as an arch enemy and had known that he was a scout spying upon the agricultural ants' homes and that had he not been destroyed, he would have carried word to his fellows.

Unquestionably, also, the three, whom we and our bombardiers had destroyed, had also been scouts. No doubt scores of other scouts had been lurking about for days, and the attack had been most carefully planned. Very probably, I thought, our presence had troubled the raiders and they had deferred their attack until we had absented ourselves. I was rather puzzled to account for the fact that I had never seen any of the big warriors accompanying the leaf-carriers on their legitimate business, and I came to the conclusion—which I later found was correct—that the fighting individuals invariably remained in their homes, except when required for actual warfare or scouting. Obviously, too, they were not numerous, for which I was most thankful, for, had their numbers equalled those of their working fellows, life would have been impossible in the forests.

Fortunately, too, the raiders were strictly vegetarians and hence, once they overcame the resistance of their victims, they contented themselves with taking possession of the agriculturalists' stores and crops, and did not attempt to destroy the ants or their young. Hence, although scores of our friends had lost their lives, the bulk of the colony had sought safety in their subterranean burrows where we found them, huddled together, frightened out of their senses, and reminding me most forcibly of human beings panic-stricken by some catastrophe they are powerless to overcome or avert.

But not an ear of corn or a grain of wheat remained in the colony. The place was stripped bare and our own hut had been completely cleaned out. It would be months until another crop could be harvested, and starvation faced the unfortunate ants. But unless the neighboring colonies had also been raided, supplies could be obtained from them, and, already, the ants, assured by our presence that the enemy had gone, were hurrying off towards their neighbors in search of help.

Until this time I had never fully realized the feeling of friendliness I had for these ants. I was as angry, as worked up and as upset by the raid as were the ants themselves, and yet, as far as Tom and myself were concerned, we were really none the worse for the visit of the droughers. But somehow it affected me as a personal matter and my mind was filled with far from peaceful thoughts, and I was busy trying to formulate some plan by which I might even up scores and prevent any future raids. For us two to attempt to destroy or even attack those hordes of giant robbers, with their powerful fighting corps, would be the height of folly, and I well knew that it would be equally hopeless for me to attempt to induce the agriculturalists to carry war into the enemy's country, so to say. They were far too peaceful and peace-loving to fight, except in defense of their lives or property, and I had no means of conveying ideas to them, even had they been born fighters.

But there was one thing certain. Steps must be taken to render the colony less open to a raid than it was. No doubt, as I have said, the droughers had swept upon the colony many times in the past, and yet the victims of their attacks had never done anything to prevent the robberies. The low wall was no defense, and the entrances or gates were always open. To be sure, the leaf-carriers could climb any wall it would be possible to build, but a higher wall would hinder them, a gate which could be closed would prevent their dashing in and out freely, and there was no reason why the storehouses should not be fitted with doors or gates which could be closed from within, thus preventing the robbers from making off with the accumulated food supplies.

I tried to convey my ideas on these matters to the ants, but of course without success. But if they could not understand my gestures or my words, they were quick to grasp an idea once they had it demonstrated to them, and they were wonderful imitators. So, trusting they would fall-to and help us, once they saw what we were about, Tom and I began gathering materials and preparing to construct movable barriers. The material which seemed best adapted to our purposes was bamboo. It was light, strong, easy to cut and handle and was, I knew, about the only material we could expect to work with the hunting-knife as our sole tool. It was not difficult to build doors or gates from the bamboo and we progressed rapidly. My method was to lay a number of lengths of the bamboo side by side, lash these together with tough vines, place a second layer across these at right angles, and lash these to the first. To be sure, the first door we made, and which was designed for our own home, was crude, but it was strong and stout, and when hung in place by means of bark loops over pegs for hinges, it was indisputably a door. In fact I felt quite sure that it would resist the efforts of even the most powerful ants and that it would prove an effective barrier to a human being unless he were armed with an axe. Needless to say, the ants were intensely interested and curious. But their curiosity and interest gave way to obvious amazement and surprise when they saw the door in place. They ran excitedly about, opened and closed it, tested its strength and even tried ineffectually to force it But it was not until Tom and I carried loads of bamboo to the vicinity of their main storehouse, and commenced work upon a second door, that they realized that it was not a device intended solely for our own use. But the moment they saw us constructing another barricade beside their own building, they understood and fell to work with a will, bringing in vines and bamboo and aiding us in every way possible. Often I laughed to myself at thought of the strange picture we must have presented working there in the midst of the great, truly terrifying-appearing creatures. And yet, so accustomed to the ants had we become, that it seemed perfectly natural for us to be laboring in their midst and, to me at least, they no longer seemed insects; rather they seemed strange, primitive but friendly savages. They were wonderfully skillful and resourceful creatures. Their jaws were as useful as saws, knives and axes; they were incredibly strong, and their six leg's were all brought into play at one time. Their intelligence, too, was remarkable.

ANTS, of course, are noted for their intelligence, but hitherto, I had always felt that this was much overrated and that a great deal of the supposed intelligence of ants was in reality purely instinct. But here were ants, who had never in the history of their race seen doors or any structure of bamboo or timber, but who, nevertheless, were showing themselves far more skillful in the strange undertaking than were we two humans. By the time the door to the granary was completed and in place, the ants were perfectly capable of constructing their own doors, and all I had to do was to indicate the opening to be supplied with a door, by placing some material beside it. I was truly amazed also at the mathematical accuracy with which the creatures fitted the doors to the openings. They would scramble about apparently aimlessly, feeling the walls with their antennae, and would then build a door to exactly fit the opening which, in many cases, was irregular, arched or even oval in form. Finally, every aperture in the buildings was equipped with a door and only the opening in the wall remained. This was an undertaking that required several days and it was while the work was proceeding that another idea occurred to me. I had been puzzling my brain over some means of producing a defensive wall or barrier, when I thought of our escape from the army-ants. Here was the solution. We could construct a moat about the settlement and the water would prove an insurmountable barrier to the droughers. The land was practically level, a good-sized stream flowed within a few yards of one side of the fields, and while it would be a tremendous undertaking to dig a wide deep trench about the entire colony I felt sure it would be worth the trouble and could be done.

But it was a job that Tom and myself could not hope to accomplish. The ants must do this for themselves, and the difficulty was how to show them what I had in mind and for what purpose the ditch was intended. I had seen them digging irrigating ditches—and trenches to drain the surplus water from their fields, but how was I to make them understand that they must dig a huge ditch completely encircling their domain? However, I did not give the ants enough credit for their intelligence or their confidence in me. Digging ditches was one of their normal and everyday occupations, and I had merely to start digging, to have a husky gang of workers digging like mad, wherever I turned the earth. I would have given a great deal to have known what their ideas were, what purpose they thought I had in mind. But I feel sure that they associated the ditch with the doors and with the recent raid, and that their quick intelligences had jumped to the conclusion that both were designed for their own protection. At any rate, trench digging went on apace, and I thought, as I watched the creatures, what wonderful aids they would prove to an army and how easily and rapidly a regiment could dig itself in if accompanied by a corps of these giant insects. But the next day the ants sprang a surprise on me. Each ant appeared carrying one or two of the white blind termites I had seen within the galleries. The instant these creatures were placed within the trench, they commenced to burrow like mad, each doing the work of several ants, and fairly making the dirt fly. All the ants had to do was to carry out the loosed earth and guide the termites and keep them going, for the pale-bodied creatures had a tendency to stop digging as soon as they were a few feet below the surface. They were in effect living drills, and I was more astounded than ever at the resourcefulness of the ants in thus availing themselves of the natural tendencies of the termites. Here at any rate, the inquilines had been forced to earn their keep. Several weeks were required to complete the moat, but when it was done at last and connected with the stream and filled rapidly with water, I felt quite sure that the colony was fairly safe from further raids by the droughers. In fact, I had a rather amusing and perfectly convincing demonstration of the efficiency of my trench when we returned to the gate in the wall. I had quite overlooked the fact that we would be cut off by the moat; but here we were on the wrong side of the trench accompanied by our gang of tired ants. To Tom and myself the moat was nothing. It was not over six feet in depth and barely twenty feet in width, and either of us could swim it in a few strokes. But to the ants it was an insurmountable barrier. They were as completely cut off from their homes and friends as by a raging torrent. Wildly excited, they rushed up and down the banks, while on the opposite side their friends were just as troubled at seeing their fellows unable to return to their homes.

Wondering if it was merely fear of the water on the part of the ants or if they actually were unable to swim, I plunged into the moat and after a few strokes climbed out on the opposite side. The distress of the ants was really pitiful. One poor fellow, braver than the rest, tried to follow my example and was saved from drowning by the narrowest margin. It was evident that they could not cross and, not wishing to trouble or excite them further, and somewhat afraid they might turn upon me as the author of their predicament, I again swam the moat, and, with Tom's help, cut a number of bamboos and with these formed a crude bridge. Hardly were the bamboos in place before the ants rushed across them to be welcomed by their friends as though they had been miraculously raised from the dead. To build a light, strong bridge of bamboos was our next undertaking, and this we arranged like an old-fashioned draw-bridge, so that it could be raised or lowered from our side of the moat. This was a never-ending source of delight to the ants who, I feel sure, made many wholly unnecessary trips into the nearby forest merely for the sake of traversing the bridge. But I was not yet wholly satisfied. I remembered the ingenuity the army-ants had shown in attempting to reach us by forming a living bridge across the stream, and I did not feel at all sure that the droughers might not be equally clever. All the time we had been working on our defenses I had been thinking, trying to evolve some plan to strike a decisive and salutary blow at the droughers. How I wished I had my medicine-kit. If I had possessed a few bichloride of mercury tablets, or my calomel, I could have wiped out the droughers or so decimated them that there would be no danger of attacks for years. Ants, as I had often demonstrated when they became troublesome in any tropical camps, are strangely affected by mercurial poisoning. It appears to drive them insane, and once they have tasted it, they will fall upon one another ferociously, fighting to the death, and as each one swallows more of the poison as it bites its maddened adversary, an entire colony is soon destroyed much after the fashion of the famed Kilkenny Cats. But I had no mercury bichloride, no means of securing any, and I knew of no natural ant poison in the country. Bisulphide of carbon would be as efficacious as mercury, and while there was an abundant supply of sulphur in deposits about hot springs and fumeroles on the mountain sides, I had neither the apparatus nor the chemical skill to produce the volatile bisulphide. But the thought of sulphur gave me an idea. Would it not be possible to locate the droughers' nests, surround them with sulphur, and setting fire to this, destroy the ants with the fumes? I had no compunction about resorting to such means. Despite the fact that they were giants in size, the leaf-carriers were merely ants, and it speaks volumes for the state of my mind and the vagaries of human psychology that, while I regarded the droughers as vermin to be destroyed by any or all means, I looked upon the agriculturalists as friends and fellow beings.

To secure a supply of sulphur was easy enough, but to locate the homes of the droughers was a more difficult matter. To be sure, it would be easy to follow their trails to their nest, once the trail was found; but oddly enough, during all our stay in the country and on our innumerable trips, we had not met the leaf-carriers more than three or four times, and each time, they were far from the colony of the agriculturalists. That the raiders had come a long distance, I felt sure; but a long distance to us humans would be but a short trip to the droughers, who, as I have mentioned, moved at terrific speed and traveled farther in a half hour than a man could walk in two days.

THE WORLD OF THE GIANT ANTS

MOREOVER, we had no idea where to start. The raiding ants had left no visible trail, but I knew that, like bees, ants returning to their nests, usually travel by the straightest most direct route, and I decided that our best course would be to start at the spot where our bombardiers had attacked the raiders and follow as nearly as possible the course they had been taking when we had surprised them. It was an easy matter to locate the spot where we had met the raiding droughers, and after a few moments consideration, we decided upon the general direction they had been following. All through the first day we tramped on. Nothing of any great interest transpired, but we made one or two interesting discoveries. Among others, we found a most interesting example of protective coloration—not the type whereby a defenseless creature imitates its surroundings, but of the more remarkable form wherein a defenseless creature mimics in form or color some dangerous creature. Quite unexpectedly and suddenly we came upon a gigantic solitary ant resting quietly upon a stone at the edge of a clearing in the forest. Without our bombardiers, which we had left at home fearing they might apprise the droughers of our proximity, we were practically at the mercy of the terrible creature. But apparently he had not seen or scented us, and hoping to escape his notice, we drew hastily back trying to step noiselessly. But Tom unfortunately tripped upon a root and crashed backward. Instantly, at the sound, the ant was on the alert. He reared himself on his hind legs, raised his great head and swung quickly around towards us. Terror-stricken, I sought about for some spot, some refuge wherein we could battle against the monster which I felt sure was about to rush at us.

Then something about the creature struck me as being peculiar. I peered intently at the giant insect and roared with laughter, while Tom gazed at me, apparently thinking I had suddenly gone mad. The next moment he had every reason to think I had taken leave of my senses, for I deliberately approached the dreaded creature, picked up a stone and tossed it at him. Tom yelled in terror, expecting the ant to dash at me. But instead, the huge, ferocious-looking insect turned tail and scurried off as fast as his six legs could carry him. He was in fact an out-and-out fake; a sheep masquerading in wolf's clothing. He was not an ant at all, but a harmless beetle, so incapable of offensive or defensive tactics, that Nature had protected him from enemies by fashioning him in the form of a solitary-ant. My first close scrutiny of the creature showed me that he possessed no powerful mandibles, although at first sight he appeared to, owing to the manner in which black and white markings were arranged about his mouth. Neither were his antennae those of an ant, while his seemingly slender waist, his round thorax and ant-like abdomen were all optical illusions produced by white markings upon his stout, heavy thorax and bulky abdomen. But he was a most remarkable counterfeit, and would have passed as a true ant anywhere, unless his make-up was detected by the trained eye of an entomologist.*

IT was a short time after unmasking this fellow that we luckily came upon an abandoned road of the leaf-carrier. Although partly overgrown with weeds and grass, it was still recognizable, and I had no doubt it led to the nest and had been abandoned when the supply of proper vegetation at its other terminus had been exhausted. I was not mistaken. A few hours later we came to a cross-road, and although no ants were visible, I knew from its appearance that it was daily in use.

I had no desire to be seen by the droughers, for memory of their giant warriors still was uppermost in my mind, although I had no fear of the ordinary workers. Moreover, if my plan was to be successful, I would have to approach the nest when its occupants were at home and resting. To attempt to walk about the nest and arrange my sulphur would be impossible with endless streams of busy ants passing back and forth; and I had no definite knowledge as to the hours when the leaf-carriers ceased their labors and betook themselves to their underground chambers. Ordinarily, I knew, they were most active during the day, and in the tropics, as a rule, the relatives of these ants retired to their nests at night. But I also knew that they frequently made raids during the night-time and, on several occasions I had found the ants passing the day underground. Just what the hours of labor and rest might be with these particular ants must be learned by observation. So, making a short detour, we cautiously approached the road once more. Several times we repeated this, until to my satisfaction, I saw a large cleared space in the forest, and in the centre

[* A very common form of protective coloration among insects is that in which a harmless species or genus imitates a dangerous or offensive species or genus. Many flies bear such a close resemblance to bees that they are left undisturbed. Beetles imitate hornets and ants. Moths imitate bees and wasps, and many butterflies, which are edible to birds and other enemies, are colored to imitate noxious or inedible species.]

of this, the enormous mounds of refuse and earth which marked the home of our enemies. From hiding places back of the trees, we watched and saw a number of the big droughers come rushing from another pathway and vanish in one of the openings in the mound. No others were in sight; none emerged, and as it was near sundown, I assumed that the ants' labors were over for the day. Retiring to a spot at a safe distance, we ate our dinner and waited patiently until nearly dark. Then we again approached the ants' nest, and as no ants were visible, I decided our time was ripe. Treading softly, for I felt sure the ants beneath the ground would be aroused if they heard the unusual vibration caused by our steps, we worked diligently, encircling the nests with a pile of leaves and twigs, scattering sulphur among them, and arranging a pile of inflammable material and sulphur in each of the openings that led to the underground galleries. At last all was ready, and striking fire, I ignited the leaves, and rapidly we spread the flames from pile to pile.

Choking and coughing with the fumes of burning sulphur, we stamped, shouted and danced above the homes of the ants, anxious now to arouse them and bring them forth. Then, holding our breaths, we dashed through the ever-thickening fumes and took up positions of vantage on the windward side of the clearing.

Our noise, our pounding and the smoke had almost instantaneous results. Ants by scores came pouring, struggling from their burrows. But as fast as they emerged, they fell victims to the fumes of the sulphur. Over their dead bodies poured others—workers, warriors, great fat-bellied queens; drones and even inquilines. The whole place was a writhing, squirming, dying mass.

Terrified by the fire, overcome by the smoke, killed by the fumes, utterly disorganized and at a loss, the ants fell by the thousand. A few broke through the encircling fire, only to succumb a few yards beyond, and by the time the fire had burned out and the last pale-blue flames of the sulphur had died down, not a living ant was visible. Moreover, the mound itself had caught fire and was a smouldering red-hot mass, and I knew that any ants, any young or any eggs that might remain within the chambers would be utterly destroyed.

We had wreaked vengeance in full; we had entirely annihilated that den of robbers. While there were doubtless others in the forest, I felt sure that we had eliminated the greatest source of future raids on our friendly agriculturalists.

CHAPTER SIXTEEN

MOST amazing things have happened since last I wrote. We have made the most astounding discoveries and have come nearer to death than at any time since we have been here. For a time all went smoothly and peacefully after our return from our successful destruction of the drougher-ants. We made several trips as the weather improved, always seeking for some means of escape. It was on one of these trips that, for some inexplicable reason, the humor seized me to go out of our way and visit the black savages. Heaven knows I had no sane reason for wishing to do so. They were bestial, horrible creatures, far less human in many ways than our clean, friendly agricultural ants, and I ought to have been content to let them mind their own business, while I minded mine. But something, some uncontrollable urge, led me on.

As we reached the aphis orchard, we heard strange sounds from the distance; guttural cries and most peculiar animal-like noises. Wondering what could be up, and thinking the savages must be holding some sort of dance or ceremonial, we hurried towards their village. But as we came within sight of the open area and the mound in its centre, we halted abruptly and drew quickly into the shelter of the trees.

Before us a terrific battle was in progress. Everywhere upon the clear space about the blacks' village there were fighting, struggling knots of the black savages and light, yellowish-red creatures which I at first took to be some species of giant ant. Everywhere, too, lay dead bodies and wounded combatants. Never have I seen such savage, vicious fighting, not even between the most ferocious insects, and for a moment I stood spellbound, watching as if in a trance, the savage warfare before us. Despite their repulsiveness and their bestial characters, my sympathies were all with the blacks, for they were human at least. But despite my sympathies and my desire to aid the savages, I had no desire to throw myself into the fray. I had long ago exhausted my pistol cartridges; our weapons were crude bows and arrows and spears, and—yes, I had almost forgotten it, very useful slings such as the Andean Indians use—and while I had no doubt that we could give a good account of ourselves and could injure or kill a number of the enemy, still I knew that the ultimate result would be our own destruction. As I watched, I noticed that while the blacks used every effort to kill their adversaries, the latter appeared more anxious to capture or disable the savages than to annihilate them.

But the most astonishing thing, that which held me spellbound and oblivious to all else, was that the strange creatures were not ants, as I had at first thought. What they were I could not even imagine. In many ways they were ant-like. They possessed six legs, they resembled insects in the arrangement of thorax, head and abdomen; their enormous nipper-like jaws were those of warrior ants; but there all resemblance to ants or other insects ceased. Their eyes possessed lids, and instead of being fixed, glassy and expressionless, like those of insects, they were movable and as capable of expression as those of a mammal. Their antennae were almost rudimentary and they had well developed ears. And, instead of all six legs and feet being similar, each pair differed from the others. The rear legs were heavy, strong and terminated in broad clawed feet admirably adapted for supporting the creatures and gripping the earth. The central pair were flexible, slender and ended in digited members most astonishingly like hands, while the front pair were short, immensely powerful and bore terrible pincer-like claws somewhat like those of a gigantic lobster. Moreover, the creatures did not behave in the least like ants or any other insects. They stood, most of the time, erect; they moved swiftly and with amazing agility upon their hind legs; they used their middle pair of limbs like hands, and they wielded their front claws like weapons. That they represented an entirely new order of animal life, a peculiar connecting link between the true insects and the crustaceans, seemed certain, and yet their eyes and their actions appeared to be almost those of vertebrates. So intensely interested in the creatures had I become, that I scarcely noticed the battle or other incidents of the scene, and I had quite forgotten our tame bombardiers until one of the beetles rushed forward towards the struggling combatants. Instantly I realized that his interference would prove equally disastrous to both the black savages and their foes, that his deadly gases, released among those struggling close-locked figures, would overcome all alike. Then an amazing thing happened. The bombardier checked its onward rush, sniffed suspiciously, and turning tail, came dashing back with every symptom of terror. At the time I had little chance to marvel at this. From the opposite side of the open area a column of the strange red creatures was issuing. Without attempting to aid their comrades in their ferocious battle, they hurried directly towards the low wall surrounding the village of the blacks, swarmed over it, and vanished within the subterranean galleries of the savages. By now the fighting was almost over. Nearly all the black beings were dead, wounded, or prisoners, but they had given a good account of themselves. Far more bodies of their enemies, than of their own, lay scattered about the battlefield. Perhaps a dozen were still fighting, but they were rapidly overpowered, and, with their prisoners surrounded and completely cowed, the red creatures stood waiting. Presently, from the blacks' homes the strange invaders began to emerge, each I noted, carrying a burden.

The next moment I gasped in astonishment. The burdens they were carrying were the young savages I had seen in the underground nurseries. Squirming and yowling, but firmly held in the powerful claws of their captors, the infantile savages were being borne towards our hiding place. Terrified at thought of being discovered, realizing too late the danger we were in, we turned to rush for safety among the denser growth. Before we had taken a dozen strides, terrifying figures surrounded us, huge claws darted out and seized us, and screaming, fighting but helpless in the vise-like grips of the monsters, we were borne triumphantly back to the horde of awful creatures with their human loot.

EVEN in our extremity, during that terrifying time, I was astonished that our captors did not offer to harm us. The creatures who held me were in fact most considerate, even gentle. For brutes who, a few moments before, had been fighting so savagely and exhibiting such ferocity, their present actions were astonishing. Of course I did not struggle or resist—such a course I knew would be worse than useless, and poor Tom was too far overcome with terror to do more than move one foot before the other, as his captors led him forward.

Our arrival before the horde of the creatures caused tremendous commotion. One huge beast, who appeared to be a leader, hurried towards us, examined us minutely and uttered strange squeaky sounds which reminded me more of the creaking of rusty hinges than anything else I had ever heard. Instantly my captors released me. But not so with Tom. With scant ceremony he was hustled to the groups laden with their kicking, squirming black captives. The next instant the throng commenced to move away from the open space, with its litter of dead and dying, and headed to the right with the captives, Tom included, in their midst, and surrounded on all sides by the comparatively few unburdened creatures. They gave no heed to me and it was obvious that I was free and of no interest to them. Why this should be so I could not imagine.

Although the comparison was not flattering, yet it must have been evident to the beings that the blacks and myself were equally human. And it must have been equally evident that Tom was also a human being. Why then should they have attacked and carried off the youthful black savages, taken possession of Tom, and freed me? The only answer I could think of was that it was a matter of color.

Both the savages and Tom were black, while I was white, or rather I should say red, for I was tanned and burned by the sun until no one would have recognized me as a white man. Possibly, I thought, these weird, puzzling, ferocious beasts might classify human beings by color alone. Tom being black would be considered in the category of their victims of the battle, while I would be regarded as a friend, or at least no enemy, because my color was somewhat like theirs.

It seemed a far-fetched theory but it was the only one that occurred to me. But I had no mind to remain there while Tom was being carried off to some terrible fate. So, hurrying forward, I joined the procession, and presently, growing bolder now that my first terror of the things was overcome, I managed to push my way in towards the creatures guarding Tom. Even then the red giants paid no more attention to me, than if I had been one of their own sort.

But when I tried to force myself between Tom and his captors, the latter roughly shoved me aside and indicated that I was to remain at a distance from their captives. But they could not prevent me from talking to Tom and I did my best to try to reassure him, and to assure him that I would stand by him no matter what happened. The sound of my voice appeared to amaze the creatures, and the entire company came to an abrupt halt and stood staring and listening.

But Tom's voice simply astounded them. At his first words his captors sprang aside in fear. But their surprise was only momentary.

As we again marched onward, I studied the creatures minutely, and once more I revised my idea as to their identity and place in the animal kingdom. Now that I could observe them closely, I was once more convinced that I had been correct in my first surmise, and that they were ants. But if they were ants, speaking from a zoological viewpoint, they were assuredly most remarkably specialized ants. And yet, aside from their lidded eyes, their well-developed ears and their unusual feet, they were distinctly and unmistakably ant-like. They were, in fact, exactly what one might expect had evolution proceeded along insect lines and had ants, the most intelligent and advanced of insects, reached a stage comparable to that of the Pithecanthropus in the mammalian genesis of evolution.

Antennae had become of secondary importance as auditory organs were developed. Movable eyes had developed through necessity, and variable lenses and pupils had made soft eyes essential and consequently lids were needed to protect them. And with advancement and specialization of characters, the variable feet might well have resulted. The fact that they communicated by means of sounds was not so surprising, now that I came to consider it. For all we know, ordinary ants and other insects may communicate by means of sounds pitched too high or too low for the human ear to detect. And the fact that the voices of these creatures were audible to me merely proved that their vibrations happened to come within the range of my own sense of hearing.

Realizing this, realizing that the creatures were nothing more than huge, highly specialized ants, comprehension came to me like a flash of light, and all that had puzzled me was made clear. They were slave-keeping ants; they were the warriors of some colony who had made a slaving raid, and instead of fellow ants, they had taken possession of the degenerate human beings and were carrying them into slavery. And Tom was destined also to be a slave to these super-ants. All our common, well-known slave-holding ants, so abundant in many lands, are red; always they make slaves of black ants, and here these gigantic red ants still ran true to Nature's laws and chose black beings for their slaves. It solved the problem of my treatment and freedom also. Not being black I could not, to the ants' way of thinking, be made a slave, and hence I was of no value or interest to them, for they made war and attacked other creatures solely to obtain a supply of slaves.*

[* Many species of common ants possess slaves. Oddly enough the slave owners are red and the slaves black. The slaves—which are reared from the captured pupae and eggs of the black ants—are faithful, industrious and perform practically all the labor of the colony. So dependent upon their black slaves are some red ants that they are unable to feed themselves. When on a slave- hunting raid, these ants send scouts ahead to locate the nests of the black ants and conduct the attack on military lines, with skirmishes, rear guards, flanking parties, shock troops and reserves.]

THE WORLD OF THE GIANT ANTS

IF I were right in my surmises and deductions, as I felt convinced I was, then personally I had nothing to fear from these semi-human ants. But my blood boiled and I was furiously angry at thought of their calmly taking possession of Tom as if I had no rights or say in the matter. Still there was something extremely ludicrous in the thought of Tom being a slave to the ants.

I could picture him trying to act as nursemaid to a young ant, scurrying about seeking food to supply his owners, laboring at building the ants' nests or digging subterranean tunnels. He would, I imagined, be about the most useless and inefficient slave the ants had ever owned. And with this thought came a new fear. I had watched and studied the habits of our common slave-holding ants far too often not to be thoroughly cognizant of their customs, and I well knew the fate that befell their black ant slaves if they failed to fulfill their allotted tasks or to satisfy their cruel owners. Death swift and certain was their portion, and Tom, I felt certain, would fail utterly, even if he did not assert himself and submitted to his slavery. A human being serving as the slave to ant masters! It was unthinkable, monstrous, impossible. And yet, the black savages were human, and before me the red ants were carrying off the savages' infants. For the first time I noticed that not a single adult savage had been borne away as a captive. Although many had been taken alive and unharmed, all had been released when the victorious raiders had departed. It was all very clear to me, now that I realized they were slave-holders and were following precisely the same habits and customs as any ordinary slave-keeping ants, with the sole exception that they had substituted black human beings for black ants. And while they were acting much as do human slave-raiders, yet they showed far greater wisdom and foresight. Instead of carrying the adults into slavery, and being forced to expend a vast amount of time in teaching and training them, as well as in forcing them to labor and in addition losing many through one cause and another, they were making slaves of the infants who, reared among their owners, knowing no life but that of slavery, would be easily trained, would never rebel at their lot and would grow to maturity as ideal slaves. No doubt, too, the red giants had other and equally excellent reasons for leaving the adult blacks behind, and for taking pains not to kill more than was essential to their victory.

LEFT unmolested, the blacks would continue to breed and increase, for I could not imagine them having sufficient intelligence to move to a new locality or to provide defenses against further attacks, and they would thus provide a constant source of supply for the slave-raiders whenever the latter required new slaves. No doubt these red fellows had been systematically raiding the blacks for generations. But all this, as I mulled it over in my mind, did not pacify me in the least regarding Tom's plight, nor did it account for the reds taking possession of him, an adult. The only answer I could find for their thus making an exception of him was that they had looked upon him as my slave, a trained slave from infancy, like their own, and had calmly taken possession of my property. The more I thought of it, the angrier I became. The creatures were no better than highway robbers. I was tempted to attack them single-handed, to attempt to recover possession of Tom, for somehow my first intense dread of these super-ants had given way to a supreme contempt for them. But my common sense prevailed. I realized that it would merely mean defeat, injury and probable death for me, and that in that case Tom would be irretrievably doomed. No, it was far wiser for me to control my feelings, follow along with the procession to the ants' destination, and trust to some chance of rescuing Tom without endangering ourselves overmuch.

Up to this I had been too preoccupied with my thoughts to notice that our bombardier beetles had deserted us. I was puzzled, but then the actions of these beetles had puzzled me from the time of our first meeting the slave-raiders. Why had they appeared frightened? Why had they failed to attack these great ants with the same ferocity they had always exhibited towards others? Surely they must have recognized them as ants. And why had they now deserted us? I could not even think up a theory to account for their actions.

Meantime we had made a wide detour, had left the aphis orchards far behind, had passed at a considerable distance from the colony of agricultural ants, and were approaching a portion of the valley I had not previously visited. Eventually, as we topped a low hill, I saw that we were close to the area which on several occasions I had viewed from a distance and which I had always assumed was a second colony of the black savages with their neighboring aphis pastures. Now, as we drew near, I discovered that I had made a great mistake. The orderly expanses of trees were aphis groves to be sure, and the herds of clumsy bovine aphids we saw were being herded by blacks, but here and there among them stalked great red slave-holding ants. They were the owners of the aphids, the masters here, and the black herders were merely their slaves. Unquestionably we were close to the homes of the slave-raiders, and presently we left the orchards behind and came out upon a broad open space with a great conical mound in the centre. Everywhere were the red giants and everywhere, hurrying about on numberless duties, laboring in the broiling sun, toiling under heavy burdens, were scores of the subjugated human slaves. And yet, even then, I could not avoid feeling that of the two, the ants were the superior beings, that the naked, misshapen black savages were far inferior to their insect masters. Here, in this remarkable spot, the whole order of things seemed to be reversed. Insects dominated, the only indigenous human beings were degenerate, miserable brutes and were entirely subservient to the forms of animal life, which man is accustomed to consider are the lowest orders of creation.

I noticed, too, that there was a great diversity among the giant slave-holding ants. Those whom I had accompanied and who had raided the blacks were obviously warriors or soldiers. A few of the same sort were to be seen around the immense ants' nest towards which we were now proceeding, but there were far more of totally different forms. Many of these others had enormous heads, weak bodies and almost atrophied legs and were apparently blind, for despite the fact that they possessed fixed fishy-looking eyes, each was being guided and led about by attendant black slaves. Others were burly, heavy-bodied creatures with small heads, inconspicuous jaws, great staring eyes, well developed antennae and such long, slender legs that they appeared almost more spider-like than ant-like. It was this type I had seen with the aphid herders, and I now saw that they were all engaged in watching the blacks and in keeping them at their work. We had now reached the summit of the mound and paused at the verge of the great crater-like depression in the centre with the various dark openings to subterranean burrows piercing its sides. As we halted, a horde of horrible-looking creatures emerged from the tunnels. That they also were ants and belonged to the colony was evident, but they were totally distinct in form from any of the others I had seen. Their jaws were huge, but were blunt thick-edged affairs. Their eyes were minute, almost invisible; their bodies were swollen and their legs short, stout and terminated in peculiar blunt-ended claws that somehow looked like pudgy, toil-calloused hands. As these slovenly, almost grub-like beasts reached the waiting warriors, the latter handed over their squalling, infantile captives to the newcomers. With skill, which could only have been born of long practice, these creatures seized the black youngsters, holding them securely but without injury in their powerful mandibles, and hurried with them to the burrows whence they had emerged.

BUT Tom was a problem. As he cowered and yelled and struggled at the approach of the things, one after another would examine him, and apparently satisfied that he was not an infant—and perhaps recognizing the fact that he was not of the same race as the other blacks, they would move off without offering to take charge of him. The warriors squeaked, croaked and evidently became insistent, but without result. The nurses, for I knew that was what in reality the blunt jawed individuals were, would have nothing to do with the big adult negro. Their duties were to care for infant slaves, to rear them, train them perhaps, until old enough to labor for their masters, and they had no interest in grown-up slaves. Like all the rest of their kind, they were highly specialized for their particular place in the complex social and communistic life of these ants and had been developed through countless generations to perform one set of duties and only one. It was the same with the warriors. They had become specialized for conducting raids and taking prisoners and were at an entire loss when it came to any other matter. And it was very obvious that they were now at a most complete loss when it came to ridding themselves of Tom. Throughout their lives and the lives of their innumerable ancestors, warriors had gone forth, had battled, had returned with captives and had delivered the captives to the proper individuals. Not until they had been relieved of every prisoner were their duties at an end, and here they were with a captive of whom they could not rid themselves. So intensely socialistic were they, so synchronized their brains or instincts, that the whole army was as much affected as though each individual were personally responsible for Tom. There they stood, all completely upset, all waiting on the two who had Tom in their custody. More than ever was I impressed by the shortcomings of ants' boasted intelligence, more than ever I realized the futility of communism when carried to the extreme, and more than ever I appreciated the fact that ants, no matter how huge, no matter how super-developed, would never attain the heights of human beings. As long as everything went smoothly and along accustomed lines, they were capable of accomplishing anything, and exhibited what appeared at first sight to be real intelligence and reasoning. But once their accustomed line of action was interrupted, once anything without precedent took place, they were helpless. And there was no one individual, no group of individuals, to get them out of a dilemma, to meet unforeseen circumstances and find a way out of difficulties, to give orders or to be obeyed. In short, there was no head, no leader, no ruler among any of the ants, and therein lay their greatest weakness.

All these thoughts flashed through my mind in a moment. The next instant I was hurrying forward. Here was my opportunity. The warrior ants had no thoughts, no ideas except to get rid of Tom and thus fulfill their allotted duties as ordained by their special development, their duties and their instincts. Probably, I thought, they would not care a jot who took their troublesome captive in charge, as long as he was off their hands. And quite confidently, with these convictions in my mind I strode to Tom's side, seized him by the arm and started to drag him off. Without offering the least resistance, his captors released their hold and instantly, as if I had given them an order, the assembled warriors broke ranks and scurried off to their underground quarters.

I was delighted, immensely pleased that my deductions had proved so correct. And Tom, poor fellow, was almost speechless with delight. But we were not to get off so easily. As we hurried down the slope of the mound and started across the cleared area towards the woods beyond, one of the long-legged slave drivers glanced up, stared in our direction with his protruding, almost crustacean-like eyes, and the next instant came racing towards us.

Just what his intentions were I neither knew nor stopped to enquire. With Tom at my side I dashed forward at topmost speed. But we were no match for the big ant. Now I realized why these fellows possessed such muscular bodies and long legs; they were built for speed; they had been developed through centuries, ages, for the sole duty of watching and guarding slaves and for chasing those who attempted to escape. Evidently the fellow racing after Tom and myself thought Tom was a runaway slave. What he thought of me was of no particular interest at the time. And what punishment was customarily meted out to slaves who attempted to escape, I did not know. But I had no doubt it would be drastic and that I, as an abettor of Tom's break for liberty, would be treated far from gently.

Neither Tom nor myself had any intention of submitting to capture tamely. We had been surprised, taken at a disadvantage, when we had been made prisoners by the raiders; moreover, they had outnumbered us fifty to one. But with this single long-legged fellow after us, it was a different matter, and even in the excitement of the time, I saw that he was alone, that none of his fellows had joined in the pursuit. Realizing we could not outdistance him, I gave a sharp command to Tom, and halting, we both wheeled. Quickly we fitted arrows to bows and let drive. Tom's shaft went wild; he was still trembling and shaky from his experience, but mine struck the oncoming ant fairly in the thorax. He plunged forward on his head, turned a complete somersault and lay helpless, paralyzed.

But as we were about to turn to hurry on, another of the long-legged fellows came speeding towards us. There was nothing to do but stand and fight. He was still far off but to run would merely be to exhaust ourselves. His six, long, powerful legs would carry him twice as fast and countless times farther than our legs. And to battle with him, even if by good luck we were as successful as with his companions, would not better us much. There were dozens of his sort scattered about the plain, and I had no doubt but that as rapidly as we destroyed one, another would take his place. Why several did not start for us in unison was a mystery, but I assumed it was age-old custom and instinct for individuals to recapture runaways, and I let it go at that.

As I have mentioned, Tom and I possessed slings which we had found quite serviceable in the past, and now, not caring to waste arrows which were valuable, we whirled the primitive weapons and hurled a shower of rocks at the oncoming ant. Several struck close to him, one or two whanged against his body, and one struck and broke the second leg on his left side. Here was something quite unexpected and new to his experience. With the same lack of initiative, with the same utter failing of intellect and reason which I have referred to when face to face with any novelty, the fellow stopped in his tracks, not knowing whether to retreat or advance. He made a tempting mark, and as rapidly as we could load and whirl our slings we continued our fusillade. Whether we killed or wounded him I do not know, for all our interests were centred on an unexpected development.

Our ammunition, rough stones of various sizes and shapes, was not conducive to accuracy, and the majority of our shots went wild. Some thudded harmlessly upon the open ground, but two or three dropped into the midst of a group of black savages attending some of the blind fat ants. Whether the slaves were actually struck or not, I do not know; at any rate the falling stones brought cries of terror and frightened screams from the blacks, and completely forgetting their charges, thinking only of getting away from the descending missiles, they took to their heels as if the devil had been after them, as no doubt they thought he was. Instantly every long-legged slave driver within sight was up and going. Here, to their minds, was a slave-break, and almost before we had recovered from our surprise at this unexpected denouement, the chase was in full swing and heading directly away from us. Our way was clear, and making the best of our opportunity, we gained the shelter of the forest.

CHAPTER SEVENTEEN

SINCE I last opened my notebook to record events, I have gone through a greater trial than has been my misfortune since entering this place. But thank God all ended well, and it is now a thing of the past. Much as I suffered, poor Tom suffered a thousand times more.

Having escaped from the red slave-owners, who no doubt found too much to occupy their attentions in recapturing their slaves to bother chasing us, we reached our home (we now called this agricultural-ant colony our home), in safety.

For a time nothing of great moment happened. We made many new discoveries and found many new things, and we also vastly improved our weapons. Now that we knew of the warlike slave-owners, we felt the need of weapons more than ever. Not only did we make better slings, but having proved the value of these primitive weapons, we spent much time searching for pebbles of uniform weight and size, and as rounded as possible, to be used as missiles.

And, having nothing better to do, we spent many hours chipping and pounding uneven pebbles into spheroidal form, until we possessed a large store of ball-like stones. Then we made a discovery which caused us to feel that all our labor in this direction had been wasted. In a clay bed near the upper waters of a stream, we came upon great quantities of perfectly spherical nodules of great weight, veritable bullets in fact, nearly as heavy as if made of iron, which I recognized as cassiterite or stream-tin. Commercially, this would have been a great find, and, had I been free and within reach of civilization, my fortune would have been made, for a short search revealed the fact that the bed of the stream was literally paved with the valuable ore.

Here, ready to hand, were missiles for our slings which were immeasurably superior to ordinary pebbles, and for several days we carried loads of the nodules to our hut. I laughingly remarked to Tom that if we had only possessed a cannon and powder we would have had most excellent ammunition and could make short work of any attackers. In fact this started me on a new train of thought, and a wild scheme of actually making powder and firearms entered my head. I had no doubt that powder could be made, for as I have said, there was a boundless supply of sulphur; charcoal was to be had for the trouble of making it, and I knew that by a little experimenting I could produce saltpeter by means of a rubbish pile or "nitraria" such as I had seen used in Paraguay. But I could think of no way of making any sort of a cannon or gun. Of course I knew that in ancient times the Chinese used firearms of bamboo or even of wood, but even to fashion such things was beyond our capabilities. However, just to pass the time and to satisfy myself that it was possible to do so, I decided to experiment with gunpowder. I therefore proceeded, with Tom's help, to accumulate a quantity of rotten vegetation, dung, offal from game we killed, and other waste material, and built up a good-sized mound in a remote spot. As it would be several months before this would decay and produce the nitrate I desired, we set to work on other matters.

Our hatchet-like weapons had proved most useful, and in pondering how we could improve upon these, I remembered the saw-edged swords of the Aztecs, and it occurred to me that we might construct something of a similar sort. Where we had destroyed the drougher-ants there were a number of the hard, extremely tough and sharp jaws of the defunct warriors, jaws like enormous shark's teeth, and we gathered several dozen of these. Then, with a great deal of trouble, we hacked and whittled out sword-like pieces of palm wood with serviceable handles. Along the edges of these we fastened the ant-jaws, securing them in place by means of fibre cords and a cementlike wax that I made by a mixture of bees' wax, pitch and the juice of some species of rubber tree. I cannot lay claim to any inventiveness on my part in making this, for it was nothing but the "karamani" wax used extensively by the Indians of Brazil and Guiana for attaching their arrow-heads to the shafts; but it served our purpose admirably. The savage-looking weapons, when completed, were fearful things, and Tom grinned from ear to ear as he swung his about his head and expressed a desire to try it upon some enemy. Little did we dream how soon that wish would be fulfilled.

THE WORLD OF THE GIANT ANTS

So accustomed had Tom become to the weird creatures and unusual conditions, that he frequently went off alone in search of game or for other purposes, and it was not unusual for him to be absent for several hours at a time. Oddly enough, too, the gigantic insects had apparently acquired an instinctive dread of us humans, and for a long time we had not been attacked by any of the inhabitants of the forest. Indeed, several times when we met creatures which, a few months previously, would have attacked us savagely, they showed every desire to get away from us. Whether this was due to that remarkable inherent dread of human beings which animals acquire after a short acquaintance with man, whether it was the result of our activities, or whether it was the result of experience, I cannot say; but even the predatory hornets, the terrible solitary-ants and the ichneumons seemed to avoid us. Still, we were usually accompanied by our domesticated bombardier-beetles. These were now of the fifth generation, and having been bred in captivity and descended from tame ancestors, they were most docile and intelligent creatures. The agricultural-ants even had become thoroughly accustomed to them, and they came and went about the colony and made friends with the various inquilines and insect guardians of the place. Also, I must not forget to mention that the latter creatures had become equally friendly with us, evidently having come to the conclusion that we were recognized and accepted members of the colony. The huge dragon-flies in particular showed great intelligence and would sail down and alight near us, waiting expectantly for us to toss them bits of meat while we ate. It was fascinating to watch these creatures, which I could only liken to living airplanes, as they turned their enormous thin-necked heads from side to side and watched us with their goggling many-faceted eyes and licked their chops and protruded their remarkable folding jaws. As far as our good-natured ant hosts were concerned, matters proceeded much as before. We had never learned to communicate with them except by signs, but we had developed a fairly complete sign language, and despite the fact that the ants about us now were many generations removed from those whom we had first met, they seemed to have inherited all their ancestors' knowledge of us, and acted exactly as if they had always had us with them.

All of these things I have mentioned at some length, for all have a very direct bearing upon that great calamity which befell us. Tom had gone off on a hunt, but when he had not returned late in the afternoon, I began to feel uneasy. Then, when late at night his two bombardiers came home, and I saw that one was limping and badly injured, I felt certain that some accident had befallen my faithful friend, for I no longer looked upon him as a servant.

Throughout that long night I paced back and forth, unable to sleep, torn with fears, and conjuring up visions of the awful future in store for me in case Tom had been killed and I should be forced to remain alone in this terrible land of insects. As soon as it was dawn I started out, but it was, as I knew, an almost hopeless undertaking. I had no idea in which direction Tom had gone and all I could do was to wander aimlessly, shouting and hallooing. At night I returned discouraged, saddened, despondent and utterly heartbroken. But I pulled myself together. I must not give up. My life depended upon finding Tom. Alone I could not exist here, and I determined that, should I fail to find him within a week's time, or should I find his dead body, I would do away with myself, rather than face the certainty of insanity which I knew would result if I dwelt for long alone.

SO, day after day, I tramped the forest, the valleys, the plains and the mountains, searching for my only fellow man in all this land. Forcing myself to think calmly, I laid out a regular course, covering a different area each day, until, on the sixth day, only that section near the slave-holders' colony remained unsearched. I hated to go near this spot and I put it off until the last, partly from my inborn fear of the slave-owners, and partly because I felt sure that Tom would never have gone in this direction. One day more of fruitless searching and I would give up. In fact I was far more occupied with thoughts of how I could commit suicide, than with thoughts of facing the slave-holders, as I set off in the direction of their farms. Nevertheless, I proceeded cautiously. I had no desire to fall into the clutches of the big red brutes a second time, even though I could take my own life as readily among them as elsewhere—a strange psychological state of mind to be sure. And neither did I fail to shout Tom's name and to halloo as I proceeded. I had gone far and felt I must be nearing the country of the slavers when I stopped, my breath suppressed, my ears strained. From somewhere in the distance I thought I had heard a faint call. Could it be possible? Was Tom somewhere in this neighborhood?

Having no fear that my cries would attract the attention of the ants, for I felt certain they were deaf to all human voice vibrations, I bellowed at the top of my lungs. Again I listened, and again it seemed to me I heard an answering cry. But it might be echo, it might be an hallucination; in short, it might be the result of my overtaxed nerves and brain. Forgetting caution, I rushed forward, shouting as I ran. Suddenly, beyond the fringe of forest, I saw open country, and instinctively I halted and proceeded more cautiously. Before me stretched a newly-cleared space about the trunks of the aphid trees I knew so well.

Here and there black slaves were toiling under the watchful eyes of their horrible red masters, and for a moment I watched them. Tom, I knew, could not be here, and I was about to turn away when I caught sight of something which caused me to stare with wide incredulous eyes. Close to the forest edge beyond the other slaves and their masters, two great red ants were standing, and beyond them, working like the other slaves, was a single being as black as his fellows but who was clad in rough garments! Instantly, as I rubbed my eyes and convinced myself I was not delirious, I knew it was Tom. Strange that I had not thought of this possibility before, that it had not occurred to me that he might have been captured by these slave-owners. But the joy that filled my heart at seeing Tom alive and apparently unharmed, drove all other thoughts from my mind. But how to reach him; how to free him from his masters? To rush blindly forward and attack his guards was, I knew, suicidal. Although the red ants had not harmed us before, I felt quite sure that should I attempt to rescue Tom from their clutches, or should I attack them, they would fall upon me and end my career in short order. For a moment or two I pondered. Then an idea, the only one I could see, although mad and desperate enough, occurred to me. Tom was working close to the forest, within easy call, and by carefully circling the area within shelter of the trees I could, I thought, reach a spot within a few yards of him. Then if I could attract his attention or could talk to him without his captors' knowledge, it might be possible for him to make a quick dash. For what might follow I did not plan. I felt sure that his two guards would be the only ones to start in chase, and these we might destroy, once they were out of sight of their fellows.

Cautiously retracing my steps, my heart beating hard with excitement, I crept through the jungle until I felt I had reached a spot about opposite the place where I had seen Tom. Stealthily, for while the red ants might be deaf they possessed keen senses, I stole forward until I could peer through the dense growth. Yes, there, within a dozen yards of the forest edge, was Tom, and at sight of him at such close quarters, unbridled rage at his captors possessed me. Evidently he had not submitted tamely to captivity nor to forced labor. His skin was covered with wounds, and I knew from the expression on his face that he was suffering. Regardless of all else, willing to take the risk of the vibrations of my voice alarming the red ants, I called his name and a cautionary warning. I saw him start, listen and glance up, but by no other motions did he betray his surprise. But to my dismay I saw that the giant ants had also detected my voice. They were glancing about and waving their antennae, evidently trying to locate the spot whence the unusual vibrations had come. Luckily for us they were drivers and not warriors, for the latter possessed true ears and would no doubt have located me instantly.

But even as it was there was no time to be lost. Whatever we did must be done quickly and before the ants realized what was afoot. Desperate measures were essential, and all my preconceived plans were cast aside. Tom, of course, had no weapons, and like a flash I realized that he must pass close to one of his guards if he dashed to me as I had planned. Quickly fitting an arrow to my bow, I raised my jagged sword with my other hand, swung it, and shouting to Tom, "Here, Tom, grab this and run!" I hurled it towards him. The weapon fell almost at his feet, and scarcely had it touched the earth when my arrow flashed through the sunlight and buried itself in the soft skin between the thorax and abdomen of the nearest ant. Everything happened at once. As the ant doubled up and fell, Tom seized the sword, leaped forward, dealt the prostrate ant a terrific blow that crushed its head to pulp, and gained my side. The other ant, dazed at the suddenness of it all, hesitated a moment. Then he was after Tom, while his fellows nearest to him came hurrying towards him.

Again I fired but missed. There was no time to fit another arrow to the string. If we tried to run we would be overtaken. There was but one course open: to stand and fight, to destroy this nearest creature that was now within a dozen feet of us, and then rush off before the other ants saw us. In terse rapid words I said as much to Tom, who seemed unable to grasp the fact that he was free, unable to speak for the moment. But he could act, and backing against a tree and grasping his sword, he prepared for battle. My only defensive weapon was my knife, aside from the sword, my bow and arrows and my sling, and this would be hand-to-hand fighting. But Tom gave me no opportunity to use my weapon. He had scores to settle with the brutal red beast, and all the long-dormant savage blood of his African ancestors was aroused. With a hoarse yell, he leaped forward, swung the jagged sword, and with a vicious side-sweep, sliced the head from the oncoming ant at a single blow. In the winking of an eyelid the fight was over. The way lay open before us, and at top speed we rushed off through the forest.

BEHIND us, now and then, we could hear sounds of the pursuing ants. How far they followed us I cannot say, but at last the sounds ceased, and feeling we were in no danger, we slowed down to a more comfortable gait. Poor Tom was all in. He had been weakened by his wounds, he had been almost starved, and the excitement of the duel and escape had about finished him. But as he limped slowly along, he told me bits of his story. He had been surprised in the forest by two red warrior ants, and though he fought savagely, he had been overcome and made a prisoner. Some of his wounds had been received in this struggle, but the others were the result of his refusal to herd with the repulsive blacks or to work for his masters. He shuddered and actually wept, as he related how the red ants had bitten and tortured him, although with devilish ingenuity they avoided maiming him so he would still be able to work. How they had seized his limbs in their jaws and had bitten until he felt as if his bones would crack; how they had nipped pieces of flesh from his back and chest until screaming with the pain, he had submitted. And during the six terrible interminable days he had had no food, except the stinking offensive stuff fed to the horrible half-human blacks.

Undoubtedly the ants had thought him an escaped slave and had therefore punished him the more severely, but that made his condition no better, and it was days before the poor fellow was able to be up and about. Meanwhile I was filled with a new dread. If the red warriors roamed the forest searching for runaway slaves, they would be a constant menace. No doubt, too, they were untiring, skilled trailers, possessing all the marvelous powers and instincts of ants combined with a super-intelligence, and sooner or later, they would locate us. At any moment, if we ventured into the forest, we might be discovered and attacked, and I had little doubt that, after their recent experience, they would be in force. And if we remained within the confines of the Agricultural-ants we would not be safe. Although I had done everything to render the place as nearly impregnable as possible, still I knew that the red soldiers, if numerous enough, could reach us and that we could not count too much upon the resistance of the agriculturalists. The more I thought on this matter, the more certain I felt that sooner or later we would have to wage a decisive battle with these slave-holding ants. And the more I thought of them and talked the matter over with Tom, the more I began to hate the creatures and to wish that we could wipe them from the face of the earth. In fact, I even thought of training our peaceful hosts, of equipping an army, and of going forth to attack the slave-owners, instead of waiting for them to take the offensive. But before I reached any definite decision in this direction, another event transpired which, for a time, drove all thoughts of the slavers from our minds.

Whenever we went on any hunt (we had long since given up our hopeless seeking for an exit from the valley) we kept as far from the district of the slave owning ants as possible, and invariably bent our steps in the opposite direction. I thought that we had pretty well explored the valley within a radius of eight or ten miles of the colony of agriculturalists, and that we knew practically every square mile of this side of the country. But a tropical forest can hide most conspicuous things within a very small compass, and I soon had another proof of this. Passing through a rather dense stretch of jungle, Tom stubbed his toe upon a stone, and, glancing down, I saw that the object was a squared and sculptured piece of masonry. Instantly, my curiosity was aroused, and intently I examined the thing as we cleared away the moss and dead leaves about it. It was beyond question the work of human hands and a sudden wild hope seized me that there might be other men in the valley after all. A moment later I realized how groundless were my hopes, for the fragment of stonework was immeasurably ancient. But it proved, at least, that human beings had at one time dwelt in the valley, and the work upon the stone showed that they were no savages, that they were cultured, perhaps civilized beings.

Where there was one bit of sculptured stone there must be others, and excited, my interests all aroused, we sought diligently amid the tangled vines and trees. Presently our efforts were rewarded. Overgrown and hidden so that even a dozen feet away they were invisible, we came upon the ruins of a great stone building. Concealed as it was, I recognized it instantly as being the handiwork of the same race that had built Tupec. Here indeed was an amazing discovery, and yet I should have known, from the fact that the tunnel from Tupec led to this valley, that the race must have known of the spot. Everything else was for the time forgotten, and we devoted our time until dark to clearing away the jungle and exposing more and more of the ruins.

Determined to learn all I could of the place, although what earthly good it would do me, I do not and did not then know, we returned the following day with our hammocks, prepared to camp by the ruins and pursue our investigations.

Each hour that we worked increased my wonder and my interest. The first building we had found was but one of a dozen or more, each surpassing the last in workmanship, in beauty of sculpture and in archeological interest. Indeed, as we wandered about in the forest, we soon discovered that we were in the midst of ruins far more extensive than those of Tupec; ruins of what must once have been a magnificent and large city. What, I wondered, had become of the race that dwelt here? Why had they vanished? Why had no descendants remained? Cudgelling my brains for answers to these puzzles, I arrived at the conclusion that the inhabitants of this city must have deserted the valley and established Tupec, for all my investigations proved more and more conclusively that Tupec was the more recent of the two, although that, I knew, must go back for countless thousands of years. What, I wondered, were the conditions of this valley in those far-distant times? Was it inhabited by overgrown giant forms of insect life or had they been the result of development after human beings had vanished from the district? And then one day the mystery was cleared up. In many places the massive masonry was only held together by the binding roots and vines, and as we cut away a mass of these, a large section of a wall gave way and came crashing down. Behind it yawned a great black opening, and, peering into this, I saw that the entire walls were occupied by innumerable niches, and that in every niche was an earthenware jar or vessel. Here was an archeological treasure-trove, although as worthless to me, in my present plight, as were the dead and twisted lianas we had hacked away to expose it. But while I fully realized this, still my scientific ardor was in no wise diminished, and I was as filled with interest and delight as though I could carry the specimens and my story to my fellow men at any time.

THE light within the chamber was dim, but on the following morning, with the sun shining into the aperture, all was bright and clear in the great room, and I gazed fascinated and entranced at the rows and rows of magnificent decorated wonderfully moulded pots. I should not, however, say pots, for aside from the fact that they were all more or less pot-like in form, I knew at my first glance that they were not vessels in the true sense of the word; rather they were effigy or portrait-jars, of a type new to archeology and modelled with truly amazing fidelity to nature. There were human figures in every conceivable attitude, figures of birds, mammals, crustaceans, insects; figures of reptiles and molluscs; figures of monsters unknown to me, and representations of fruits, vegetables, flowers, leaves and of every imaginable combination of all.

So perfectly were they made, so beautifully colored, that I knew they must have been made from life and I gazed spellbound at the counterparts in miniature of the ancient inhabitants of the valley and of Tupec.

Then, as I moved about studying these archeological marvels, it suddenly dawned upon me that they were not placed within their niches hit or miss, but were arranged in some definite order, that they were all symbolic, and that their relative positions conveyed some meaning. I felt sure of it. I felt convinced that before me was a history, a codex, telling the story of the ancient race. A story, written in effigy jars instead of in carved symbols on stone or in written characters, but a story none the less. If I only had the key! If only I had some hint of the cipher! Now they were as meaningless to me as so many cooking utensils. I did not even know where to begin, whether the symbolic figures started from right or left, from top or bottom, or from which one of the four walls of the chamber. I stared at them as though I might hypnotize the inanimate objects into revealing their secrets. And slowly, as I gazed at the nearest jars a strange, almost uncanny feeling came over me.

It seemed to me that I was beginning to see light, that comprehension was dawning upon me, that my mind was actually penetrating the secret of the symbolic vessels. There, before me, was a vessel bearing the perfectly modelled figure of a stooping man, and upon its surface was depicted human beings busy at some labor. In the man's hand was a tool, a hammer or maul, and before him a slab. It was plain enough now. He was cutting a stone and the painted figures were working on a stone building. The next jar on the right bore the figure of a woman and child, and on the right side of this the next vessel showed a bird with wings wide spread. But on the left side stood a magnificent jar showing a man in elaborate headdress and costume holding his hands aloft and above him was a flaming sun. To the left of this was a vessel of strange squarish form and covered with a painting clearly showing a sacrifice being held upon a pyramidal altar. Eureka! I had it! I fairly danced and-leaped about, until Tom must have felt sure that I had gone mad in contemplation of this "trash" as he called it. I was more excited than I had been for years. I forgot my plight, my surroundings. I had made an astounding discovery, and I felt convinced that presently, with a little study and patience, all the mysteries of the ancient race and of Tupec would be solved for me. There could be no doubt of it. I could grasp the system now. Here was the stone cutter, symbolical of building; next the completed edifice and the high priest worshipping the sun, and then the sacrifice. Almost feverishly I examined the jars further to right and left. The woman and the bird seemed to have no relation to the stonecutter, and those farther to the right seemed to have even less. I felt sure that I was right; that the symbols should be read from right to left, and carefully I examined those to the left of the sacrificial scene. Here were jars bearing effigies of corn, of cacao, of various vegetables, and with painted scenes showing planting, harvesting and preparing food plants. Now that I had solved the puzzle of the system, I grasped the meanings of the jars readily. First the erection of a temple, sacrifices to the gods, the tilling of land and cultivation of food—a veritable genesis stood before me. With the utmost difficulty I controlled myself. For all I knew I was beginning in the middle of the story. I must search about until I found a beginning. Then calmly, patiently I would set myself to decipher the whole. Never once did it occur to me how absolutely futile was this labor, how foolish my elation, how ridiculous my interest. My scientific brain demanded that the history be read, my archeological interests drove all other thoughts and considerations from me. For the time, I was oblivious to all else.

Then, as I examined the innumerable jars, striving to find some hint, some indication of where the strangely recorded history commenced, I noticed that here and there were empty niches; that in others the jars were plain, monotone vessels. Here were puzzles. What did the vacant places and the ordinary jars signify? Were they meaningless or had they some significance which I could not fathom? Or were they—yes, I believed that was the answer—were they representatives of lapses, of years, or of decades, when no unusual events occurred or of which no records had been kept. If so, if the latter were the case, I reasoned that in the earlier periods of the race's history there would be more lapses, more periods forgotten or lost, and hence the portion of the walls where the empty niches and plain jars were most numerous would be the spot where the records commenced. And I cannot adequately express my elation when I found that in one of the walls the lowest rows of niches were almost all filled with meaningless red or brown jars, and that many of the spaces were empty. To the left the symbolic jars increased in number, and to the right all were symbolic and obviously of much more recent date than those on the left. Beyond question, beyond doubt, this was the beginning of that marvelous, unique history, and only patience and concentration were needed to make clear to me the whole story of the people, who had once dwelt within this weird land, and who, I felt convinced, had left the place and had erected those magnificent buildings at Tupec.

But all this had occupied a great deal of time. The sun had passed far beyond the meridian, the room was filled with dark shadows, and only here and there did enough light enter to enable me to distinguish the designs upon the jars.

It was useless to try to do more until there was better light, and regretfully I left the chamber, though much to Tom's satisfaction. He, poor chap, was half famished, although I had quite forgotten that we had eaten nothing since the previous afternoon.

CHAPTER EIGHTEEN

I CANNOT spare the space to record in detail our work of the next few days. Controlling my impatience, I set to work with Tom to clear away vines, branches and debris until at all hours of the day the sunlight could enter the room containing the jars. Then methodically, as painstakingly as though identifying and cataloguing museum specimens, I worked upon the symbolic jars.

As I worked, the meanings became plainer and clearer, and within a few days I could read the story they told, as readily as I could decipher the graven symbols of the Mayas or the codices of the Aztecs. There is no necessity to enter into the details of this work. If I ever escape, I shall make it known to the scientific world, and, if I do not, of what use will it all be? In fact I hardly know why I am writing at all, why I am taking the trouble to record anything, unless it be merely from force of habit and for my own satisfaction. Suffice to say, that the history revealed by those magnificent examples of the ceramic art was most fascinating, most tragic and most remarkable. Whence the race came or who they were is still a mystery, for, as I have said, the early periods of their existence in the country were mainly blank or vague. But that they came from overseas and migrated across vast stretches of country was evident. Also my supposition that they were a white race was borne out by both the painted and modelled figures. Not until they had settled in this valley had history been recorded systematically. Then it proceeded almost without interruption. Each cycle of a certain number of years, as nearly as I could judge approximately each century, an empty niche indicated the beginning of a new cycle. And if I am right as to the length of these cycles, then the race dwelt here in this accursed spot for at least ten thousand years. Originally the place was the home of some sort of huge bird, or rather, judging from the representations of the creatures, some long-extinct flying-lizards, which preyed upon the insect life. Even in those far-distant days the insects here were of most unusual size, for repeatedly, upon the jars, insects were shown in company with human beings and nearly as large as the latter. Unquestionably the giant bird-like creatures kept the insects in check, and, being harmless creatures so far as human beings were concerned, they were soon hunted and killed for food. With the short-sightedness of all human beings, the inhabitants continued to destroy the feathered creatures until the last had been killed. No longer kept within bounds by their natural enemies, the insects increased in numbers and in size. Crops were destroyed, human beings attacked, and existence in the valley became a constant battle between man and the insects. Life became impossible, and the inhabitants sought to migrate to another land. But during the thousands of years since they had entered the valley, great changes had taken place. Great walls of rock barred the pass through which their ancestors had come; but in their desperate search they found a cave, a tunnel-like cleft in a mountain. Exploring this, they found it led through the cliffs, and driven by necessity, thousands of men were put to work enlarging and strengthening this natural passage until they had drilled a tunnel through the mountain. Often terrific battles took place between the workers and the giant ants. But in the end, the human beings won. Deserting their great city, taking with them only the essentials of life, they prepared to leave, and to prevent all possibility of being followed by their insect enemies, they planned to arrange the opening to the tunnel so that it could be closed behind them and could not be opened from the valley side.

During all these years another race had lived in the valley, a race of bestial black beings (the savages we had met, beyond doubt) and though the civilized white race was forced to leave or succumb, the semi-human, primitive savages continued to exist—a strange comment on the boasted superiority of civilized man over primitive man, in the matter of survival. Here then were all the puzzles and mysteries of Tupec made clear to me. No doubt, after escaping from the valley and founding Tupec, a second history of symbolic jars was maintained. No doubt, somewhere amid the ruins of Tupec, that priceless ceramic story still lies hidden, and my greatest regret is that I am doomed to know this and shall never be able to find it and learn the full history of that ancient vanished race of white men. But the sculptured figures and carved effigies, which had so puzzled me at Tupec, are puzzles no longer.

They represented bits of the past story of the Tupecan. The giant insects, the great feathered creatures—birds or flying lizards, I cannot say which—the terrific battles with the giant ants, all were perpetuated there in Tupec, yes even the black savages. And within that tunnel, the fragments of horny matter and the bones, which we found, were the grim reminders of those hand-to-hand conflicts waged between the builders of the tunnel and their insect foes.

So interested had I become in this story of the race, and so much had I dwelt upon the history of the escape from the valley, that I became obsessed with thoughts of possibilities of escaping that way ourselves. Might it not be possible, I thought, to dig away about the entrance until we two could enter? Would it not be possible to pry, cut or by some means break through the stone doorway? I thought of the herculean labors of primitive races in stone cutting, of the seemingly superhuman feats men had performed. If one man could overcome such apparently insurmountable obstacles, could not we two do as much? We had been too easily discouraged, I decided; we had been supine, lacking in determination. At any rate, we would have another look at the place, and so, regretfully leaving the ruins and its treasures, we returned to our hut, and a day or two later, set out for the tunnel.

Upon our way, we met with many adventures and constantly came upon new things, but these were in a way merely repetitions of those that had gone before and are not worth the trouble of relating. But when at last we came to the tunnel and I made a careful examination of the massive stone portal that blocked it, my heart sank. At a distance, thoughts of forcing a way through had seemed reasonable. Plans for patiently chipping away the rock day after day, month after month, year after year, had not seemed visionary. But now, beside the flinty mass of stone, we seemed so puny, so incapable of making any impression upon it, that I was thoroughly discouraged. A thousand wild, impossible schemes passed through my mind. I even thought of employing a horde of those ghostly, blind, mining termites to dig under the door, only to discard the idea the next moment. I could not direct their movements, they burrowed aimlessly, and, moreover, I could not use them without making our efforts known. Once they had burrowed beneath the door, the way would be open for all the terrible creatures of the valley, and even for the sake of escaping myself, I would not let loose the horde of giant insects to overrun the country beyond, and very probably spread over the entire face of the earth.

MY thoughts were interrupted by Tom. "Beggin' yo' pardon, Chief," he remarked, "Ah was thinkin' if how we had powder we right well might blow open tha door. An' Ah was rememberin' yo' was thinkin' of makin' powder one time."

I slapped Tom on the back until he coughed. His mind had seen light where mine was groping in the dark. Why not? If I could make powder, even a miserable apology for the explosive, a charge properly placed might well dislodge the door and, once we had crawled through, we could block the opening again, even if to do so, we were obliged to blast the tunnel down behind us.

Fired with the idea, more optimistic than I had been for months, we hurried back to the ant colony. Going to my dung-heap, I raked the pile carefully apart, and to my delight saw that clusters of dull yellowish-white crystals had formed in the mess. Touching these to my tongue, my hopes were confirmed. They were unquestionably saltpeter, and although in small quantities and very crude, I had no doubt they would serve our purpose. Gathering every crystal with the utmost care, I found I had nearly a pound of the precious chemical. But we would require many pounds to make powder enough for our purpose, and for the next few days we worked feverishly, making additional and larger "nitratarias."

It would, I knew, be weeks before we could hope for saltpeter crystals from these, but time was no object. In fact, we had long before lost all reckoning of time. Meanwhile we would gather sulphur, make charcoal and carry on a series of experiments on a small scale, in order to learn the best proportions of the three ingredients to give us the explosive needed. It is not necessary to recount the details of this. We had many failures before we had even a modicum of success and on the day when, touching fire to the result of our labors, the black mess puffed up with a flare and a cloud of smoke, we felt as elated as though we had made a momentous discovery. Still we were far from having powder, which could by any stretch of imagination be classed explosive. It was slow-burning, and although a charge placed in a section of bamboo, split the tough fibres apart with a satisfying pop, still a similar test with a pottery tube was an utter failure, the powder blowing out the plug without smashing the inch-thick terra-cotta. Patience and perseverance will accomplish wonders, however, and by the time our new crop of nitrates was ready, I had discovered the secret of mixing and grinding powder which, although far less powerful than ordinary blasting powder or gun powder, would, I felt sure, serve our purpose. But it would require great care and the utmost caution to prepare a sufficient amount to blast a way into the tunnel and it would be a long time before we could hope to make the attempt that might win us freedom.

And long before that day arrived, other events transpired which completely upset our plans. We had been absent for two days at our sulphur deposit, and upon returning found death and destruction in the peaceful industrious colony we had left. Our hut was torn to bits, our belongings scattered. Dead and wounded agricultural ants strewed the ground, and the survivors rushed aimlessly about, terrified out of their wits. It was not hard to discover what had happened. One or two dead slave-holding ants told the tale. But for a moment I was puzzled. Why should these creatures have raided the agriculturalists except in search of us? They never molested other insects without reason, they made slaves only of the black savages, and if in search of us, why had they attacked and destroyed the others, when they failed to find us? But those questions were soon answered. Cowering in a dark corner of the agriculturalists' underground dwellings, we found three of the black slaves. My reasoning jumped to a conclusion at once. The poor creatures had seen Tom's escape; they had seized an opportune moment and had fled from their red monsters, and, either by savage instinct or by chance, they had found refuge among the agriculturalists. Then the reds had trailed them, and failing to recapture them had vented their anger and their vengeance upon the peaceful colonists who had given sanctuary to the slaves, as they had to us. No doubt the agricultural ants had fought valiantly, no doubt their insect allies had aided them; but the details of the fight we never learned.

This murderous raid made me determined to settle once and for all with those uncannily human and brutal slave-owners. I flatter myself that I am a peaceful man and I have always decried war, but now I was possessed with a most warlike and belligerent spirit. Neither was I content to wait until the reds should again take the offensive. I determined then and there to carry war into the enemy's camp, to attack the reds in their own territory. But there were many obstacles in my way. For Tom and myself to attempt such a campaign alone was out of the question. Even had we possessed fire-arms we would most certainly have sacrificed our lives in such a Quixotic attempt. And it seemed almost as hopeless to think of inducing the agricultural-ants to aid us. In the first place, we could not communicate our ideas or wishes to them; in the second place, they were not a warlike race. Then I thought of the black savages. They, after all, were the most intimately concerned with the slavers and they had the greatest reasons of all for wishing to have their oppressors destroyed.

But how could I communicate with them? How could I make my plans and wishes clear?

Help came from an unexpected quarter and in an unforeseen way. The three slaves had, willy-nilly attached themselves to us and particularly to Tom. Perhaps his color gave them confidence; perhaps the fact that he had also been a slave of the reds inspired them, or possibly they realized that we were enemies of the slave-owners, friends of the agriculturalists, and hence friends of them. Low as they are in the scale of humanity, I believe even these ape-like human beings possess some sense of gratitude. Otherwise I cannot explain why they acted as they did. Why they watched our every move, our every expression and listened attentively to our conversation as if striving to understand us; why they should have been so anxious to interpret our wishes, and to labor for us. If Tom started to do any simple task, a black would leap forward and perform the duty for him. If I wished an object I had to point and a black would hurry to bring it to me. And to my amazement, I found they were not the unintelligent dumb beasts I had thought. Though bestial in appearance, though unspeakably filthy in habits, yet they possessed brains and reasoning powers far above those of the most intelligent quadrupeds. To be sure, all three were young specimens—mere infants in point of actual age, but they were fully developed, for like the apes, these savages mature in an astonishingly short time. Undoubtedly, they had been reared from the embryo stage by the ants, and so had been trained to work. But their aptitude for reading our expressions, for interpreting our gestures and even the meaning of our words and orders, was truly marvelous. Here, I thought, were creatures capable of being trained, and if men can train elephants, lions, seals and other creatures as they do, why, I reasoned, could I not train these savages to a far higher degree? Once trained, they would be ideal soldiers, for I had seen enough of them to know that they were born fighters, that they had the brutes' blind courage and lack of fear, once their fighting spirit was aroused. And if I could train these three individuals, would it not be within the bounds of possibility and reason that I could make them understand my object, that I might be able to make them convey that knowledge to the rest of their tribe, and that, eventually, I might have a horde of savage blacks to accompany me on my attack upon the red ants?

BUT I had not foreseen events which amazed me even more and made my task far easier than I had dared hope. Within a week after being with us, one of the blacks astounded me by pointing to my bow and clearly pronouncing the word "bow." Almost dumbfounded at this demonstration of the fellow's intelligence and adaptability, I decided to test him further, and addressing him, said "arrow." For a brief moment he hesitated, moving his thick lips as if pronouncing the word to himself. Then, with a glad cry he bounded off and came back carrying my sheaf of arrows. I cannot express the astonishment that I felt. The fellow actually had learned a smattering of English! Had the others done the same? I was not left long in doubt. All three had not only learned the names of various articles, so they could pronounce them, but had learned to recognize the names of many more objects when I uttered them. From that time on I bent all my efforts to teaching the fellows to speak and understand English, and with far better results than I would have believed possible. To be sure, there were certain words that were impossible for them to utter or to understand, but I soon found that we got on famously, by using words of Spanish, French or some Indian dialect in place of these. Also, I was trying my best to acquire a working knowledge of their gibberish. I cannot say I succeeded well in this, but Tom very quickly learned their almost unintelligible and guttural words, probably because of some inherited aptitude for the tongue of his African ancestors. Of course this took time. Weeks passed, but so interested had I become in this work, that I had almost forgotten my scheme to escape from the valley and my determination to attack the red ants.

In the meantime, too, I had made still another epochal discovery. I say epochal, for had it not been for this, I doubt if my plans ever would have materialized as far as they have. This was the fact that our blacks could understand and even communicate with the ants. No doubt, while they were slaves of the reds, they bad acquired some means of grasping or receiving the vibrations by which their masters communicated with one another. But it came as a distinct surprise to find they could converse—there is no other name for it although it was not conversing in the ordinary sense—with the agricultural-ants also, and as a natural result, with the giant dragon-flies, the huge bees, the Carib-beetles and even with our bombardiers. Do not imagine, however, that I meant to convey the idea that the semi-human beings could carry on a discussion with the insects or could talk freely with them. They could convey meanings to the ants and their allies and could understand the insects' meaning to a certain extent.

At the time, this impressed me merely as being useful, for it paved a way for Tom and myself to get in closer touch with our hosts by using the blacks as interpreters, but later it proved of inestimable benefit in a wholly unforeseen way.

I must, however, curb my desire to write so fully of all that has transpired during the past months. I must confine myself to the most important facts and events. Suffice it to say, that eventually I set out with Tom and our three blacks for the savages' headquarters beyond the aphid-orchards. Of that memorable visit I need only mention the results. With our meagre knowledge of the blacks' language we caught only a word here and there as they conversed with their swarming, curious fellows. No doubt they related marvelous tales, but the main point was that they followed my instructions and explained my ideas and plans. And of still greater importance is the fact that their fellow tribesmen unanimously were with us in our plans to attack the red ants. Heaven knows they had suffered enough to make them welcome such an opportunity, but by themselves, so great was their terror of their hereditary enemies, they would never have attempted such a thing. The first matter then was to provide the blacks with weapons. Unarmed as they were, they were no match for the natural fighting-machines in the shape of warrior-ants. But with bows and arrows, even with hatchets, spears and clubs, they would be in a different state indeed. Much time was devoted to the preparation of weapons, and still more to teaching the savages to use them, and I am sorry to say that there were not a few casualties among the blacks, before I could make them understand that they were to confine the use of their weapons to their enemies, and were not to practice on one another. The things were so new and strange to them, that for some time they could not overcome their curiosity to test them upon any living thing they saw. Repeatedly one savage would fire an arrow into the body of a fellow savage, and both he and the victim would stand gazing with most ludicrous expressions of utter amazement at the result. Never did I hear a wounded savage utter any sound denoting pain, and I am not sure that they actually do feel pain. In fact they are a most puzzling lot, and at times I cannot settle in my own mind whether they are men, apes, or insects. This may sound like the ravings of a lunatic, but these fellows have some of the attributes of all three.

DURING all this time I had a vague fear that the reds might raid the blacks prematurely, for I did not desire a battle until I was morally sure that we could emerge victorious. But luck or nature have been with us, and so far no reds have put in an appearance. My blacks are fairly well trained in the use of their weapons, and before very long I feel we will be in a position to give a good account of ourselves. Moreover, I believe the agriculturalists will join us. They appear to have grasped the idea, but they are naturally and by instinct so domestic and peaceful that I have little hopes in that direction. I have often thought of using my powder in connection with my attack upon the reds, but I hesitate to use it for such a purpose. I am still intent upon blasting a way to the outer world, and I only wish I had an inexhaustible supply of explosive, for I feel sure that properly used, it would prove more destructive to the red slave owners than anything else. Perhaps, however, it would so terrify my own forces that its effects would be nullified.

And now I must set down some incidents that might seem incredible. To us, in this amazing place, they do not appear so remarkable as many other experiences.

Discussing one thing and another with Tom, and recounting our adventures, we brought up the matter of the giant tortoises, and into my mind flashed that joking remark I had made to the effect that the giant land-turtles were like army-tanks. An inspiration came to me. Was it not possible to transform that semi-humorous comparison into a reality? Could not those monstrous, armor-clad beasts actually be used in our forthcoming war?

I had no expectations of training the beasts, for I well knew that the chelidae are among the most stupid of creatures, and as far as I know, no one has ever been able to train a tortoise of any species. But a turtle, once headed in a certain direction, will usually travel in that direction almost as inexorably as fate. The immense beasts, moving across the ants' country, even over the ants themselves, would smooth down mounds and earthworks and crush the insects as effectually as a steam-roller, and no ant, not even the giant solitary species, could make the slightest impression upon the tough skins of the turtles. Moreover, and this was I felt the most important point, a man or men mounted upon one of these living fortresses would be in a far more favorable position to bash in the heads and jab spears into the vitals of his enemies, or even to shoot arrows or sling stones, than from the ground. Possibly I was a little mad, perhaps I am still; but the idea took possession of me, and the very next day, accompanied by our three blacks, we set off for the turtle hill. We had no difficulty in locating the brutes, and no trouble in mounting them, but to drive them back to our home was a very different matter. I have said that a turtle, once started in a certain direction, will continue to move in that direction. But while I found this quite true in the case of the giant tortoises, the direction in which they moved was not our direction. Try as we might, we could not start them in the desired direction. For the first time the black savages showed signs of enjoyment and a sense of humor. Never before had I observed either of these human attributes among them, but here, in our tussle with the ponderous but harmless turtles, they were as gleeful and joyous as children. For hours we labored, trying to induce the turtles to head towards our distant home. We tried every device we could think of—without success. If a turtle was turned in the direction we desired he would either refuse to move, and would withdraw into his shell, or instantly would wheel about and head another way. Never have I dealt with such obstinate beasts. An army mule is the most tractable of creatures by comparison, and it was as hopeless to try to use force as it would have been with an elephant. At last we gave up in despair, and weary with our effort, left the tortoises to their hillside.

But our trip to the turtle hill brought results of a very different sort. As we were returning, we came upon a column of the terrible army-ants. To be sure it was not a large army such as that from which

Tom and I had so narrowly escaped long before. Nevertheless it was big enough to strike terror to our hearts, and turning, we were about to flee for our lives when we stood rivetted to the spot at sight of the three blacks. Instead of racing away from the voracious creatures, they were calmly approaching them. In a moment the foremost ants would be upon them. The huge scissors-like jaws would seize the savages and tear them to bits before our eyes.

And then an amazing, an absolutely incredible thing happened. The three blacks began dancing and leaping about, shouting shrill metallic sounds, and instantly, as if obeying an order, the advancing column of great blind ants came to an abrupt halt. I could scarcely believe the evidence of my eyes. By some uncanny power, by some miraculous means, the three fellows had stopped that army of the most terrible of all ants, and there they stood, hissing and squealing, uttering strange high-pitched notes, as if actually conversing with the army-ants. And that in effect was precisely what they were doing. What they said, how they managed it are matters entirely inexplicable to me; but the fact remains that somehow they controlled the creatures and conveyed their meaning to them.

But still more incredible developments were to follow. Leaving his companions, one of the blacks came hurrying to us, and in his broken, half-comprehensible manner, suggested to me that we should enlist the army ants in our service.

Now I was perfectly sure I had gone mad. I began to feel that it was all an hallucination. That the savages, the ants, my plans for a battle, perhaps even the valley itself were all figments of my mind. The idea was unthinkable, too preposterous. And yet I felt as sane as ever in my life. At any rate, I thought, if this is madness, if all I have suffered and undergone are merely my fancy, if it is all the workings of a diseased mind, I might as well carry on in the same insane manner. But in my heart, I knew that it was no question of insanity; that I was neither dreaming nor suffering from any mental derangement, and that, considered calmly, it was no more remarkable that these blacks could communicate with army-ants, than that they could do the same with the red ants or the agriculturalists. And if they could communicate with them, why should they not induce the army ants to join us as allies? For all I knew, they also were natural enemies of the red brutes; for all I knew they were friends of the savages. And if the army ants did join us, Heaven pity the red slave owners, when we attacked them.

CHAPTER NINETEEN

EVENTS have moved rapidly since last I wrote' describing our preparations for war upon the red ants. It seems scarcely believable, but it is nevertheless true, that the army-ants have proved most tractable, and have exhibited the most astonishing intelligence. Neither Tom nor myself have any influence over them, but our three blacks appear to be able to control them absolutely. I have come to the conclusion that it is some form of hypnotism, that these savages, only a step above the animals and insects, are much closer to the lower forms of life, mentally, than are we, and that their minds, although far below ours in development, are yet so immeasurably above those of the insects, that they can dominate the latter by will or hypnotic power. To draw a parallel, just as the hypnotist with a powerful will and personality can hypnotize a weaker-minded man, so these savages can control the actions and wills of the weaker-minded ants. Unquestionably it is this power that has enabled them to survive and hold their own in this land, from which the civilized white race was forced to flee. Or possibly it is the other way about, and self-preservation and necessity have led to these humans developing their hypnotic power over their natural enemies. Certain it is that, without some such power, these beings, ignorant of the simplest weapons, never could have survived amid the countless hordes of giant, ravenous insects.

But the most surprising thing to me is, that they have not used the same power to control the red slave-owners. The only explanation is that these super-ants are not subject to the mental power of the blacks. Also, it seems strange that, being able to enlist such beasts as the army-ants in their cause, the blacks have not long ago led an attacking force against their red enemies.

But no doubt it never occurred to them, for they have no inventive ability, no foresight and no imagination, and, having been for countless generations subject to the slave raids, they have grown to regard their plight as a natural condition. Not until I brought the matter to their minds did they dream of organized action to protect themselves.

But I am wandering from the more important matters of my records. Fortunately the army-ants needed no especial training, for they were naturally born soldiers and possessed an organization and discipline far more efficient than I could have evolved. All I would require of them would be to head them for the red ants' colony and they would do the rest, and, as I thought of this, I wondered why neither these slave-holders nor the agriculturalists had been attacked and overwhelmed by their army-ant cousins. Our peaceful hosts had been raided by the droughers and by the reds; I had witnessed battles between them and the solitary ants, and yet, for some reason, they appeared to me immune to attacks from the far more voracious and savage army-ants. There must be some explanation, I felt sure, and I noticed that, even with our ant-army near at hand, the agriculturalists came and went and showed no fear of the terrible creatures. But the ways of the lower animals are past human understanding, and despite the years of study which have been devoted to them and the voluminous works that have been published, we really know nothing about the mental processes, the innermost motives and the instincts of the creatures all about us. We observe a certain trait or habit, a certain reaction, and judge the reasons and the causes thereof by our own reactions and point of view, which, for all we know, may be totally at variance with the lower forms of life. Never had these facts been made so obvious to me as since I have been in this valley, where insects rule and predominate, and such humans as there are, are the lower animals, if I may so put it.

But again I am getting off my subject and must stop dissertating. I could not determine the reason for our agricultural ants being on peaceful, if not friendly terms with our army-ants, and there was no use troubling my mind over it. It was fortunate that it was so and that was enough. Having seen the strange power which the blacks exerted over the army-ants, I decided to determine if they possessed the same or a similar power over any of our other neighbors, such as the giant bumble-bees, the dragon-flies and the Carib-beetles, for if they did, and they could enlist these creatures in our service, we would possess a fighting force which could attack from the air as well as on foot. The idea tickled me immensely, for it savored of modern warfare with airplanes, and this conceit brought another and more fantastic idea to my mind. Why not go a bit farther and use other methods of modern war? Why not employ bombs, even gas, in our attack? I might not be able to make firearms, but I certainly should be able to design and construct some form of explosive bomb or grenade. And sulphur fumes would be as deadly to the red ants as the most terrible of destructive gases to human beings. But would it be possible to train the giant dragon-flies to carry and drop such things? That was a great question, and I greatly doubted if the broad-winged insects had enough intelligence to enable them to grasp the idea, even if, by some means, I could communicate with them through the medium of the black savages. However, even if this were not possible I could make grenades which could be hurled among the ants, either by hand or by some mechanical contrivance.

THERE is no need to relate in detail all my efforts, my failures, my disappointments and my experiments. I had comparatively little difficulty in inducing the dragon-flies to carry objects into the air, and there was still less difficulty in getting them to drop these objects. The trouble was to get them to drop the things at the right time and in the right place. They appeared to regard it as a sort of game, and I sincerely believe that these insects possess a sense of humor. Repeatedly they would let their burden fall within a few feet of me, and I swear they actually grinned when they saw me jump hastily to one side. It was hopeless to waste time and effort in trying to train the creatures, and I could foresee that if given explosive bombs, they were as likely to drop the contraptions upon their friends as upon their enemies. But if my ambitions in this direction were doomed to be abandoned, my experiments had led to another idea. I had observed that both the dragon-flies and bees were natural retrievers, and would swoop with the speed of lightning, the moment an object that glittered was tossed into the air. I could not train the creatures to obey my signals or my voice, and the blacks had as little control over them as I had. But by throwing objects into the air, I could bring the insects dashing earthward. Hence, if when we attacked the reds, I could manage to throw missiles of some sort into the air, my flying squadron would come swooping down, and, seeing their friends fighting with the red ants, they would undoubtedly fall upon the slave-owners with all the fury of their savage natures. Meanwhile, the idea of using grenades and bombs was still uppermost in my mind. We now had a sufficient supply of saltpeter to make a large amount of powder, and I decided that most efficient bombs could be made of pottery. By making globular vessels with thick walls, and leaving a small orifice for a fuse, we would have fairly good substitutes for the old-fashioned spherical bomb-shells. Of course they could not be accurately timed, neither was it possible to arrange them to explode by concussion, for I had no fulminate and no means of making it. But it would not matter if a fuse spluttered and smoked for some time after it fell among our enemies. They would not know what it was, and would never dream of attempting to extinguish the fuse. But there was another and more important problem to be solved.

Once we attacked the red ants, it would, I knew, be a hand-to-hand fight and a general melee, and to attempt to throw grenades into the struggling mass would be to kill and maim as many friends as foes. No, if my bombs were to prove of any value, we must manage to hurl them at the ants before the actual battle began, and to do this, we must have some sort of engine or machine.

Small grenades might be fired from bows by being fitted to the tips of arrows, much as grenades known as "whizz-bangs" were fired from mechanical devices during the Great War. But the larger ones, on which I counted most, would be far too heavy to be used in this way. The only device I could think of was a sort of catapult, and I spent many days experimenting and working on that idea.

Under normal conditions, it would have been an easy job to rig up a small catapult, but we had no tool worthy of the name except my hunting knife, and the simplest undertaking became a stupendous matter under such conditions.

But at last I had the satisfaction of seeing my crude affair complete, and I was as delighted as a boy with his first gun when we tested the machine, and sent a dummy bomb sailing far over the tree tops. We could not well use more than one of the things, and I contented myself with this first catapult. Meanwhile, our army-ants were literally eating their heads off. Our black fellows had them in charge and allowed them to roam about, always accompanying them and keeping them under control, in order to forage for themselves. As a result, the country for miles about was stripped clean of almost everything edible, and food became a serious problem for us. But we were now nearly ready to launch our attack and, in two days more, would start on our march for the red ants' stronghold.

Then all our plans were upset. Exhausted, terror-stricken, two of the blacks came rushing to our camp. The red ants had made another raid; they had carried off more of the savages as slaves, and had left scores of dead and wounded behind them. Despite the resistance made by the blacks and the good use they had made of the weapons we had supplied, they had been overpowered.

But they had given a very good account of themselves, and the reds had not gotten off unscathed by any means. For every black killed, at least two of the raiders had been destroyed; but the odds in numbers had been overwhelming, the hereditary fear of the red ants had had its effect upon the savages, and, having no leader and having been taken by surprise, they had fought without order or system. Too late, I realized my short-sightedness in not having posted scouts to warn of such a raid. But there was no use in lamenting that now.

The allies on which I had counted the most had been demoralized and decimated, but, to my surprise, the savages, instead of being terrorized or anxious to avoid further conflict, were all the more eager to even scores with their foes.

There was no use in waiting longer. The blacks were eager to regain their fellows who had been made prisoners, and to revenge themselves. Our army-ants could not be maintained in idleness indefinitely. We had a supply of bombs and our catapult, and I determined to set off on our campaign at once. My Chelonean Army, as I called it in honor of the turtles we did not get, was a strange, weird organization; the strangest army that eyes ever looked upon. There were the horde of brutal, ugly, naked, black savages—half human, half-beasts; the swarming, blind, terrible- jawed inexorable army-ants; the great hard-shelled, rapidly- moving, metallic-hued Carib-beetles; the peaceful agricultural ants, like ploughboys and farmers drafted into a real army; our retinue of tame bombardier-beetles, and Tom and myself, while overhead buzzed and whirred the dragon-flies and bumble-bees like scouting airplanes. And never was there an army more difficult to control, to handle and to deploy. It would have been bad enough with the savages alone; but with all the diversified units, each a law unto itself, each with distinct ideas, instincts and habits, the most experienced and efficient general on earth could not have prevented it from being chaotic. The Carib-beetles would dash off after prey whenever they pleased. The blacks pranced and shook their weapons and uttered bestial shouts.

The agricultural-ants were thinking far more of their crops and fields than of military tactics. The dragon-flies and bees flew here, there and everywhere, and only the army-ants, under control of their savage masters, moved steadily, irresistibly onward like well-trained troops. I had strapped our catapult to the back of our largest bombardier, another carried our ammunition and bombs, and these docile, domesticated beasts could be counted upon. Despite the seeming control exercised over the army-ants by the savages, I had little confidence in these blind scimitar-jawed creatures, and Tom was deadly afraid of them. Hence, for the sake of safety, and partly because they were to serve as our shock-troops, the army-ants were in the advance with the blacks behind them, and the agriculturalists, Tom, myself, and our cohorts of domestic insects bringing up the rear.

CHAPTER TWENTY

LOOKING back upon it, I do not think that any of the members of my army actually understood what it was all about, with the possible exception of the blacks. They, of course, had semi-human minds and an idea of revenge, of righting personal wrongs and of fighting for a principle. But the others were merely insects with insects' minds and habits, and in the insect-world, I doubt whether there are such things as vengeance, wrongs or principles. Certain species are predatory, certain species are not; some insects live on friendly terms with others; some are always at war. But all this is a condition of nature, a part of the Great Plan, and as there are no family ties, no feelings of blood relationship, no such emotion as affection among insects, there can be no ideas of right and wrong, of vengeance or of enmity, aside from natural inherited instinct. All warfare among insects, as far as I have observed (and it makes no difference whether or not they are tiny things or giants creatures) is either in self-defense or to secure food. Countless millions of larvae have been destroyed by ichneumons, but the butterfly or moth that develops from a larva which has escaped bears no enmity towards the ichneumons, and has no fear of these terrible enemies of their kind. A wasp may swoop down and seize a spider, but the spiders never go out of their way to attack the wasps. A Carib-beetle dashes in and seizes a victim from among a busy colony of hornets, but the hornets never take concerted action against the Carib-beetles nor attack one whenever it is seen. I could mention thousands of similar cases, but I must confine myself to more important matters. And it was this lack of the true militant spirit, this entire absence of a true purpose, which I had not foreseen and which, I now feel convinced, was our undoing. It must be remembered also, that we could not really communicate with any of our allies with the exception of the semi-human savages. To be sure, all the various members of my army had thrown in their lots with us, but I feel sure now, that it was owing, not to a desire to destroy the red ants, but was due entirely to the strange hypnotic power of the blacks, and to the fact that Tom and myself were, instinctively perhaps, regarded as beings so superior that we were dangerous and must be humored. Possibly, too, the agriculturalists felt that we were members of their colony, and as such must be supported, while their insect protectors accompanied them as a matter of course.

I hate to record what transpired on that day. I had given far too little credit for intelligence to the red ants. Perhaps they were apprized of our approach by the swarm of dragon-flies and bees in the air. Possibly they had scouts posted in the forest. Perhaps, by some inexplicable instinct or intuition, they learned of our proximity or again perchance it was merely the fact that they had developed far more intelligence than their relatives, and through countless centuries of life maintained by warfare and raiding, had developed military instincts and tactics. I confess I do not know. All went well until we came close to the orchards of the slave-owners. Before us the forest ended and the sunlight streamed upon the clearing in whose centre was the red ants' citadel.

The place seemed strangely quiet, strangely deserted. No slaves toiled under the watchful guardianship of the reds. Onward we marched. For a moment the army-ants hesitated as they reached the cleared space. They moved their antennae about nervously, stroked one another, seemed perplexed, and then suddenly, wheeling abruptly, they swung sharply, to one side and hurried on away from our objective. In vain the blacks strove to control them. All their power over the creatures seemed to have suddenly vanished.

Heedless of the fellows, the army-ants swept on their course and presently were out of sight. I was amazed, thunderstruck. What had so abruptly influenced them? Was there something about the red ants, as about the agriculturalists, which prevented the army-ants from molesting them, prevented them even from trespassing on their domains? No doubt it was something of the sort, but I had no time to ponder on the causes of their desertion.

The most powerful division of my army had vanished, our forces had been deplorably reduced, and still there was no sign of the enemy. Quickly unlashing our catapult, I fitted a bomb to it and hurled the missile into the red ants' mound. The next instant it exploded, and a cloud of smoke and sand flew up from the spot. This should bring the unsuspecting ants swarming out, I thought. But still there was no sign of life. Another bomb followed, and then, as perplexed, wondering, we started forward, a black savage threw up his arms, uttered a terrified cry and vanished in the solid earth. Before I realized what had happened, two more followed. Then a Carib-beetle was swallowed by the earth, and a dozen agriculturalists went with him. Scarcely had they vanished, when from every side came rushing the red warriors. Bursting through the ground they had undermined to trap us, they surrounded us, their great jaws clashing, their armor-clad bodies gleaming red as blood in the sun.

INSTANTLY the battle was on. Valiantly our agricultural friends fought. Body to body, jaw to jaw they slashed, bit, wrestled with their red foes. And like the savages they were, the blacks threw themselves into the melee. Clubs and swords swung, spears darted, arrows flew. No quarter was given and every man and insect fought for himself. Had our forces equalled or even approximated those of the red ants, we would have utterly routed them, perhaps annihilated them. But they were three to our one, and despite the advantages of weapons, I knew our forces were doomed. Tom and I were in the thick of it, but we had a tremendous advantage. We possessed explosives, and each time a red warrior or a group of warriors rushed at us, we hurled a grenade with ghastly results. In this way we managed to keep a cleared space about us, and, as fighting groups separated from the mass and our friends fell, we threw bombs into the knots of victors and helped even scores. Had it not been for these missiles, not one of us, I believe, would have escaped. As it was, the red ants, blown to pieces in groups and singly, unable to face this new form of battle, overcome by the acrid fumes of the powder, began to give way. Scores, hundreds lay dead and wounded all about. As many more lay writhing, helpless, overcome by the sulphurous smoke. But the number of dead and wounded agricultural ants and savages was appalling. Few of the agricultural ants survived. Over half the blacks had succumbed, and even the armor-clad Carib-beetles had fallen before the maniacal fury of the giant red ants. Only the great bees and dragon-flies had escaped without great loss and they had taken little part in the fray. Once or twice a bee had dashed down and had stabbed a red warrior with its terrible sting. Once a dragon-fly had volplaned down and had nipped off the head of a red ant and had triumphantly borne it aloft, to drop it, a moment later, into a struggling knot of fighters. And two of the dragon-flies had fallen victims to their habit of dashing after any bright object and to my bombs. Swooping down as I hurled the missiles, they had seized them in mid-air, and, an instant later, had been blown to bits by the explosives.

As far as the red ants were concerned, the fight was over. As quickly as they had materialized from nowhere, they vanished into their subterranean burrows, and we were left alone with our dead and dying.

The only consolation in the whole miserable, disastrous affair was that not one of our allies had shown fear or had given way. There was no thought of retreat in their minds, and so filled were they with the lust of battle, that both savages and agricultural ants fell upon the dead and wounded reds and tore them to pieces. And greedily, deliberately, the Carib-beetles gorged themselves upon the bodies of the fallen warriors.

For a space I considered pushing onward and destroying the homes of the slave-holders. But I feared the whole area had been undermined, and I felt morally certain that we would find no occupants within the citadel. It was obvious that the red ants had been prepared for us, that they had made the pitfalls to trap us, that their warriors had lain concealed underground until ready for the attack, and I had no doubt that they had provided for all contingencies and had removed all their fellows and their slaves to some secret hiding place to keep them from falling into our hands in case we were victorious. No doubt, too, the scent of the hidden red warriors had aroused the suspicions of the army-ants, and had caused them to turn aside and thus avoid the pitfalls.

Throughout, the red ants had exhibited a high degree of intelligence and a knowledge of military tactics. We had been rather squarely outwitted, outgeneraled and beaten, and there was nothing to be done except to retrace our way to the colony of the agriculturalists.

To return to our homes was more easily said than done. Throughout our weary march we had to fight our way, for the red ants had closed in behind us and beset us on every side. Only the fact that they were, so to speak, out of their element, saved us from utter destruction. They were, however, insects, of the open rather than of the jungles, and were accustomed to fighting in clearings and not in dense growth. And they had acquired a very great respect for our weapons. Whenever we caught sight of a red warrior at a distance, a discharge of arrows and missiles from our slings would end in victory for us, and I thanked Heaven that these creatures had not reached a stage of development that had enabled them to make use of other weapons than their powerful jaws and feet. Often, however, they would come unexpectedly rushing at us from concealment, and desperate hand-to-hand duels would ensue. But our black allies appeared rather to enjoy fighting, now that they possessed weapons, and they took the keenest delight in bashing in the heads of the red warriors or slicing through their attenuated necks with their saw-edged swords. As for the agricultural-ants, they appeared to take the whole affair as a matter of course. In every respect, they always have reminded me of yokels or farmers among humans, having the same dogged determination, the same bulldog persistency, the same methodical way of doing everything—fighting included. They would plod along, the most peaceful-appearing of creatures, until a red ant would rush upon them, when—presto! they would become fighting machines, alert, fearless; possessed with a sort of calculating, calm ferocity that was far more terrible than sudden anger or rage. And, more than half the time, they would come off the victors. Tom and I had our share, also. To be sure, our superior brains, our better weapons, and the fact that we were more accustomed to the weapons, were all in our favor. But on the other hand, the fearsome aspect of these giant adversaries carried terror to our hearts, and I always felt—though I am rather ashamed to admit it, a sort of superstitious dread of the creatures; a sensation that I was fighting with some uncanny monstrous beings, not of this world. And I invariably felt chilly and shaky whenever one of the reds rushed at me.

TOM was even more affected in this way than I was. He was deadly afraid of all the huge insects, and of the ants in particular. Like all of his race, he is extremely superstitious, and while he had—by the greatest efforts of self control—overcome his dread of the agricultural ants, he still insisted the others were not real insects, but "jumbies." Moreover, his experience among the slave-owners had served to make him still more afraid of the red ants.

But he is not lacking in courage and will fight as desperately for his life as anyone. And it is a brave man indeed who can stand up and face a monstrous six-foot creature all shining chiton, with its six-armed, many-jointed legs, its fierce, staring eyes and its great clashing keen-edged jaws capable of biting a human body in twain. Neither of us escaped without a scratch, however. Tom's body and limbs were covered with blood from cuts and slashes of the ants' claws, and one beast had taken a good sized piece out of my shoulder. But I thanked

God that his snapping jaws had missed my neck by the fraction of an inch.

Most of our losses, however, were among the agricultural ants who fought with nature's weapons; but several of the blacks were killed, others were badly wounded, and only the Carib-beetles and our bombardiers escaped unscathed. The former did good work and more than once pulled down and destroyed our enemies, while the latter, although for some reason refusing to use their gas discharges at the red ants, were most useful in giving us warning of the slave-owners lurking in ambush.

It was a pitifully small remnant of my army that at last reached the colony of agricultural ants, only to find that disaster had overtaken it during our unsuccessful foray.

Obviously the red ants had had full knowledge of our activities, for I cannot convince myself that it was mere coincidence, that the red ants had reached the colony by a roundabout route and had vented all their savage fury upon it, while we were attacking their stronghold.

They had slain for the mere lust of slaying, had destroyed crops and harvested grain, had even entered the burrows and galleries and had ruthlessly killed the inquilines, the larvae and every living thing they could find.

Scarcely an agriculturalist remained alive and uninjured, and, worst of all, we could not retaliate or even pay off a few of the scores, had we been able to do so, for the raiders had completed their destruction, and had departed before we arrived on the scene.

With the diligence and industry so typical of their kind, the agricultural ants in my army instantly fell to work repairing the damages to their galleries and homes. Presently several went hurrying off and within an hour they returned leading a long column of their fellows, each bearing a burden of grain or corn. I was astonished. The messengers had gone to a neighboring colony, had besought aid in their extremity and their fellows had come to their rescue. For hours the string of ants came and went steadily, until enough grain had been stored to supply all immediate needs. But the neighbors did not stop there. Several hundred remained at the stricken colony and aided in repairing damages, in starting new fields and in bringing order out of chaos. Even larvae were brought to replace those killed or injured, and in an astonishingly short time the colony, as far as outward appearances were concerned, might never have been attacked. Surely, among these creatures, a friend in need is a friend indeed.

CHAPTER TWENTY-ONE

SINCE our defeat by the red ants, a most deplorable state of affairs has developed. We have been driven out by the agricultural ants and have been forced to take up our abode among the black savages. How strange are the ways of an inscrutable Providence, or of Fate. How strange a turn of the wheel of fortune that we should find our only friends and allies in all this vast land are the beings whom we so despised and shunned, the beings who first showed hostility towards us.

I cannot say and do not know why the agricultural ants would not permit us to dwell with them longer. Provisions were short and it would have been a long time before the new crops were ready for harvesting, and meanwhile the larvae would have matured and there would have been far too many mouths to feed. Perhaps it was due to this fact, and a fear that we would take some of the slender supply of provender that induced them to get rid of us.

Perhaps it was due to the fact that they regarded us as responsible for the defeat by the red ants and the following raid. Or perhaps they felt that we were the primary cause of all the trouble with the slave-holders, and that they would not be free from future attacks as long as we remained in the colony.

Whatever their reasons, we were soon made to understand that we were no longer welcome guests. We returned from a hunt to find all of our belongings moved outside the walls. I wondered at this but did not then realize what it meant, and Tom and myself, together with the two blacks (one had been killed in the battle) patiently carried the things back to our hut. A little later, several ants appeared and began picking up our possessions and moving them again. Still failing to take the hint, I seized our goods and had quite a tussle with the ants before I recovered them. Then, as if by preconcerted arrangement, a horde of the ants swarmed down upon us and not only bore all we owned outside the colony walls, but commenced tearing our hut to bits before our eyes. No one could mistake the hint, and dumbfounded, we stood beside our few belongings like excited tenants in a city; homeless, friendless and unable even to demand an explanation. To be sure we could again camp in the forest as we had done at first. I also thought of returning to our cave in the mountain side. But somehow, after dwelling for so long with the ants, we felt inexpressibly lonesome and friendless and I felt more miserable and disheartened than at any time since entering the valley. But for the time being, there was nothing to do but to camp as best we might, and with the help of the blacks—who still stuck by us and were most faithful, willing fellows—we gathered what we had, under a clump of trees, put up a rude shelter and spent a miserable night.

But worse was to come. The agricultural ants, having turned against us, had no intention of allowing us in the vicinity, and it was barely light the next morning when they appeared in force, and, by actions and manner, told us as plainly as in so many words to "move on." They pushed and urged us, though without roughness or violence, and despite my resentment and my regret at thus being treated like a malefactor or other undesirable, I could not but marvel at the ants' persistence and bravery. Though they well knew our strength and the efficiency of our weapons, they laid hold of us and showed no signs of fear that we might resist and fight. No doubt we could have inflicted serious damages and killed many had we resisted, but I well knew this behavior would only make matters worse. I had seen enough of the agricultural ants to know they were determined, dogged, valiant fighters, with an obstinate, bulldog persistency, and even if we beat off the ants for the time, scores, hundreds of others, would take their places and, in all probability, our lives would be sacrificed for nothing. At all events, there was no reason why we should remain in that spot more than in another, and so, shouldering our burdens, we left the ants and their colony and headed towards our cave in the mountains.

Our way led near the aphis-orchards of the blacks, and as we neared these, the two savages with us showed the greatest delight, evidently thinking we were headed for their home. After all, I thought, why shouldn't we take up our abode near the black fellows? They were degraded, filthy, brutal, little above the insects in the scale of evolution, but they were, after all, human.

We need not come into very close contact with them; need not share their dens and food, any more than we had shared the quarters of the agriculturalists. And surely, if we had lived months with a colony of ants, we should be able to exist among human beings, low as these were. Moreover, here was cleared land and we could cultivate and raise crops, for we were sorely in need of some food other than meat and the grain we had obtained from our ant friends. In addition, I felt a greater interest in the blacks than I had before the battle, for they had exhibited a deal of bravery, had proven that they were capable of being trained and educated, and I believed I might be able to do a great deal towards uplifting them. Of course, I still had in mind my scheme for blasting a way to freedom, but I had exhausted my supply of powder in our ill-fated attack on the red ants, and weeks, even months, would be required to accumulate a new supply. Meanwhile I could keep my mind busy in my effort to educate and teach the savages, while finally they would prove most useful in aiding us, by carrying the sulphur and doing other heavy work.

Hence, considering these various matters, I turned aside and headed for the stronghold of the black savages, although as I neared their settlement I began to have some doubts as to the reception they would accord us. After the battle they had gone off, and while the two who were with us had remained faithful and friendly, I was not at all sure that the others might not have grown resentful when they thought over their losses, and might, therefore, treat us very much as had the agricultural ants.

BUT I need not have feared any such developments. As we came in sight of the clearing, our blacks shouted and yelled, and instantly, out from their burrows swarmed a crowd of the savages. One glance, and with wild whoops, and dancing and leaping like mad things, they came rushing towards us. Their greeting was vociferous, enthusiastic, and far too odorous for comfort. But there was no doubt about our being welcome here. To them we no doubt appeared as most superior beings (which I flatter myself we are) and even though they had lost heavily in the battle, yet they must have realized that we were their friends and had done our best to free them from the ever-present dread of their oppressors. I was rather surprised that the red ants had not included the blacks' village in their foray upon the agriculturalist. But when I came to consider the matter, it was not surprising. To have wrought havoc here would have availed them nothing and would have greatly decreased their ever available supply of slaves. Also, no doubt, they felt that we might fall upon their rear if they delayed too long, and hence confined their attack to the agricultural ants. Looking back upon it now, I am fairly certain that the red ants' attack on the agricultural ants' colony was a most devilishly planned scheme to get rid of us. I believe the creatures reasoned that if they injured the agriculturalists, the latter would blame us and would turn against us, exactly as they did; and no doubt the red ants thought that the agriculturalists would go to extremes and destroy us.

Having made up my mind to remain temporarily, at least, with the blacks, we lost no time in preparing a suitable dwelling. With hundreds of hands to help us, this was not difficult, and it was surprising how rapidly our hut was built and how much easier it was to direct the savages than the ants. Here were beings with whom we could at least converse after a manner, whereas among the ants our sole means of communication was by a most unsatisfactory lot of signs. Moreover, low as they were, the blacks possessed semi-human manners of thought and psychology, whereas, the ants, despite their intelligence and size, were, after all, out and out insects with insects' instincts, ideas and habits, and by no possible means could they ever acquire anything approaching human intelligence.

Our house here was built of stones and clay, and was a far better structure than was our former residence in the ant-colony. It was at some distance from the blacks' dwellings and pleasantly situated in the shade of some large trees on the farther edge of the cleared apace. By nightfall we were quite at home and would have been comfortable enough had it not been for the friendly though rather unwelcome attentions of our savage hosts. They insisted upon gathering about and brought us innumerable offerings of aphis milk, decayed insect meat and other things which they considered delicacies, but which were nauseating to us. All carried the weapons we had provided, and to my surprise and delight I discovered that they actually had made duplicates of their own. Several had slings that were as serviceable, though more crudely made, as those we had furnished; one or two had clubs which were wicked-looking things, though ungainly and cumbersome, and one fellow had an apology for a bow with which, to my astonishment, he could shoot far more accurately than with the bows I had made. Here was proof positive that these miserable ape-like beings were far more intelligent than I had surmised; they possessed an imitative instinct to a high degree, and in addition actually had a germ of inventiveness and ingenuity in their dull brains.

How long, I wondered, would it take to raise these blacks to the plane of ordinary savage races? They bred and matured so much more rapidly than other human beings, that I had no doubt that the undertaking to develop them would be far simpler and quicker than with barbarous races possessing more of the human attributes. In a way, it would be like training anthropoid apes, creatures which, at four or five years of age, are fully developed mentally and physically. But on the other hand, would acquired habits and characters be inherited? If so, with their rapid growth and increase, as much could be accomplished in a few years, as in centuries with ordinary humans. It was a fascinating idea, and my scientific curiosity to experiment along these lines was so thoroughly aroused that I almost decided to delay attempting to escape from the valley. But common sense overruled scientific ardor. If I escaped, it would always be possible to return and experiment to my heart's content.

And what was to prevent me from taking our two black adherents with me? They would prove most useful on our long, dangerous return to civilization, and they would provide most perfect subjects for scientific investigation. Yes, when I made the attempt, I most certainly would try to carry our two savages along with us.

CHAPTER TWENTY-TWO

WE have been among the blacks for several weeks and many new events have transpired which I think worth recording, although I am getting woefully short of space in my notebooks. However, if worst comes to worst, I can make a fair substitute for paper from the inner bark of the seda virgin tree, or I might even use parchment. But I still hope to escape from this valley before my paper is exhausted. I have found the savages even more quick to learn than I had expected or hoped. I have a number of them well trained as agriculturalists, and they take as keen an interest in watching the plants sprout and grow as any suburbanite in the springtime at home. Others I have taught to dress and cure skins; others to prepare bark-cloth, and I have spent a good deal of time trying to teach the women to spin and weave the wild cotton that grows here and also the silk from the huge cocoons. What a find this place would prove for silk manufacturers! Here are silk-worms a yard and more in length, which spin cocoons containing thousands of feet of silk so strong and perfect that it could be wound upon spools and used as thread without any preparation.

Also I have employed a large proportion of the men in fortifying this place, for I am sure that, sooner or later and probably sooner, the red ants will raid the blacks in their customary manner. Although the savages' settlement is admirably adapted for defense, and with a sufficient force could be held against a large body of attackers, more especially now that we are well provided with weapons, nevertheless we could not have hoped to make a successful resistance. It is seldom that any great number of the denizens are present during the day. They are obliged to be absent tending their aphis-herds, cultivating the gardens we have established, and attending to other duties, and an attack would find us short-handed. My first undertaking was to surround the centre of the clearing with walls. These were not so much for defense—for the red ants could surmount any wall with ease—but to give our people the advantage of being able to hurl missiles down upon the enemy, and so to take the latter at a disadvantage, as they scaled the defenses. It was a huge undertaking, but the blacks—though without the least idea as to plans or purposes—took childish delight in erecting the walls, and the place is now completely encompassed by a strong stone, earth and clay wall, nine feet in height and nearly six feet in thickness. There are no openings in this, and the blacks and ourselves enter and leave by means of ladders which are drawn up, very similar in many respects to the way in which the Pueblo Indians of our Southwestern States protect their homes from attacks. In addition, I have had a vast quantity of stones piled here and there along the summits of the walls. These can be quickly rolled and hurled upon an enemy, and I have also provided many roughly-made containers which are kept filled with powdered sulphur, for I feel sure that the giant red ants will be overcome by sulphur fumes as quickly as are ordinary ants.

It was while I was having this sulphur prepared that another means of defense occurred to me. This was to mine the area beyond the wall so that an attacking force could be blown up at the proper moment. The red ants had demoralized us by their pitfalls, but explosive mines would go them one better. The only trouble was to secure enough powder for the purpose. I had prepared quite a quantity of gunpowder since my arrival here and much of this I had used in making grenades or bombs to he thrown from the wall in case of an attack. But to make enough explosive to lay a series of mines would be next to impossible and would require many months of labor. And if I did succeed and used the precious powder for this purpose, it would mean that I would have to abandon my hopes of blasting into the tunnel for nearly a year. One half the amount required to lay the mines would be enough to blast down the tunnel door, and hence I decided that the idea, excellent as it was, was not practical.

But a few days later a discovery we made completely altered my viewpoint.

THE WORLD OF THE GIANT ANTS

To the south of the aphis-orchards was a stretch of country we had not previously explored. Several times we had started in that direction, but each time something had happened to prevent us from carrying out our intentions. The first time it was the discovery of the aphids that had sidetracked us. The next it was the raid of the red ants upon the blacks, and at another time it was the discovery of a stream, which, I thought we might divert to provide an ample supply of water for ourselves and the savages.

It was not a promising looking country from a distance, and appeared to be a barren, sterile waste, much like the desert of the tarantulas, but on a smaller scale. Beyond it, however, the mountains were very broken and rough and their slopes were covered with a vegetation that appeared to be different from anything else I had seen in the valley. There really seemed no valid reason for my desire to visit the place, but very often I had little to occupy my mind, and despite all my experiences, my scientific ardor for exploration at times took possession of me.

We found the place even more of a desert than the tarantula desert I have already described. The surface was composed of jagged, broken rock and hard-packed sand with numerous low ridges of rock laid bare by the wind, like the half-buried skeletons of some gigantic pre-historic monsters. Not even cactus showed upon the waste, and I was about to turn back from the forbidding spot when a shout from Tom drew me to him.

"T'ank de Lord, Chief!" he exclaimed. "We don't been have to go without salt no more, Chief. No, sir, just looka here 'bout. Here's salt a growin' in tha sand."

He was pointing at small veins and outcrops of dull-whitish crystals in a seam of the outjutting rock. Our need of salt had been most acute, and delighted that Tom had discovered the much needed mineral, I picked up a few particles and touched them to my tongue. My first taste was enough. The sharp, bitter taste told me instantly what it was, and while I was disappointed at finding we must still go saltless, I was overjoyed at Tom's discovery. The material was salitre, crude nitrates much like those of the Chilean desert, but apparently far purer, and instantly I realized that powder-making henceforth would be an easy and simple matter.

No longer need we gather spoonfuls of nitrate crystals at a time from our rubbish piles. Here was a natural deposit large enough to supply all our needs and more, and while I felt sure it was most crude and contained many other chemicals, yet I felt certain that even if it proved unsuited for powder in its natural form, it would not be difficult to clean and refine it.

OUR trip to the desert had not been in vain, and gathering all we could carry of the stuff, we hurried back to our hut. I was eager to test the quality of our new find and busied myself mixing the other ingredients with the best salitre. The result was not by any means as satisfactory as I could have wished. The powder, to be sure, exploded, but it lacked the power and rapidity of the powder I had hitherto made. But this I was sure was due to the impurities in the saltpeter and I set about experimenting at refining it.

I racked my brains trying to recall all the details of the process as I had seen it at the nitrate officinas in Chile, but not being a chemist, and lacking many of the essential requisites and apparatus, the best I could do was to put the mineral through a washing and recrystallization process.

The result of this was far better than I had hoped. The resultant saltpeter was even superior to that we had secured from the initrarias, and the powder made with it was the best we had produced. The next day we returned to the deposit accompanied by a dozen or more blacks, and at the close of our labors, we had several hundred pounds of the salitre ready for refining and use.

There was now no reason why I should not go ahead with all my plans to blast our way out of the valley and also, in the meantime, lay mines about our territory.

For days we worked like slaves, for I dared not mix powder in large quantities and prepared the explosive in small batches at considerable distances from one another. Realizing that we might at any time be raided by the slave-owners, the first lot of powder went to placing my mines. These were earthenware jars filled with powder and buried a foot beneath the sand, and with powder-trains leading to convenient spots within the wall. I had found it so difficult to make reliable fuses, even of short lengths, for my grenades, that I abandoned the idea of using fuses for the mines, but instead laid conduits of bamboo sections under the surface of the earth and scattered a powder-train through these. I was so anxious to prove the efficiency of my mines that as soon as the first one was in place, I touched fire to the end of the powder train. Almost instantly the mine exploded with a roar, sending a shower of stones and sand high in air.

For an instant the savages threw themselves down, fairly quaking with terror. Then, as they realized that they were not harmed, and I tried to explain the purpose of the mines, they leaped up, howling and shouting, as though they had actually seen their enemies blown to atoms.

With a number of the mines laid about the clearing, I felt we were fairly safe from a successful attack by our enemies, and turned all my attentions to manufacturing enough powder to blast down the gateway to the tunnel.

This I knew would be a far more difficult undertaking than to blow a few hundred pounds of sand into the air, and I used the greatest care to mix the ingredients to produce an explosive of high power. Of course the resultant powder was miserable stuff compared to ordinary commercial gunpowder or blasting powder. But what it lacked in quality I could offset by quantity and, having done my best I decided to test the result upon solid stone. This was somewhat difficult for there were no large masses of stone near the blacks' homes and I wished to make a thoroughly practical and convincing test, for upon the results our freedom and# probably our lives depended.

The best and most available spot where this could be done, was on the rocky mountain side, and carrying a fairly large supply of the best powder, Tom and I started off. After a short search, we found a large mass of rock practically identical with that of which the tunnel door was composed, and with a small deep fissure running across one outjutting mass. Into this crack we forced and rammed several pounds of powder, tamped it with sand and clay, laid a fuse, and touching fire to it, beat a hasty retreat. Several moments passed. I began to fear my fuse had gone out or that the powder had failed, and was on the point of stepping forward to investigate, when there was a terrific report, and bits of broken rock rained about us. Rushing forward, we found a mass of stone weighing several tons had been dislodged and cracked. Like boys, Tom and I locked arms and danced and pranced about. Our powder was a huge success. There was no doubt that we could force the tunnel door and escape from the valley, and we saw freedom near at hand.

All we needed was enough powder to insure tearing down the door at the first blast, for if we merely cracked or moved it slightly, our own efforts might defeat us. A bad crack which would not permit us to escape might render it impossible to place a second blast properly and might very probably form apertures or openings through which the exploding gases could escape without exerting any force upon the rock itself. So, satisfied that our powder was all that we required, we hurried home and made preparations to produce enough of the explosive to shatter the stone portal to fragments. We worked with light hearts and with greater enthusiasm than at any time since we had entered this place. At last we were on the road to freedom and we laughed and joked and made plans for our futures as though we were already quit of the valley. In a few days the place, with its gigantic insect inhabitants, its terrifying creatures, its strange half-insect-like savages, and its ancient ruins of an unknown white race, would be merely memories of the past. We would have our black servitors and our primitive weapons and garments to assure us it was not all a dream. In a few weeks we would be far beyond Tupec and approaching the outskirts of civilization, and within six months we would be back in a land of electricity, radio, motor cars and modernities where our adventures would appear so unreal and fantastic, that they would seem, even to ourselves, the figments of imagination.

ALL went well. Our powder-making progressed rapidly and no signs of the red raiders caused us any uneasiness.

We transported our explosive to the tunnel entrance and examined the massive door minutely in order to locate the best spot in which to place our blast which was to prove our open sesame. It was a difficult matter to find such a spot. The door was perfectly fitted and not a crevice or crack showed into which we could hope to ram enough powder to even shake the portal.

For a time I began to think that I was to be balked at this late stage and I wondered how I could have been so stupid as to have failed to investigate, before going to all my trouble and making all my plans. Then I remembered that when we had passed through the door there had been quite a high step from the floor of the tunnel to the earth outside. Of course the lower edge of the door must fit against this ledge cut in the rock, and if I could somehow manage to get some powder between the door and this inside sill, the explosion would probably force the door open even if it did not crack or break it. With this idea giving me renewed hope, Tom and I set to work digging away the earth about the lower edge of the massive stone. We worked feverishly, as if our lives depended upon it and in a fairly short time had scraped away enough of the sand and earth to expose the living rock below the tunnel mouth. As I had hoped, there was a fairly wide crack between the door and the sill behind it, a crevice as wide as my thumb, and by inserting sticks in this and probing about, I found that the crevice extended upward for nearly a foot and narrowed until the door and sill fitted tightly together at the upper limit of the crack. To push powder up into this opening was a slow and difficult job, for it kept dropping out as fast as we put it in. But I solved the problem at last by wrapping the powder in packages of thin papery bark, and after each was in place, puncturing the covering. It was in fact the same method that was used in loading big cannon, and by the end of the afternoon we had stowed fully fifty pounds of powder between the door and the solid rock behind it. By the time this was tamped and the fuse laid, it was dark. Well satisfied with our day's labors and with every expectation of being out of the accursed valley before another sun had set, we started back towards the savages' clearing. Half way there, and at almost the exact spot where the blacks had first attacked my Indians, we were met by a knot of wildly excited blacks led by our two special friends. They were so excited and appeared so terrified that I could not make head or tail of what they said. All I could gather was that ants had come to the village. Thinking that the red ants' raid was under way, Tom and I dashed forward as rapidly as our weary muscles would permit, while about us, and urging us on, were the gibbering blacks.

But as we came within sight of the place there was neither sign nor sound of battle, although I could see crowds of the savages gathered upon the wall. Hurrying forward, and wondering what all the excitement was about, we clambered up the ladder. Even then I could not understand what was the matter. But Tom, who was far more proficient than myself in interpreting the so-called dialect of these creatures, at last grasped their meaning.

"He do say the ants been come," he exclaimed. "He say a-plenty come this side an, show himselfs an' not been make fight. He say they over yander behin' we house. They don' been tha monstrous red ants, chief. They been tha farmer specie an' they desire to meet with yo', chief."

What, I wondered, had caused the agricultural ants to come here? Why did they wish to see me? How had they made their wants understood by these savages, and why did they remain hidden over by our hut? At any rate it was a relief to find it was no murderous slavers' raid, and feeling sure the agricultural ants were on a peaceful mission, I hurried down the ladder and across the clearing to our hut. As I came close to it, a score of most fearful, terrible-appearing creatures suddenly appeared from where they had been concealed. So monstrous and dangerous did they look that I uttered an involuntary cry and leaped back, expecting to be attacked and destroyed the next instant. No insects I had yet seen had been so formidable in appearance. Unquestionably they were ants, but they were little more than living, gigantic, serrated jaws and powerful clawed legs. Their bodies were slender, attenuated and lithe, their motions were so rapid, the eye could scarcely follow them, and yet, somehow, somewhere, they bore a strange familiar resemblance to something else. All this rushed through my brain in the fraction of a second. Then, among the creatures appeared several agricultural ants, and instantly the solution of the mystery flashed upon me. The monsters were agricultural ants! Not the ordinary, hard- working, peaceful creatures we had known, but highly specialized fighting units; ants developed, transformed— Heaven alone knows how—by some treatment of the larvae until, just as special treatment of a bee-grub results in a queen, the larvae, instead of becoming ordinary workers, had become veritable warriors.

What amazing, incredible super-intelligence the agriculturalists must possess to have done this! Here was exhibited reasoning powers equal to those of human beings. They had suffered at the hands or rather at the jaws of the red ants. They had realized that to successfully combat trained warriors, they must also have warriors and, casting aside all the age-old habits and traits of countless generations of their species, they had produced a race of super-fighters. In a few generations, perhaps in one generation, they had developed physical characters totally distinct from those of the normal agriculturalists. How I wished I had had these fellows with me on our attack upon the red ants. But it was too late to think of that now. Tomorrow I would be out of the valley forever; the ants could fight it out and be the masters of their own destinies, and the blacks would have to work out their own salvation. But why, I wondered, had the agricultural ants brought their newly evolved warriors to me? What was their idea? Did they wish me to return to their colony or was it a threat?

I was not left long in doubt. Our two blacks possessed an uncanny faculty for understanding these ants and now, in their scarcely intelligible, half-human lingo, they explained that the agriculturalists had come to offer their services in repelling and destroying the red ants. They had driven off a foray of the slave owners in a second attack made by the latter, and now they had come to volunteer their services as allies of the blacks. No doubt, if the reds again attacked the savages, these terrible fighters would prove most valuable aids, but I could not see that it was of any interest to me. I was through with them all, and within twenty-four hours I would be beyond reach of reds or any others. I tried to appear nonchalant, to make it understood that I was in no need of reinforcements, but I did not care to make known my plans for tomorrow.

And so here we are, Tom packing our few belongings ready to take with us; myself writing these last few lines of the record I have kept for so many many months—or is it years—and, outside our hut, the newly created warriors herded, if I may use the term, by their agricultural fellows, for so specialized have these fighters become that they cannot feed themselves but must be fed by the others. Moreover, they are practically devoid of antennae, these organs having been reduced to mere rudiments in order to give room for their awful mandibles, and as a result they have to be moved and handled like so many automatons. I wonder why on earth they insist upon remaining here. The savages have not taken them into their village and seem to be rather in fear of the creatures. They act for all the world as if they were keeping some sort of a watch over Tom and myself; as if they suspected we were planning to leave the valley and were ready to prevent us from going. Heaven help us if that is in their minds, though why they should care whether we left or not, after evicting us from their colony, is beyond my comprehension. Anyway, tomorrow will settle the question. By the end of another day we will either be outside the valley or torn to pieces, for I am determined that no beings here shall interfere in my plans as long as I am able to lift a hand to prevent any interference.

CHAPTER TWENTY-THREE

HOW futile are man's best laid plans. Another day has passed since last I wrote. How glibly I stated that before another sun had set we would be out of this valley. How confidently I stated that we would be either free or torn to pieces. Yet we are still here, and as yet unharmed. Rapid and unexpected have been the astounding events that have taken place within these past twenty-four hours.

THE WORLD OF THE GIANT ANTS

Now I know only too well why the warriors of the agricultural ants refused to move away; why they came here. Faithful fellows they have proved, friends to the last even though they did drive us from our home among them. Would that I might have been able to communicate with them, to understand them fully.

I must hurry on. A battle is impending. But I forget, things so plain to me may be a puzzle, a mystery to everyone, if anyone ever should read these notes.

This morning—though it seems much longer—one of the black aphis-herders came dashing in from the groves, terror upon his face. Even I grasped his meaning. The red ants were approaching. The long expected raid was about to take place. Almost at the same time several agricultural ants came rushing into the clearing. Hurrying from one to another of their fellows, they whistled and touched antennae. Almost instantly the crowd of warriors was upon the move. Never have I seen better disciplined, better drilled troops. As if with one accord they formed into columns, each led by the workers, and wheeling, deployed and took up their stations about the clearing. I was astounded. Beyond doubt the agriculturalists had known that a raid was being planned; unquestionably they had come to us to aid us in repelling the attack; obviously they had posted scouts to keep them informed of the movements of the reds. But while I appreciated their acts, their friendliness and their value, yet they hindered and hampered my own plans. I had counted upon my mines, and these allies were now stationed over the hidden explosives. To set them off when the reds were attacking would be to destroy as many friends as enemies. In vain I tried to make the warriors move. In vain I endeavored to explain, but they were mere fighting machines endowed with life, creatures understanding, knowing only battle and the manipulation of their huge jaws. It was useless. My only hope was that when the reds attacked, the agriculturalists would fall back, that my new Chelonean army, as I called it, would slowly retreat before the reds and take its final stand close to the wall. Upon the wall they would be useless. Their sole weapons were their jaws and to use these they must come to grips with the enemy.

As far as we were concerned, all was in readiness. I had no fear of the ultimate outcome. Our combined forces, our defences, those terrible specially developed warriors would destroy the power of the slave-holders forever.

Hours passed. I had begun to think there had been a false alarm, when, among the trees of the aphis-orchards, we saw the advancing host of red ants. I gasped. There were thousands, tens of thousands, it seemed. They were everywhere; they came from every side.

And they showed no signs of making an immediate attack. I wonder if they are besieging us, if they have some devilish scheme of which we are ignorant? They first appeared three hours ago. I have had all the subterranean galleries destroyed so they cannot enter by the tunnels opening in the aphis-orchard. I have stationed blacks below ground to destroy any red who happens to dig his way through. But I am beginning to fear for the result of the battle, if battle it is to be. I have talked it over with Tom, I have pointed out that no matter what happens, if one of us is killed, wounded or captured, the other must make his way to the tunnel, blast the door open and escape. For the survivor to remain here alone would be unthinkable. I hope and pray that such an eventuality will not arise; but we must be prepared. I have made Tom promise, though with great difficulty, that if I fall he will take charge of my notebooks and leave the valley and make his way to civilization or die in the attempt. Then I will know that my story has one chance in many thousands of reaching my fellow-men.

THE first skirmishes have taken place. A shock-column of red ants rushed our agricultural allies near our hut. But few returned from their foray. They were mowed down, cut up as if they had charged a row of slashing steel blades. A little later we discovered a patrol of the reds approaching across an area temporarily unguarded by the agricultural warriors. Rushing to the powder-train leading to the mine in that spot, I fired it. The next moment only a yawning hole in the sand and fragments of dead ants remained to mark their attempt.

I fear we are in a bad fix. We have little water, little food, and the reds are in incredible numbers all about us. If only I could induce our agriculturalist warriors to rush the enemy. If only the reds would come on and attack. But the agriculturalists developed their fighters with one point in view and one only. They produced creatures with fearful natural weapons, great strength, quick motions and utter lack of fear, but in doing so, they sacrificed all intelligence, all individuality and initiative. The reds, on the other hand, seem to have developed even greater intelligence and a greater instinct for military tactics than before, and yet they have retained all their fighting characteristics. To attempt to make a sortie with the blacks would be suicidal. My handful of savages would literally be eaten up by the hordes of reds. And the latter have learned to keep beyond reach of our weapons. At first, arrows and slings did considerable execution among them, but now they have withdrawn just beyond range. I am beginning to feel that we are doomed. How I blame myself for not having attempted our escape sooner. Had we made our preparations to blast the tunnel door a day earlier, we would now be out of the valley and safe. And now, with all prepared, with only a spark needed to open our way to freedom, we are more helpless, more prisoners than ever. But of what avail to regret what cannot be remedied? There is a chance, a very slender chance, that we might escape through the lines of the red ants under cover of darkness.

They are strictly diurnal and are dull and semi-dormant at night. But they are so sensitive to the slightest sound or vibration, to sounds or perhaps scents undetectable to humans, that such an attempt would be a most perilous and desperate undertaking. Moreover, I feel that it would be a cowardly, despicable act to desert these blacks who look to me for their salvation. My presence in the valley—though Heaven knows I had no wish to remain here—has been the cause of all this trouble and warfare. I am in a way responsible, and in addition, I have developed a hatred of the reds more intense than I would have believed possible. To me they seem living incarnations of everything evil. And yet I suppose they are merely following out their natural instincts, are merely fulfilling their destinies as planned by the Creator. Most of all I am worried and troubled over Tom.

I have got him into this mess, and he, poor boy, must be sacrificed on the altar of Science because of his faithfulness and devotion to me. My own life is of little consequence. I am well along in years, I have done my part—small as it is—in the scientific world, and it is no worse to meet the end here at the hands of savage insects, than elsewhere at the hands of savage men, or by some accident or disease. I do not hold life cheaply, but in many ways I would prefer death to longer imprisonment in this valley. My greatest regret would be that all I have learned would perish with me, that the place would remain unknown and unsuspected indefinitely, that no fellow scientist would be able to complete my work and thoroughly investigate the marvelous ruins of the pre-historic white race. I had hoped, planned, to return with a large party and proper equipment, but I can see no hope of that now. I could face my future, my probable death with equanimity, if I could only be sure that my notes would reach the outer world. But I fear that Tom, if I fall, might forget his promise and would remain, faithful to the end.

THE suspense is getting unbearable. I am determined that in a short time I will force the issue. Unless the reds change their tactics and attack us, I shall lead an attack upon them. The inaction is more trying than the most desperate hand-to-hand fighting.

* * *

I HAVE been thinking deeply upon the matter of Tom's escape. I believe he, with his latent savage instincts and his African ability to move stealthily in the darkness, might get safely through the red ants' lines, especially as there seems to be an area to the west that is not so closely guarded and patrolled as elsewhere. If he could do this, if he could reach the outer world with my notebooks, my own fate would not matter so much. Moreover, if he could reach the outposts of civilization—and I have no doubt that he could do this if he gets through to Tupec—he could summon aid and return with a large party equipped with fire-arms. If I still live when they arrive, I will be rescued and none the worse off; the valley can be pacified, the red ants annihilated and the scientific world enriched by a study of this place. My life may be sacrificed, it is true, but if Tom remains and the reds are triumphant, his lot would be worse than any death. He would be made a slave of the inhuman monsters and treated far more brutally than the ordinary slaves.

I must use every argument to induce him to attempt to get away without me. I must play upon his terror of falling into the slavers' clutches again. I must promise that if the reds are defeated I will follow him; but the all important matter is to save him from the fate that I feel sure will be his if he remains, and to carry my notebooks to my fellow men. I do not feel at all confident that I can induce or force Tom to do this. But he is obedient, he is brave, he is resourceful and it is my only hope.

DECIDED Tom will attempt to reach Tupec. He will go through the tunnel as planned and I believe he can make it. Giving him my notes as only proof. Tom can bring a rescue party back from Tupec. He has full instructions as to forces, arms, etc. The Chelonean army will attack today.

MY Cheloneans victorious. The Reds annihilated. Am mortally wounded. Tom leaving at once. No use for rescue party now. My last words—

THE END

If you've enjoyed this book, you will not want to miss these terrific titles...

ARMCHAIR LOST WORLD-LOST RACE CLASSICS, $12.95 each

- **B-48** **THE DRUMS OF TAPAJOS, Illustrated Edition**
  by S. P. Meek
- **B-49** **THE TEMPLE OF FIRE, Illustrated Edition**
  by Fred Ashley
- **B-50** **THE FACE IN THE ABYSS, and Other Fantastic Tales, Illust, Ed.**
  by A. Merritt
- **B-51** **INLAND DEEP, Illustrated Edition**
  by Richard Tooker
- **B-52** **THE SILVER GOD OF THE ORANG HUTAN, Illustrated Edition**
  by David Douglas
- **B-53** **THE KING OF THE DEAD**
  by Frank Aubrey
- **B-54** **THE BOATS OF THE GLEN CARRIG, Illustrated Edition**
  by William Hope Hodgson
- **B-55** **THE SECRET OF THE EARTH**
  by Charles Willing Beale
- **B-56** **THE WORLD OF THE GIANT ANTS, Illustrated Edition**
  by A. Hyatt Verrill
- **B-57** **PHALANXES OF ATLANS, Illustrated Edition**
  by F. Van Wick Mason

ARMCHAIR CLASSICS OF SCIENCE FICTION SERIES, $12.95 each

- **C-80** **OPERATION: OUTER SPACE**
  by Murray Leinster
- **C-81** **THE FIRE PEOPLE, Special Illustrated Edition**
  by Ray Cummings
- **C-82** **THE BLACK STAR PASSES, Special Illustrated Edition**
  by John W. Campbell

ARMCHAIR SCI-FI & HORROR GEMS SERIES, $12.95 each

- **G-29** **SCIENCE FICTION GEMS, Vol. Fifteen**
  Milton Lesser and others
- **G-30** **HORROR GEMS, Vol. Fifteen**
  Henry Kuttner and others

If you've enjoyed this book, you will not want to miss these terrific titles…

ARMCHAIR LOST WORLD-LOST RACE CLASSICS, $12.95 each

- **B-5** **ATLANTIDA**
  by Pierre Benoit

- **B-6** **FORGOTTEN WORLDS**
  by Howard Browne

- **B-7** **THE LOST WORLD**
  by Arthur Conan Doyle

- **B-8** **THE CITADEL OF FEAR**
  by Francis Stevens

- **B-9** **A STRANGE MANUSCRIPT FOUND IN A COPPER CYLINDER**
  by James De Mille

- **B-24** **THE PURPLE SAPPHIRE**
  by John Taine

- **B-25** **THE METAL MONSTER**
  by A. Merritt

- **B-26** **THE YELLOW GOD**
  by H. Rider Haggard

- **B-27** **UNDER THE ANDES**
  by Rex Stout

- **B-30** **LAND OF THE CHANGING SUN**
  by Will Harben

- **B-31** **SHE (The Ultimate Illustrated Edition)**
  by H. Rider Haggard

- **B-32** **JOURNEY INTO LIMBO**
  by Scott Michel

- **B-33** **THE LOST CONTINENT**
  by Weatherby Chesney

- **B-34** **TWO THOUSAND MILES BELOW**
  by Charles W. Diffin

If you've enjoyed this book, you will not want to miss these terrific titles…

ARMCHAIR SCI-FI & HORROR DOUBLE NOVELS, $12.95 each

D-161   **THE TIME-RAIDER** by Edmond Hamilton
WHISPER OF DEATH, THE by Harl Vincent

D-162   **SONS OF THE DELUGE** by Nelson S. Bond
DAWN OF THE DEMIGODS by Raymond Z. Gallun

D-163   **HIS TOUCH TURNED STONE TO FLESH** by Milton Lesser
ULLR UPRISING by H. Beam Piper

D-164   **WOLFBANE** by C. M. Kornbluth & Frederick Pohl
THREE AGAINST THE ROUM by Robert Moore Williams

D-165   **LET FREEDOM RING** by Fritz Leiber
THE MACHINE THAT FLOATS by Joe Gibson

D-166   **EXILES OF THE MOON** by Nat Schachner & Arthur Leo Zagut
DEATH PLAYS A GAME by David V. Reed

D-167   **THE COUNTRY BEYOND THE CURVE** by Walt Sheldon
EMPIRE by Clifford D. Simak

D-168   **ARMAGEDDON** by Rog Phillips aka Craig Browning
THE LOVE MACHINE, THE by James Cooke Brown

D-169   **THE LAST TWO ALIVE!** by Alfred Coppel
OUT OF TIME'S ABYSS by Edgar Rice Burroughs

D-170   **BEYOND THE GREEN PRISM** by A. Hyatt Verrill
ALCATRAZ OF THE STARWAYS by Henry Hasse & Albert dePina

ARMCHAIR SCIENCE FICTION CLASSICS, $12.95 each

C-67   **POWER METAL**
by S. J. Byrne

C-64   **THE PROFESSOR JAMESON SAGA, Book One**
by Neil R. Jones

C-64   **THE PROFESSOR JAMESON SAGA, Book Two**
by Neil R. Jones

ARMCHAIR SCI-FI & HORROR GEMS SERIES, $12.95 each

G-19   **SCIENCE FICTION GEMS, Vol. Ten**
Robert Sheckley and others

G-20   **HORROR GEMS, Vol. Ten**
Manly Wade Wellman and others

If you've enjoyed this book, you will not want to miss these terrific titles...

ARMCHAIR SCI-FI & HORROR DOUBLE NOVELS, $12.95 each

- **D-171** **REGAN'S PLANET** by Robert Silverberg
  SOMEONE TO WATCH OVER ME by H. L. Gold and Floyd Gale

- **D-172** **PEOPLE MINUS X** by Raymond Z. Gallun
  THE SAVAGE MACHINE by Randall Garrett

- **D-173** **THE FACE BEYOND THE VEIL** by Rog Phillips
  REST IN AGONY by Paul W. Fairman

- **D-174** **VIRGIN OF VALKARION** by Poul Anderson
  EARTH ALERT by Kris Neville

- **D-175** **WHEN THE ATOMS FAILED** by John W. Campbell, Jr.
  DRAGONS OF SPACE by Aladra Septama

- **D-176** **THE TATTOOED MAN** by Edmond Hamilton
  A RESCUE FROM JUPITER by Gawain Edwards

- **D-177** **THE FLYING THREAT** by David H. Keller, M. D.
  THE FIFTH-DIMENSION TUBE by Murray Leinster

- **D-178** **LAST DAYS OF THRONAS** by S. J. Byrne
  GODDESS OF WORLD 21 by Henry Slesar

- **D-179** **THE MOTHER WORLD** by B Wallis & George C. Wallis
  BEYOND THE VANISHING POINT by Ray Cummings

- **D-180** **DARK DESTINY** by Dwight V. Swain
  SECRET OF PLANETOID 88 by Ed Earl Repp

ARMCHAIR SCIENCE FICTION CLASSICS, $12.95 each

- **C-69** **EXILES OF THE MOON**
  by Nathan Schachner & Arthur Leo Zagut

- **C-70** **SKYLARK OF SPACE**
  by E. E. "Doc' Smith

ARMCHAIR MYSTERY-CRIME DOUBLE NOVELS, $12.95 each

- **B-11** **THE BABY DOLL MURDERS** by James O. Causey
  DEATH HITCHES A RIDE by Martin L. Weiss

- **B-12** **THE DOVE** by Milton Ozaki
  THE GLASS LADDER by Paul W. Fairman

- **B-13** **THE NAKED STORM** by C. M. Kornbluth
  THE MAN OUTSIDE by Alexander Blade

If you've enjoyed this book, you will not want to miss these terrific titles...

ARMCHAIR SCI-FI & HORROR DOUBLE NOVELS, $12.95 each

- **D-231** **THE TRANSPOSED MAN** by Dwight V. Swain
  PLANET OF DOOMED MEN by Robert Moore Williams

- **D-232** **NEWSHOUND, 2103 A. D.** by Milton Lesser
  ZERO, A. D. by Robert Wade

- **D-233** **SPACE-ROCKET MURDERS** by Edmond Hamilton
  D-99 by H. B. Fyfe

- **D-234** **EXPLORERS INTO INFINITY** by Ray Cummings
  DESIGN FOR DOOMSDAY by Bryce Walton

- **D-235** **LAST CALL FROM SECTOR 9G** by Leigh Brackett
  TIME CRIME by H. Beam Piper

- **D-236** **SCYLLA'S DAUGHTER** by Fritz Leiber
  TERRORS OF ARELLI by Aladra Septama

- **D-237** **FURLOUGH FROM ETERNITY** by David Wright O'Brien
  INVASION OF THE PLANT MEN by Berkeley Livingston

- **D-238** **THE SUN-SMITHS** by Richard S. Shaver
  THE OPPOSITE FACTOR by Chester S. Geier

- **D-239** **THE EXILE OF THE SKIES** by Richard Vaughan
  ABDUCTION by Steve Frazee

- **D-240** **BEYOND THE WALLS OF SPACE** by S.M. Tenneshaw
  SECRET OF THE NINTH PLANET by Donald A. Wollheim

ARMCHAIR MASTERS OF SCIENCE FICTION SERIES, $16.95 each

- **MS-13** **MASTERS OF SCIENCE FICTION, Vol. Thirteen**
  Robert Silverberg, The Ace Years, Part Three

- **MS-14** **MASTERS OF SCIENCE FICTION, Vol. Fourteen**
  H.G. Wells, The Amazing Stories Collection, Ultimate Illustrated Edition

ARMCHAIR MYSTERY-CRIME DOUBLE NOVELS, $12.95 each

- **B-45** **NIGHTSHADE** by John N. Macriss
  ONCE IS ENOUGH by David Wright O'Brien

- **B-46** **NAKED FURY** by Day Keene
  MURDER IN BARACOA by Paul E. Walsh

- **B-47** **FRENZY** by James O. Causey
  IN THIS CORNER—DEATH! by Emile C. Tepperman

Made in the USA
Las Vegas, NV
24 December 2024